MARSHALL RYAN MARESCA

THE FENMERE JOB

A *Streets of Maradaine* Novel

DAW BOOKS, INC.
DONALD A. WOLLHEIM, FOUNDER
1745 Broadway, New York, NY 10019
ELIZABETH R. WOLLHEIM
SHEILA E. GILBERT
PUBLISHERS
www.dawbooks.com

Cover illustration by Paul Young.

Cover design by Adam Auerbach.

Edited by Sheila E. Gilbert.

DAW Book Collectors No. 1847.

Published by DAW Books, Inc.
1745 Broadway, New York, NY 10019.

First Printing, February 2020
1 2 3 4 5 6 7 8 9

DAW TRADEMARK REGISTERED
U.S. PAT. AND TM. OFF. AND FOREIGN COUNTRIES
—MARCA REGISTRADA
HECHO EN U.S.A.

PRINTED IN THE U.S.A.

Raves for the novels of Marshall Ryan Maresca:

"[*The Way of the Shield*] is a political story, one which both demands and rewards your attention. It's a personal story, dealing with pain, loss, heartbreak and forgiveness. It's a story about morality, about sacrifice, about what people want from life. It's a fun story—there's quips, swordfights, chases through the streets. It's a compelling, convincing work of fantasy, and a worthy addition to the rich tapestry that is the works of Maradaine." —Sci-Fi and Fantasy Reviews

"Veranix is Batman, if Batman were a teenager and magically talented. . . . Action, adventure, and magic in a school setting will appeal to those who love Harry Potter and Patrick Rothfuss' *The Name of the Wind*."
—*Library Journal* (starred)

"Maresca again gives us a book that is just a pleasure to sit back, read and enjoy. Have fun with it."
—Speculative Herald

"The perfect combination of urban fantasy, magic, and mystery." —Kings River Life Magazine

"Marshall Ryan Maresca is some kind of mad genius. . . . Not since Terry Pratchett's Ankh Morpork have we enjoyed exploring every angle of an invented locale quite this much." —B&N Sci-fi & Fantasy Blog

"Maresca's debut is smart, fast, and engaging fantasy crime in the mold of Brent Weeks and Harry Harrison. Just perfect."
—Kat Richardson, national bestselling author of *Revenant*

"Maresca offers something beyond the usual high fantasy fare, with a wealth of unique and well-rounded characters, a vivid setting, and complicatedly intertwined social issues that feel especially timely."
—*Publishers Weekly*

DAW Books presents the
novels of Marshall Ryan Maresca:

Maradaine:
THE THORN OF DENTONHILL
THE ALCHEMY OF CHAOS
THE IMPOSTERS OF AVENTIL

*

Maradaine Constabulary:
A MURDER OF MAGES
AN IMPORT OF INTRIGUE
A PARLIAMENT OF BODIES

*

Streets of Maradaine:
THE HOLVER ALLEY CREW
LADY HENTERMAN'S WARDROBE
THE FENMERE JOB

*

Maradaine Elite:
THE WAY OF THE SHIELD
SHIELD OF THE PEOPLE
PEOPLE OF THE CITY*

*Coming soon from DAW

Acknowledgments

Five years ago, *The Thorn of Dentonhill* was released, and amazingly, with that, I started a ball rolling that I've been frantically trying to keep on course. And it's been a thrilling journey, but not without its challenges.

Fortunately, I've had a good team with me in this crazy ball-rolling business, especially in the course of bringing *The Fenmere Job* into your hands.

First off, there's Dan Fawcett. Over the years, his ear has been the one I've bent, and he's added more to Maradaine, and especially to Asti and Verci, then I could ever calculate. As I've mapped out this crazy idea with all its moving parts, he's remained someone I lean on.

Way back when I first dropped my Big Plan on him, he said, "That's fantastic, but for it to work, for you to be able to do what you want to do, you're going to need the right editor and the right publisher."

Fortunately for me, Sheila Gilbert and DAW Books were very much the right editor and the right publisher. Were it not for Sheila—two time Hugo winner for Best Editor, so very well earned—and her astounding faith in this work and my big plan, we wouldn't be here. Everyone at DAW and Penguin—Sheila, Betsy, Katie, Josh, Leah, Alexis—have been fantastic partners on this endeavor.

Of course, there were also my two amazing beta readers, who've seen every stage of this endeavor through several revisions: Kevin Jewell and Miriam Robinson Gould. They have been there to help me make each book as strong as I can make it. My agent, Mike Kabongo, has been instrumental in making this big, mad plan happen.

Further thanks are owed to my parents, Nancy and Louis, my mother-in-law, Kateri, and my son, Nicholas.

And highest and first in my heart, my wife Deidre. None of this, absolutely none, would have come about without her. She's the north star by which I can always navigate my way.

The Fenmere Job

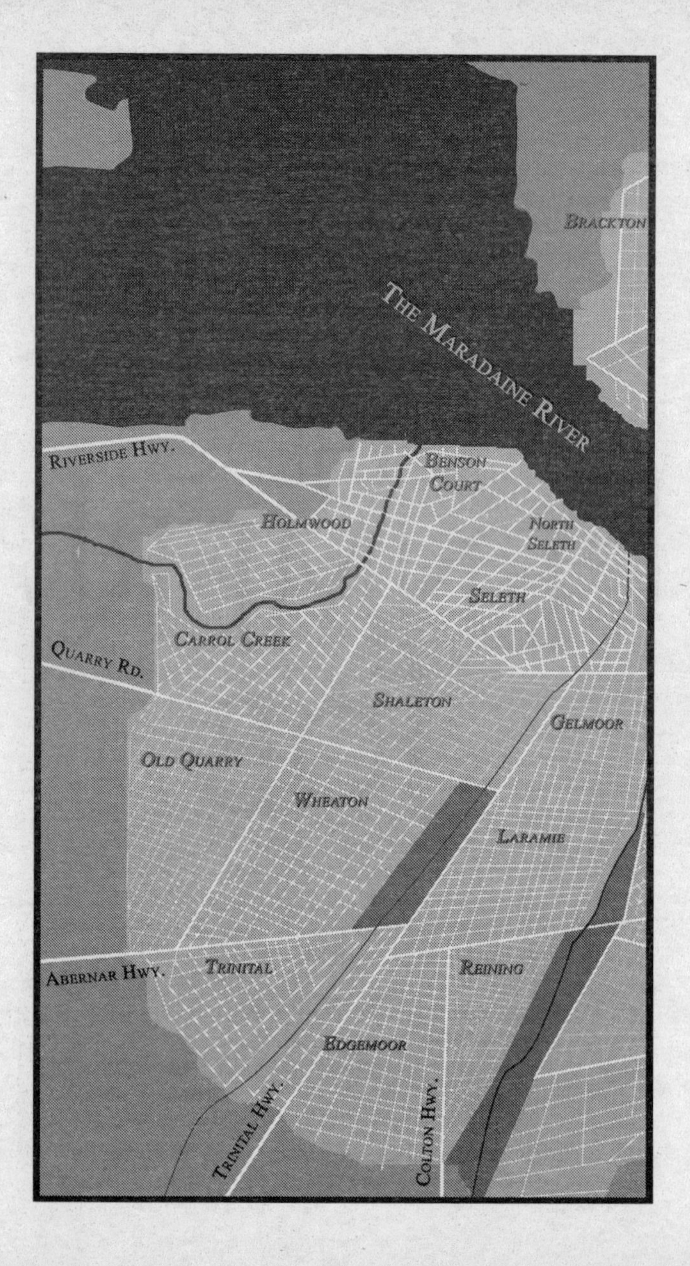
Brackton
The Maradaine River
Riverside Hwy.
Benson Court
Holmwood
North Seleth
Seleth
Carrol Creek
Quarry Rd.
Shaleton
Gelmoor
Old Quarry
Wheaton
Laramie
Abernar Hwy.
Trinital
Reining
Edgemoor
Trinital Hwy.
Colton Hwy.

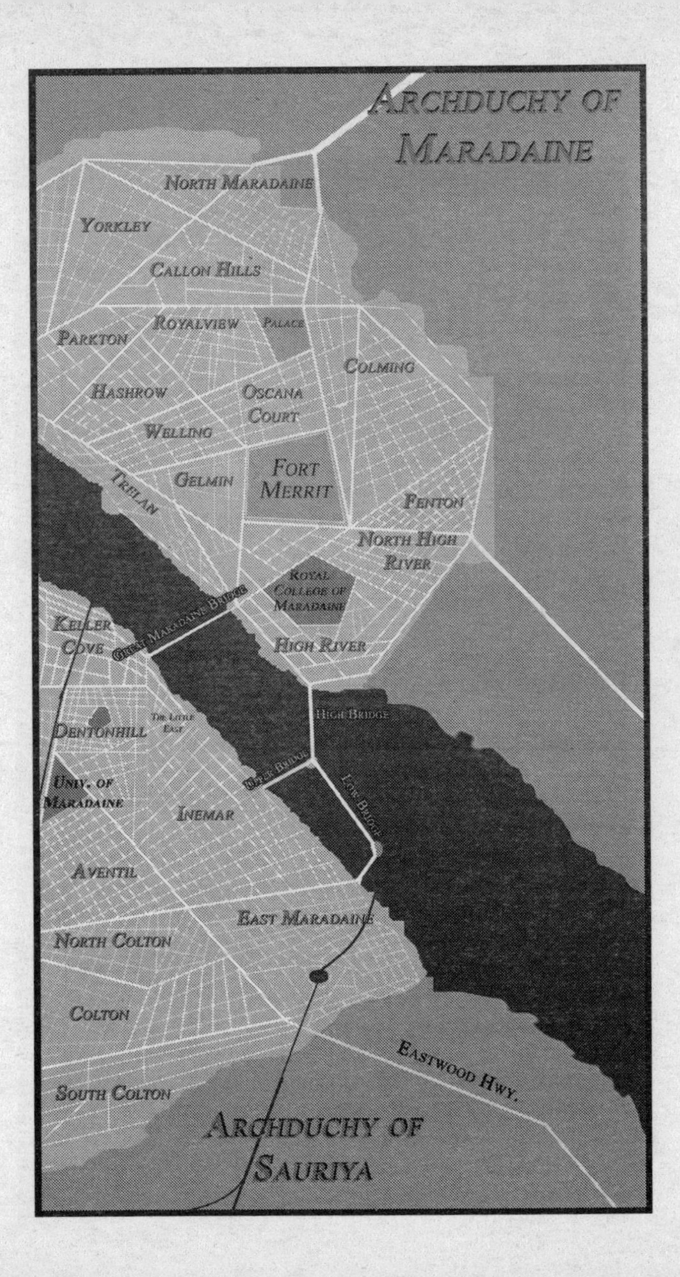
Archduchy of Maradaine
North Maradaine
Yorkley
Callon Hills
Parkton
Royalview
Palace
Colming
Hashrow
Oscana Court
Welling
Fort Merrit
Gelmin
Trelan
Fenton
North High River
Royal College of Maradaine
Keller Cove
Great Maradaine Bridge
High River
High Bridge
Dentonhill
The Little East
Low Bridge
Univ. of Maradaine
Inemar
Aventil
East Maradaine
North Colton
Colton
Eastwood Hwy.
South Colton
Archduchy of Sauriya

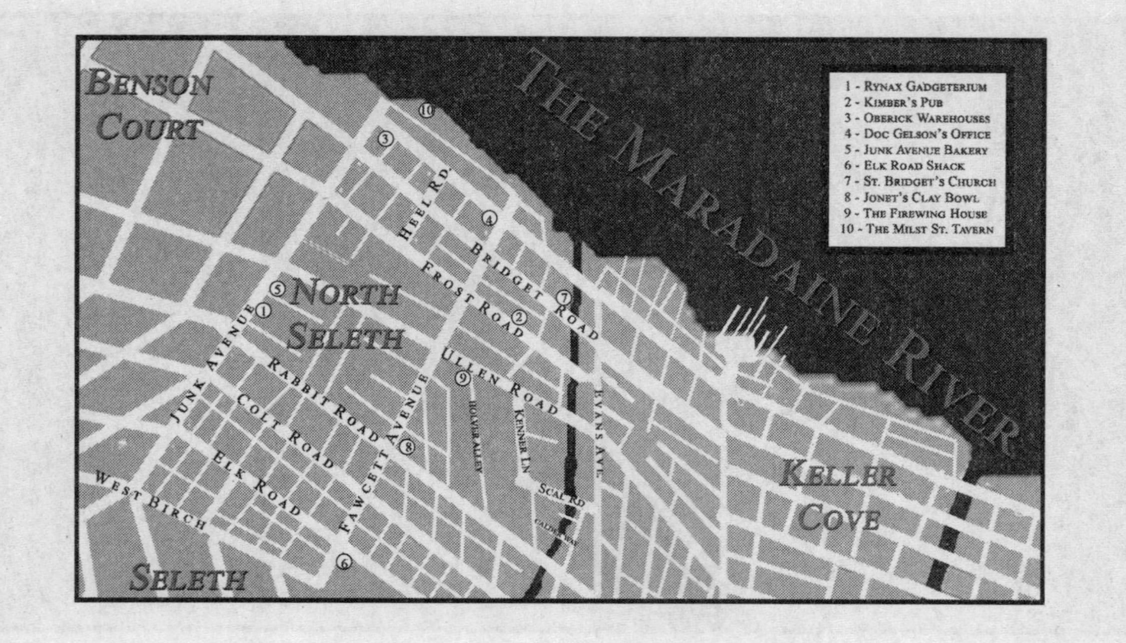
The Maradaine River
1 - Rynax Gadgeterium
2 - Kimber's Pub
3 - Oberick Warehouses
4 - Doc Gelson's Office
5 - Junk Avenue Bakery
6 - Elk Road Shack
7 - St. Bridget's Church
8 - Jonet's Clay Bowl
9 - The Firewing House
10 - The Milst St. Tavern
Benson Court
North Seleth
Seleth
Keller Cove
Heel Rd.
Bridget Road
Frost Road
Ullen Road
Evans Ave.
Holver Alley
Kenner Ln
Scal Rd
Junk Avenue
Rabbit Road
Colt Road
Elk Road
Fawcett Avenue
West Birch

Chapter 1

THE STREETS OF NORTH SELETH were quiet again, according to all the folks at the Keller Cove Constabulary House. But that was a lie.

Lieutenant Jarret Covrane knew that quiet was really a low murmur, a teapot ready to boil. Despite being told that the neighborhood wasn't his problem, he made a point of walking his own patrol in North Seleth each evening. Almost no constables from Keller Cove bothered going west of Evans, save those being punished with a posting at the waystation, and none from the Seleth house went north of Elk. And the folks in the Benson Court Constabulary House weren't worth talking about.

So he made the walk every night, uniform coat crisp and buttoned to the collar, despite the heat. Summer had been brutal, and even though it was now autumn, the heat hadn't broken. Even now, with the sun going down, there was little relief.

He waved amiably as he passed the lamplighter crew—two young boys and old Missus Terrendill. They diligently lit the streetlamps each night, even though within the next hour, half the lamps would be snuffed and robbed of their oil. That's how it went every night.

A handful of young men spotted him and scurried into Nander's Pub. Crease Knockers, by the look of them. There were handfuls of these little gangs popping up around the neighborhood. Crease Knockers, The Potato Boys, The Three-Fingers. He had lost track. The Scratch Cats ruled the roost right now, and he heard that Bessie's Boys were gone. The rumors were that Miss Bessie was killed in the Election Riots, but Covrane didn't take those seriously.

He turned the corner onto Kenner Street, which was still fairly busy, even with most of the shops locking up for the night. He wondered how many people were crammed up in the apartments above each one. Rents were getting higher, people were making less, and half the shops in the neighborhood were abandoned. After the fire, the riots, the squeeze from the gangs, the people who could leave did, and few people were opening new shops in this part of town. One new business, however, was one Covrane made a point of visiting each night on his rounds.

"Wondering if you were going to make it before I was done," the proprietress said as he walked up. Helene Kesser pulled shut the wrought-iron gate that protected her cheese and charcuterie shop. "You running late?"

"Paperwork," he said. He leaned in as he approached. "Too late to get a nibble of something?"

"I'm afraid so, Constable," she said with a wicked smile. Closing the distance, she added, "You'll have to settle for this." She kissed him, quick and fierce, and then pulled away.

"That's all for now?" he asked.

"Definitely all for now," she said. "But maybe you can knock on my door around ten bells, once Julien is asleep."

"I'd like that," he said. "I should probably finish up my rounds."

"Yes, you should," she said. "For all the good it does."

He chuckled ruefully and continued down the alley. Helene Kesser, she was—she was exactly like this neighborhood. He was certain she had a crooked past—she knew far too much about crossbows for him to believe otherwise. But despite the dirt on her soul, she had a decent heart and wanted a simple, clean life. Surely some chicanery was involved in her going from slinging goxies to running her own shop with her cousin, but whatever that was, she seemed determined to build a better—and honest—life now.

That was the case all over North Seleth. Covrane knew there were hundreds of Helenes. He would help keep their lives better and safer. He saw no need to dig up the past of people who were clearly on a path to reform.

"Evening, Constable," a pudgy man said with a tip of his round hat as Covrane came out of the alley. Simple man in a simple suit, probably working an honest job at the docks or a counting house. "Good to see you about."

"Good evening to you, sir," Covrane said with a nod. Respect for these people, for this neighborhood. Covrane would bring it, even if he had to do it all on his own.

Hal Elman was pleased to see a constable strolling the street as he made his way from the office. First to the bakery to fetch his wife, and then home, and hopefully another quiet evening of the two of them. Quiet evenings were, it seemed, starting to be the norm again, which Hal deeply appreciated. After the fire had uprooted Lian's sister's family, followed by weeks of madness and danger, things had settled. Maybe soon Lian would be willing to walk home from the bakery on her own again. Not that he minded, it was a pleasant nightly ritual of fetching her and walking home, but he didn't like that she was always so frightened. Despite that, she had insisted on continuing to work in the bakery with her sister, Raychelle. He was proud of her for that.

But the bakery itself made him nervous. Possibly because Raychelle's husband had "inherited" the place under mysterious circumstances which Hal had never fully understood or believed. And, to be honest, Verci Rynax smelled of trouble, and his brother, Asti, even more so. Disreputable, to say the least.

Not because they're Kieran, Hal said to himself. There were plenty of fine folks who were Kieran. Some very respectable businessmen. Hal was not like his boss, Mister Bradford, who would spit and mutter, "Stinking greasy piries" all the time. But he understood why some of them—like that Asti Rynax fellow—made people nervous.

There were plenty of people who made Hal nervous, of course. The new folks who moved into that Magic Circle house on the corner of Ullen and Holver Alley, for example. One of them was walking by right now: a striking woman with sharp, drawn features, standing out even more because she wore trousers, waistcoat, and thin-brimmed hat of burning yellow and orange. Hal had seen her and a couple of the others on a few occasions on his way home from work, but he had never found the courage to even say hello.

They were neighbors, after all. But, mages. That was a bit frightful. He didn't know anything about magic. He had never met a mage in his life. In his University years, there was the one chap who lived on his dormitory floor who was supposedly a magic student, but he turned out to be a chemist or something who later was kicked out.

Still, Hal couldn't help turning his head to watch her as she passed by. Something mysterious and poised and even regal about the woman really—

"Oof, watch it!"

He had plowed into some kid on the walkway.

"I'm so sorry, young man," Hal said. "I wasn't—"

"Yeah, I know what you weren't," the kid said. "Stop being such an oaf!" He darted off.

Hal shook his head. He needed to be more careful, especially on these streets. Half the people here would rob you as much as look at you.

Suddenly realizing, Hal checked his coat pocket. His coin purse was gone. Again. And that kid was well out of sight.

He sighed. Fourth time in as many months. He needed to wise up and stop letting that happen, if he and Lian were ever going to save up enough to get out of this neighborhood. He had a feeling they needed to do that soon.

The fat man in his stupid hat was always an easy mark. Enick had stolen his coin purse at least four times in as many months, and the fool was never any wiser. Enick almost felt bad for him, but that guy clearly had enough to eat. He dashed down the alley, went around the back of the tenement, and climbed the iron back ladder to the crash flop.

"Enick decided to show up," Mister Pent said. He was, as usual, half drunk on turned wine and walking around in his skivs. Peeky and Telly were sitting on the floor—the part of the flop where the wood wasn't so rotten you'd fall through—counting coins.

"Yeah, I been running about, getting things done," Enick said. He didn't like Cobie Pent, but for some reason Peeky and Telly latched on to him. Sure, he had escaped from Quarrygate and, when he was clear-headed, told them some pretty smart things. Not that there was much of anywhere else to go. Bessie's Boys were no more. Jede was dead, Tarvis was in the air, Conor was in with the Scratch Cats and Lesk's crew. Peeky and Telly were all Enick had left. They needed a place to crash, and this flop with Mister Pent was as good as any. That one time a Crease Knocker had chased them here, Mister Pent thrashed him solid, cut open his throat, and got rid of the body in the night. Even Enick had to admit, Mister Pent was good for protection, didn't beat any of them, and mostly just wanted food and wine while he stayed hiding in the flop.

There were worse arrangements.

Enick dropped his takings on floor. "Doing all right. Was able to walk right into Porky because he was eyeing some bright skirt walking by."

"Nice," Peeky said, counting the coins out. "So that's two crowns eighteen and nine pence today."

"That's good work it is, boys," Mister Pent said. "All right, you take that, get to the bakery and get a couple loaves." He looked out the window. "Sun's down, so the cheese shop is shut, same with the butcher. Split up and get to the grocer if you can."

"We know the play, boss," Telly said. He was the oldest of the three of them, nearly twelve. He was the oldest, Peeky was the fastest, and Enick had the hands. "Bread, onions, cheese, ham, and wine."

"And tea. And cream if they got it."

"The cream'll be spoiled by morning, boss. Ain't like the ice truck drops off to us."

"Right," Mister Pent said. "Sorry, kid. Being dumb. I'm hungry. Scat."

Telly scooped up the coins and scrambled out the window, and Enick tagged behind him. When they hit the dirt, Telly dropped a few coins in his hand. "You get the bread, Peeky and I will go to the grocer."

Enick ran over to the Junk Avenue Bakery. He always wondered why they would steal money but never just steal bread from the bakery. Mister Pent said that wasn't done, especially that bakery. "Treat it with respect."

He reached the bakery as the lady was blowing out the lamps inside. But still, she hadn't latched the door.

"Closing!" she said as he came in.

"I just need whatever loaves you got!" he said. "I got money!"

The baker lady squinted at him. "Do you?" She walked about around the rack to behind the counter. Moving like she wanted to keep something between him and her. "Let's see."

He held out the coins.

"I have three loaves that I'll give you for six ticks," she said. "How's that?"

"Deal, Missus Junk!" he said, putting the coins on the counter.

"I'm not—" she shook her head. She grabbed the loaves off the rack and wrapped them up. "Be safe out there, hmm?"

"Always am," he said, grabbing the bread. Still, she looked like she meant it, unlike most of the other shopkeeps on this street. Maybe that's why Pent respected the place. Maybe this bakery was special.

Raych Rynax latched the front door shut once the little urchin was gone. She was happy to get rid of those loaves, actually. They'd be stale by the morning. She was used to one of those boys showing up at this hour, she made a point of having something to sell to them. No need for them to go hungry.

She was pretty sure he was one of the boys who would hang about Mila at the beginning of the summer, when all the Henterman business was going on. She wondered if they'd be better off in Gorminhut or with the church, but that wasn't her place. She had enough problems on her shoulders. Blowing out the last of the lamps in the front of the shop, she went to the kitchen, where Lian was finishing up the cleaning.

"Last sale?"

"Locked up," Raych said, heading over to the crib. Corsi was already dozing, the little saint. Verci had built a clever little—well, it was a cage, but it was a cozy cage, and that meant Corsi could rest and play contentedly in the bakery kitchen without much supervision. It really made everything much easier for her and Lian to run the place without one of them constantly running upstairs to the apartment to check on him.

"Then that should be it," Lian said, and as if on cue there was the usual rap-clack-rap of Hal knocking his special knock on the back door. Hal did it that way, he said, so they would know it was him knocking. Of course they knew, no one else would knock. Certainly the hooligans who broke in here a couple months ago didn't.

Still, Raych found herself instinctively making a sudden, tight-knuckled fist.

Lian opened the door for Hal. "Ready to go, my dear?" he asked.

"Yes, of course," Lian said, kissing him on the cheek. "You're all set?"

"Rather," Raych said.

"Good night," Hal said, waving to her. "Best to Verci!"

"I'll let him know," she said, and Hal and Lian went off.

Raych gently pulled the levers and catches on the crib—it had taken her forever to learn it, but Verci had been a patient teacher—and extended the wheels. She could now push Corsi along in his own little carriage, all without disturbing him from his rest. As was her habit every night, she was going two doors down to the Rynax Gadgeterium—still not open for business—to see Verci hard at work on getting the shop ready. In part to make sure that he was, in fact, hard at work at that, and not on some other scheme.

Asti had gained a bit of odd affect in the past couple weeks that gave her doubts. They were proper business owners now—bakery and a shop, making honest money. No need for schemes or revenge anymore. She wheeled the crib out the back door, latching it with her key, and out the alley to the street, almost clobbering someone as she emerged.

"Mister Scall!" she said with a cry. "I'm so sorry!"

"No, no . . . no trouble," he said. Jared Scall was a muscular bear of a man, with nothing but a kind, wounded heart inside. She remembered seeing him weeping days after losing his butcher shop in the fire. And his wife, she—

That was too terrible.

"Still, I apologize," she said with a nod. "You have a pleasant evening."

"And you, Missus Rynax," he said, and wandered off down the street.

Jared Scall hadn't even remembered walking on Junk Avenue. He must have been in another fog. Raych Rynax had been kind enough, but he saw the pity in her eyes. He didn't need pity. He needed a drink.

He let his feet take him where they clearly wanted him to go—Kimber's Pub on Frost. There a few ciders and a few beers would do their job and clear his head just enough to get the sound of wet, ravaging coughs out of his memory. Just for a few hours.

But that sound still echoed about in his head. Those horrible coughs that would never stop. Until they did.

Kimber's was warm and inviting, though only a few people were about tonight. Doc Gelson, of course, was at his usual stool, and there was a young girl sitting at a table with a pile of books. She looked about his daughters' age. Theny and Poun were staying with their aunt, far on the south side of the city. Best for them to stay away.

"Jared," Kimber said from behind the bar, her voice firm. "You can't have that in here."

She pointed to his belt, where his mace was hanging. His, his father's, his grandfather's, his . . . who even knew how far back. The only thing to survive the fire. Jared had fallen into the habit of keeping it on his person since then. Not that he had used it on another human being since his war years, but . . . but given everything, he felt better having it on his belt.

"Of course," he said, taking it off. He handed it over to her. "I forget that I have it sometimes. Cider."

She poured a cider for him, judgment and pity in her eyes. "You know you can—"

"Cider."

"Right," she said. "Your weapon will be returned to you when you leave."

"Fine," he said.

A few ciders in, a kid ran into the place, making a line right for the reading girl.

"Miss Bessie!"

"I ain't Miss Bessie," she said.

"I don't care, you got to—"

"I told you," the girl said sharply. "I ain't Miss Bessie."

"Conor is taking scratches!" the kid said, not deterred. "If you come, he'll listen. If you—"

Kimber came over, putting herself between the girl and the kid. "This girl is busy studying, and she isn't the person you're looking for. And this is no place for you."

The kid glared at Kimber, then at the girl, who avoided his gaze.

"Fine," the kid spat out. "I'll do it alone." He left.

Kimber rubbed the girl on the shoulder and went back to the bar. "Another, Jared?"

"Yeah," he said. He kept his eye on the door, though. It was good for that kid to learn some harsh truths now. He should know that, in the end, everyone was alone.

Nikey stormed out of the pub and down the street. Stupid Miss Bessie. Wanted to pretend she was too good for them now. Wanted to pretend she didn't care. Wanted to pretend that the Boys—her boys—didn't matter no more.

Nikey still called himself a Bessie's Boy, though, even if he was the only one left. Some were dead or gone or who even knew what, but Nikey had gotten his face stomped for being a Bessie's Boy, so he wasn't going to give it up now.

And he wasn't going to let Conor do it either.

He ran down Fawcett as fast as he could, all the way to Colt Road, and then around the alley to the abandoned workhouse where the Scratch Cats would hole up. He found the broken window and slipped inside. The Cats were there—at least a dozen of them—surrounding a fire in a metal barrel. Conor was in the middle of them all, with the ugly one—Tummer, that was his name—standing in front of him.

"Are you going to give your heart, give your blood, give your fight, for all your brothers here?"

"I will," Conor shouted out. Saints, he actually was doing it.

"Are you going to earn their trust, earn their respect, and earn your scratches?"

"I will!"

"Are you going to—"

"Stop it!" Nikey shouted. "Conor, you got to stop this."

"Who the blazes is this pip?" someone asked.

"The rutting what?" Tummer asked. All dozen of them stared at him, hate and rage in their eyes. They all wanted to tear him apart.

Nikey ran close. It didn't matter. He had to reach Conor. "Come on, buddy, don't do this. We can both just walk out of here, go to a different part of town, and—"

"Nikey," Conor said coldly. "Go home."

"Home is where you are!"

"Conor," Tummer said. "Earn your scratches."

Nikey didn't even see the punch coming. Then another, which knocked him back. Then another, and he fell to his knees. Another, and a tooth flew out of his mouth. Another sent him to the floor. And another. And another.

All of them had been from Conor.

"That's a Scratch Cat!" Tummer shouted.

Nikey couldn't move from the floor. There was no point. It would only earn another punch from Conor. He couldn't take another one.

"Come on," Tummer said. "Let's take you to the Honey Hut, let those girls make a man of you."

"You kidding?" another Scratch Cat said as they all walked away from Nikey. "That Bardinic slan won't let you in."

"Of course she will," Tummer said as their voices faded. "Ia loves us."

That was the last thing Nikey heard. He waited a while to be certain they were gone, then slowly pulled himself to his knees and crawled out. So be it. He'd stand on his own, and when the time came, he'd show them who he was.

"You boys have got to be kidding."

Ia Estäan stood in the doorway of the Honey Hut as the handful of Scratch Cats huddled on the stoop, wanting to get their latest recruit—a child—some time with one of the girls. There wasn't a chance she would let that happen.

"Run the blazes off," she said. Even if she wasn't standing a step above them, she'd still loom over them. As it was, she was towering. "Don't come back here until you can look me in the eye."

None of them moved, all of them quivering in terror. Boys.

"Scat, *bijërka*!"

They ran. Her native tongue had that effect. She shut the door and strolled back to the parlor. Five of the girls were lazing about, waiting for clients to show up. There hadn't been a decent amount of business so far, but it was still early. By ten or eleven bells, once the gents of the neighborhood were fully in their cups, then it would be hopping. Running the place, minding the girls, it was a good gig. She knew why Lesk had put it on her—she could be the rose and the muscle, all in one. The girls appreciated her being in charge as well. Apparently in the past months, the place had been run by a *clöke* named Upscitch who liked to take his own liberties with the girls. When Lesk took things over, Upscitch found himself taking swimming lessons while tied to a rock. He didn't do too well with that.

"Jelsha," she called to the smartest, most seasoned girl in the parlor. "I'll be in the back with the chief. Don't call me unless there's a real problem, *sjat*?"

"Got it," Jelsha said, not looking up from her newssheet.

She didn't need to go to the office, but she knew that Lesk had slipped a couple fellows in the back under the cover of darkness. A meeting. She hated having men under the roof that she hadn't checked out. And if Lesk had had a problem with that, he wouldn't have brought them here.

"So right now the *Opportunity* is moored out of sight on Cordorin Island," she heard as she came in. She knew the voice, and certainly knew the *Opportunity*. And, indeed, in the back office Lesk and Poller were sitting with Ben Choney and his Ch'omik ship's mate Ka'jach-Ta.

"Ben!" she exclaimed as she saw him.

"Ia!" He laughed that big, brassy laugh of his. "Have you fallen in with these disreputable fools?"

"Damn right I have," she said.

Ka'jach got to his feet, sheepish smile on his beautiful dark face. "Ia, *nu luotkåun min måuku midin*." Her native Bardinic, spoken in his Ch'omik accent, still made her heart flutter.

"And yet I've not seen you for years," she said.

"The sea calls, and you stayed here."

"Can we get back to business?" Lesk asked.

"Certainly," Ia said, sitting down. She raised an eyebrow at Lesk as a challenge. He may have assigned her to this place, but she wasn't going to get pushed out of his circle.

"Good," he said. His face showed a hint of begrudging respect. He knew she was the smartest one in his circle. "I'm told your contact will meet you out there, give you the goods, and then you just get them to us at the warehouse on the bank."

"River Patrol is on fire of late," Ben said. "I don't know what stirred them up, but they are making it harder to smuggle anything in."

"That's why we need you, Ben," Lesk said. "Because you're the best."

"Hardly."

"The best who knows the downriver islands," Lesk said.

"It's exactly because of Patrol acting up that this opportunity landed on us," Poller said. "It's hot here, but it's positively blazing down by the Pellistar Docks, which is what these folks usually use."

"Ah," Ben said. "So, this is an audition."

"Exactly."

"I hate auditions."

Ia didn't know all the details, but she knew that Lesk had been looking—under the Old Lady's orders—to expand his fingers into every bit of business in North Seleth. All but for the few blocks that the Old Lady said to leave alone. But he was also looking to cooperate with the players in other parts of the city. The Old Lady had said—or Ia was told she had said—that this was how they avoided another incident like the fire. Which was fine by Ia.

Jelsha knocked and opened the door at the same time. "Hey, ma'am. We got someone making trouble upstairs."

"Fine," Ia said, getting to her feet. "Ben, Ka'jach. Hope to see more of you soon. Right now, I have to empty out the sewage."

"Right now, I have to empty out the sewage."

Asti Rynax was impressed how well the flue scope had worked. After all these years, he was still surprised by his brother's genius for invention. He could hear everything they were saying. And his instincts to stalk after Ben Choney were right. That old pirate hadn't been in Maradaine in years, and he showed up on a river barge with Ka'jach, going through customs? No, that was very suspicious. But why was he working with Josie and Lesk?

"So what's your timeline?" Lesk asked.

"That depends. We get the delivery tomorrow, then we should be able to uncrate it, load the smuggle packs under rowboats by the next evening, and row our way up to meet you about an hour after sunset on the fourteenth."

Lesk was silent for a moment. "I'm not crazy about that, but I understand. Rather you take the time to do it right."

Asti was a little impressed. Maybe his time in Quarrygate had given Lesk a bit of sense. Or maybe that was Josie's influence. But Lesk had always been so impulsive, so foolhardy, for him to show respect and the patience to do a job right?

It was almost a shame. Lesk was getting better, and Asti was going to ruin it for him.

"Seven bells, at the Oberick Warehouses," Ben said.

"Which one?" Ka'jach asked.

"Number four," Lesk said.

"Then we can get it to the new house by nine," Essin said. Lesk made a hissing noise—Essin always said a bit too much, and that was just what Asti wanted to know. Whatever this was, it was tied to the new house—the mage house—on Holver Alley. And that was likely tied to the fire.

Ben coughed. "Unless we don't get the shipment, then we'll send word."

"Good," Lesk said. "While you're here, you want to visit a girl or two?"

"Tempting," Ben said. "But we should use the darkness to get back to the *Opportunity* without River Patrol mucking us up too much. Even still, we might have to dodge them all night. Best not waste time."

They exchanged pleasantries and left. Asti pulled the scope up through the flue and packed it back away. Good. He didn't know the full scale of what Lesk was up to yet, how it tied to the Mage Circle house that had been built on the Holver Alley wreckage, or Josie's machinations for the neighborhood, but right now he had a time and a place. That was somewhere to start.

He heard Ia outside on the front stoop, making some noise with a client she was tossing out on his ear. Asti crept across the roof and looked down. Ah, Innerick. The old oddball who always made gross comments to Helene when she was working in his goxie shop. Asti was glad she didn't have to deal with that anymore.

He needed to reach out to Helene. And Julien, of course. Kennith, Almer. Maybe Pilsen and Vellun. And Mila. He knew he shouldn't get her involved. She was moving on to better, heading to the University of Maradaine next week. But he also knew her too damn well. She would be in the thick of this until her first class day, if not after. And as much as he hated to admit it, he needed her. Her and the rest of the crew.

They now had a job to do.

"Well, I don't want your stupid girl anyway!" Innerick yelled at the shut door. That monstrous Bardinic woman had no right throwing him out. No right at all. He paid good money and should get what he wanted.

Now he would probably have to wander over to Benson Court and get one of the poxy girls there. Not much to look at, but they'd do anything for a couple ticks. He chuckled as he stumbled in that direction.

"Hey, man," someone said from the alley. "Seems you aren't too happy."

"No, I'm not," Innerick said. "Stupid girl was no fun."

"I know that, I know that," the man said. "You want to brighten your mood."

"No, thank you, sir," Innerick said. "I only do that with girls."

The guy laughed emptily. "Nothing like that, man. Nothing like that. I've got something else you might like. You ever run the violet?"

This man was talking about *effitte*. "I heard that's a bit dangerous."

"Well, yeah," the guy said. "The old stuff, it'd knock your brain out of your skull. But I got the new stuff."

"New stuff?"

The guy flipped his hand over, showing a tiny glass vial, but it wasn't filled with the thick purple liquid that Innerick had seen before. Instead, it was a fine powder. "This stuff sends you to the stars, but you'll still land on your feet."

Innerick's hand went forward almost of its own will. "So, like *effitte,* but cleaner?"

"Cleaner, stronger, better."

Innerick had always wanted to know what it was like. He had heard the stories, and he knew he should be afraid, but . . .

Roll it all.

"Yeah," he said. "What do you want?"

"For this?" the man said, holding up. "First time, half-crown."

"Deal," Innerick said, passing over the coin. "How do I . . ."

"Just rub it on your lip is all."

Innerick started to open the vial.

"Not here, friend," the man said. "Move along. Be discreet."

"Discreet, yes," Innerick said. "I'll do that."

He briskly started walking west. Maybe with this, one of those Benson Court slans would be satisfactory.

Another easy sale. Camping outside the Honey Hut was the best idea Weskie had had. Folks going in and folks coming out—especially sour-faced ones who clearly were not satisfied—were always looking for something to rattle their skulls. He had had his doubts about the new stuff when he was told to sell it, but the kick from that delightful purple powder was nothing to ignore.

He needed another knock himself. He slipped into the alley and opened up one of the little vials getting just a dash of the dust on his fingertips. Just a little, just enough that no one would notice. He stuck his finger in his mouth and rubbed it over his gums.

In moments they went numb and then warm and then that numb warmth spread up through his head and down his body all way to his toes, taking a little extra time in the tenders. He shuddered in joy as he put the cap back on. Maybe he should go into the Honey Hut himself. Rolling while riding on the powder would be amazing. Maybe he should try to get the girls inside hooked on it too. Good customers all around. Bosses would be pleased.

He started to put the vial back in his pocket, but his arm wouldn't move. He hadn't even noticed at first, but it was stuck.

No, not stuck. Bound. A rope was coiled around it.

"How did—"

Before he finished that thought, he was wrenched off the ground and dangling by his arm from the rooftop over the alley. Dangling from a rope that twisted tighter and tighter around his arm, as it coiled its way down his body.

Holding the rope was a shadowy figure, somehow a man but also the night itself—like he could see the sky and stars through the man, and they moved with him. All of the man was in darkness, except the bottom of his face.

Weskie thrashed about, desperate to get back to the ground, but terrified to even cry out.

"Hello, Weskie," the man made of darkness said.

He knew his name. The darkness knew his name. Weskie knew that the sinners were here for him, to drag him to the blazes for all eternity. The numb warmth became cold as ice, except for the wet warmth that filled his pants.

The figure reached out and plucked the vial from Weskie's hand.

"Now," he said, his voice seeming to echo about, so it was all at once right in front of Weskie, and yet also bouncing around from every direction. "You're going to tell me what this is, and where it's coming from."

"I—I—what?" Weskie gibbered. "Who are you?"

"Oh, Weskie," the figure said. "You're working for Fenmere and they didn't tell you? That's a shame."

He was real. The stories—he had heard guys like Lemt and Jendle talk of it but he hadn't really believed—the stories were true. "You—you're him?"

"Right," the Thorn said. "So start talking."

Chapter 2

VERCI HAD SPENT THE LAST three months falling in love with the new Rynax Gadgeterium. He had no idea what strings Major Grieson had pulled to put the shop in Verci's name and transfer the debt from the old location to the new one, but he didn't care. The shop was exactly what he wanted it to be. Open space for the storefront, with great morning light. Plenty of space in the back for his workshop. Three apartments on the upper floor: one for him and Raych, one for Asti, and one they could rent out for extra income.

It was everything they had wanted before the fire. Most days, Verci could let himself forget about the fire and focus on the future. Getting the shop ready to open, setting up his workshop, building up an inventory for sales. Asti had helped with all of that.

But Asti's head was definitely elsewhere. He had spent the first few days with a sledge, cracking through the floor in the back room. His instincts led him to an old storm cellar, sealed off and abandoned. He put his energy on cleaning it out, searching it thoroughly. Verci left him alone to that, but quietly built stairs and a hidden trapdoor in place of the hole Asti had made in the floor.

"Why even bother?" Raych asked after a week of that.

"No surprises," Asti had said. "We've done our best to lock down all the underground tunnels to the bakery, but maybe there's one we don't know. We need to know everything about this place, every secret it holds, and every secret it *can* hold."

"But this is just about knowing, right?" Raych stressed. "So we can hide and protect ourselves. Not for you all to run off on some new gig or scheme out of there."

"Right," Asti had said. Verci knew better than to believe that, he also knew better than to bring it up. Asti had respected the promise he had made that day in Kimber's Pub. He put up the show of respectability, and he didn't talk with Verci at all about a plan.

"But when it's time, we'll be ready," Asti had said that day. And Verci feared that "time" was coming shortly. Asti was out in the street most nights, watching, planning, and the bunker below them was his war room. He had been asking about inventions, getting him to build things that, according to Asti, would theoretically be useful. Then going out at all hours.

But Verci also had to admit, he was a little envious. As much as he loved working the shop, as much as he loved quiet evenings with Raych and Corsi, there was the thrill of a job that the straight life would never give him, and that he hadn't had for three months.

Well, almost hadn't. Last week Grieson abducted him and dragged him to the Parliament to defuse a monstrosity of a machine, built to kill over a dozen people. Then the next night he rescued a young woman from a personal deathtrap. Both of those were quite a thrill. If he was being honest with himself, they put the itch back in his fingers.

He hadn't told Asti whose daughter it was in the deathtrap. Asti had been stable of late—no spells or rages since the night at Henterman's. A good sign, and Verci wasn't about to do anything to make him spiral. Certainly not mention Cole Pyle or anyone else in that Constabulary household.

"What did you get done today?" Raych asked him. She had come in the back door—Verci had designed a special lock that wasn't opened with a key, but turning the knobs in the right order. Only he, Raych, and Asti could get in the back door, and it would damn well stay that way.

"Springboxes—music and jape-snaps."

"You've been focusing on toys." She wheeled in Corsi in his crib-carriage. One of Verci's better contraptions, in his own opinion.

"Well, Terrentin is coming. I'd like to open in a few days, so people can buy gifts for their children."

"That is brilliant," she said. "What's left to get the shop open?"

"Not much," he said. "Musclework with the shelves, setting up the displays. Nothing Asti and I can't do quickly."

"Then maybe we should spend a little on a paper job of the grand opening," she said. "For a week from today?"

"That's perfect." He got up from the work stool and crossed over to his wife, kissing her.

"Where is your brother?" Raych asked, her eyes fixed on the secret trapdoor to the basement.

"Out and about," Verci said. "Probably just having a few drinks at Kimber's."

She raised an eyebrow. "Hopefully just a few."

"Where are we staying tonight?"

"Here?" she asked. The apartments upstairs were not that comfortable yet, and the apartment above the bakery was better furnished. But Raych hadn't slept easily there since election night. Their apartment above the Gadgeterium was certainly habitable, it just needed more work.

"Sure, here."

Things would be stable and normal once the shop opened. The life he had promised Raych. They would be safe, and Josie Holt wouldn't bother them unless they crossed a line.

Verci tried not to think about the fact that Asti was fixing to cross that line.

Mila had had enough of studying. Her eyes were about to bleed out of her skull. She knew she had to keep at it, and she was grateful that Kimber had taken it upon herself to mother the blazes out of her to make sure she kept on it. In another week she'd be checking in at the University of Maradaine. She had had three months to make up the schooling she had never had.

Asti's solution to that problem, she had to admit, was pretty damned clever. He had gotten a ton of books—history of Druthal, foundation of law and government, plays, and novels—and just told her to read it all. He had also gotten a bunch of sword pulps, pennyhearts, and chillers. "Read those in between the other stuff. Read it all. Train yourself to love reading."

That helped. There was plenty of stuff she slogged through, but balancing that with reading things that were just fun made a big difference. Over the summer she had devoured all five of *The Pirates of New Acora*, though she wasn't as thrilled with the last two, where the main romantic couple was replaced by a far more insipid pair.

Then there was the arithmetic. She had never learned any, and that was where Kimber stepped in. Kimber knew all her numbers and sums and such—doing her own books at the pub—and drilled Mila up and down each evening. Then Kimber made Mila do the books herself. That, at least, was in trade for a room at the pub. But that also was so Kimber could keep an eye on her.

"Where are you going?" Kimber asked when Mila got up from the table, packing her books and notes together.

"To sleep," Mila said. "Head is pounding."

Kimber came around the bar and took the numbers sheet Mila had been working on. "All right, this is good."

"Damn right, it's good," Mila said. "Good night."

She went up to her room, but with little intention of sleeping. Once she was washed up and in her room, she changed into darker clothes, belted her rope and a couple knives, and slipped out the window.

Asti had been teaching her plenty of other things this summer.

She took to the roof, and from there worked her way to Ullen Street at the mouth of Holver Alley. From the vantage point of the roof across the street, she had good eyes on the mage house that had been built over the ashes of Mister Greenfield's shop.

She wondered how Mister Greenfield was doing. She hoped he was happy in his new life—with a new name—serving in a fancy house. He deserved that after all he went through.

The mage house was quiet. She had been keeping an eye on it most nights, determining who lived there, who came and went, and so forth. The mage house—the Firewings—that had been her priority. Whoever they were, Treggin had been one of theirs. He had been part of the plot to manipulate Lord Henterman, organized the gangs and street chaos in the neighborhood. The fact that his Circle suddenly put up a house here, in a part of town that never had a Mage Circle house before? Suspicious. She was going to find out whatever she could. Watch them, study them, learn everything about them.

There were at least three people—mages—who definitely lived there. One, an older man—older like Mister Greenfield, not Mister Gin. Fit body, half bald, trimmed beard and mustache. Usually wore waistcoat and suspenders, and left his shirt unbuttoned halfway down his chest.

Then, two women. One, oddly elegant, always in bright colors, always walking with poise. The other, slovenly and unkempt. And with an eyepatch. Mila was watching for a month before she finally recognized the woman—the same mage who worked for Mendel Tyne in his emporium. What was her name? Ecrain?

There were a few others who gave Mila a "mage" impression who came and went, but none of them stayed more than a day or two. Those three were the only permanent residents.

Then there was Enanger Lesk. Mila had seen him go in a couple times a week. He was coming up the street now, with a handful of thugs in tow. Scratch Cats, by the look of them. Conor was with them.

That hurt. He had been a good kid, one of her Bessie's Boys, one she could count on. But she had to leave that behind now. Conor already thought she had failed them, let them all get arrested. That was the part that stung the most: Conor and most of the other boys had been busted because of Josie's plan, and now Conor blamed Mila and worked for one of Josie's gangs. Didn't make any sense.

"What do we have?"

Asti had slipped up to her, mouse quiet, but she didn't let herself show any sign of surprise. She waited for him to situate himself next to her.

"The usual suspects inside. Ecrain, Fancy Lady, Creepy Jerk."

"We need names," Asti said.

"Does it really change things?"

"It's just good form," Asti said. "And Nange?"

"With a group of Scratch Cats tonight. Which includes Conor."

Asti sighed. "Sorry."

"He made his choice," Mila said. Even still, Nikey came to her, begging her to stop Conor. She might have done something.

"Nange coming in with a handful of street muscle means he's trying to show some strength to them," Asti said. "I'm betting he's still got something to prove to them."

"They're mages. I imagine they're not easily impressed."

He pulled out a lensescope and peered down at the place. "I imagine not."

"You have news?" she asked. He had an excitement about him that she hadn't seen for a while. The past few months had been more workmanlike, methodical scouting of the mage house and Lesk's crew. But tonight, he had the twitch.

"Why do you ask?"

She looked at him, and saw the slightest of grins on his stubbly face. That clinched it. "There's news."

"Maybe," he said. "Definitely something we *can* act on. Question stands if we *should*."

She turned so she could get a better look at him. "Hesitation? From you?"

"We rushed with Tyne, and we rushed with Henterman, both times because we had to. And we got lucky both times."

"Bit of talent."

"Bit of talent, a lot of luck. I don't like to rely on that." He shook his head. "Henterman's was rutting sloppy, Mila. We went in not even clear on the goal. And now—look, new players."

Mila turned back to spot the couple that was walking up to the house. Man and a woman, both about Asti's age. Not fancy people, not service people either. They had a look of clerical work. Bookkeepers, pencil-pushers. Perhaps a little more refined.

"Lawyers?" she asked as the two went in.

"Could be," Asti said. He shifted his legs to sit on the roof. "So, there's a shipment coming in the day after tomorrow, will be smuggled in around seven bells, then brought here at nine bells."

"What kind of shipment?"

"That's what I want to know. I've got an instinct that this is what Lesk wants to prove—to the mages and these other folks."

"Why them?"

Asti passed the scope to her. Following his direction, she saw through the window. Sitting room, the two newcomers were sitting in chairs, and Fancy Lady and Creepy Man on a couch. Lesk and his boys were standing, Lesk in the center with them at his back. He was doing all the talking, while the rest focused on him.

"Looks like he's telling them what's what," she said. "He's in charge in there."

"He's talking, but it's to get their approval. The new people came in last, but they're given chairs. He's left standing. He's deferring to them."

"So they're the boss?"

"No, they represent the boss," Asti said.

"So who's the boss?"

"That's the big question," Asti said, shaking his head. "Depends where they're coming from, what they're peddling. It would be someone who Josie would be humble toward. That's a short list to guess from, but I'd rather have information than speculation."

She had a suspicion what he was thinking. "You want to hit that shipment, don't you?"

He sighed. "Instinct is telling me that it's an opportunity to knock these guys hard, but—"

"But we've only got one shot for a solid hit, and if we miss . . ." She let it hang.

"Unless we do it mouse quiet," he said.

That made sense. Hit the shipment in a way that Josie and Lesk's crew would never suspect them. "So how do we do that?"

"I'm still just thinking," he said. "And it might not be we. You're leaving in a week."

"You're talking about the day after tomorrow. I'm still here."

"Everything is in the air at the moment," he said. "What was that?"

Mila looked back to the house. The businesswoman had opened a case and taken out a single vial, handing it to Lesk. The case held several more vials, but she couldn't see what they were.

"Payment?"

"Sample?" Asti said back. "Did you get a good look?"

"No," she said. The two lawyer types were getting up to leave. "We need to get close. Drunken Steve and Nervous Doxy?"

"You're not dressed for that."

"Honeybee?"

"Definitely not dressed for that. And that doesn't work too well with a man and a woman."

"They are a bit too polished for that." She thought for a second. "Can you give me a Drunken Steve and follow my lead?"

Asti paused for a moment. "You've got a play?" She wasn't sure how to read his face, but there was an odd pride in his smile.

"Yeah, I do," she said.

"Then lead on."

She shimmied down the drainpipe, and once on the ground, ditched her rope and one of her knives in the gutter. As Asti came down behind her, she stripped off her shirt, tore her chemise, and smudged her face and collarbone with dirt.

"Ready?" she asked as he took off his jacket, so to look less like a rooftop thief.

He nodded and roared, "Get back here!" She darted out of the darkened niche into Holver Alley, as the lawyerly couple were starting to walk down Ullen. Mila tore at them at top speed.

"Oh, help me, help me, he's a beast!" she said, barreling into the man. In a frantic performance, she clawed and pawed at him, while Asti came stalking at them all.

"Get your own girl!" Asti snarled at them. Mila's quick search didn't yield anything like a billfold or papers, but the man did have a knucklestuffer in one of his pockets.

"Protect me, sir, I know you can," she said, scurrying behind him and clutching the woman. The phrase that let Asti know the man was armed.

"Be on your damned way, folks," Asti said. "I got business with this strumpy tart."

"I'm a good girl, I am," Mila whispered in the woman's ear. "I was just walking home when he spotted me . . . and grabbed me . . . tore my . . ." She went into heaving sobs, while her free hand sliced a hole in the woman's case. She slid two fingers inside, grabbed a vial, and pulled it out. "Oh, please help me."

"Do something," the woman said firmly to her companion.

"Be about somewhere else," the man said with authority. "Surely there are appropriate slatterns to slake your lust on. No need to dally with this child."

Mila winked to Asti to let him know she had it, and slipped the vial into the hidden pocket of her slacks with her knife. Mission complete, time to extricate themselves.

"Maybe I'll slake it on your face!" Asti shouted, swinging wildly at the man. It was a good feint, showing none of Asti's usual fighting prowess. He barreled into Mila and the woman in his missed punch. Mila screamed again and ran off. She heard Asti take a hit from the man. She couldn't hear what happened next as she worked her way back around to the alley to fetch her shirt and weapons. By the time she was back up the drainpipe to the roof, Asti was there as well, sporting a bloody lip.

"Sorry," she said.

"It's nothing," he said. "So what is it?"

She handed over the vial. He held it up to the moonlight.

"No clue," he said. "Let's go see Almer. He'll figure it out."

Asti paced about Almer Cort's apothecary shop, one of the few surviving bits of the old Holver Alley, while Almer examined the powder in the vial. Mila sat in a corner, reading *The Seas to Khol Taia*, a war novel by the same fellow who wrote *The Shores of New Fencal.* It was a decent enough historical account of the Island War while being an entertaining read. Asti was glad that Mila was enjoying reading, enjoying learning. Hopefully, she'd enjoy getting the blazes out of this neighborhood and live a proper decent life.

But he would miss her. Blazes, she had a good instinct for the trade. In seconds she had a scheme to swipe a vial off those two and put it into action. They didn't even need to plan, she just had her instincts, matched with his rhythm. Just like he and Verci had back in the day.

Or you and me.

The voice in the back of his head whispered to him.

"Shut it," Asti whispered back.

"Hmm?" Mila asked, looking up from her book.

"Nothing," Asti said. The voice just chuckled. It had been there since Henterman's. Now his skull had three residents: himself, the beast, and the voice.

Her voice.

Mila gave him a look, raising her eyebrow.

"Really," he said.

"You let me know."

She's going to betray you, like they all do. Even Verci is going to.

Asti closed that off, refused to listen. It wasn't saying anything new. He went over to Almer, who was looking at several rats in cages.

"Why do you have those here?" Asti asked.

"To run tests like these on," Almer said.

"Why did you *already have them*?" Mila asked.

"To be ready for moments like this." He frowned, as he sprinkled a bit of the powder into a beaker of liquid, which changed color. "Where did you get this?"

"Stole off a pair of swells who met with the mages and Lesk."

"Hmm," he said. He looked at the rats again. "Saints, most of them are dead."

"You killed them?" Mila asked.

"This killed them." He took a small baton and prodded one of the other ones. "I gave less to these." He pulled on a leather glove and opened the cage. He cautiously grabbed the rat, but it didn't put up any struggle as he picked it up. With his ungloved hand, he opened its eyes and inspected it.

"What do you think?"

"I'd have to run more tests, but . . . my gut? This is *effitte*."

"I've never seen *effitte* look like this," Asti said. He looked to Mila.

"I never even seen it."

Almer put the rat back in the cage. "I've never seen it like this either, but that's my best guess. If it is *effitte*, it's a lot stronger. More effective, probably more dangerous."

"What do you mean, more dangerous?" Mila asked.

"People probably get latched to it faster, harder. Easy to do too much, look at these rats. Not to mention the number who'll go into the trance." Almer pushed the vial away in disgust. "Is this going around the neighborhood?"

Asti scowled. "It might be. If so, it's something we need to contend with, regardless."

"What do you mean?" Mila asked.

"I mean, we've been playing quiet until we have our moment to strike at Lesk, the Old Lady, and the folks in that house, and to find out who or what was really behind the Holver Alley fire."

"The Andrendon Project," Mila said darkly.

"And we're really not closer," Asti said. He picked up the vial. "But if it involves them bringing this sewage into Seleth, I don't think we can sit around and let it happen."

"You're right there," Almer said.

"What if this is what's coming in on the shipment?" Mila asked.

It clicked together. "Ben Choney was saying the River Patrol has gotten more intense upriver. Effitte smugglers, they probably need to use a new part of town, so they're coming here."

It's like you can't help yourself.

"So those swells, they work for the *effitte* dealers."

"No," Asti said. "They work for Fenmere. And he's coming here."

Mila picked her book up off the floor and tucked it into her waistband. "So, everyone, tomorrow? Safe-house?"

Asti nodded. "Everyone, tomorrow at the safehouse."

Helene Kesser went to her room, letting Julien finish up with the dishes from supper. For the past few months, he had been really happy. They were selling cheese and cured meats. He was working hard each day, smile on his face. They were doing good business, making an honest living. She had an honest-to-the-saints suitor who called on her regularly, the sort of decent fellow a girl could marry. Saints, a constable, and a good man at that. It was everything she should want.

And she rutting well hated it.

But for Julien, and his happiness, she'd endure it. Her cousin had been through enough, used by folks like Josie Holt or Nange Lesk for his strength, beaten so hard in the process he sometimes forgot what he was doing or where he was. But not with the cheese shop. Every day they worked, he was a little brighter, a little happier, a little more the sweet boy she had grown up with before that horrible job.

And he was all she had left. The Orli Fever had taken Mom, the job had taken Dad and Uncle Holsten, and the fire had taken Grandma. She made a promise she would take care of him, and she would hold to that, even if it made her rutting miserable.

In her room she opened up her wardrobe—the one Verci had made for her. With a click of the hidden catch, the secret compartment opened up, with her working clothes and her crossbows. She wasn't sure why she had decided to keep them hidden. It wasn't like Covrane didn't know about them.

Maybe it was better for her to keep them out of sight, out of memory.

She kept coming back to them, though.

She laid out a leather tarp and put each of the crossbows on it. Orton and Holsten, the two snap-shot hip-hangers. Simple, easy loading, short range bows. The kind to keep loaded while on a job, ready to fire as fast as she could draw it. She checked them both, oiling the wood, cleaning the mechanisms. Then the Rainmaker. Long range, high power sniper bow. She could thread a needle five blocks away with her, but not the sort of thing one carried around easily. Right now, it was disassembled. For practice, she put it back together, checked the gears, checked the tensions. All good. After it was assembled and checked, she took it back apart again.

Finally, The Action. This was her real beauty, the Verci Rynax original. Fast reload, light, durable, and accurate enough to nick the wings off a fly at a hundred paces. If she ever was in a scrap, this was the one she wanted in her hands.

Julien came into the room. "There a job coming up?"

"Don't think so," she said, putting the things back away in the wardrobe. "Just maintaining my gear, you know?"

"Right," he said. "The lieutenant, he's at the door."

"Good," she said, closing up the wardrobe. She brushed herself off. "Leave me a bottle of wine out, and go to bed, hmm?"

"Sure," he said. His big hand rested on her shoulder. "It's all right, you know. If you want to do a job."

Saints, he knew. "Just want to be ready, for when Asti needs us."

He scowled for a moment. "What was the signal for that again?"

"Chalk mark on the kitchen window, with a lit candle," she reminded him.

"Right. That's what I thought. Because it's out there right now."

He had seen it and forgot what it meant. She tamped down the urge to admonish him. His memory was never very good. "All the more reason for you to get some sleep. Looks like we've got a busy day tomorrow."

He went into his room. Helene went back to the kitchen, put her own mark and candle up for a countersignal, and opened up the jug of wine. Taking a deep breath, she went to the door to let in Lieutenant Jarret Covrane, the man whose heart she'd have to break, eventually.

Chapter 3

VERCI CAME DOWNSTAIRS IN THE morning to find Asti hard at work in the front of the store, putting up the display shelves. As it was with most mornings, Raych was already up and gone to the bakery before he woke up. He had long since gotten used to that aspect of their marriage.

"Something's up," Verci said. If Asti was getting all this work done before Verci was even there, he had a plan in the works.

"Safehouse in an hour," Asti said. He pointed to a teapot on one of the tables. "Made tea."

"Why?"

"Because you like tea in the morning."

"Why the safehouse in an hour?" Verci went and poured himself a cup. "I presume we're meeting everyone."

"I'm not calling in Pilsen and Vellun, not yet. Those two are still need-to-know." He kept at the work, setting up another shelf.

"And what am I?"

"What do you mean?"

"I mean, you've decided this, which means you've

probably already talked to Mila, Helene, everyone else. Am I last?"

"I didn't want to wake you."

"Wake Raych."

Asti put down his tool. "Right now, it's definitely better if she's need-to-know as well. And you know that."

"She doesn't want us doing this anymore."

"And you?"

Verci clicked his tongue, unsure what to say. "That depends on what 'this' is. What did you find out last night?"

"Few things. Lesk and his people are having something smuggled in through the river. Ben Choney is bringing it."

"Ben? How's he doing?"

"Oh, fabulous. After I spied on them, we had a few beers and talked about the old days."

"Don't be a jerk." Drinking a few sips of tea, he went to the other side of the shelf. "Let's get this one on the wall. So something is being smuggled in. And this concerns us, why? Is it about the fire, or the Andrendon?"

"Not directly, but—."

"So it shouldn't be our concern. Long game." Verci didn't think he should have to remind Asti of these things. "Keep watching, keep planning. Surgical strike." Verci picked up his side of the shelf.

"It is connected to the mage house."

Verci put it back down.

"You're sure?"

"Yeah. The shipment will be delivered to the mage house. Tomorrow night, delivered to the warehouse at seven bells, and then to the mages by nine bells. That's the plan."

Verci swore heavily. If it was about the house, then it likely was about Andrendon. And he couldn't ignore it.

"And it might be *effitte*."

Verci's heart jumped. "Wait, for real?" For all the

ills North Seleth faced, at least it didn't have that poison in the streets.

"It's something like *effitte*, but it has Almer baffled."

"Saints above and sinners below," Verci said. He decided not to make anything about Asti bringing this to him after everyone else, since Asti was right. If this involved the mage house, and it involved *effitte*, it was something big. More importantly, it had to tie to Josie making deals with Gemmen and all the Neighborhood Kings—*effitte* meant Fenmere and the Dentonhill cartel.

They needed to know more, if nothing else.

"Pick up the shelf," Verci said. "If we've got an hour, let's get this done."

Measures were taken in case Josie had people watching the shop, watching Asti and Verci. Verci set a few windups in the shop that would make enough clacking and banging to give the illusion that they were in there working. Then they put on quick disguises—nothing that would pass close inspection—and slipped out the back door. Verci prayed they weren't under any serious scrutiny from Josie, as none of these measures would hold up. "Now the safehouse?"

"Now to Kennith. I left him a signal last night, but didn't see a countersignal this morning. Let's make sure he got the word."

Verci shrugged. He'd more than happily go see Kennith. He was hoping, once the Gadgeterium was up and running, to work with him on some legitimate projects. Kennith was a good carriage driver, and he loved his horses, but he also was a damn good builder. Working with Kennith on the carriages, designing new ones, was always a treat. They had made the spring-powered carriage that shot down eight blocks faster than an unencumbered horse could gallop it. Ken had had some ideas on how to improve it, make it last longer, and Verci was all for that project.

Maybe spring-powered, unhorsed carriages were the future.

They went to the North Seleth Inn, passing the inn itself to walk along the back path to the carriage house, where Kennith worked and slept. It had been a familiar enough place that they went in without knocking. One of the carriages was in the middle of the room. A pair of legs stuck out from under it, and the familiar sounds of a wrench tightening the axle bolts filled the room.

"Hey, Ken," Verci said. "You busy today? Because we've got a thing."

"Oh, there is a thing?" The voice from under the carriage was not Kennith's. Too female, too accented. The owner of the legs pulled herself out from under the carriage. A Ch'omik woman, but nothing like Kennith. Kennith was Ch'omik: ebony dark skin, thickly curled black hair which he kept cropped short. But he had been born and raised in Druthal, and regardless of the color of his skin, he was as Druth as Asti and Verci were—utterly, despite some people constantly claiming otherwise. And Verci knew Ken got it worse than he or Asti ever did.

This woman was truly Ch'omik, as in born in Ch'omik-Taa. Strong accent. Muscular arms bare, with swirling tattoos and scarification. Hair in long, tight braids. Multiple rings in her ears, with a chain leading to the stud in her nose. She looked at the two of them with an intense bearing, before a wide smile broke out on her face.

"You must be the brothers Rynax," she said. Turning to the back of the carriage house, she called out, "Kennith! Your Rynax boys are here, and they say there is a thing!"

Kennith came out from the back, pulling on a shirt. "Hey, boys. Something going on?"

"There's been a development," Asti said. "We're all meeting to . . . discuss it."

"There is something they want to steal, and they need you to drive the carriage!" she said, a bit too loudly for Verci's comfort.

Kennith grinned sheepishly. "I see you, uh, met Jhoqull-Ra."

Asti raised an eyebrow, but then said, *"Ahgdekh Eka, E-ra."*

"Dekh'rra Qha," she said back with a nod of her head. "Was that all your Ch'omik, Rynax?"

"I can also say thank you and goodbye politely," Asti said. "I've learned those in several languages."

"Smart," she said. Turning to Verci, she said, "So you must be the inventor man. Gadgets and creations of wonder."

"Guilty," Verci said.

"So, we need to go?" Kennith asked with a nervous laugh.

"Just a second," Verci said, crouching next to the carriage. "What are the two of you doing to this?"

"Just an idea I had," Kennith said, until Jhoqull coughed. "That is, *we* had."

"He means I had it," she said. "Though he mentioned the spring-powered pedal drive."

"That's the name?" Asti asked.

"It's a work in progress," Kennith said.

She went on. "In that first run you had, it was all bouncing and pounding. At that speed, of course it would be."

Verci shrugged. "I was on a horse at the time, trying to keep up."

She looked to Asti.

"I wasn't even there at the time. You were talking about that?"

"We were talking about carriages," Kennith said defensively. "She's a driver, too."

"The best in the Hodge," she said with a grin. "If he lets you down, give me a shout."

Verci's attention was under the carriage. The axles were completely redesigned, so each one was independent and connected to springs, able to move up and down. Verci stood up and pushed the carriage down on one side, and it bounced back up. "So if you hit a bump or a hole, it bounces with it."

"That's the idea," Jhoqull said.

Verci liked it, but he saw some problems. "You're going to need more steel reinforcement on the shafts, if not just make them out of steel to begin with."

"I told you!" Jhoqull said, smacking Kennith in the chest.

"I didn't want to—"

"He doesn't want to go to the forge my cousins have in the Hodge," she said to Verci. "He doesn't like to show his face there." Kennith had never spoken of why he didn't care for the Hodge, but he had made a point of saying he had no interest in living there, even though he had some people there. People, clearly, like Jhoqull.

"We're running a bit behind," Asti said.

"Oh, yes, go have your secret crime meeting," Jhoqull said. "I think that's wonderful." She grabbed Kennith by the chin and pulled him close to her, kissing him. "Have a wonderful time, and if you need a real driver, let me know."

She left the carriage house without another word.

"She's entertaining," Asti said.

"It does get lonely here," Kennith said sheepishly.

"No judgment," Asti said. "We need to move forward with our lives. Glad to see you doing it."

"I'm right about the steel," Verci said. "And the wheels as well, I think."

"I'm listening," Kennith said, as Asti led them out of the carriage house.

"Did I tell you about what I saw last week? A pared-down pedalcart, so it was just a pedalcycle. Now that's a brilliant idea . . ."

The new safehouse was not ideal. Asti had been spoiled by the grand warehouse headquarters Josie had set up for them before. That space had been secure, filled with amenities that made working and planning their next move so much easier. But that space was Josie's, lost to them now.

This was what he could get while keeping a clean appearance: the empty apartments above Doc Gelson's office. Gelson had lived up there when he had a wife and children, but he was alone now. He had moved himself into the back room of his office, sleeping there when he wasn't seeing patients or drinking the night away at Kimber's. He rented it out to Asti with no questions and a firm declaration that he wanted to know nothing. That was an arrangement Asti could live with.

The apartments had their own front door and stairwell directly to the street, as well as another stairway from Gelson's office, an ironwork back ladder to the alley, and easy trapdoor access to the rooftop. The roof had a good view to the docks, the river, and to Saint Bridget Square.

Asti went into the alley, while Verci and Kennith went into Gelson's office, going up from inside. He climbed up the ladder and slipped into the window, disarming Verci's snap trap as he entered, and rearming it once the window was shut.

"I love these little paranoid rituals of yours." Helene was in the sitting room, boots on the table, while Julien was in the kitchen. "All we did was bring tea, cheese and ham, bread and preserves. Because I, at least, have a sense of how to meet people in the morning."

"Tea?" Julien asked.

"Please, and all the rest." Asti went over to the table. He appreciated Julien bringing food and hospitality. He hadn't seen the big guy as happy as he was working their new shop. And their meats really were excellent. "You doing all right, you two?"

"The shop is good," Julien said.

"We're actually making a good, clean living," Helene said. She gave him a look that spoke volumes, though.

"Hopefully, nothing we're talking about today will change that. But we've got to decide our plan."

"It's time for a plan?" Julien asked, coming over with the tea and a plate of food.

Verci and Kennith came up the stairs, Almer with them. "That is the question, isn't it?"

"We need to decide that," Asti said. "And, I know each of you has your own thing right now. Each of you got your deal from Grieson, your lives are clean and honest."

"Until the next card is played," Helene said.

"We don't know—" Kennith started.

"You think the fire was just to build a mage house?" Helene shot back before Ken could finish. "No, that is just the next step in, what is it called?"

"The Andrendon Project," Asti said.

"Yeah, that. Whatever it is, it's deep in money and trouble. It's going to deliver more pain to this neighborhood."

"So what's happened?" Kennith asked.

"We should wait for Mila."

The trapdoor to the roof opened up, and Mila dropped down. She was dressed in a smart professional suit, with woolen skirt and waistcoat, carrying a valise. She even wore a set of specs that made her look a few years older. "I've been waiting five minutes for one of you to say that."

"Should soundproof that roof," Asti muttered.

"You've been busy," Verci said, giving her appearance a nod of approval. "And here I thought you were just studying."

"I've been studying," she said, sitting at the table. She tossed the valise over to Asti. "But I've also been working an angle, just like you have. Namely, I've been working this from the legitimate end of things."

"Legitimate?" Helene asked. She nudged the tray of bread and cheese closer to Mila with her boot. Mila helped herself to it.

"The bureaucratic side of it. For the past three months I have—or at least, Jendly Marskin has—" she gestured to her outfit.

"You've been a terrible influence on her," Verci said to Asti. Leaning in to Mila, he asked, "Who is Jendly Marskin?"

Mila stood back up and put on her Jendly persona—prim body language and clipped, educated accent. "She's a very harried young secretary and clerk who is constantly put upon by her superiors. But she's made very good friends with several clerks in the City Archives offices. And with a wink here, a crown there, an idle favor elsewhere, she's been able to get her hands on files and papers that other folks might not so easily acquire. For example, what do you know about Circle Law?"

"Very little," Verci said. Asti watched his face, which was absolutely beaming. Verci was just as proud of Mila as Asti was, and for damn good reason. In the past months she had gone from a gifted street rat with talented hands to the kind of operator who could con, spy, or plan. Anything she wanted.

All the more reason to send her to University and give her real options.

"Well, Circles are obligated to register with the city, and those registrations include membership rolls, real properties, charters, but—they are protected documents. No one is supposed to even look at them without an order coming from the level of the Archduchy Court, and even that requires a suit which would be challenged by the Circle lawyers."

"What good does that do us?" Kennith asked.

Mila shrugged. "The good it does is, that protection is largely based on the honor of the clerks of the bureaucracy. Who aren't supposed to let someone like the young Miss Marskin down into the archives, but when she shows up with pastries and pleasant conversation . . ."

Asti opened up the valise. "You have the files on the Firewings?"

"I have the files on the Firewings," she said. Her face fell a little. "I'm still trying to find the ones on the Creston Group, Andrendon, all that stuff, but I haven't been able to figure out where in the archives they are."

Kennith grunted in annoyance. "Can we get to why we're here?"

Mila glared at Asti. "Didn't you tell them?"

"I was getting to it," Asti said, thumbing through the files. It really was excellent information. Mila was, once again, a treasure. He was going to hate to lose her. "So, this is what we know: Lesk, and therefore Josie, is having something smuggled in through the riverside warehouses, using Ben Choney and the *Opportunity.* After the drop, it's to be delivered to the Firewing mage house in Holver Alley. This shipment is likely this new powdered form of *effitte.* The Firewings may or may not be in league with Willem Fenmere, which suggests an alliance between Fenmere and the Old Lady."

Helene leaned forward. "You think she's looking to take a piece of the *effitte* trade?"

"I have no idea," Asti said.

"Or is she going to let him sell here, in exchange for something else?" Verci asked. "There's a lot of things we don't know."

"We need to find out," Julien said. "So we all stay safe."

Kennith walked around the table, grabbing a piece of cheese off Asti's plate as he talked. "That's not what you're thinking, is it, Asti? You want to steal that shipment before it gets to the mage house, but you don't want to sacrifice our well-earned stability to do it. So you want to know if we're willing to take that risk, not knowing if the shipment is this new *effitte*, not knowing how big of a wrench this throws at the Old Lady, or more importantly, the folks behind the fire. There's too much we don't know, but there's also too much at stake to ignore it. Is that the size of it?"

Kennith had nailed it perfectly.

Almer spoke up. "This new *effitte*, whatever it is, it's ridiculously dangerous. I was up all night running tests. A lot of dead rats. It's bad news, all around. I don't know about you all, but I do not want to see it hitting our streets. Not if we can do something." Verci made a grunt of vague agreement.

Asti took another sip of his tea. "I don't want the drugs here, and I definitely don't want the Dentonhill cartel that comes with it. So we need a plan. A clever plan that keeps us in the clear, but takes this out of their hands. So what do we have?"

"Isn't that usually your job, boss?" Helene asked.

"Yeah," Asti said. "But we're a team in this together. We do this together, all in the same book. I don't blame anyone for not wanting a piece of it."

"Julie and I are in," Helene said. Julien's face didn't say the same thing at all, but he nodded along just the same.

"You even have to ask?" Mila said.

Asti looked to Verci. His face was uncharacteristically unreadable.

"You say Ben Choney is bringing this in with Ka'jach?"

"Far as I know," Asti said.

"Then maybe—and this is ridiculous I'm even suggesting it, but *maybe*—what we need is a Middleman Game."

Asti groaned. Verci was right. It was terrible but yet kind of perfect for what they needed.

"What's a Middleman Game?" Mila asked.

"It's damned near impossible," Asti said. "So many ways it could go wrong."

"True," Verci said. "But if it goes right, no fighting, no chasing, and no one even knows what happened until it's too late. They certainly won't know we had anything to do with it."

"What the blazes is a Middleman?" Kennith asked.

"The idea is this," Asti said. "You've got a drop happening—someone delivering the merch you want, someone else getting it. Sort of thing that happens every day, right?"

"Right," Kennith said.

"So, a Middleman Game means you put yourself between them. You pretend to be the sellers for the buyers, and the buyers for the sellers. If you do pull it off, you walk off with both the merch and the money, and both of them blame each other for it going wrong."

The room was quiet for a moment, and then Kennith asked, "Well, how do you even do that?"

"I don't have any idea. Like I said, damn near impossible."

"Damn near," Verci said. "But I was thinking, at night? In the moonslight? Ben and Ka'jach?" He pointed to Almer and Kennith. "The resemblance isn't too bad."

Verci was right. That could rutting well work.

"Do we have the people we need to pull this off?" Verci asked as they came in the back door of the Gadgeterium. "I mean, I put up a good face in there, but—"

"A good face?" Asti asked back. "You pitched the plan."

"I know!" Verci said. "And I know how impossible—"

"Your idea. Why would you even—"

"Because we don't have good options. I'm sorry, Asti, but . . . there's a lot of things we don't know."

"We know tomorrow night, seven bells, Oberick Warehouses. Number four."

"That's a start. Who owns that warehouse? What sort of setup is in there? Guarded? Security?"

"I would assume," Asti said.

"And is Lesk going to be there? One of his lieutenants? Or just underlings? We need to know more about their whole organization."

"Verci, you wound me," Asti said. He opened up the trapdoor to the bunker. "What do you think I've been doing for the past three months?"

Verci followed down the stairs as Asti lit a couple lamps, revealing a wall covered in papers, drawings, maps, and notes. Near the ceiling was a drawing of Josie, and below her, Enanger Lesk, Kel Essin, Ren Poller, Sender Bell, and Ia Estäan, each drawing labeled. Then further networks of people, organizations, locations. Asti had even compiled sketches of the doxies at the Honey Hut, regular customers there and at the Elk Road Shack. And there was a line leading to the

Firewing house, with sketches of three mages. One, with the eyepatch, labeled "Ecrain," and the other two unlabeled.

"Do you even sleep?" Verci asked.

"Not much," Asti said back. "Now, thanks to Mila, we've got names to attach to the mages in the Firewings." He grabbed a charcoal stylus and a sheet of paper, writing names and attaching them to the sketches. "Ecrain Jelsen," "Pria Mandicall" for the man, and "Larian Amalie" for the other woman.

"Why didn't you tell me about this?" Verci asked. "I would have helped."

Asti sat down in a chair. "First of all, you needed to be focused on getting the store together. Especially building up our inventory."

"Fair enough."

"And you deserve to spend your evenings with your family. I don't have anything better to do. I need to stay busy or . . ." He paused in silence for a moment. That silence confirmed Verci's worst fears: Asti was getting worse and keeping it from him. "The work keeps me focused, and focus holds everything together." He tapped the stylus on his temple.

Asti hadn't spoken much of the night at Henterman's, where he had acted like a mindless windup toy, mercilessly killing guards, and then trying to kill Verci, before snapping out of Liora Rand's control. And that was how he spoke of it, in the rare moments when he did: control. Like he had no will to act, save what she put to him.

Verci didn't know what else he could do, so he went with Dad's old advice: just drive forward. "So, the warehouses. That's right near where our old safehouse was. We have to assume there're Josie tunnels leading there as well."

"Not that I've found," Asti said. He went to the map of the neighborhood and lifted it up, revealing another map underneath. "The scope of what's under the city is . . . frankly, it's awe-inspiring. I've only managed to map a little of it. I wish I had time to explore it fully. Much of what Josie used, she inherited."

"This is beyond sewers," Verci said.

"Sewers, catacombs, I don't even know what. Some of it was just pure quarrying out stone to build the city back in the day."

"Centuries ago."

"And no formal maps or records of it all, at least that Mila and I could find. Which is why I've had to make this map myself. The bakery is a hub, which is why she made that her center of operations back in the day."

The map Asti had drawn was wild. It was like a whole extra city, several layers below them. "How deep does it go?"

"Once I found a ladder that went down fifty, seventy-five feet at least." Asti shrugged. "I'd love to find out, but that's not a priority right now. I mostly wanted to confirm our security here, and in the bakery as much as I could, and anywhere else with our people." He pointed to spots on it that corresponded to Almer's shop, Kimber's Pub, the safehouse above Gelson's, the cheese shop. "As far as I can tell, all of those are cut off from Josie's tunnels."

"Nothing by Saint Bridget's Square?" Verci asked. "That's surprising."

"Nothing I've found," Asti said. "Maybe there were church catacombs that don't connect to the rest, or . . . I don't even know." He added two new facial sketches to the board—he really was quite gifted at drawing—and added a label under them. "FENMERE LIEUTENANTS."

"The ones you and Mila saw last night?"

"Yeah."

Verci looked over the whole of the board again. "So, what do we know about the Oberick Warehouses?"

"It's a whole block of warehouses by the riverbank. High-fenced enclosure. It's all owned by some east-town company, who then rent out the individual warehouses to other companies."

"Including Josie?"

"At least one of them. Maybe all of them. Mila and I dug through city records, but there's a lot of financial and ownership information that I don't really understand."

Verci chuckled. "Asti Rynax admits he doesn't understand something. That's new."

"Shut it."

"Fine. But she owns at least one."

"Presumably warehouse number four. Sender Bell is in charge of a few crews of bruisers and wagon men, at least one of which works out of the Oberick."

"Legitimate?"

"On its face. Uptenning Holding Company. They handle storage and distribution of dry goods, cloth, other merchandise. That's where your wife gets the flour for the bakery."

Verci frowned at that. A reminder that everything they did in this neighborhood was tied to Josie, tied to the illegitimate. Even if he lived a straight life from now on, it would still be touched by her and the rest of the underworld corruption. Just like the tunnels beneath them, there was no telling all the ways she twisted and wound about the entire city, especially North Seleth.

"What about the physical layout?"

"Haven't done a sneak inside, not yet. Was planning on that tonight."

"I'll go with you on that. I wouldn't hate it if Helene found a perch, Mila paced the perimeter."

Asti gave him a smile. "I was hoping you'd say that. I was ready to go myself, but—"

"No, brother," Verci said. "We're a team. And I'm getting a bit of an idea of how we can pull this off, but I'll want to see what it all looks like to see if it'll work."

"Sounds good. I'm thinking of a problem with a Middleman, though. We have Almer and Ken pretending to be Ben and Ka'jach, presuming no one in the Oberick knows them. We need a plan to account for that, by the way."

"You have one?"

"Not yet. But here's my main concern there: We send Almer and Kennith into warehouse four for a fake drop—phony product for their real money. We need to do that first, so then we can trade the real money for the real product once Ben and Ka'jach deliver it."

"Give them real money?"

Asti shrugged. "Ben was always a good sort. I don't want him to get shorted."

Verci accepted that. "I see the problem. Who's playing the warehouse boys for the sake of Ben? He knows us. I think he knows Helene, too."

Asti grit his teeth, muttering a low curse before he said, "I think we need Pilsen and Vellun."

Chapter 4

ASTI FELT GUILTY FOR NOT having gone down to the West Birch Stage since Pilsen and Vellun had gotten their deal from Grieson after the events at Henterman's. While both of them had been vital parts of the operation for several gigs, Asti had kept them at arm's length for the past three months. He didn't trust either of them. They were not part of the plan to lay low and strike when they were ready.

Pilsen and Vellun were actors by trade, but conmen at heart. More importantly, Pilsen had been close to Josie for decades, and Asti couldn't be sure if the old man was loyal to her. Asti couldn't be sure about a lot of things. Pilsen appeared to be slowly losing himself—he was an old man after all—and his memory wasn't what it used to be. Or it might be a brilliant, calculated act. As much as he loved Pilsen, Asti knew the man was utterly capable of that level of deception.

Vellun was a decent sort—or as close to that as a dedicated conman could be. Asti had originally taken the pretty young man as dim but well-meaning, wanting to follow the old man's schemes out of love and loyalty. But in the moment of the offer from Major

Grieson, Vellun showed he was much smarter than he had let on. Asti hadn't ever trusted him, but that had made him even more cautious.

Despite that, he needed their skills right now. They were planning a con job, and that required the best conmen they could get on board. Asti didn't trust Pilsen and Vellun, but he liked them much more than anyone else who could do what they could.

"Last time we were here, it was a shabby, run-down rut hole," Verci said. "Now it looks downright respectable."

Indeed, the West Birch Stage had been all but rebuilt—fresh paint, new siding and doors, bright awning and marquis. The outer walls were papered over with posters of the current and upcoming shows, as well as slateboard stands on the walkways advertising the performance.

"They've got quite a season planned," Verci said, looking at the poster. "I actually think they might be too busy for us."

"Let's hope not," Asti said.

They went inside, to see several actors rehearsing a scene, while a few other people were working in the background, building the set, hanging drapes. Pilsen was center stage, on his knees, looking impossibly feeble, with three other actors surrounding him.

"How dare you, who once called yourselves sons? Who once called yourself blood! A taste of greed has infected your mouths, and now you drink deep every drop. Were my holdings not enough for you? My rents and dues? You deny me the smallest comfort, even food and bed? Where is the love you swore? Where is the loyalty? Must you suck out even the marrow from my bones?"

"Seek your mewling daughter, old man," one of the others said. "Perhaps she will give you rest."

"Perhaps she still cares for your empty shell."

"Perhaps she will feed your hungry bones."

"Oh, you traitors! Unworthy! To the rocks and shoals I go, to die, to drown, on your head!"

"*The Autumn of Corringshire*?" Verci whispered to Asti.

Asti nodded. Whatever thoughts or memories Pilsen may have lost, his towering talent remained. He was thunderous and tragic as Corringshire. But perhaps Pilsen was in a unique place to understand a man who had lost almost everything.

"Our heads are clean," one of the actors said.

"Clear!" Pilsen said, getting to his feet and abandoning the character. "Your heads are clear, and then it's 'Clear also your mind, then, and think never again of your father, your lord.'"

"Right," the actor said. "Should we—hey, who are those two?"

A worker—a tall, muscly fellow—came over quickly to Asti and Verci. "This isn't open to the public, friends, you'll have to step away."

"Oh, we were looking for—" Asti said.

"They're all right!" Pilsen said, stepping off the stage. "Silent backers, you could say. Let's take a moment, and then start again with the top of Act Four."

He crossed the seats, one of the other actors with him, while the rest wandered off. It wasn't until they closed the distance that Asti realized the other one was Vellun.

"You seem to be doing well," Asti said. "Finally playing Corringshire?"

Pilsen chuckled. He seemed quite in his senses right now. Perhaps the work had given him new purpose. Or perhaps it had all been a ruse. "Corringshire now, and then in a few weeks we do *The Tavern Tables* so I can play Menslin, and then . . . it's the new one, right?"

Vellun nodded. "We've got a young playwright at the University, fellow named Kirklin, who's writing something specifically for us. The pages are quite impressive."

"No title yet?" Verci asked.

"He wants to call it *A Thrice of Famine*, which . . . I have mixed feelings about. It's that or *The Rude Mechanics*, which isn't very descriptive."

Vellun was definitely not the pretty dullard he had played at being.

"You're not here to talk theater, are you?" Pilsen asked.

"Not specifically," Asti said. "But it's good to see you're doing well. When does this go up?"

"The eighteenth," Vellun said. "But we're in good shape."

"Good," Asti said. "Because I was wondering if you and your troupe might be interested in, let's say, a command performance tomorrow night."

Verci added, "One that might test your improvisational skills."

"Of course we would," Vellun said. "Actually, we just did something like that for the City Constabulary."

"You what?" Verci asked, not trying to hide his surprise.

"Out in Inemar, they hired us to pretend to do a crime as a training exercise. It was actually quite a bit of fun."

Asti was agog. "You got paid, by the sticks, to pretend to commit a crime?"

"Sounds absurd, doesn't it?" Pilsen said. "Who knew that's what happens when you are legitimate?"

Vellun nodded. "But that means I can tell the other folks in the troupe we're doing the same thing again, and they won't ask any questions. Though . . . it won't be dangerous, will it?"

Asti didn't want to lie. "The plan still has some moving parts we need to figure out, but in theory, your side of things won't involve any direct threat. If it does, things have gone terribly wrong."

"Terribly," Verci said. "If things go smoothly, we do the gig and walk into the cool night, no one the wiser."

"For a piece of the take?" Pilsen asked.

Asti hedged. "Strictly speaking, there won't be a take. This is more of a . . . personal project."

"You'd prefer we not know more than we need to?"

Pilsen asked. He nodded. "I get it, it's fine. But these folks do have rents to pay."

"There's not a take, but we can handle some operational expenses," Asti said. "A hundred crowns for the lot of you?"

"Like I said, our silent backer," Pilsen said. "We'll be glad for the gig. But, remember boys, I'll be very cross if you don't come and see the real show on the eighteenth."

"Where have you been?"

Mila was surprised to hear that much intensity in Kimber's voice as she came into the pub. Kimber had certainly been protective of Mila over the past months, even a bit maternal, but not emotional.

"I was out," Mila said. "I've been reading plenty, thank you. Finished that history book this morning."

"I don't—no, that's good—" Kimber stumbled over her words for a moment. "Look, I went to find you, and you were gone—"

"And I'm going to be gone for good soon, so don't worry," Mila said. "Another week, I'll be at the University, and you can—"

"Saints, girl, let me speak!" As soon as Kimber said that, she gasped and covered her mouth, and then kissed her knuckle and touched it to her heart and forehead while saying a quick benediction. "I was looking for you for a reason."

"You don't need to check on my studies."

Kimber pulled Mila behind the bar. "Will you listen? Your boy came here."

"I don't have any boy," Mila said. "Certainly no one is calling on me."

"Not like that. I meant the one who . . . from before. When you had another name." She hissed that last part out in a whisper, and looked out at the folks in the taproom. "Do you understand?"

"That . . ." Mila faltered. She didn't want to think about Nikey or Conor or any of her old Bessie's Boys right now. "That's not my problem."

"Well, I have too soft a heart, because an injured boy is my problem, and so it's your problem as well."

"Injured?"

"Room three," Kimber said. "Doctor Gelson is with him. Go find out what's going on."

Mila nodded mutely, unsure of what she could even say. She went upstairs to room three, and knocked gently. After a moment, the door opened. Doc Gelson looked at her with unfocused eyes—he was already sauced and it wasn't even midday—and then stepped back to let her in. "You here with the fresh bandages?"

"No," Mila said. "You need—"

She saw Nikey on the bed. His face was a mass of swelling, blood, and bruises. If it wasn't for his raggedy coat, she'd never have recognized him. Her heart stopped in her chest and she stumbled, almost fainting before Gelson caught her and steadied her.

"What happened?" she asked.

"Conor and the Scratch Cats happened."

Mila turned to the corner of the room where the voice had come from—the tiny voice full of rage. The dirty boy there was easy to miss—small and wan, not even seven years old—and sat on the floor there, idly sharpening a knife on a stone.

"Tarvis!" Mila exclaimed. She hadn't seen him since the night his twin brother was killed and he had slipped off into the darkness with murder on his mind. He looked up at her, his eyes showing that his anger had only grown in that time. His looked at her with the eyes of a seasoned soldier, one who had long ago succumbed to hate.

"He tried to stop Conor from joining," Tarvis growled out. "Conor did that to him. Took me most of the night to drag him here."

"But . . . why . . ."

"I remembered this was where the doc was," he said. He pointed his knife at Gelson. "He's the one who paid for Jede to get buried proper, have a marker. So he's not someone to stab."

"You saw what happened to Nikey?" Mila crouched down in front of Tarvis, hoping he would listen to her.

"I keep an eye on the Cats, the Knockers, rest of those bastards," Tarvis said. "Stab some of them in the kidneys when I get a chance. Saw what they did to Nikey. Nikey was good to me and Jede, so . . . I dragged him here. To you, I guess." He got to his feet. "Now you're here, so I can go."

"Wait, Tarvis . . . where are you going? What are you doing?"

He looked at her with empty eyes. "You don't care."

And he left the room.

"And what about this one?" Gelson asked Mila, pointing to Nikey. "He's lucky someone found him."

Mila sat on the bed. "Nikey? You awake?"

"Not quite," Nikey muttered. "Where . . ."

"At Kimber's," Mila said. "You're safe."

"Conor—"

"I know all about it," Mila said. "Tarvis . . . Tarvis found you, told me what was what. And the doctor is here for you."

"You—" His swollen eye struggled to open. "You're here, Miss."

"Yeah," she said, taking his hand. "I'm sorry I let you down, Nikey."

He squeezed her hand back.

"He should sleep," Gelson said.

"Yeah," Nikey muttered, closing his eye.

"You do that," she said, kissing his forehead. "I'm . . . I'm leaving the neighborhood soon, Nikey. I'm sorry. But I promise you, I promise, I won't leave until this is sorted."

And she damn well would do that, she told herself.

Verci returned to the Gadgeterium in the late afternoon, Asti having left on his own to confer with Helene and Mila before tonight. There was still time to put up the last two shelves before Raych would come. That would be a good amount to get done for the day.

He opened up the back door to find Raych already there, sitting in a chair in the workroom while reading a newssheet and eating cheese and cured spiced lamb sausages.

"So you haven't been in for much of the afternoon," she said as he came in. "You and Asti both. I found this odd, especially since I had already gone to the charcuterie to get sausages and cheese, and wouldn't you know it? Julien was working alone. Helene out and about."

"Raych—"

"Wait, it gets even better. I thought to myself, you know who needs bread? Kimber. And maybe we could trade for her preserves and mustard. Wouldn't that be lovely?"

"I can—"

"And I know that Mila has been staying there, studying like Saint Arrianne most of the time. But Kimber was concerned because Mila has been in and out all day." She put down the paper and assembled the cheese and sausage on her bread.

"I really—"

"So, all four of you are flitting about during the day. What could that mean?"

She bit into the sausage and kept her eyes locked on Verci.

"Do you want to know?" Verci asked.

She chewed for a moment, drawing it out with clearly deliberate intention. She swallowed hard, and then picked up a teacup and sipped slowly.

She was enjoying this a bit too much.

"Things are going on," Verci said.

"I'm aware that things are going on, dear," she said. "I was under the impression that we were done, and that they didn't need to go on anymore. That you and

Asti and your gigs or jobs or whatever you call them were at an end."

"They were," Verci said. "Until now."

"Why now?" She put down her tea and stood up. "I mean, you said the reason you weren't doing anything was because Josie paid you off, explicitly so you all wouldn't make a stink and go after her! So what are you doing?"

Verci tried to think of the most diplomatic way to phrase their intentions, and came up with nothing. "We're making a stink and going after her."

"And this is not a stupid idea, why?"

"Because if things go right, she'll never know it was us?"

"You're an idiot! If I figured out something was up, why do you think she wouldn't?"

"No one who isn't you would know that Asti and I weren't in here today," Verci said. "Nobody else can even get in here without getting killed—"

"A lovely trait for a shop."

"And the windows are still covered, we have the windups running so it sounds like work is going on. Asti is—"

"Yes, Asti is very cautious and terrified about anything and everyone," Raych said. "It's one of his most endearing qualities, that he balances his absurd need to do stupid things with a meticulous care borne out of the overwhelming fear that something might go wrong." Her voice grew to a magnificent crescendo as she went on.

"That's about right," Verci said.

"Yet somehow things always go wrong!"

"That's more or less accurate."

"Verci!"

"We're really going to try for nothing going wrong this time."

"Why is there a 'this time'?"

Verci went to the chair and sat down, taking some bread and a slice of the sausage for himself. "If it were just about Josie, affirming herself as the underworld queen of the neighborhood, I wouldn't care. Let her have it, pay whatever duties or levies she asks of people under her protection."

"We don't—"

"We don't yet. But I figure six months, a year, that'll change, we'll need to start payoffs. Price of doing business here in North Seleth."

"That's terrible!"

"Terrible, but if that's what us being clean would look like? Fine. I can live with that. But this is not just Josie and her aspirations, or Lesk and his flunkies. This is the mages in the house where Win's shop used to be. This is the people who burned down the alley. This is Fenmere moving in to sell drugs in this neighborhood."

"Who?"

"The who doesn't matter as much," Verci said. "What matters is further steps are being taken that jeopardize our home, our business, our safety. And if we don't put a stop to it now, there may not be a chance to do it later."

With that, he took a long deliberate bite of the sausage and bread. Both were excellent. Of course his wife's bread was excellent, she did an incredible job in the bakery. And Julien's version of a Patymic sharp-spiced dried sausage, paired with the mild tang of the sheep-milk cheese, was bliss. That was what this was for—honest businesses doing good work for the people of this neighborhood.

"And you're convinced of that?"

"Quite," Verci said.

"Then I trust you're right," she said. "What's the play?"

"Soft run to scout tonight, real gig tomorrow."

"And what—"

She was interrupted by a knock on the door.

Verci put his finger to his lips and grabbed a pair of darts from the table.

"Verci, don't be an idiot."

"What?"

"Someone knocked on the door. Of a shop. It's not an attack."

"It might—"

"Attacks don't knock."

She had a point. Still, he palmed the darts instead of leaving them on the table, and went to the door. Whoever had knocked had knocked again. Verci disabled the alarm trip and opened the door, noticing that Raych was right at his shoulder.

"Oh, you are here!" the man at the door said. Gentleman in his middle years, decently dressed, a bit out of place in this part of the city. Carrying a portfolio case. More suited for the middle districts like Laramie or Gelmoor, or more likely north side. Looked like a lawyer, maybe. Or a clerk. "You are the infamous Verci Rynax, are you not?"

"Infamous?" Verci asked. He did not like the sound of that.

"Verci Rynax, of the Rynax Gadgeterium, yes? I came across town for a purpose."

Verci was glad to have the darts in his hand, but this fellow did not look like a physical threat. A bit doughy in the face and neck, and the suit did not make him look like a man of action. But that could have all been subterfuge. "And what is that purpose?"

"May I come in, and we can talk in a civilized way?" the man asked. "I don't want to just be here on the stoop."

"You don't?" Verci asked.

"Oh, by the prophet's blessing," Raych said, pushing the door all the way open, as well as shoving Verci out of the way. "Please forgive my husband, he's been working night and day to get this shop ready to open before Terrentin."

"Of course, of course," the man said as he stepped inside. "It should have been obvious to me. The store isn't open, though I do like your signage out there. Very well done, very prominent. Eye-catching."

"My brother has a good hand for painting," Verci said cautiously. "But we're not quite ready for customers."

"Certainly not for daily sales, but I was wondering about special projects. Commissions."

"Commissions?" Raych asked. "As in you would pay for Verci to build something?"

"Well, assist in the design, but—"

Too much, too fast. "Wait, do what? Who are you, and how do you know of me?"

"My apologies," he said. He put the portfolio case on a counter and reached into his pocket, producing a card. "Garibert Carrigan, of Carrigan, Fisher and Elvert."

"Lawyers?" The card only had the names.

"Nothing of the sort!" Carrigan laughed a bit. "Though I can see why you would think so. The three of us, we . . . well, what we do isn't all that different from you. We envision the future, and put it into practice. Design devices, have them built, improve the quality of life in this fine city. So, no, we are not lawyers or a business partnership, but rather a mechanical firm."

"Mechanical?"

"Well, that's what our letters from U of M call it," he said. "They say 'Mastery in Mechanical Application,' though I wonder if that's just so much bunk. I mean, look at you. No colleging, am I right?"

"Right," Verci said cautiously.

"And yet," he said, picking up one of the windups on the shelf. "You've clearly got an innate genius for this. That can't be taught. Look at what you've done."

"Well, that's just a toy—"

The man tossed it up in the air and caught it again. "But it shows what you are capable of. And it's what we could use."

Verci held up a finger. "Let's walk back to 'infamous.' How do you know of me?"

"Well, what you did at the Parliament," the man said.

"I—" Verci felt his palms go sweaty, and every muscle in his shoulders tightened. "I did not—"

"My husband lets his modesty go too far," Raych

said. "You have to understand, he thought it far too unseemly to crow about his accomplishments that day. It was . . ."

"An atrocity, from what I heard," Carrigan said, bowing his head.

"Yes, but how did you find me?" Verci asked. This was deeply troubling. "My name was kept out of it!"

"My apologies, Mister Rynax," Carrigan said. "If it makes you feel better, it wasn't easy. I'm old friends with a King's Marshal, who told me about the fellow who disarmed those devices, and then I did a fair amount of legwork. Fortunately for me, there are only so many mechanical geniuses with Kieran heritage and a westtown accent."

Verci kept a lid on his panic. "You have to understand, if you could find me and my family, the monster who built those atrocities could as well."

"No, I fully understand. But still, Mister Rynax, lives were saved thanks to your know-how. And we've got a problem that, while nowhere near as dire or . . . mortal, well, it requires that same level of genius."

"What sort of problem?" Verci asked. Even though everything about this made the hairs on the back of his neck stand up, his curiosity was stoked.

Carrigan flashed a broad smile, and opened up the case.

"So, we're designing an engine, of sorts. You have some idea of what that is?"

This man both wanted his expertise and to treat him like an uneducated fool. Verci wasn't sure how he felt about that. "If you want to build a carriage that doesn't require a horse, I've got some ideas, but it doesn't go more than a short distance—"

"You have?" Carrigan asked. "Great saints, that's fascinating. We should talk more about that. Perhaps that can be a further collaboration, as we do have access to capital, and none of our competitors are even considering such a thing . . ."

In other words, they had money to spare.

Wait . . . competitors.

As Verci came over to look at the sketches, he had a moment of clarity about what was going on. They needed his expertise, yes, but why did they seek an unknown gadgeteer in an unopened west side shop? The story about finding him after learning what he did at the Parliament was probably true, but that wasn't why this fellow came.

Carrigan came here because he and his people couldn't solve a problem, and they couldn't go to anyone else, because they were the competition. People with capital. People who could steal the idea. Verci Rynax was in no position to do that, as far as this fellow figured.

Clearly, he had no idea what Verci Rynax was capable of stealing.

Verci looked at the sketches, which were meticulously drawn out, with numbers notated next to each gear, bit, and bob. The numbers were meaningless to him, in fact most of it seemed quite incomprehensible to him. It must have shown on his face.

"I apologize, there's a lot there that's the mathematics of it, probably not what you're used to."

"It's fine," Verci said. "It's just . . . well, not what I'm used to. What's the scale of this supposed to be?"

"Quite sizable," Carrigan said.

Verci couldn't help but think there was something missing in the picture. There was something that looked like a carriage, of sorts, but with dozens of wheels, and possible seats for as many people. It seemed to be connected to a cable, which was connected to the gearbox engine. But Verci couldn't quite make sense of it.

"You've built this?"

"We've built models to scale, but not yet the real thing."

"So, what's going wrong? Is it that the carriage here just crashes into the machine?"

"Something like that."

"And what powers the gearbox engine here?"

"Steam," Carrigan said. "But the boiler system for that is separate."

"Let me understand if I'm getting this—you've got this gearbox engine pulling the cable, which pulls the carriage, right? Where is this supposed to be?"

"That's still being worked out by the people who hired us," Carrigan said. "It's our job to make it work. And we'll pay you five hundred crowns for your assistance."

Raych squeezed Verci's shoulder at that. He was interested, but he also had too many questions. "Can I hold on to these, see what I can make of it. I'm sorry, but—"

"This is a complex problem, so of course," Carrigan said. "I didn't expect an answer in seconds, when you have no idea what this is all about."

"I appreciate that," Verci said.

Carrigan nodded. "You have my card, so whenever you're ready, come to the offices, and we'll see what we can make work. I won't take up any more of your afternoon." He tipped his hat to Raych, and went out the door.

"That was very interesting," Raych said. "That's what legitimate business looks like."

Verci reactivated the alarm traps. "Maybe. But something seems off."

"You just don't know what to do with yourself with an honest living."

She might have been right about that, but Verci wasn't kidding about his fear of reprisal from the Gearbox Killer. Verci had seen what he was capable of up close. It was terrifying.

Verci tried to push that out of his head as he looked at the sketches. There was something intriguing about it. He could guess part of the trouble they were having—inadequate control, the cable yanking the housing off the carriage, so many possible problems. "Perhaps so." He turned to her and kissed her.

"What am I going to do with you, Verci?"

"I don't know, but—"

"But you're going to be going on your 'soft scout' with your brother, so I suppose I should get some food into you, yes?"

"Yes." She came over and kissed him once more, but in her eyes he saw through the facade of her support. She hated this, and hated that he was going out tonight, that this was still a part of their lives.

But she understood and stayed supportive, all the same. And he loved her for that.

Chapter 5

AFTER SPENDING TOO MUCH OF the day trying to read, Mila was more than happy to do something constructive. Namely, help with the scout of the warehouses. Hopefully that would quiet the guilty voices in the back of her head, drumming her conscience for what happened to Nikey. She needed to figure out how to make Conor pay for that.

She waited in the back-alley courtyard of a tenement apartment as the sun was setting, already far out of view. It was only a block away from the Oberick Warehouses, and dressed as she was—old, ragged clothes from when she was street begging—no one would think much of her. At worst, someone in one of the apartments might chase her away, but this was the exact sort of place she and her sister had spent their nights back then.

She hadn't thought about Jina for some time. How could she do that? She should be enraged about her, all the time. But now she wondered if Jina was better off. They were regularly hungry, chased, attacked . . . every day was a struggle. Now, hopefully, Jina was with the saints, and wasn't suffering anymore.

And Mila wasn't suffering either. Her life had become quite comfortable, and was on the verge of becoming even more so.

She hoped Jina could forgive her for that.

A few notes of whistling startled her out of her reverie.

"Just going to stand there?" Helene in her deep plum vest and slacks with violet blouse and cap, case for her crossbow slung over her shoulder.

"Waiting for you," Mila said. "What's the play?"

Helene went to the ironwork back stair and started climbing, and Mila followed her.

"There is no play tonight," Helene said. "We're just doing eyes on."

"Eyes on is a play," Mila said. "I take it you're scope scouting from up here, and I'm going to check the perimeter, count the guards, and mark their patrol, and Asti and Verci slip in to take note of the layout and figure out how we're doing what."

Helene stopped at the top and looked down at her. "So what are you following me up here for?"

"Make sure you know."

"You think I'm that dumb?"

"No, I know—"

"Yeah, you do know." She got on the roof and unpacked her crossbow. Then she looked up, and for a moment, Helene's eyes spoke volumes of sorrow and anger. She looked away, burying her head into her crossbow case. "You do know."

"We're not going to be doing this much longer," Mila said.

"You're going to miss skulking about in the dark, Mila?" Helene asked. She gave a grin. "You'll probably steal half that college in a week."

"Won't be the same without you perched on some rooftop, raining death down."

"I rarely actually rain death," Helene said. A smile crept its way across her face. "It's more like lightning. But let's hope you don't need it tonight."

Mila nodded. The last thing they wanted to do was do anything that was noticed, that would put folks on alert. That would make tomorrow night that much harder.

"Get on the street," Helene said. "No need to hang around up here."

Mila scurried down to the street again, and made her way to the gates of the Oberick Warehouses. The deliberate, unassuming pace that was second nature to her, the way she would walk back when she would regularly have to beg and steal to survive. Head low, eyes up, seeing everything, noticed by no one. Certainly no one would recognize her as Mila, that nice girl always reading in Kimber's. Or as Miss Bessie. Just a nameless beggar who people would make a point of looking away from, as long as she didn't spend any time on their stoop.

She had already done part of her diligence for the Oberick Warehouses, going back to City Archives, looking through ownership papers. She had wondered if that was what University was going to be like: libraries, researching. She could do that, she was certain of that now. Blazes, if she wanted to, she could probably fake her way into a job as a city bureaucrat. That would be a clean, honest life.

Asti probably could have done the same thing, if he had wanted to. Why didn't he? Just to stay loyal to the neighborhood, work with Verci? Or was it because of the storm in his head, that he didn't trust himself?

The warehouses took up about half a block here, the property surrounded by a low slat fence. The fence was in disrepair, plenty of places to see through. A few places where the wood was rotted through, especially at the ground, so she could easily scurry her way inside the yard. Also easy to climb over. But the street was busy right now, and there was still plenty of light, so it would be foolish to try. When they needed to pull this tomorrow, it would be much the same. So, she needed to find a place that was well out of sight, at least here on the ground level. She rounded the corner to the gate.

"Gate" was a strong word. It was a gap in the fence, with a turnpike arm blocking the drive into the warehouses. There was a single guard booth next to the turnpike, but at the moment no one was in it. Perhaps nobody manned the gate at all.

She didn't stay still, continuing her walk of the perimeter. Eyes on everything. Get every bit of information that Asti will need for the plan tomorrow.

The sun was down, but the moonslight was rather bright as Asti watched the grounds of the Oberick Warehouses from the rooftop across the street. Bright enough to see, and far too bright to slip in.

"How many warehouses are there?" Verci asked as he dug through his pack.

"Looks like eleven," Asti said. He turned to look at the river. "There's no proper docks here, but there's the back deck of the Milst Street Tavern on the shore. One of the gigs we did with Ben, we brought the boats in there."

Verci glanced over that way. "Not like there's many sticks that patrol the waterline."

"But River Patrol does send a few boats out this way." He could see the silhouettes of them in the distance, small sailing skiffs with blue-tinted lamps on their bows and sterns.

"Ben knows how to get around them, I'm sure."

"Right, but presume he'd rather spend more time on the boats. He said 'pack the rowboats.' So, we're looking at least two boats' worth of stuff."

"The hide packs!" Verci said suddenly.

"The what?"

"That gig with him, about six years back?"

The memory hit him. "Right. You built him those waterproof cases that went on the bottom of the rowboats so—"

"So he could get through a checkpoint with the contraband hidden underneath," Verci finished. "Got to presume he'd still be using them."

"They were good." Asti looked to the river with his scope. "All right, here's the big problem I see. We're presuming he's sneaking in *effitte*, or this new stuff. We know what a vial looks like, but we have no idea how much of it is expected, how much space that takes."

"So we need to assume that they're using my cases, and how big those cases are, and from that, how much they're bringing in."

"And we can only do that as they're coming in," Asti said.

Verci scratched at his chin, his fingers twitching. Despite what he said earlier, he was excited to be doing this now. "All right, here's how I see it—we've got to figure out which of those warehouses has nobody in it—"

"And get Ben and his folks to come there instead of the right warehouse. All while sending Almer and Ken to the right warehouse, to trade an amount of the fake drug that we can't know until Ben gets here."

"Couldn't be easier," Verci said. "And somehow also beat Ben there, so we do his side of the drop first, so we have the money to give to him. And also get ourselves both sainted."

"Verci—"

"I mean, that part I've got worked out. Letters of beatification, documentation of miracles . . ."

"Verci!"

Verci sighed. "Pulling off this one would be a miracle, you know that."

"Right. So right now, here's what we need to do. First, figure out if Lesk has folks working in warehouse four every day, or if they'll just be there for the drop."

"I thought you knew who his people were."

"I do. This stuff is under Sender, and he's got two street bosses and twelve guys beneath him, and they work the warehousing and shipping part of his operation. But the question right now is, are they here *now*?"

"Fair."

"Second thing, find out how each warehouse is labeled."

"What?"

"I mean, warehouse four has to have a 'four' on it somewhere, right?"

"Well, sure, but—oh. That's good. If it can be done."

"Right. And then we need to figure out which place is unused enough to be *our* 'warehouse four.'"

"Mila's signaling."

She was around the corner, away from the entrance gate. The streetlamps here weren't burning—no one had bothered to fill the oil or light them up, but the moonslight was enough to see her clearly. Tomorrow would be just as bright. For now, though, there weren't too many people in the streets anymore. Made sense—up here there were mostly warehouses and workrooms. No shops, pubs, or tenements. Hardly a place to wander about unless one was up to no good.

They slipped down to the street level and met up with Mila.

"Gap in the fence back that way," she said. "I think your best bets are numbers five, seven, and twelve. Those are long-term rentals by eastside consignment houses. Odds are against anyone doing daily work there."

"Good work," Asti said. "Keep an eye out for Constabulary or Lesk's people. Bird call if you spot either."

She nodded and slouched off.

"I can't help wondering if it's a good thing or a damned shame we're pushing her out of this business and to the University," Verci said. "She's on her way to being a legendary thief."

"I don't wonder," Asti said. "She can do anything she wants, and she deserves to be able to do it."

Verci clapped him on the shoulder and squeezed. Asti knew he understood. They had gotten in this because their father had pushed them to it, given them nothing else. Hadn't given a moment's thought that there could be something else. And as much as Asti still loved their pop, he wondered what might have been if Dad had set their sights a bit farther.

Of course, Asti had gone farther, farther than any of them had imagined possible, falling in with Intelligence. But, he mused as they slipped through the fence hole and found their way to warehouse twelve, the life of a spy and the life of a thief was shockingly similar. Same skills, same planning and groundwork, and virtually the same consequences if caught.

"It's isolated," Verci said as they looked at warehouse twelve. "I mean, it's farthest away from the entrance and the guard booth, presuming that would be manned."

"It's also impossible to believe this could be number four," Asti said. He pointed to the sign above the door, with the number painted in red on a white placard, slightly worn and faded. "I mean, this is twelve, and those are ten and eleven. We would have to renumber everything to sell that."

"And farthest from the exit may be to our detriment," Verci said. He did a quick jog about the building and then came back. "All right, just the one sign over the main door. But those signs are high up, I'm not seeing good handholds. Or a great way to get those down and back up quickly."

They made their way over to the part of the yard where warehouses five and seven were. Both of them were dark and unoccupied. Four, on the other hand, had lamps burning at the barn doors, and more light coming from the windows.

"Well, that answers one question," Verci said. "Definitely people here in number four right now."

Asti took that in, looking at how the buildings were laid out here. One through three were closest to the gate. Then four through seven were in a diamond pattern, with four and seven on the ends and five and six in the middle.

"Seven is our best bet," Asti said. "You can easily

believe that they could be numbered the other way around, and it's farther away from number four."

"Let's give it a look."

Warehouse seven was dark, and the lock on the barn doors had signs that it hadn't been opened in a while, nor was it well-maintained.

"Rust always makes these harder to open," Verci muttered as he struggled to pick the lock. "I do miss having Win around for this sort of thing."

"Though he'd hardly appreciate being on this run," Asti said. Win had gotten out of this life, out of this side of town, starting a new life under the identity they had crafted to infiltrate Lord Henterman's estate. Asti wished Win all the best, he deserved it. The poor man had been a completely legitimate tradesman, with a shop, wife, children, before the fire had taken all of that. Asti had worried that Win would never recover. Hopefully his new life as the underbutler for Lord Henterman would help him move past that all, find some measure of peace.

Peace that Asti knew he would never have.

But that was what all this was for, so that Verci and his family could have that. Asti was well aware that wasn't in the stars for him. He'd help Verci in every way he could to establish the shop, establish himself as an honest businessman, and let Raych and Corsi live a clean, legitimate life with him. Asti would gladly give his life for that.

He couldn't live much longer, not with this beast and this other monster living in his skull. He never could dare let down his guard, so he would guard over them, the only family he would ever have.

Verci got the lock to release and opened the barn doors. The place had plenty of shelves, plenty of crates, and just enough dust that it was clear whoever owned these goods didn't come out to check on them very often.

"Yeah, this is good," Asti said. "A few lamps, a bit of sweeping up, and with Pilsen and Vellun and their people, make it look like this is the place for the drop-off."

Verci went back out and in again. "And do you have a plan to make that seven look like a four, and the reverse over there, without Lesk's boys knowing what we're doing?"

Asti nodded. "I do, but it's a bit out there. It's going to put you to work building tonight, and rely on Helene being able to hit clean on target with a new toy."

He went back outside, Verci right on his heels.

"What sort of new toy?"

Asti looked over to the rooftop Helene would be perched on right now. It was a good sightline for what he needed. Straight on at the signage for this warehouse. He pointed to the signs and then gave her a signal to shoot. In a moment, there came the familiar *thwack* of her bolt striking the sign dead center. So she could hit this far perfectly with the regular crossbow.

"What sort of new toy?" Verci asked again, closing up the barn doors and shutting the lock in a way that it appeared latched, but could easily be opened back up.

"The sort that will change the sign," Asti said. "Let's get out and meet up with the ladies. I know what we need to do now, I just got to figure out who to put where."

Helene saw the boys leaving after she took the shot. She knew she shouldn't have to prove anything, not to them, but she also knew Asti liked to make sure he was gauging distances and feasibility of his plan; it wasn't about questioning her skills. At that distance, she could hit true with The Action just fine, no need to break out the Rainmaker. She wondered just what Asti was planning, but he seemed satisfied that the shot she made from her current perch would suit his needs. The scout was done, and from what she could see in her scope, the boys looked more satisfied than discouraged. They also weren't leaving the warehouse grounds in a panic, which meant no one was noticing or chasing them.

Or they didn't notice anyone doing that. Helene kept her place for a few minutes, scanning about with her scope, looking for any signs that they had attracted unwanted notice. Everything looked clean so far, though. No sign of anyone raising alarm or following them. Once she saw Asti and Verci were out of the yard and back down the street, she packed up her crossbows and went back down to the alley.

She made it back to the safehouse above Doc Gelson's before the rest of them, and went into the icebox to pull out something to eat while she waited. There was a nice Forleon sheep-milk cheese, and a Rinaser region rabbit-and-venison sausage that Julien had made which would be quite nice with the crusty remains of the bread from this morning.

Asti and Verci came in through the roof trapdoor as she finished eating. "Took you boys long enough."

"We weren't exactly racing," Verci said as he looked at the crumbs on the empty plate. "How long have you been here?"

"I left the roof as soon as you all were out of the lot and I saw that no one was tailing you. Thought you'd all be here faster than rabbits."

"We doubled around and checked the path from the river to the warehouses, figured what Ben is going to do when he lands."

She nodded. "So, I presume you have some crazy sewage idea of how to swap the signs for warehouses four and seven, yes? And that's on me?"

"You and Julie, most likely," Verci said. He looked over to her crossbow cases. "I'll take the Rainmaker with me to make some changes, but odds are you're going to need him to hold it."

"Good," she said. She liked plans that put Julie up in her perch with her, instead of on the street in danger.

"He might not stay up there all night," Asti said. "You might not either."

"What do you mean?"

He shook his head, tapping a finger to his temple. "I'm clocking through this whole thing in my head, and we have a bit of a numbers problem. You and Jules might have to do a few different things. Same with Mila. All of us."

Helene didn't care for that, but she knew the way Asti Rynax planned a gig, his first goal was to keep everyone safe. Everyone but himself. She had seen more than once he'd throw himself on a fire if it let everyone else get away.

"Just make it a plan Julie can keep in his head. He doesn't improvise well."

"I know that," Asti said with a bit of a snap. Then he cooled a hair. "I know what all of you are capable of. Trust me."

"Not hardly," Helene said with a smile.

"Wise."

"I need to build and sleep and build some more," Verci said. He grabbed Asti from behind. "A bit of sleep would probably do you some good."

"I'll get some," Asti said. "I've got to work out the moving parts."

"I do moving parts," Verci said.

"You know what I mean."

"Boys!" Helene said. "What do you need from me tonight?"

"Rest, get yourself and Julien in the right headspace," Asti said. "Can we meet at four bells to go over the plan?"

"Four bells?" she asked. That would only give them three hours to go over things, get the job in Julien's head, and get to work. But it also meant closing the shop early—which she was fine with—but Covrane would notice she was gone.

She wasn't sure how she felt about that. Of all the things going on in her life, Covrane was one that she genuinely liked, and the fact that sooner or later she would have to disappoint him weighed on her.

Not like you were going to marry a stick, she thought.

"Is sooner better?" Asti asked. "I don't know if we can go much later."

She noticed something in Asti's eyes she didn't usually see—concern. He always cared, and she knew he cared for her, but that usually manifested mostly as righteous anger. Not sympathy. She wasn't sure how she felt about that.

"It's fine. Just have to plan ahead. But I should go."

"Night," Verci said. He picked up the case for the Rainmaker and went to the door, looking back to Asti. "You coming?"

"I'll wait for Mila, make sure she's set, and. . . . I got to think this ploy over. Plus send word to Almer, Ken, and Vellun."

"We're bringing in Vellun and Pilsen?" Helene asked. "You sure?"

"I'm not seeing other options. We need bodies, we need face-men. They . . . we can trust them in this, I think."

"But—"

"But I'll be ready if we can't," he said, his attention turned to the table. He looked like he was deep in his head, probably working out all the details of the plan like only he ever could.

There was the Asti Rynax she knew.

"Go, sleep," he said, clearly well into his thoughts. "Before I change my mind and want to keep you here."

"Going," Helene said, pushing Verci out the door. She turned back to Asti. "You all right?"

He shrugged. "As much as ever. And having this . . . something to do. That helps." His attention was still over at the table. Worryingly so.

"Get some sleep," she said. "Need you sharp tomorrow."

Chapter 6

ASTI LATCHED THE DOOR BEHIND Verci and Helene, and let out a long, slow breath.

"I'm still here, you know."

Not the beast, growling on its chain. That was firmly within his skull, where it belonged.

He had been hearing her since that night at Henterman's. First a quiet whisper, then it grew louder. A few weeks ago, he started seeing her out of the corner of his eye. And now . . . the voice was external now. And familiar.

It now manifested with the vision of Liora Rand, sitting at the table patiently.

He knew, firmly, that it was a complete figment of his broken mind. But everything about her felt real. Voice, appearance . . . he even imagined her scent. But maybe that was just memory or . . .

Or worse.

"Locking the door won't make a difference."

He sat down at the table determined to ignore her. She wasn't real, she was just his damage, his doubt, made into unreal flesh.

"It's not going to work, because it's too risky a plan,"

she said. "Too many unknowns. Too many moving parts. Too much risk."

"Risk we have to take," he said. Then he bit his lip. He shouldn't have even acknowledged.

"I mean, let's look at what you have," the imaginary Liora said, getting to her feet. "First, you have Almer and Kennith, playing their parts. That's the most solid thing you've got on the board right now. Of course, neither of them have ever done real face work like that."

"Ken has."

"Kennith played an idiot show role for popinjay fools. This is trying to trick actual players that he's a specific person. And the folks they're meeting might even know the real articles."

"Someone should be with them," Asti said, more for his own benefit.

"You and Verci can't do everything. Who's in warehouse seven? Not just Pilsen and Vellun?"

"Mila—"

"A child!" Liora said. He would have sworn she was right there with him, looking exactly as she did the day she had betrayed him. Same crimson blouse. Same tanned skin and sun-bleached hair from their months in Napoli. Same alluring smile. "After all this, who do you have? A child, an idiot, a couple untrustworthy actors, a couple honest boys who are over their heads, a wild horse who's a decent shot, and your brother, who is at most humoring you."

"Shut it," Asti whispered.

"It's amazing you've accomplished anything."

"Shut it."

"Verci wants nothing more than to drop this and stay with his family, and you drag him back down with you. You are going to get him and all the rest killed!"

"Shut it!" Asti shouted, snapping out a knife and throwing it right at her heart.

The knife embedded into the empty chair. No one there.

"You all right?"

Asti looked up at the roof trapdoor. Mila was looking at him, her eyes full of concern. He had no idea how long she had been there.

"I—I'm fine."

"You haven't been fine since Henterman's, and we all know it." She dropped down into the room. "I mean, you've been holding it together well enough, especially around Verci, but . . ."

"It doesn't matter," Asti said. "I've got it under control."

She looked at the knife in the chair.

"Mostly," he said.

"This is beyond the beast on the chain."

"Liora . . ." he said.

"You aren't hunting her, are you?" Mila asked.

"I wouldn't know where to start."

She glared at him.

"All right, I would know. I'd dig out her old aliases, remember every detail I could about her, put together a journal. Run down every name, every old haunt, check all the contacts . . ."

"Where's the journal?"

He tapped his head. "I'm not letting myself write it down. That would give her . . . that would be—" He felt hot tears push their way to the corners of his eyes. He turned away from Mila and went to the icebox for a cider.

"What did she do to you?"

"It doesn't matter." But it did. She had controlled him, made him into her killing machine. He had nearly killed Verci, mindlessly. It was only by some miracle of his will that he had been able to snap out of it before he did it. Maybe that was the one thing she couldn't break.

Mila frowned at him. "Fine, it doesn't. You've got the plan for tomorrow?"

"Putting it together."

"Should I sleep here tonight?" she asked. "It's clear you're going to stay here—"

"No, I'm . . ." he said reflexively. "You should go to your place."

"My place is wherever it needs to be. If you need someone . . ."

"It's probably better for you to not be here. In case."

"In case you throw more knives?"

He got up, pulling the knife out of the chair. "Exactly."

"That's why I shouldn't—"

"Mila," he said, trying not to let his voice rise. "I know what I need to do. I need to come up with the plan for tomorrow, I need to work it all through. So I just need . . . I just need a cool head, and it's better for me to do that alone right now."

She didn't look convinced. "So you know, I circled back through and checked warehouse four myself. Overheard two guys in there, griping about Sender coming for the business tomorrow."

Asti groaned. If Sender Bell was there, that was going to make things even harder. Sender wasn't the brightest of folks, but he certainly knew Ben and Ka'jach, and he had been in the neighborhood plenty enough to probably recognize Almer. And he knew Asti and Verci all too well.

"Good to know," he said. "I'll keep that in mind when I put this together. Now scat."

"You're sure—"

"Go!" he said forcefully. "I promise I will be better alone. And I'll even sleep."

She just nodded, and hopped up to the rooftop trapdoor and pulled herself out. Asti shut it and set the bell wires.

He would be better. He'd hold it all together, he'd have the plan in the morning, and no beast or Liora or any other manifestation of his broken mind would stop him.

Because he had to. This was his only chance.

Verci had gone to bed late, after sketching out his designs for the night's gig, and laying out his tools and workspace for what he would do in the morning. Despite that, he was up before Raych in the morning, which was highly uncommon. He started water for tea and tended to Corsi before coming to kiss her awake.

"That I could get used to," she said sleepily. She got up and took the baby from him. "I see you're both already having a good morning. Probably because Daddy is going to do bad things tonight and wants to make Momma happier about it."

"It's probably a factor," Verci said.

"It's a good instinct," she said. "So, what's the plan?"

"Build some fun toys to use tonight," Verci said. "And if I know Asti, he'll be knocking any moment now."

The door knocked right away. Raych looked at Verci amazed, and he let her think he was a genius about these things, and not that he heard Asti come up the steps to the apartment. She opened the door to reveal Asti, looking rather well-groomed and shaven, carrying a basket of food. He was clearly hoping to engage Raych's good side as well.

"I come bearing cheese and ham," Asti said, holding it up for Raych to see. "And I have a jar of preserves from Kimber in my pocket there. And another of mustard."

Raych narrowed her eyes at him a little. "I wasn't really looking for those things yesterday."

"Even still, a peace offering."

Raych deposited Corsi in Verci's arms and gave him a rueful smile, and then crossed over to Asti to take the food from him. "I supposed this means you're staying for breakfast."

"I wouldn't object, but I don't want to impose."

"Sit," she said. "There's already tea, and if I know you—"

"I did sleep a little."

"Where?" Verci asked, sitting at the table. They hadn't had many proper meals here, and the place was a bit of disorder, covered with notes and paperwork and other odd bits of paper. "Sorry, we should—"

"I've got it," Asti said, scooping up the papers. "Organization isn't your strongest suit."

"And it's yours?" Raych asked.

"It actually is," he said as he flipped through the papers, shuffling them around. Verci focused his attention on Corsi, playing a game of silly faces. He felt he should be victorious in the game, but Corsi hit back with some real winners. "I mean, come on, Verci, you have design sketches with bakery invoices. We need to keep things in order. Archive boxes, and separate ones for the two businesses. Let alone your sketches should—" Asti's voice darkened. "What's this?"

"What?"

Asti flipped a calling card over to show to Verci. "Sergeant Cole Pyle? Of the city constabulary? Why do you have his calling card?"

Verci hadn't told Asti about it, but he couldn't lie now. Not about this. "He . . . he handed it to me."

Asti slammed his hand on the table. "He handed it to you? The stick that killed Dad just, what, walked up and passed out his card to you?"

Raych came over, putting a cup of tea in front of Asti. "Keep it under control," she said.

"It was last week. Tied to that business Grieson pulled me into."

"He's answering for that, let me tell you," Asti said, his face starting to take on a ruddy pallor. "And, what, Pyle was there?"

"No," Verci said. "Sit down."

"Why should I—" Asti raved.

"Sit down and hold it together," Verci said. "I can't have you—"

"Lose control? Because you hid *this* from me?" He held up the card again, almost shoving it in Verci's face.

"I didn't hide it, I just didn't mention it."

"Didn't mention this," Asti snapped.

"Cool down or walk out!" Raych shouted. Corsi started crying, and Verci rocked him in his arms. That seemed enough to startle Asti down a bit.

"Sorry," he said. He took a sip of the tea. "I've got

my hand firmly on the chain, really. But what happened? Why didn't you tell me?"

"I know where he lives," Verci said quietly. "I was in his house."

"In his house?" Asti grit his teeth and took a moment before letting out a sharp exhale. "How?"

"I'm not entirely sure how, but . . . that Gearbox fellow from the papers, from the Parliament, he had put a girl in a horrific machine. The inspector—the one Grieson brought me to—she, she found me. All so I could save the girl."

"Well that's good," Asti said.

"The girl was Pyle's daughter."

Asti exhaled sharply. He was calmer now. "All right, that makes sense. Still, I don't know how you didn't tear his heart out."

"There were about a dozen sticks in that house," Verci said.

"You did better than I would have."

"Damn right I did."

"Well, you know where to find him, so we can—"

"We're not doing anything, Asti." Verci shook his head. "I'm drawing an absolute line there. We do what we need to here, against Josie and the mages and the Andrendon and all that, because that keeps our people and our homes safe. But that's the line. No settling scores with sticks, no revenge for Dad. None of that."

"You think he would—"

"I know what Dad would say," Verci said. "And so would you. You have to take out a stick or a guard, they knew the risks, that's a fair game. Because you *know the risks too*. Dad never went on a gig without knowing, and I mean knowing, that something could go wrong and some stick might iron him—"

"Or shoot a bolt in his heart."

"Yeah, it kills me," Verci said. "It killed me to stand in that sitting room while that man thanked me profusely for saving his daughter. I got out, ran half a block, and threw up in an alley." The bile rose in his throat just from the memory.

Raych had come around behind Verci and wrapped her arms around his shoulders.

"You're right," Asti said quietly. He got up from the table. "No, you're absolutely right and I'm sorry. I'll go."

"Don't," Verci said. "It's—"

"You haven't eaten," Raych said.

"I—it's fine, I don't need . . ."

"Nonsense," Raych said. She went back over to the stove and came back with plates of melted cheese and ham on bread. "You two are going to do something stupid tonight, so I want you well fed, so you don't get your brother killed."

Asti nodded and sat back down. "May Saint Senea hear you on that."

"Speaking of stupid, you said we have a problem," Verci said, taking a bite of his breakfast. Raych sat down with her own plate.

"Yeah, that we need Kennith playing Ka'jach in the fake drop, but we also need him driving a carriage."

"Someone else drives the carriage," Raych said.

"Normally yes," Asti said. "But Almer's also tied up playing Ben, you and I need to already be two different places, Mila as well. Maybe Julie—"

"Julie can't drive a carriage."

"Right. So, unless Raych is going to do it . . ."

Raych almost spit out her tea. "You can't be serious."

"Not really," Asti said.

"Good," she said.

"No, not Raych," Verci said. But then the answer was obvious. "Kennith already told us who."

Mila watched the spice shop from across the street, not sure if she should go in or not. She had a suspicion that she would get answers in there, answers that Asti wouldn't give her. She knew the spice merchant was

Poasian, and a spy of some sort. Maybe a former spy, who now helped Druth Intelligence? And he was Asti's friend? Or at least an associate. She had no idea.

But she had a suspicion that he knew what had happened to Asti, and he understood what was happening now. Because Asti, regardless of whether he would admit it or not, was getting much worse.

"So here's my question," a young man said. She hadn't realized he was standing next to her until he spoke. "Why would a Poasian spice merchant set up shop out here?"

She looked at him, about to give her best Miss Bessie crack at him, when her voice left her for a moment. He was about her age, maybe a year older or so, with a wild mop of hair and a maddeningly pretty smile. Skinny—almost too skinny—with a dusky complexion that made her think that he might not be Druth, but she couldn't be sure.

"Ah, wha—?" was all she managed.

"I mean, it is odd. But what's also odd, is that you can't seem to decide whether or not to go in."

She now was really going to snap at him, but then she noticed the coat he was wearing. "You're at U of M?"

He looked down at himself, as if he wasn't aware of what he was wearing. "That I am," he said. "Starting fourth year in a few days."

"Same," she said. "Well, first year, but still."

His eyebrow went up. "Really?"

She remembered she was dressed as a street rat, not in her smart suit that would make her look like a University student.

"I—well . . . I haven't gotten my school uniforms yet."

"They itch like crazy," he said. With a shrug, he added, "I'm guessing you didn't have traditional schooling, but have gotten some sort of special patronage to go to the University."

"You sound like you're familiar with how it works," she said.

"Quite." He sighed. He glanced over at the spice shop, and then looked at Mila again, like he was really looking at her for the first time. Saints, his eyes were delicious. But he had a moment of indecision, as if he wasn't sure if he should say what he wanted to.

"Go on," she said.

"There will be people—a lot of people—who'll talk. Behind your back, to your face. People who never had a day without a solid meal or a warm room in their life. And they're going to assume you don't deserve to be there."

She held up her chin. "I'll show them otherwise."

"Good," he said. "It won't shut them up, but . . . just know that there are a few of us out there who know different. And we know that you're there for a damn good reason."

She turned away so this pretty stranger wouldn't see her tears well up. "So, you're from around here, too?"

"Me, no," he said. "Grew up in a circus caravan. You been to campus yet?"

"Going in a few days for the first time."

"The Girls' Schools are on the north tip, near the social houses. I'm on the south end, in the Holtman Cluster, but if you ever see me about . . . you'll know one person."

She extended her hand. "Mila Kendish."

He hesitated for a moment, and then took hers. "Veranix Calbert. Friends call me Vee."

"Good to meet you, Vee," she said, giving her best win-over-the-folks-in-the-records-office smile.

He laughed nervously. "I shouldn't tie you up. You were going to go into the spice shop."

"Weren't you?"

"No, I was just . . . curious," he said. A hint of darkness in his voice. "I'll let you be on your way."

He let her hand go, and went off down the street, vanishing into the crowd.

Mila took his words as a sign, though, and taking a deep breath, walked across the way and into the spice shop.

The scent in the air was heavy—rich and earthy, oppressing her nose. The shop was dimly lit and cramped, clay jars crowding the few shelves in the tight space. A few flickering candles were on the shop counter, where the Poasian man looked up from his books to greet Mila with a disturbing smile.

"Child," he said. "While I understand you may wish to wander off the street, this is not the place for you."

"I'm where I mean to be," she said.

He made an unreadable expression. "So, you have entered with intention. You don't give the appearance of a usual customer, but I will happily help you with whatever you might wish to purchase."

It seemed that, despite this man knowing Asti, and being a Poasian spy himself, he didn't know who Mila was. Of course, he could just be pretending.

"I thought you had your ear to the street," she said.

"Well, any good businessman needs to know about his city, his neighbors, and what is going on around him," he said. "To do otherwise would be very poor practice, indeed. But I fail to see how that connects to the purchasing of spices. If I perhaps knew what sort of dish you are hoping to supplement? What sort of flavor profile are you seeking?"

"I'm not seeking spices."

"Then you are in the wrong store."

"I'm seeking you, sir," she said.

"Me? Just the humble spice merchant. I would hardly know why you would seek me if spices were not your gain."

"Don't pretend you don't know who I am."

"You might be a girl who enjoys something that could bring out a certain rich sweetness, say in a warm cup of milk. I have *chondier* for that . . ."

"You are a spy," she said. She wasn't sure what else she should say, but she decided there was nothing she could do but be direct.

He sighed. "It seems the reputation of my people has been a poison against me."

"Your people," she said. "The Poasians. The ones who make *effitte*?"

At that, he spat to the ground. "I do not sell drugs, my child. Spices are a different matter. Now, some of these can have interesting effects on the body and mind, but I assure you—"

"Let's talk about what the Poasians do to minds," she said. "I've heard quite a bit about that."

"Surely rumors and exaggerations, my child."

"Like what they did to Asti Rynax."

"I don't know who or what you mean," he said. But there was a hint of sweat on his brow.

"You do—"

She had put her hand on the hilt of her knife, hidden under her ragged coat, and in a flash the Poasian was over the counter and holding her wrist.

"Enough of that, young woman," he said. "I am not going to be taken by an urchin like you."

Mila twisted her arm to try to free herself, but the Poasian man—the scent of him hit her like a punch in the nose—held strong. She brought up her leg to kick him, but he dodged it while holding on.

"Far better than you have failed at killing me," he said. "I'm slightly insulted."

"Not trying to kill you," she said.

"That's good, because your attempt is pitiful. Walk in brazenly, ask leading questions, obvious grab for the knife." He pulled the blade out of her waistband and dropped it to the ground, kicking it away. "The quality of assassins seem quite lacking in this country."

"Not an assassin!" she said.

"Certainly not," he said. He let her go, taking three quick steps away to the other side of the room. He was standing on her knife. "But, no, not here from Druth Intelligence, and certainly not from any other government. No, your reasons are personal."

"Your people did something to Asti Rynax," she said. "To his head. When he was in your prison."

"Asti doesn't know you're here, does he?" the spice

dealer said. "Did you come here hoping I had some means of, what, fixing him?"

"Do you?"

"Child, if I had such means, would I be here, in the crotch of the world, actually having to eke out a living as a spice merchant?"

"You're a spy."

"If I were, I would point out that the intelligence business, like every other game, has its winners and losers. Trust me, I would very much be one of the losers. And for that matter, so is Asti."

"He's getting worse," she said. "What did they do to him?"

"I can only imagine," he said. "And you? Tell me, Miss Kendish, what do you hope to gain?"

"You know—"

"Of course I know," he said. "You, the Kessers, the fellow who left to become a butler. I'm familiar with all of you."

"But—"

"I may be one of the losers, but I know how to do my job." He shook his head, and then kicked the knife back over to her. "There is nothing to be done for Asti. I am amazed he's as capable as he is. For all our dealings, I have a strange admiration for him."

Mila picked up her knife. "I just want to know what's going on."

"Talk with the brother, girl," he said. He sighed as he went behind the counter. "Let Rynax know many things that come from Poasia—be it honest import or otherwise, are shipped by a broker named Adfezh. A dangerous man." He started measuring out a few spoons of a spice and putting it in a bag.

"I'll let him know."

"Adfezh does not place much trust in new players. Be aware of that."

She wasn't sure what he was trying to tell her. "Meaning?"

He gave a weary sigh. "Children, this is what I'm

reduced to. Dealing with children. All right, girl, I'm letting you know, that if Adfezh was testing a new channel to bring in goods, it would definitely not go unsupervised."

That came through clearly.

"I'll let him know."

"I'm sure he'll appreciate it," he said with an exaggerated shrug. "It's also good business to support the neighborhood one lives in, no?"

Chapter 7

ASTI HAD RARELY BEEN IN any of the Little East, and never in the handful of blocks called the Hodge. The other enclaves had pretty specific populations—Asti had always wondered why Dad had settled down in North Seleth instead of the Kieran district of Pirietown—but the Hodge was the part for folks who didn't have a proper enclave of their own: Xonacans, Bürgs, Turjin, Napolic, Jelidan.

And Ch'omik. Abrennick Alley was almost exclusively Ch'omik, which Asti was acutely aware of as he followed Kennith. The folks staring at him were likely born and raised in Ch'omikTaa. Asti was surrounded by bare arms of dark skin, each of those arms telling a story with scars and ink.

"Asti," Kennith hissed by his side. "You're being weird."

"How am I weird?" Asti whispered back.

"I should have come myself."

"No, it's fine," Asti said.

"Haven't you, like, traveled the world?"

"Really just the Napolic Islands."

"It's over here," Kennith said with a sigh. He led the

way over to a brick building with a wooden door, half hanging open, heat pouring out into the alley. Metal-working shop, the forge blazing in the center. Jhoqull-Ra was hammering away at something on the anvil, her powerful arms glistening with sweat.

"Hey, Kh'enta," she said with a smile as she looked up. "Didn't think you'd come out to see me here."

"Well, there's a thing," Kennith said.

"I see you brought your friend along. *Q'anach*, Rynax."

"Same," Asti said. "I don't know how much you know about what we all do."

"I know you have Kh'enta here do stuff that should tear carriages apart. Why he's always having me and mine hammer things out for him."

"Your cousins aren't here, are they?" Kennith asked.

"No, they're about elsewhere," she said. "They don't want to kill you, you know."

"And I don't want them to, and not seeing each other keeps things that way."

"As you fit," she said with a shake of her head. "But, yeah, Rynax, I know you do things that the law would frown upon. I also know this one's a good stone, and he's said the same about you and your brother."

"And you said you can drive," Asti said. "We need someone to do that. Tonight."

"I can. There a reason he's not doing it?" She crossed over to Kennith and grabbed the front of his shirt with what Asti would only describe as aggressive affection.

"I need to do a different job on this one," Kennith said.

She widened her eyes at that. "Oh, that is interesting, boy."

"Kennith says you're good, and he vouches for you. I'm not inclined to trust easy, but I believe in him."

"Is there a spot of coin for me in this thing you're doing?"

Asti sighed a little. "To be honest, this one . . . it's not so much about that."

"This is one of those 'matter of honor' things, rather than profit?"

"You could call it that," Kennith said.

She nodded. "I respect that, I do. Most folk on Abrennick would. And it's Kh'enta's honor, so that matters to me. But I still need a bit of something."

Asti couldn't argue with that. "There might be some spoils at the end, and we'll give you plenty of that. If not, I'll pay you from my own pocket."

"Mothers of my mothers, this is the real thing," she said. "I never would have guessed a Kieran would part with money so easy."

"Kieran blood, Druth birth," Asti said. "Like Kennith."

She patted Kennith on the cheek. "Poor boy doesn't know what he is."

"Hey."

"It's truth and you know it."

Kennith frowned, and Asti wanted to move forward before they started arguing. He didn't know enough about her or their relationship to know how that would play out. "We've got to take care of a few more things before tonight. Four bells at our safehouse. Kennith knows where it is."

"Meet me at my stables half a bell before that," Kennith said.

"Half a bell isn't near enough time," she said, and kissed him far more passionately than Asti was comfortable watching. "I'll come at three bells, and you be ready."

"Absolutely," he said. He staggered a few steps away from her.

"It's a pleasure, Rynax," she said. "You'll be impressed."

"I already am," he said, and Kennith pulled him out of the forge and down the alley to the main street.

"She really is a good driver," Kennith said. "And Verci would probably appreciate her metalwork."

"I'm sure he would." Asti couldn't let something go,

even though the hairs on the back of his neck told him he didn't need to ask. "Kh'enta?"

"It's a—she thinks that Kennith isn't my 'proper' name. And makes a point of that whenever I come out here. Most of the folk out here do." He tilted his head a bit and sighed. "But she's the only one I don't mind it from."

"I'm glad, Ken," Asti said. "We all need a bit of, you know, normal. A bit of happy."

"Yeah," Kennith said. He looked at Asti again. "You'll find yours."

"Mine is you all finding it," Asti said. "That's the most I expect, and that's fine with me."

Verci was the last one to arrive at the safehouse. He had spent the day building and modifying the gear they would be using tonight, and had lost track of time. He almost wanted to forgo the usual safety procedures and just go straight to the safehouse. But this was not the time to be sloppy about anything. Better late right now, instead of having anyone taking notice. He knew damn well he didn't know who else in this neighborhood could be trusted. Josie probably had eyes places he didn't expect.

He hated that. Of all the things that needed to change, that he wanted to fix, it was the situation with Josie. They were about to break the truce with her. If everything went well, no one would be looking at any of them for tonight. But if it went wrong, they would be at war with Josie Holt and her entire empire.

Verci wasn't sure what would be worse: losing that war, or winning it.

He reached the safehouse at half-past four bells, and everyone else was waiting for him. Asti, dressed like a dockworker in shirtsleeves and suspenders, his belt of knives hidden under the waistcoat. Helene in her purple coat and slacks, hair tied back. Julien in charcoal grays, Mila in the same. Almer and Kennith dressed as sea captain and his mate. Once again, he was wearing a Ch'omik sleeveless leather shirt, as was Jhoqull-Ra. She sat a little apart from the rest of the group, watching intently as Helene painted fake Ch'omik tattoos on Kennith's arms.

"That is just nonsense you are writing," Jhoqull said.

"You can do it if you want," Helene said.

"Oh, no," Jhoqull said. "I'm not shaming the mothers of my line by casting lies on any arm."

Kennith looked at her, shaking his head. "We're committing crimes, you know."

"Druth crimes. That does no shame. Very different."

"We're just about there?" Verci asked. "Where are Vellun and Pilsen?"

"Not part of this aspect," Asti said. "We keep a wall between them and the plan. They only know what they need."

"Wise," Helene said. She finished a symbol on Kennith's arm. "How does that look?"

"Like blasphemy," Jhoqull said. She inspected closer. "But surely passable to Druth eyes."

"Hey, Verci," Julien said from the kitchen. "Kennith brought the kra-dock, since it's a gig."

"*Chr'dach*," Jhoqull said, as if Julien's voice brought her pain. "And that is not Kennith's atrocity. I had my cousin Ochqaa make it, so you would know the proper thing."

"It's really good this time," Julien said, a wide grin on his face.

"Really, Jules?" Kennith asked, almost pained.

"We're already running late here," Asti said. "Can we move on?"

He did not look happy, even less so than this morning.

"Right," Verci said. "I've got some toys. Helene, here's yours for tonight: a modified Rainmaker." He took the monster crossbow out of the case, with the new housing and specialized shots.

Helene looked terrified of the thing. "Is this to shoot a bear trap at someone?"

"Not far off," Verci said. That was the basis for the device he built. "You and Julien, start to get a feel for that, because you won't really get to practice the actual shot."

"What the blazes am I shooting?" she asked, taking a closer look at the thing.

"These," Asti said, reaching into his own bag. He pulled out two wooden placards, painted with FOUR and SEVEN. "From your perch, you're going to change the signs on the two warehouses."

She grabbed one of them. "These aren't too heavy, all right. And—" She looked again at the contraption Verci had devised. "Oh, I see. Slams four nails on impact, releasing and securing. The wood might snap. At least it'll crack."

"That's fine," Asti said. "Old and worn would look better."

"You can do it?" Verci asked.

"Of course I can," she said. "I presume the idea is to land them over the original signs."

"Ideally," Asti said.

"So that's the switch," she said. "To get Ben and Ka'jach to the wrong warehouse. Not too hard."

"That's the easiest part," Asti said. "While that happens—after sunset—Verci and Mila are in the water."

"We're in the what?" Mila asked.

"I'm in the water," Verci said. He had a feeling this would be on him. "You're on the bank, waiting for my signal."

"What is with the water?" Mila asked. She looked over to Asti.

"Show them," Asti said. Verci opened up the other case, taking out the visor and mask, with a series of tubes on them.

"I'm swimming with this on. The tubes let me breath under the water, and you'll be able to talk to me and hear me."

"That's some madness," Jhoqull said. "Why would you do that?"

"We're working on the presumption that Ben Choney is smuggling the drugs in under the longboats, packed in watertight cases Verci designed."

Verci pulled out one of them. "Just like this. We see how many cases he's got on the boats, we can figure out how much of the drug he's bringing in."

Almer stepped up. "I've made a bunch of vials of our substitute drug. I'll check how much one holds."

Helene nodded. "So we know how much we need to bring. And your goods will pass the muster?"

Almer shrugged as he filled the case. "Looks right. Smells right." He looked over to Asti. "Unless they have a chemist with them, it'll pass any reasonable inspection. But beyond that, we'll just see."

"Well, I'm in there with you, as part of 'we'll just see.'"

"Won't you be recognized?" Mila asked.

"Hopefully this is a good disguise," Asti said. "I'll leave you to the talking, Almer. You're the captain."

"We're hoping that no one in that warehouse really knows Ben," Helene said. "That's a big ask."

"He isn't that connected in this neighborhood," Verci said.

"Ia knows him," Asti said. Helene groaned loudly at her name. "Him and Ka'jach. I think she knows Ka'jach *very* well."

"Then let's hope she's not there," Verci said.

"Her or any of Lesk's inner circle," Asti said. "Almer's cooked up a plan for that contingency. Once the trade is made, I'll take the money to the other warehouse, where Vellun and his folks will be waiting to take the real merch from Ben."

"How are they getting in?" Verci asked.

"Mila will ride with Jhoqull to the West Birch, pick up the actors, and deliver them, as well as Ken and Almer, to the warehouse. Jhoqull, you're driving them in, and then driving Verci and Mila out."

"So, what am I driving?" she asked.

"The wagon I've got in the carriage house," Kennith said. "I've done it up so it looks like it's full of crates, but you can hide a dozen folks in there."

"That's useful," Jhoqull said.

"Moving on," Asti said. "Jhoqull brings you back out, and that's when you two hit the water."

"I am staying out of the water," Mila said forcefully.

"Sixty vials in the case," Almer said, finishing his load. "Do we have more of these cases? Might look better if I have a few packed?"

"I can get them," Verci said. "What's the most we expect?"

Asti furrowed his brow. "My gut says six, but do we have enough to do eight cases? That's a good safety."

"I can do that," Almer said.

"Now," Asti said. "Once you get a count, Verci, Mila signals Helene, who signals us, and that's when we go do the drop."

Jhoqull spoke up. "So I take Verci and Mila out to do their water game, and, what, wait in the street?"

"You plant yourself where you can look out. And you might need to help hold up Ben and Ka'jach."

"And the Poasians," Mila said.

"The what now?" Helene asked.

Asti scowled at Mila. "We should be prepared for the idea that the Poasian smugglers will ride herd over Ben. Everything goes to plan, they'll just see everything going like it's supposed to: they deliver the drugs to us. Let's be clear: this is the real objective. Everything else is cream on the top. If we have to skunk everything and get the drugs, no matter what, that's the play."

"If that's the case," Helene said. "I mean, I already know what you're going to say, but why aren't I just dropping two bolts in them as soon as their boat lands, you and Verci pulling the goods, and we run like blazes? I mean, there's no reason to suspect a play like that would be us, right?"

Asti sighed, and chuckled a little. "I got to admit, I

really would love to just smash and grab. But I worry that it could start Josie and Lesk—and Fenmere's folks—doing a teardown of the whole neighborhood. This play, as crazy as it is, at least keeps the drugs off the street, and keeps the point of failure a mystery. No one starts tearing up our homes."

"Plus, it's Ben," Verci said. "He's a decent one."

"There is that," Asti said. "But that's the goal—for the night to end and no one even guesses that anything went wrong."

"Fair," Helene said. "So, no kill shots?"

"I didn't say that," Asti said.

"Please save our lives if we're in trouble," Ken said.

Jhoqull chuckled. "Oh, fathers of your fathers, see how brave you stand."

Kennith scowled at her. "You know that's not my faith."

Her tone deepened, getting very serious. "They look down on you, and they know, even if you don't believe."

"And next?" Mila said.

"Next, ideally, Ben and Ka'jach come in, they sell us the drugs, walk out with money and go back to their boat. Jhoqull moves the wagon to the back wall, everyone sneaks out and we're back here to destroy the drugs."

"That simple," Helene said.

Julien popped a *chr'dach* in his mouth. "I think it is."

Verci went over to the kitchen and grabbed one of the *chr'dach*. "What could go wrong?" he asked as he bit into it.

The burning fire from the bite made Ken's version of the dish taste like a wet rag. Verci coughed and went to the icebox for a cider.

Asti sighed. "All right, let's move. Time's running short."

Chapter 8

THE BEGINNING WENT SMOOTHLY. Everyone got to position, Asti and Verci slipped onto the warehouse grounds without a hitch, and Mila rode down to West Birch with Jhoqull. Despite not being sure what to say to her, Mila was deeply intrigued by the woman. She had remembered that at the Henterman party Kennith had played at being a Ch'omik national, with the tattoos and scars, but this woman was the real thing. She didn't say much as they drove down to West Birch, picked up Vellun and Mister Gin with their troupe, and came back.

"So what can you tell me about this gig, dearest?" Mister Gin asked as they were riding back up. "Asti didn't give a lot of details."

He seemed far more lucid than he had the last time she saw him. "We're delivering you to Asti, he'll tell you what you need," she told him. "I don't know much more."

"You all need to make like crates of merchandise back there," Jhoqull said. "So let's have a bit of quiet."

Mister Gin started to object, but Vellun took him by the shoulder and pulled him back. The two of them and the rest of their troupe, as well as Kennith and Almer, were all hidden away in the compartment that looked like a bunch of crates.

"Hope that's not too uncomfortable for them," Mila said.

"It's about as big as the cargo hold we all came up here in," Jhoqull said. "Twenty of us."

"Why did you come to Maradaine?" Mila asked. "If you don't mind me asking."

Jhoqull sighed. "My father and his bond-partners were pledged to the *en-cha* of our city. The *en-cha* made some trades with a Fuergan merchant, and that included those pledges. My father and his bond-mates were obliged to follow this Fuergan, and the family stayed together."

"Wait, traded? Like slaves or something?"

"The pledge is not like that," Jhoqull said. She frowned. "The words do not translate into Trade very well, but our family—our root—it is now tied to the Hieljam family through ties of honor. We live our lives here, and if the call is made, we would go to war for them."

"War? Like, actual war? Has that—did you?"

"A few months ago, the head of the Hieljam was murdered. We were ready to tear the Little East apart if the call was made, but the local constables arrested the malefactor, so it did not come to that."

"Local constables don't do much in this neighborhood," Mila said.

"Nor ours," Jhoqull said. "But they pay attention when a rich man dies."

They passed into the warehouse grounds with little trouble. Mila was ready with a whole story for the man at the entrance gate, but he just waved and let them in when they approached. Mila was a bit disappointed at how easy it was. They reached warehouse seven—it still had the seven sign, which Mila found a bit troubling—and rolled in when Asti opened the doors.

"When are the signs getting changed?" she asked as

Asti closed the door. Vellun, Pilsen, and the rest unloaded and started milling about, looking for direction from Asti.

"Later," Asti said. "It's going to make a blazes of a sound, so we need to misdirect when we do it."

"How?"

"I got a plan. But Helene's in place. You ready, Verci?"

Verci was wearing an outfit that was as tight as his skin. "Ready as ever."

"What are you wearing?" Mila asked.

"I'm told it's sealskin, whatever that is," he said. "It's very tight."

"It's great for this sort of job," Asti said. "I've told you."

"What the blazes is a seal?" Mila asked.

"Bardinic animal," Asti said. "I held on to it from Intelligence. It's very useful for swimming."

"It fits him, not me," Verci said.

"You got fat on bread," Asti said. "Not my fault."

"Easy," Verci said. "I'm the one going in the water. Be nice."

"Are we all set?" Mila asked, hoping to keep this from dragging out. "Let's move."

She hopped onto the carriage and looked to Jhoqull, who just glared back at her.

"Please?" Mila asked.

"That's something," Jhoqull said, taking up the reins. "Druth fools need to learn about politeness."

She drove them out, and Mila went into the hiding spot with Verci, as he fiddled with his gadgets—a pair of helmets, a series of hoses, a box with bellows, a crank wheel. "All right, what do I need to do with all this?"

"First and foremost, don't let the hoses get tangled," he said. "That happens, and I'll suffocate."

"That's bad."

"Quite." He handed her one of the helmets. "Put this on."

"I'm not going in the water."

"This is how we talk when I'm down there. Like the

ear funnels in the bakery's hiding rooms. The hoses are direct between us."

Mila put it on, and he put on his own headgear and latched it to his shoulders. He looked ridiculous, with the hoses coming out of his head. "Can you hear me?" His voice was hollow and echoey, but she could hear.

"Fine," she said. "Do I look as silly as you?"

"Impossible," he said, taking his back off. He pointed to the pump on the floor. "Now, you got to keep pumping that, so I keep getting fresh air."

"I can't help but think I'm going to be very noticeable with this whole getup," Mila said as she removed her helmet.

"You're going to hide under the tavern," he said.

"The tavern?" Mila asked. She already didn't like sound of it.

"We're here," Jhoqull said. They unloaded, only the moonslight showing them the way down to the patch of dirt under the deck of the Milst Street Tavern, right at the edge of the river. Jhoqull helped Mila carry the pump down, though with her powerful arms she could have done it alone.

The river rushed west, out to the distant ocean, and the brackish scents of the city's waste hit Mila in the nose. The hiding place under the tavern deck smelled like sewage and rotten river mussels, and the ground was littered with empty mussel shells and other detritus. They hid the breathing pump behind a support post, which Verci also tied a rope to.

"I doubt we have much time," he said, lifting up the headpiece. "Jhoqull, you should make yourself scarce."

"Where do you need me?" she asked.

"Park the wagon. There's a real dive pub between here and the warehouses—the Wrath Cellar. It's a perfect position. Lean against the wall there and keep an eye." He checked the hoses one last time.

"They'll think I'm looking to dox," she said.

"That's not the worst thing for our purposes," Verci said.

"If you see the captain and his mate coming with the merch, and don't see us, stall them," Mila said.

"How do I do that?" Jhoqull asked.

Mila shrugged. "Like you said, they'll think you're looking to dox. That's one way."

"I can wallop you, girl."

Mila instinctively skittered back, her hand going to the knife at her waist.

"I'm sure you can," Verci said, stepping in between them. "But we don't have the time for this. Let's drive forward."

Jhoqull nodded and went off into the dark. Verci went under the dock and lit a taper.

"Now what?" Mila asked.

"I need a lamp under there," he said, taking a glass ball attached to one of the hoses. "Hopefully this works, and won't be too noticeable from the boats."

"Hopefully?"

"Never really tested this before," he said. He pulled on his helmet and signaled for Mila to get her head-piece on, and to start pumping. He lit and closed the lamp, which gave an eerie glow as he waded into the river.

"That current looks strong," she said.

"It rutting well is," Verci said.

"Cold?"

"Not really," he said. "But that's what sealskin is supposed to do."

"Now what?" she asked.

"Keep an eye out for the rowboat," he said. "Or row-boats."

"I'll let you know," she said, continuing the pump. "What happened with Asti at the Henterman house?"

"You know what happened."

"No, something happened in the house. With him, you, and that lady."

"Nothing important," Verci said.

"And since then, his control has been slipping more and more. He's been getting worse."

"He's handling it." Now she couldn't see him, or even the soft glow of his lamp.

"He's worse. And I control your air, so tell me."

"Saints, you're cold," he said. "Fine. I don't pretend I fully understand. Somehow Liora just said a bunch of nonsense words to him, and that put him under her spell."

"Magic?"

"Probably not, but who knows."

"Telepaths," she said. "Asti said the Poasians tortured him with telepaths."

Mila could hear the breathy sighs echoed through the tubes. "Keep pumping. Do you see any boats?"

She looked out down the river. "I think I see something coming. Maybe two boats."

"All right," he said. "Let's get to work."

Verci had been ready for the current, he had been ready for the darkness, and he had been ready for the cold. He hadn't been ready for the raw, irrational panic that clawed at his heart once his survival became dependent on a thin piece of hose piping precious breaths of air into the metal box on his head. The regular beats of the hiss and push of air when Mila pumped were not a source of comfort, but a reminder of how tenuous his situation was. He held it together, keeping himself focused on the task, but the urge to scream, to get out of the water and tear everything off his body was nearly overwhelming.

Nearly.

He let out a bit slack on the rope anchoring him to the bank, keeping him from being swept out down the river, and wondered if this was how Asti felt all the time.

"I'm wrong, it's three boats," Mila said through the hoses. Hiss and push. Fresh air.

"I think I see the first one," he told her. "Let me move in closer. Keep pumping."

He latched the rope onto a hook on his belt, and moved his waterlamp to the place it attached on his visor. Bright enough to help him see a few feet, hopefully not too bright to be seen. Even though he wanted to scream in terror, he was pleased with how well things were working. The visor, the breather, the lamp, and all the gear clasps he had added to the sealskin suit. They had never pulled off a gig like this before, and there was something deliciously legendary about this.

Shame they couldn't tell anyone.

The boat was above him, and he swam up and gently grabbed hold of the bottom. He was right—the smuggled cases were attached to the bottom. With light touches, he confirmed three of them.

"Three on the first boat," he said. Hiss and push. Heart beating like a racing stallion. Had to stay calm. Use less air.

"Why aren't you just taking the merch off them now?" Mila asked. "Or we could have swapped the vials here, and they'd never know."

"Swap would have taken at least four of us in the water," Verci said. "We didn't have the gear, or the time to teach you all how to do this."

"Or take them?" Mila asked.

"Then they'd know where it happened, and Josie would guess who could pull it off." He could make out the second boat, barely, in the swirling churn of the river and the glow of the moonslight. But he was almost at the edge of the slack his hoses would give him. He couldn't be that far from Mila. Hiss and push, hoses tethering him to the deck. He wondered if there was a better way to work this device, something that let him move freely. Maybe on its own boat, or little rafts. But who could pump it?

"First boat is coming toward the bank."

Rutting blazes. He let go of the first boat and let the current take him to the second. That was too hard, too fast, and he jarred the boat as he grabbed hold of it.

"Rutting," he muttered.

"All right?"

"You tell me. They reacting on the second?"

"Just rowing."

"Can they see you?" If they spotted Mila—and more importantly, spotted the breathing gear—it'd all be skunked.

"I don't think—"

"If you have to, get the blazes out, and get the count out. Don't worry about me or the pumping."

"Don't have the count yet."

"Three on this boat," he said after he confirmed it. Now he just needed to get to the third boat. Which he couldn't see. "Where's the third?"

"About half a block away from the second. It's definitely lagging behind." She gasped. "The first boat is landing on the bank, about thirty feet away. They should be able to see me, but—"

"Get out!" he snarled.

"But—"

"The count is nine," he said. That was a likely guess, good enough to send her out of danger.

"You couldn't—"

"Get out, send the signal. Run!"

He heard her drop the helmet, and the hiss and push stopped. He took a great gulp of air, and then closed the gaskets. With a flip and a snap, the hoses disconnected. Now he could swim freely, but only had the air left in the helmet. Not much. He let go of the second boat, and released more slack in his anchor rope. He hoped it would be enough, as he flew downriver.

The anchor rope pulled tight, stopping him with a snap just as he reached the third boat.

The boat had no smuggle packs beneath it. Not a third boat of merchandise. He needed to find out who was on this boat. He slipped past the boat and came up at the aft, grabbing hold of the stern and he let his head surface.

Two voices, speaking in Poasian. Definitely not good. Steps needed to be taken. He opened the gasket—the hose connection was above the water now—and took a few breaths. He closed it and went back under, keeping one hand gripped on the bottom of the boat. The current was brutal, trying to pull him off, and the Poasians should notice the drag as they rowed upstream. He didn't have much time, and he had no idea if this would even work. He was fighting the current, could barely see, and between the cold and the sealskin, his fingers were all but useless.

Despite that, he found what he was looking for: a seam between the slats of the boat. He unclipped the knife at his hip and dug it into the seam. Just a little push, crack it open. Then another seam, another crack. About to do a third—lungs burning—when his hand slipped, and the knife tumbled off into the current and the murky darkness. Verci's first instinct was to go after it, but there was no chance he could get it. That knife was gone.

Blazes, that was a good knife.

He let go of the boat, and grabbed his anchor rope before the current yanked him too far. He kept his place, but the boat moved on. He surfaced and opened the gaskets again, finally taking a sweet, clean breath.

Ben and Ka'jach were on the bank, unloading the cases, and the second boat was almost there. And the Poasians—

He didn't speak Poasian, but he recognized the sound of panic when he heard it. That probably wouldn't stop them, but a few minutes slowing them down might make all the difference. Verci doused his lamp and swam to the bank—steep and rocky here—and climbed out of the water.

He glanced back, but the river was too dark for him to see much. He could hear the Poasians shouting, and a splash of the water. Hopefully, their boat was going under.

He'd double back for the other equipment. Right now there was enough to do, and every second counted.

"I see her!"

Julien was being a good spotter. Helene was glad the

plan involved him being up in the perch with her. She'd prefer he was out of it completely, but if he had to be somewhere, on a roof, keeping an extra eye out, carrying that monster launcher for her—that was where she wanted him.

She turned her scope to where he was pointing. Mila was in position, flashing a bit of mirror. Helene loaded her blunt tip and fired at the wall next to the girl. Mila startled, but nodded, looking up at Helene across the wide distance between them. She held up both hands, bending in her thumb. Nine.

"Nine," Helene muttered. Saints, that would be challenging.

"Jules, get over here," she said, repositioning herself to look at the warehouses. She grabbed another bolt and loaded. "Get eight bolts in your hands."

"Eight?" he asked. He picked a bunch up and slowly counted them out, and then counted them again.

"We need to send the count to Asti, and that means speed. So get ready to hand off to me as fast as possible. Ready?"

He looked at the bolts in his hand, and counted one more time. "Yes."

"All right," Helene said. "Let's go." She took aim at warehouse seven, right at the big barn door. Fire. "Next," she said as she recocked the crossbow.

Jules handed her the bolt, and she reloaded it. Aim, fire, reload. Again and again until Julie was out of bolts. She kept her scope aimed at the door for a bit. As she expected, it opened, and Asti stuck his head out.

"Nine?" he mouthed.

She looked to Julie. "You got a stylus and the order pad?"

He nodded, and dug them out of his bag, handing them over. She wrote "Yes Nine" on an order slip, speared it through a bolt and loaded it, firing it down into the door, right next to Asti's head.

To his credit, he didn't flinch when it hit, but looked as mad as she'd ever seen him. He pulled the bolt out of the door and looked at the note, then went back in, signaling her to keep her eye on the warehouse.

"Julie, take the other scope, track on Mila and Verci and the chomie girl. Make sure everything is smooth."

Asti came back out, and made a few hand signals. He must have forgotten that he had never taught her any of those codes he and Verci shared. Sometimes he made things too difficult.

Then he pointed to the building, and held up four fingers.

"Signposter," she told Julien. "We need to get that working."

"Um, Helene," Julien said. "Mila and the other girl are keeping some guys busy on the street—"

"Good," she said. "Signposter."

"And someone is trying to kill Verci."

"What?" She swung her sights over to the north. On the riverbank, Verci was in a fight with some juke with a sword. "You say that first next time!"

"What about the signposting?"

"Get it in position!" she shouted. She didn't have a shot on Verci and his attacker. Not with this crossbow. Not from up here. And with Mila engaged in some business with Ben and Ka'jach, she couldn't risk a signal shot. "Saint Senea, watch over him," she whispered. "You got it?"

"I think," Julien said. Helene checked the big device—it was loaded with the FOUR sign, but it needed to be cranked up. "Get cranking."

He started that process, while she looked through the sight to lock down the aim. She hoped to blazes Verci had this calibrated right, because there had been no time to test it. Verci might have no time either.

"Cranked?"

"Yeah," Julien said.

"Firing," she said, and she pulled the trigger.

The great shot—it was more like a harpoon than crossbow bolt—flew out across the night, sailing along until it smacked into the warehouse wall, right above the barn door. The shot then fell to the ground, but now the sign above said it was warehouse four instead of seven.

Through the scope, she could see that Asti was pleased. He whistled to the folks inside, and Almer and Kennith came out. The three of them went over to the other warehouse. Asti signaled to her to follow along.

"Saints, he wants us to post the other one now," she muttered.

"But . . . Verci . . ."

"I know!" she said. "Load the other shot!"

She picked up The Action while he was loading, looking through the scope for Verci. She didn't see him or his opponent anywhere. Elsewhere, Mila was still working her magic, doing some bit to hold up those sailor boys. If they were already walking over to deliver the merch, who was Verci fighting? What was that about? Where did he go? Was he all right?

"Loaded," Julie said. "Cranking."

She got back in position at the eyepiece, and adjusted the aim for the other warehouse. Asti and the others were now at that door. He gave her a hand signal.

"You better hope we're ready," she said. "Jules?"

"Cranked!"

She found her aim, right for the sign above the door. Asti was out of her sight, but he had already given her the go-ahead. "Firing!"

The shot went out, but she didn't even stay to see if it struck true. Grabbing The Action and a pack of bolts, she said, "Clear the perch, get back to the safehouse!"

And she raced down to the street.

Chapter 9

ASTI POUNDED ON THE DOOR just as the signposter hit the wall of warehouse four. The harpoon staff fell to the ground, and he kicked it out of the way just before the door opened.

"Blazes you pound like that?" the thug who opened the door asked.

"Wanted to make sure you heard us," Asti said.

"And half the neighborhood," the guy grumbled. "Saints almighty."

Asti wanted to say more, but he knew Almer needed to take charge of this. "This is the place, eh, Cap?"

"Right," Almer said. His voice quavered just a moment, like he only decided at the last moment not to try some kind of voice. "Let's move along." He strode forward, brushing past the man at the door, walking in like he owned it. Kennith went right with him, carrying the cases of the fake drug, glowering with each step.

Asti followed close behind, as he hoped to all the saints that no one in here knew the real Ben or Ka'jach. Almer and Kennith looked great, but there was no way they would fool anyone who really knew them, especially with all the lamps burning in this place.

"You guys get a deal on lamp oil?" Asti asked as he walked in. "I mean, saints, it's bright."

"We got a few crates of it a ways back, and the boss likes to see," one of the other guys said. Asti took in the room. Like any warehouse—shelves full of crates, boxes, and barrels. There were about a dozen guys—bruisers all—milling about. Asti wasn't sure if they were expecting some sort of fight, but by every saint, they were ready for one.

"Evening, scrappers," Almer said. "Who's doing the business here?"

"The boss isn't here yet," one of them said. "Cool your heels until he is."

Rutting blazes. Whoever the boss was, he would probably know Ben Choney all too well. He would probably know Asti, even.

"Cool our heels?" Kennith said, making his voice deep and rich with the Ch'omik accent. "What foolishness is this? Do they think we have time for this?"

"You make the time," one of the bruisers said.

Asti was assessing each of them. Size, weapons, muscles. They all had knives and knucklestuffers, but his gut told him they were more warehouse grunts rather than brawlers. Strong, certainly, the kind of strength that comes from hauling crates every day. But that didn't mean they could fight.

Even still, there were nine of them—now he had a count, now he had each one placed in his head—and fighting them all wasn't something he was too keen to do. And he presumed neither Almer nor Kennith would be much use if a brawl broke out.

"Look, we've got our delivery," Almer said, pointing to Ken with the cases of fake *efhân*. "We need to get paid and get back to the boat. We aren't supposed to be standing around all night."

"That ain't my business, salt," the bruiser said. This one—a little older, a little gray around the temples—seemed to be in charge. The others all stood in deference of him.

"You even got our money?" Almer asked. "I mean, we're here with our end."

"Oh, come on, salt," the head bruiser said. "You know that kind of coin, they ain't gonna leave it with us. Boss should be here in a click."

That was some real trouble. This boss, whoever he was, might meet up with the real Ben Choney in the streets, depending on where Mila and Verci were tying them up. At this point, it would be good if Mila was actually tying them up.

Either way, it was time for the contingency.

"If we gotta wait," Asti said, reaching into his pocket and taking out a pipe, "Mind if I smoke?"

The lead bruiser raised an eyebrow. "You talking proper smoke or that stuff?" He pointed to the cases Kennith was still holding.

"Regular smoke," Asti said. It wasn't, but this guy didn't need to know that.

"Fine," the lead said.

"I'm putting this down," Kennith said, dropping the cases of fake drugs. Asti was a bit nervous about that—if they were really here on a merch drop, he would never have any of his people let go of the merchandise until money was in sight. They should at least act like they were delivering the real thing.

"Fine, but keep your foot on it," Almer said. "I don't like these games you're all playing, gents. I was told a time and I'm here."

Asti had lit the pipe, and went through the motions of smoking it, taking care not to really breathe in the stuff, even though the three of them had taken the anti-toxin already.

"We should be fine," Almer had said when he dosed them earlier. "But if you get a real snoot of this in your lungs, you're going to be a mess."

Asti blew the smoke out, letting it pervade the room.

Kennith still looked troubled. He had voiced plenty of concerns about this part of the plan. "You say we're going to be keeping the drugs out of the neighborhood, but we're going to drug these guys?"

"There's drugs, and there's *effitte*," Almer had said. "These guys will be a little giddy, their memory will be a bit hazy, and that's it. They're not going to get hooked or violent or none of that. It's largely harmless."

"How's it different?" Kennith asked Asti.

"Look, if we were playing by the old rules of the neighborhood, we'd take the drugs, take the money, and leave them bleeding on the floor. This is . . . kinder."

"Unless it comes to that," Kennith said. "Let's not pretend that it couldn't."

Asti still wasn't sure if it would.

The barn doors opened, and three men walked in. One of them was Sender Bell.

Verci held his breath, praying to Saint Senea that the Poasian couldn't hear him. The first round of the fight had gone very badly, and had it not been for a timely kick of dirt in his face and a dash into the cover of darkness, Verci might have ended up with a knife in his heart. Now he was under a set of back stairs in some alley, with that bastard hunting after him.

And that bastard could *fight*. He moved like the wind, and came far too close to slicing Verci open in that first skirmish.

Verci touched his shoulder—no, the Poasian did get a piece of him. Damn it.

Right now, Verci had nothing but the sealskin and the breathing mask, neither of which were useful. He had lost his knife in the water. He had more weapons—another knife, his darts, and a couple little toys he'd been hoping to try out—but they were under the deck with the breathing pump. That was at least a block away—between the current and the dark, he had gotten disoriented.

"I know you are not far," the Poasian said, his accent light and fluid. "And you are not some common thief."

He was at the mouth of the alley. Which meant no way out, at least not an easy one. Alley dead-ended, and while Verci could go up the back stairs, or even climb—maybe not with this shoulder—he wasn't sure where that would take him. Not a route he'd prefer.

Verci didn't even have shoes on. That might help him slip away quietly. Same thing with the sealskin—at least it was a brownish gray. A little less moonslight, and he could be downright invisible.

He was hurting, but he'd have to dash for it. Make it to his gear, and he'd have a chance. He prodded around with his feet, finding a couple decent stones on the ground. That was something. Gripping each one with his toes—barefoot had its uses—he got two of them into his hands.

The Poasian stalked through the alley. Closer than Verci would like in this moment.

Two stones. Time to make them count. Verci hurled one—with his off hand, since his right shoulder was hurt—to the back of the alley, cracking it against one of the windows. It shattered, and the Poasian turned sharply to the sound. Verci threw the other rock as hard as he could at the man's head. That hit with a satisfying crack, but Verci did not stick around to see the results. Instead he bolted out of the alley and around the corner as fast as his bare feet would take him.

He heard the Poasian swearing and chasing behind him. No time to stop, but Verci knew where he was now. Not far to the bank. Plus, it meant he'd lead this bastard away from Mila and whatever ploy she was pulling to keep Ben Choney busy. He pounded his feet—saints, these streets were not kind to his bare flesh—and raced to the deck.

That Poasian was right behind him.

He came up to the deck, to see two of Ben's men waiting there, probably guarding the boats. No time to stop, he charged down the deck and dove right into the water.

Thank the saints he still had the mask on—no one

could see his face—but he forgot the air gaskets were open. The helmet flooded as soon as he was in the water, making it impossible to see.

Didn't matter. He turned around as soon as he was in the water, fighting the current with every stroke, swam until his hand found his anchor rope. He pulled himself to the bank, under the deck where his gear waited.

"Saints was that?" he heard one of Ben's men ask.

"Thief," the Poasian said.

Verci unlatched the helmet and pulled it off, letting the water fall away. Breathe. Air.

"Under!" the Poasian said.

Verci had been too loud. He grabbed his pack off the ground. Open it, bandolier. Darts.

Boots hit gravel. "There you are!"

Darts in hand, Verci threw two in a flash, then grabbed another two to follow them. That tore up his shoulder—a pop that radiated pain to the tips of his fingers. He prayed that was all he had to do in this fight.

Three darts in the center of the Poasian's chest. One in the neck. The Poasian fell in a heap.

Breathe. Air. One step back.

He stepped on a mussel shell, slicing open his foot. He held in a yelp, not that it mattered.

More boots on the gravel. The two sailors. "Saints, Rynax?"

"The blazes you doing?"

Curtin and Peeby. Damn and blazes.

Before Verci could answer, there was a familiar thwack. Crossbow bolt went into Peeby's chest, and he dropped. Then another, taking down Curtin. Verci dropped to his knees.

"Verci!" Helene came down under the deck, crossbow in hand. "You all right?"

"Alive," he said. "But that was in doubt for a bit."

"Raych will be happy about that."

"We'll see," Verci said, chuckling hoarsely. "Poasian there. There's at least one more in the field. I'm supposed to get to the warehouse, back up Asti, but—"

"Yeah, you're in no shape," she said. "I'll go. Get to the safehouse. Julien is on his way."

"I will," Verci said, pulling himself to his feet. "Get moving."

She ran off. Verci picked up his pack and loaded up the gear. Carrying it all with one arm would be near impossible, but that's what needed to happen. Not to the safehouse, though. Jhoqull's wagon should be close, that would do.

Once he got these three bodies into the current. Last thing this gig needed was a handful of corpses to draw attention. And Curtin and Peeby deserved to go to the water in the end. They would have liked that.

"Good, everyone's here," Sender said. "Let's not waste any time."

Asti kept his head down. He should be well disguised—the idea was to keep Ben from recognizing him, so hopefully Sender wouldn't either. Sender may have been a big muscle bruiser, but he wasn't an idiot. There was a reason Nange Lesk put him in charge of running these warehouses. The disguise should hold, but it was best not to draw too much attention to himself.

"You must be Captain Choney," Sender said, extending his hands. "And this the infamous Ka'jach. I've heard some tales."

"All good, I hope," Kennith said, laying in the Ch'omik accent.

"Ia definitely sends her regards," Sender said. "Who's that one?" He was pointing to Asti.

"He's my new chart man," Almer said. "He knows a few inlets on the Ocklet Islands even I didn't know. Useful fellow for this."

"You got a name?" Sender asked.

Asti took a pull of the pipe and blew out the smoke, not quite in Sender's face. "Ander. Tellton Ander." It wouldn't be terrible for Sender to get a strong dose of this stuff.

"Glad to have you," Sender said. He pointed to his two companions, neither of whom were the sort of muscle Asti was expecting. Both of them looked more like Almer. "Fallon there is our count man, and Heesmin is going to check the product."

Almer's face paled. He waved at Kennith, "Hand it over. And if you don't mind, I'll have Ander and me check the money ourselves."

"Certainly," Sender said, waving to Fallon to pass the valise he was carrying to Asti. Kennith took his foot off the cases of fake *efhân* and pushed it over to Heesmin.

Almer came over to Asti, opening the money case. As he went through the business of counting it, he whispered, "We have a problem."

"Heesmin, I presume."

"Yeah, I went to school with him. Never close, but, you know."

"Yeah," Asti said. "And I'm guessing he can tell the difference between real *efhân* and this stuff."

"More than likely," Almer said. "Plus the *estarrick*." He tapped the pipe. "He'll probably suss out the smell."

"Thoughts?"

Almer made a bit of a show of looking through the money. "There's the question of which will happen first: he notices the *estarrick*, or it affects him. And what he'll do about it."

Asti glanced around at the others. None of the heavies here were paying him and Almer much mind. Must be the *estarrick* was working.

Fallon, however, was more attentive. "Is there a problem?"

"Just checking," Almer said louder. "You check the goods, we check the money, everyone is happy."

"Are we?" Sender asked Heesmin.

"That is a good question," Heesmin said, looking at one of the vials, holding it up to the lamplight. "So far, so good."

"Good," Sender said. He glanced over at Asti and the rest. "Hey, where did Cando and Gado go?"

The warehouse boss looked around. "They were just here."

"That's really strange," Sender said calmly. Sender and his men were unperturbed by two men going missing. That would be an absolute crisis to him, but these guys found it an odd curiosity. The *estarrick* was working. Good. Asti nudged Almer to say something.

"We all set, friend?" he asked.

"Well, I—" Sender looked about. "I mean, I would think. Money's right?"

"Seems to be," Almer said.

"Hees?"

Heesmin looked like he wasn't sure what to say, that something wasn't sitting right with him. Kennith stepped closer to him. "It's all fine, yes?"

"Well, I think so, but—"

"Then we should be on our way," Almer said, picking up the money satchel.

"It's just this seems like a lot," Heesmin said. "Were we expecting this much?"

"That's what we were given," Asti said.

"We're not told amounts," Almer said, picking up on Asti's lead. "We just get it in and make the delivery."

"Right, yeah," Sender said. "But wait, where are Bean and Jocke?"

Asti turned. Now half of the warehouse thugs were gone, and they were starting to look spooked.

"What's up, man?" the warehouse boss asked, somehow coming off as calm and panicked at the same time. "Are we vanishing? Am I going to vanish next?" He stared at his own hands.

"Move to the door," Asti whispered to Almer. "Now."

"What's going on?" Sender asked. "This isn't funny!"

"I think it is."

The voice was a new one, echoing through the warehouse from every direction. Asti had no idea whose voice it was, and wasn't interested in finding out. "Run!"

Chapter 10

HELENE CURSED SILENTLY AS SHE slipped onto the warehouse yard. She wasn't supposed to be on the ground like this. Things had gone very badly. Verci was clipped, and she saw that Mila hadn't been able to stall Choney and his people any longer. She decided to forgo finesse and just jump the fence.

Inside, she immediately spotted Almer, Kennith, and Asti running like wildcats out of one warehouse. None of them were going in any particular direction other than out. Something had gone wrong here as well. Perfect.

"Hey," she called, getting herself in front of them. "The blazes is wrong?"

"We just ran," Kennith said. He looked scared all to blazes.

"Why?"

Asti reached her, looked just as spooked. "Something very weird in that warehouse."

"You're all fine?" she asked. "You get the money?"

Almer looked down at his hand, as if finding the case of bills was a surprise to him. "We got it."

"Are you three quite all right?" she asked. She tried

to get a good look at their faces, but that was hard to do in the cover of night. "Did you get a snoot of that smoke?"

"Did we?" Asti said. He looked around. "Maybe the antidote didn't work, Almer."

"No, no, it must have," Almer said.

Helene took the money satchel from Almer. "We're out of time, Verci got hurt—"

"How?" Asti asked.

"Poasian," she said. "The guy is dead, but Choney is on the move, so we need to be as well."

"Right," Asti said. He still seemed distracted, but he focused on Almer and Kennith. "You two, get scarce. You can't be seen here now."

"Gladly," Almer said. He and Kennith scrambled off.

Helene and Asti made their way to warehouse seven. Asti was definitely out of sorts, letting her take the lead right now. What would spook him like that? "What happened in there?"

"I think there was someone else," he said. "And . . . maybe you're right. Maybe we dosed ourselves."

"You sharp?" she asked.

"Sharp enough, come on," he said, going into the warehouse. In there, it was lit up with a few lamps, and Vellun, Pilsen, and a handful of others were milling about. They may have been dressed like dockworker heavies, but they stood like a bunch of layabouts who were just waiting.

"Show time, fools," Helene said.

Vellun straightened up. "We ready?"

"Yeah," Asti said. "Hel, money."

Helene tossed the satchel to Asti, who tossed it to Vellun. "Where do you need me?" she asked.

"Out of sight, but ready to crack if things turn left," Asti said. "Vellun, real simple show. They've got merchandise, you've got money."

"Sure, sure," Vellun said. "Look intimidating, boys! So, just straight trade."

"Give just enough trouble to not seem too accommodating. Pilsen!"

"Yes, dear boy?" Pilsen asked. "Which play is this tonight?"

Helene saw fear flash over Asti's face, then he said. "You're playing Olivette."

"Oh, why didn't you say so?" Pilsen asked. "That was one of your father's favorite bits."

"Exactly. Let Vellun take the lead, speak when you need."

"Of course," Pilsen said.

"Vellun, just get the merchandise, get them out the door. Sweet and simple." As soon as he said that, there was a knock on the door. Asti grabbed Helene's hand and brought her up one of the shelves, hidden in the shadows.

"How wrong are you thinking this is going to go?" she asked.

"I'm not taking bets," he said. "It's a losing night."

Ben Choney and Ka'jach came in with a case, and a Poasian companion. The sort of fellow who carried a longsword and looked like he had no compunction about carving people up with it.

"Already skunked," Liora said, lying on her back next to Asti. Now she was dressed exactly the same as Helene, on his other side. He wondered why his brain did that.

"Train your shot on the Poasian," Asti told Helene. "If something goes wrong . . ."

"Got it," she whispered back.

Asti couldn't quite hear Ben and Vellun talking, but no voices were being raised, and no one was going for a weapon, so that was good. Ka'jach handed over the cases of the *efhân,* Vellun handed over the money, and both sides went through the motions of checking it over.

"Just like the other side of the mirror," Liora said. "Will it go just as wrong?"

"Shush," Asti said.

Helene glared at him, but didn't say anything.

Pilsen was putting on a bit of a show, inspecting the *efhân*, counting it. Asti could tell they were delivering a lot less of it than had been part of Verci's count. Something went wrong there. Helene said Verci had gotten hurt. It couldn't be too bad, or else she wouldn't have left him. But even still—Verci got hurt. It tore Asti up not to run out and check on him. But the job had to get done. No matter what, drive forward. Assess the situation after.

"Raych will love that," Liora said.

Pilsen closed up the case and nodded like he was satisfied. Vellun said something about that being enough, indicating the money, and Ben looked perfectly pleased with things. All good. A few moments they would be gone, and all Asti and Helene had to do was clear out with the drugs. Back to the safehouse, where Almer would destroy them. And that should put a kink in the whole operation. No foothold for Fenmere. Dissolve the connections between the Firewings and Lesk's crew, and most notably, Josie. And hopefully no one would be looking at any of his people for it.

"Hopefully," Liora said. "Or they might just thrash out at you, regardless."

She was right. He hated to even admit that.

Of course, it wasn't her, it was just . . . just his broken brain telling him the things he didn't want to think about.

"If that makes you feel better."

Ben went to the door, and the Poasian took the lead to open it. Sounds of fighting came through the open door.

"Constables!" Ben shouted.

Great saints above, someone really wanted to make Asti's life difficult.

Ben bolted out the door, and the Poasian chased

behind him. Ka'jach pulled out a knife and followed. Asti scrambled out of the perch, Helene right with him.

"What are we rutting doing?" Pilsen asked.

"Getting the blazes out," Asti said. In the corner of his mind, if they got out clean, it would be perfect. Things went terrible tonight, but the sticks intervening would plaster over any of the other troubles. Certainly Josie would never suspect him of bringing constables.

Asti took the case from Pilsen and handed it to Helene. "You take point, and no matter what, keep moving. Get it to the safehouse."

"And our people?" Vellun asked.

"With me," Asti said. "I'll bring up the rear. Just follow Helene, get out of here and back to your theater."

"I've handled a sword," Vellun said.

"On stage," Pilsen said. "Not the same."

"Don't engage, just run," Asti said. "If someone grabs you, I got it."

Helene poked her head out the door. "We got a plan out of here?"

"Around the center, past warehouse six, down to twelve, through the hole in the fence. And knock out any oil lamps you can."

"But first priority—"

"Is you out of here with that case," Asti said in a low voice. No need to let Vellun and Pilsen think they were not being considered. He turned to Vellun. "And when you get home—"

"This show never happened. Let's go!"

Helene took another glance out the door, and then Asti signaled for the rest to follow. Pilsen was moving slowly, and Vellun did his best to push the old man along. Asti was right behind them.

The constables were over by warehouse four, in a full scrim with Sender and his boys. Not focused on Asti or his people. The path looked clear, and they were almost to warehouse twelve when someone jumped out of the dark and grabbed Pilsen.

"What are you, you can't, who the blazes—" the attacker shouted. He seemed completely out of his skull in terror. Asti grabbed the guy and yanked him off Pilsen. "He came out of the shadows! The shadows!"

"Run!" Asti told Pilsen. Now he could see it was Fallon, Sender's money man. Fallon was acting like a wild animal, screaming and clawing at Asti. As Pilsen and Vellun got away, Asti held the man off. Fallon was freakishly strong, though, and somehow managed to climb on top of Asti and wrap his legs around Asti's neck, while pounding on his head.

Asti took the easiest course—biting hard on the man's crotch. He then let himself drop—while still biting down—so Fallon landed hard on his back. Fallon cried out in agony, and his legs released. Asti quickly got to his feet and delivered a sharp kick to the man's tenders, even though they had already received significant abuse. That kept Fallon on the ground, crying. Asti ran to catch up with the others, though they had already gone out the hole in the fence. Asti did the same, racing down the alleyway to the street.

Someone stepped in his way. The Poasian with that wicked blade.

"Now this is interesting."

Asti was in no mood to deal with this, and turned to run the other way.

A handful of Sender's thugs came out the hole in the fence, and were running his way.

Asti turned back, knives drawn. Only one way out now.

Mila did not mean to bring the constables into the mix, but that's how it went.

Jhoqull meant well, but had no experience in any sort of street con. Jhoqull had already engaged their attention when Mila arrived, so Mila had to work with that. She had planned to go with a classic ploy, since the goal was just to tie them up for a few minutes. From the back of the wagon, she grabbed a cheap ceramic vase she had bought at the corner market. As the captain started to walk away from Jhoqull, Mila moved in with her vase, bumped into him, and let it shatter on the street.

This was a loser ploy if one actually wanted to swindle some coin, at least off of anyone other than the most naive of rubes. But Mila didn't need to actually fleece these two, she just had to keep them busy. That had gone well enough. And Jhoqull played well into this part, angrily insisting that they do the right thing and pay Mila for her broken vase.

It turned left at that moment, since a Poasian man—even more sickly pale than the spice merchant—came up and shoved a few coins into Mila's hand. "Let us not dally further." He walked along with the captain and his officer in tow. Jhoqull jumped in front of the Ch'omik officer and said something in her native tongue. It sounded like a fierce rebuke, but it could have been the recipe for *chr'dach* for all Mila knew. The Ch'omik pushed Jhoqull out of the way onto the ground, and she responded with a blood-curdling scream. The three marks scurried off at that, but Jhoqull kept going, and in a moment a few shopkeepers had come out to see what the noise was, and then that brought a pair of constables. Mila made herself scarce as the constables went after the captain, the Ch'omik, and the Poasian. Soon whistles were piercing through the air.

Mila went around the long way to get back to the wagon, finding Jhoqull already there.

"That was probably not the kind of delay we wanted," Mila said.

"It worked, yes?"

"Constables are never a good plan," Mila said. She got into the wagon, checking it over. Verci was already inside, half stripped out of the sealskin, his shoulder and his foot bleeding.

"We've had some problems," he said.

"Clearly," Mila replied. "Do we need to get you to the safehouse? Or do we wait for the others?"

"We can wait," Verci said. "Especially if we need to get into the thick of it."

"You do not look like you're in any shape for the thick of it. Should I get to the warehouse?"

"Helene's on it," Verci said. "Stay here and give me some of the rags from your outfit."

Mila tore off a strip. "We should keep bandages on hand in the wagon from now on," she said. "Instead of bleeding our way to the safehouses."

"Good plan," Verci said. "I should put together a kit."

"You carrying ninety different gadgets you never use, you'd think you'd bring something we need every single time."

"Not every time."

"Every. Time."

Jhoqull stuck her head in. "Hey, Kh'enta and the old man are running over. Do we scatter?"

"Not unless they have the drugs," Verci said. He had tried to wrap his shoulder himself, and Mila got tired of watching him struggle and did it herself.

Almer and Kennith came scrambling into the wagon. Kennith barely got inside before Jhoqull grabbed him by the shoulders, looked him over and then kissed him.

"You are good?" she asked.

"Fine, fine, but . . . I don't even know what happened. I think someone else attacked the drop."

"Where's Asti?" Verci asked. "Or Helene?"

"She's with him. They went to the warehouse to handle the drop there. We should roll."

"We need to wait," Verci said. "We don't have the goods yet, which is the whole point. Mila, scout the road between here and the back wall. Almer and Ken, stay hidden in the compartment with me. Jhoqull, be ready to drive as soon as the drugs are on the wagon."

"You mean Asti and Helene," Jhoqull said.

"I mean the merch. However they get here, we roll for the safehouse." He looked hard at Mila.

She got it. Get the goods on the wagon and run, no matter what. But she had already decided what she was going to do.

Mila got out, dropping the skirt layers that were pure disguise, as well as the ragged beggar coat. She did a quick check—rope and knives at her hips, second knife in her boot. She hoped she wouldn't need any of that.

The Constabulary whistles were really blowing now. She skirted off down the alley, but only got around the corner when Helene came running from the hole in the fence, followed by a bunch of guys who went the other way as soon as they were out. Pilsen's people. Helene charged right to Mila.

"I've got the merch," she said, her arms wrapped around the case.

Mila spun around and sprinted with Helene as they rounded back to the wagon.

"Asti?"

"Had the rear," Helene said, looking back. "Should I?"

"Get in the wagon, back to the safehouse," Mila said. "I'll go."

Helene looked like she wanted to argue for a moment, then climbed into the wagon. Mila waited just long enough to make sure Jhoqull had started driving. Asti hadn't come yet. She went back, praying to her saints that he was all right. Body, mind, and soul.

Asti was in the thick of it, fighting like blazes against a bunch of different guys. Most of them looked like typical North Seleth heavies—brawlers, but nothing Asti would have much trouble with. The real problem was the Poasian fellow—the same one who scuttled her stall. He had a real sword, and it seemed Asti could barely stay away from it while also fighting with the brawlers.

Time to even the odds.

She whipped her rope out, catching it on the Poasian's leg. She yanked as he lunged at Asti, pulling him off balance. He did not fall on his face, though, instead pivoting and repositioning himself to face Mila.

He smirked and muttered something in his native tongue, then swiped his sword. It cut the rope clean through.

"Blazing saints," Mila whispered as she pulled what remained of her rope back in.

The Poasian closed the distance faster than Mila could even imagine. She scrambled and dodged, that wicked blade coming far too close. She knew she couldn't possibly fight him with her knives. This was a real trained fighter, probably a soldier.

"Asti!" she called out.

Asti was too busy with the other heavies. She had drawn the real problem away from him, now it was on her to deal with it.

"Come on, ghost," she said, drawing a knife. "Let's see what you've got."

"Druth bravado," he said with a grin. "I do love it."

He lunged at her, and she scurried back to stay out of his range. She threw the knife, hoping he would parry it as it flew in. He did just that and she took her moment. Skipping to his side, she coiled the rope around his sword arm and danced behind him, wrapped the rope around his neck. Charging away from him, she pulled hard on the rope. He should have dropped the sword as his arm tangled into his own face.

That did not happen.

Instead his sword went to the off hand, and with two slashes he was free. Her rope was now half its original length. And he looked ready to stop toying with her.

"Now I'm—"

That was all he said before an arrow slammed into his chest. Then another. He dropped hard.

"Thanks, Hel," Mila whispered. Glad she didn't follow the plan, either. Mila looked back to Asti, who was finishing off the last of the heavies. Constabulary whistles were closer than she liked with a dead body at her feet. Asti was dashing off. He must not have seen her or realized she was nearby. That was fine. She wasn't in danger. He was fine, heading for the safehouse. Good.

She should do the same before the constables came this way. No need to end the night in irons.

Chapter 11

ASTI DIDN'T HAVE A CHANCE to catch his breath and he scrambled up to the rooftop of an apartment tenement. He wasn't sure exactly where he was anymore—maybe a block away from the safehouse, but it didn't matter. The crew had made a clean break, and he had bought them the time they had needed. They should have made it back by now.

Letting his heart slow down, pushing the beast away as it clamored for control, he walked to the other side of the building. He was close to the safehouse. He made his way quietly from roof to roof—the sort of muscle memory that never goes away—until he got there. Julien was coming up the back ladder with the crate, Verci spotting him from behind. Good.

"You all right?"

He almost startled at Mila appearing at his side.

"How long have you been with me?"

"Since I got that Poasian off your back."

"That was you?"

"With help from Helene," she said. She bit her lip awkwardly. "Helene said you were a bit out of sorts. Is everything . . . all right?"

"Oh." She meant the mess in his skull. "Well, there is precedent for that, isn't there?"

"It's good?"

He tapped his skull. "Locked up tight."

She hesitated for a moment, and then said. "Verci told me about the night at Henterman's. How you—"

"Became a windup box of death, mindlessly killing, even trying to kill Verci?" He hadn't talked about it, not even with Verci. Verci didn't push, though. Mila, somehow, always made Asti feel compelled to open up. Maybe because her eyes never showed fear or judgment.

"That was something new?" Mila asked.

"Yeah." He let himself put the weight down. "Liora, she—she said something, I can't even remember what—except for telling me to serve 'the Brotherhood.'"

"The who?"

"I don't know. I've thought about searching it down but . . . every time I start working on it, it's like my brain stops." Even now, revved up from the fight, it was like he had to push through a wall just to get the words out.

"That's . . . horrifying."

"It all is. As soon as she said the words, I was gone. And the beast was gone. And I became something else completely."

Her eyes went wide. "What . . . what did you become?"

"Their puppet. Whoever 'they' are. It was like Liora could just . . . write over my soul."

Mila shuddered. "Are you . . . are you afraid you might—"

"Terrified," Asti said. "But then something else changed. Now I hear her. All the time."

"You mean she's in contact with you?"

"No, I think . . . I think it's that part of my head, the part they controlled. It can't take me over, but it's trying to, I don't know, scare me. Or maybe it's my fear manifesting. And the beast, it . . . maybe calling it the beast is wrong. Maybe it's me. Maybe it's something I made."

"What do you mean?"

"I think—" Asti struggled to put into words the concept he had been struggling with for months. "When they tortured me, Grieson told me his telepaths said I was broken. They were amazed I was even functioning. This beast, this raging animal I keep caged in my head . . . I think it's really me."

"No, Asti."

"I mean, I think they put something in my head, this horrible puppet they could control—that Liora could control—and I shattered myself to stop it. I took the anger, the rage, I used it to make something to protect myself. It's there to keep the puppet from taking over."

"It can do that? You can . . . how does that even work?"

"I'm not even sure. I should talk more with Grieson, or the agency telepaths, get some real answers. But I'm afraid that . . . maybe this is just who Asti Rynax is, forever. A broken man, with a beast and a puppet in his skull, always holding them back."

"Well," Mila said. "I'll be here to help."

"No, you'll be at University. Being better than the rest of us." He didn't want to belabor this. "Let's go see what's what." He disarmed the roof trapdoor and opened it. "After you."

She dropped down, and he followed. Once in the safehouse apartment, he shut the door again. Everyone else was already assembled: Julien and Almer, by the trunk, Almer inspecting the goods. Verci at the table, shirt off, while Helene checked his shoulder. Kennith in the kitchen with Jhoqull. Mila quickly sat down on the couch, taking her boots off.

"So we got it?" he asked.

"We did," Almer said. "And it's a lot. Given how potent this stuff is, I can't even imagine how much this really is, what it's worth."

"Well, we got it," Verci said. "We've got it and they don't. So that's good, right?"

"Very good," Asti said. "As long as it doesn't hit back on us."

"Hopefully it won't," Helene said.

"It shouldn't," Asti said. "Vellun and the rest get out safe?"

"As far as I saw," Helene said. "I was busy getting the goods out."

"But thanks for taking care of that Poasian," Mila said. "He might have skewered me."

"Doing what?" Helene asked.

"You put a couple bolts in that Poasian," Mila said, getting on her feet. "Didn't you?"

"Just now? Not at all. Dashed back here with everyone else."

Asti didn't like the sound of that. "So who shot the Poasian?"

The trapdoor popped open, and a dark shimmer dropped down to the ground next to Asti, that transformed into a burgundy-cloaked man with a staff.

"That would be me."

"Mage!" was all Asti had a chance to shout out before the whirling staff clocked him in the head, sending him reeling back a few steps. Mila went down as well.

Asti felt the beast wanting to claw up for air, tear this mage apart, but he held it down. He couldn't let it loose, not in here, not with everyone else in the room.

Helene came up with her crossbow and fired, but the guy dove out of the way. Helene's shot almost took Almer's ear off. The guy moved in on her, but Verci got in between them, knife in his off hand. His better arm, he still held close to his body. He took two swipes, backing the guy up toward the kitchen. While Asti still tried to find his bearings, Jhoqull laid in to the fellow with several brutal punches.

The guy pivoted, clocking her with the staff and bowling her into Kennith, before leaping up, bouncing off the back wall, and laying a solid blow onto Verci. Verci crumpled to the ground.

Asti pulled himself together, drawing out his knives, but Mila was already moving in. The fellow had a rope hanging on his belt, and Mila darted in and whipped it off of him. She quickly coiled it about her arm and got ready to strike. The guy put a foot on Verci's chest.

"That's not something to play with, girl."

"I never play," Mila said, and like a shot she was on him, wrapping the rope around his arms and neck. He dropped the staff in an attempt to grab ahold of it.

"Hold him!" Helene said, leveling her crossbow at him and firing.

Despite being bound, he was surrounded by a bright red nimbus of light. The crossbow bolt stopped, midair, right in front of his chest. He then whistled, and it went flying backward, knocking Helene in her head.

"The mages found us!" Julien shouted.

"I got him," Mila said, tightening her grip.

"Sadly, no."

The rope came alive in Mila's hand, like a snake, wrapping around her while the mage was freed. He then yanked, and she went flying impossibly far across the room into Julien.

This fellow had taken out most of them single-handedly. But now Asti was spoiling for a fight. He dove in, as the fellow brought the rope back to him.

"You're going to—" Asti started.

"Pay for that?" the fellow quipped back. The rope—it was nearly a living creature in his hands—struck at Asti, attempting to wrap around his arms or legs. Asti moved a little bit faster, staying a half a step ahead of the rope in his dance, closing the distance.

"Bleed for that."

"Would have been my second guess," the fellow said, dodging from Asti's slashes. He was a slippery bastard. "And I'm not keen on the bleeding, thank you."

"Then you came to the wrong place."

"Bunch of lowlifes with a crate full of *efhân*? Nope, right place. And—" His rope lashed out to Helene, wrapping around the crossbow and yanking it out of her hand. Asti took the opportunity to strike, but then the crossbow came flying into his head. "No, thank you, miss."

Mila had darted in again, grabbing the rope as she sent her knee into his tenders. She ripped it out of his hands and then scurried to the other side of the table, next to Helene.

Asti went in for the kill, but then the guy moved in a blur, suddenly five steps away. Bow out, arrow nocked and drawn, aiming at Verci's head.

"You're an interesting crowd," he said. "But I'm not letting you have the *efhân*."

"So your boss can sell it here?" Asti snarled. "Not a chance."

"My boss?" the fellow asked. "Saints, don't you people know?"

"Know what?" Verci said from the floor. "Asti, take him out."

"I assure you I can let fly this arrow before you get a chance," he said. "Big guy, weasel. Over behind the table."

"Am I the weasel?" Almer asked.

"You're certainly not the big guy. All of you where I can see you. Even you two in the kitchen. This is not a time to be kissing on the floor."

"Is this a joke to you?" Asti asked. For the first time, Asti got a proper look at him. The red cloak and hood left him bathed in impossible darkness. There was no way to properly see his face, just his mouth and chin. But that chin was devoid of anything resembling whiskers.

"Oh, no. I am quite serious about keeping that poison off the streets."

Asti didn't know what to say to that. "That's what we're doing."

"What do you mean that's what you're doing?"

"Which part was hard to understand?" Mila spat at him. She held the rope with tight, white knuckles.

"You throw that over here right now," he said. "You have no idea what that is."

"It's your magic rope, and I'm keeping it, Firewing."

"That's a new one," he said. "New neighborhood, new nickname."

"Who the blazes are you?" Verci asked.

An answer came from the kitchen, as Jhoqull, holding a rag to her bleeding head, stepped forward. Anger made her accent even thicker. "Don't you rutting *k'aqam* know? That's the Thorn of Dentonhill, he is."

"Who?" Verci asked. This person—The Thorn of Dentonhill, according to Jhoqull—held a drawn bow over him while keeping a foot planted on his chest. His shoulder had already been through enough tonight, he did not need this. Far too often he had found himself at this end of these standoffs with lunatics.

"Just 'the Thorn' is fine," he said. "As you can see, I don't confine myself to one neighborhood."

"Saints, you westtown boys don't have a lick of sense," Jhoqull said. "You rob something that's for Fenmere and his people, and you don't even know about his enemies?"

"Wait, that's real?" Asti asked.

"You heard of this?" Verci asked back.

"Really, I'm right here," the Thorn said. "And you, broody corset girl. Slowly unlatch that belt and let those crossbows hit the floor."

"It's not a corset," Helene said.

"I don't care, I don't want to see your hands near them. In fact, Weasel, you unlatch her belt."

"Me, I—" Almer started, looking at Helene nervously.

"At least let Julie do it," Helene said.

"That's the big guy? Fine. But slow, or the handsome one gets this in his eye."

"You do well with the threats, kid," Asti said. "You sound like you'll follow through."

"Think I won't?"

Asti did something that surprised Verci—he flipped the knives over and sheathed them. "I think you can when you need to. I think you've had to plenty of times. But you came in here to put us down, not kill us."

"I came here to stop you from selling that."

"Hey, yeah, I see that," Asti said. "And we're not interested in selling it. There's folks who are, and we just wanted to take it from them. Nothing more."

"You took, what, six thousand crowns' worth of drugs, with an elaborate scheme, mind you—"

"You saw that?" Asti asked.

"Yeah. You're thieves and conmen, so why should I trust—"

"You shouldn't," Asti said. "Don't trust that, because we are. But you can tell we don't work for Fenmere, or any of his allies, right?"

"That doesn't mean you aren't looking to make your own score."

"Son," Almer said, stepping forward. "I can tell you're a passionate sort about this stuff. I feel the same way. We took it to destroy it. I'm prepared to destroy it. I can show you."

The Thorn's arm, drawn back, wavered for a moment. Saints, it must be killing his arm to hold back the bow like that. "Show me."

Almer, hands up, slowly moved from behind the table to the crate, taking out one vial. Then he opened up his leather case.

"Easy," the Thorn said. "No tricks."

Verci wasn't sure if Almer had a trick planned right now or not. Almer was definitely clever, but he was hardly brave or deceptive.

"No tricks," Almer said, taking out a small leather bag. He went back to the table and opened up the vial. Verci couldn't see what was happened, but he could see the Thorn's expression—at least his mouth, since the top half of his face was shrouded in darkness. But he looked rapt. He could hear Almer fidget and fiddle at the table. Then there was a sudden whoof of sound, and an awful smell of rot and sulfur.

"And destroyed," Almer said.

The Thorn whistled, and then hopped off Verci, back toward the middle of the room, near the roof trapdoor, and brought his bow down.

"No one get too many crazy ideas," he said. "Let's all be relaxed, friends, all right?"

"Relaxed," Asti said. "I'm guessing you want to be sure it's destroyed, yes?"

"Yeah," the Thorn said.

"And then you'll . . . do what, exactly?"

"One step at a time," the Thorn said.

"Can I get my brother off the floor?" Asti asked.

"Slowly."

Asti pulled Verci up to his feet, and then helped him back into the chair he had been in before. "Let Helene fix his shoulder. Let Almer and Julien get to work destroying it."

"I could use extra hands to make it go faster," Almer said.

"Kennith, Jhoqull? Help them?"

"Sure," Kennith said.

"Mila, you hold on to his rope for now," Asti said. "Collateral."

The Thorn nodded. "Fair enough."

"And we'll let them work." Asti stepped away from the table. He signaled Verci with his fingers. *Maybe this guy is an asset. Let's play it out.*

Fine, Verci signaled back. Asti was working to gain the Thorn's trust. Using their names, being calm. Verci knew that was probably killing Asti, but if he could do it, then Verci would go along. "Helene, if you could get back to it?"

"Sure," she said, finding the needle and thread on the table. "You want Almer to give you something?"

"No," Verci said, even though it was going to hurt like blazes. "Better to stay sharp."

"Wise," the Thorn said. "I guess while we're waiting, brothers, you two can tell me your story. Especially since you two are clearly in charge of this gang."

"Crew," Asti said. "It's not a gang, it's a crew."

"My apologies," the Thorn said.

"We've got some bread, cheese, apples," Asti said. "You want anything?"

The Thorn tensed around his shoulders. "Not if it puts you out."

"Wouldn't have offered if it did," Asti said. He slowly moved over to the kitchen, keeping his hands away from his body. He really didn't want to trigger anything from the Thorn. Verci was downright shocked at how much calm and reserve he was showing. Of course, this Thorn nearly flattened them all in a few clicks, so it probably was wisest not to aggravate him.

Helene started to sew the wound. Verci let barely a grunt out, but by every saint, it hurt. He kept his focus on the Thorn. Stared holes in the man. Let that keep his mind on something other than the pain.

Asti started to get things out of the icebox, and continued to talk. "So, I presume you followed me here from the warehouses. You must have had some sense of who we are, what we're about."

"You're clearly a cohesive group, and you care about each other," the Thorn said. "And since you're destroying the *efhân*, I'm willing to hear more."

"Willing, how about that," Mila said. "Asti, why—"

"Just, calm," Asti said. "I have heard bits and bobs about you, friend. Mostly rumor, but I know you're no friend to Fenmere."

"And you aren't either?"

"I was indifferent to him until two days ago, but if he's pushing into our neighborhood, allying with the folks hurting our people, then we take note of him and his."

"Your people," the Thorn said. "Goes beyond the eight of you in this room."

Asti came around with a board with cheese, dried sausage, bread, and sliced apples. A knife lay on the board. Maybe that was Asti's play here—put the weapon in plain sight, for legitimate reasons, so he could use it later if he needed it. "Did you hear about the Holver Alley fire?"

The Thorn shook his head, and took a piece of apple.

"A few months ago, a fire devastated Holver Alley.

Took out homes, business, destroyed lives. Most of us here were affected by it."

"All right," said the Thorn as he ate.

"We found out the fire was deliberate, part of a plan to force people out, get the land easily. For what, we're not entirely sure."

"Does the name 'Andrendon Project' mean anything to you?" Mila asked. She was really scrutinizing the Thorn as carefully as she could.

"Can't say that it does," the Thorn said. "Certainly not as something that Fenmere has his fingers in."

"Whatever it is, the people behind it are more than willing to treat us like rats, smoking us out and killing us to get it done," Asti said.

"But we've been biting back," Helene said. "Hitting those who burned us, who had it done, chasing it to the end."

The Thorn chuckled. "I can relate to that."

"The drugs are personal to you, aren't they?" Asti asked.

"The drugs, Fenmere, all of it," the Thorn said. "What he's doing to this city is already bad enough. Wasn't going to let him get another toehold anywhere."

Verci realized where that was coming from. "Who'd you lose?"

The Thorn visibly bristled at that. "We don't need to get into that."

"Just business, then." Asti sat down across from the Thorn. "So, you tracked the *efhân* trade to the warehouse, and then started the chaos in there, and when you realized we were walking out with the drugs, kept on us. Even took out that Poasian so you could follow us back here."

"Something like that," the Thorn said.

"Right, so now we've got a problem. Our goal was to sneak the drugs off the street quietly. Swap the real thing—which we're destroying—"

"Working on it," Almer said. Verci wished there was

a back room they could take that process to, if not Almer's shop. The whole thing smelled awful.

"But that quiet plan is skunked," Asti said. "We got bodies in the street, we got Constabulary's attention. The players in this game will know something went down tonight. The big question is, will they suspect if we had any part of it?"

"We can't have them looking at us," Verci said.

"We're supposed to be out of this game," Helene said.

"Like we graduated," Mila added, which Verci thought was an odd way to put it.

The Thorn nodded. "There's a truce in place, right? And if the people you went after tonight realize it was you—"

"The truce is broken," Asti said. "This isn't just about us—"

"You have people," the Thorn said. He sighed. "I get that. I don't hide my face and go by 'the Thorn' because it amuses me."

"And what do your people think of what you do?" Mila asked.

Verci winced—Helene's last stitch was a bit too tight. But Mila's question also cut hard. Verci was all too aware what his people thought. Of everyone in this room, with the possible exception of the Thorn, he was the one with the most to lose.

The Thorn sprung up on his feet, a bit too quick for Verci's taste. Verci moved to his feet, forgetting for a moment about his foot being sliced open, and the pain shot through him like lightning.

"Easy," Asti said.

"I think I don't need more questions," the Thorn said. "I don't make a habit of chatting like this."

"Fine," Asti said. "I don't—I just wanted to let you know where we stand, and that we've got some of the same goals."

The Thorn nodded. "Your truce here breaks, that's

more of a hole for Fenmere to fill. But how do we cut him off without making trouble for you?"

"There's a we?" Mila asked.

"There could be," Asti said. "This isn't your neighborhood, but perhaps you stick around for a night or two?"

"I—" The Thorn hesitated. "I need to get home, check in with my people. But I'll be back."

"Fair enough," Asti said. He gestured to the trapdoor. "You know how to find us."

"Wait," Mila said. "If he can, he should do one more thing tonight."

"What sort of thing?" the Thorn asked.

Verci looked to Mila. "What are you thinking about?"

"Lesk and his boys, as well as the Firewings, all of them, they're going to know something went wrong. So they'll start looking into what it was. Who it was. They'll look at us, unless they have somewhere else to look."

Asti nodded. He signaled to Verci. *She's got the right idea.* "The Thorn needs to do something public. So they all know he's here."

A tiny smile crept across the Thorn's face. "What sort of public?"

"I know what," Mila said. She went to one of the trunks and pulled out a few things—rope, a red hat, a dress—and stuffed them into a pack. "The rest of you finish up, get home. Get seen at home or such if you can."

"Mila—" Asti started.

"I got this," she said. She tossed the Thorn's rope to him. "Come on, Vee, let's get to work."

She went up the trapdoor. The Thorn looked stunned for a moment, and then followed. Asti hopped up and shut the trapdoor, setting the trap lines as he did.

"The saints just happened?" Verci asked.

"I'm not sure," Asti said. "But I trust her."

"You're going to let that girl go off like that?" Jhoqull asked.

"She's got it. Almer, where are you?"

"Working," he said. "If time's not a huge factor, I

can do that on my own here. No one will really mark what I'm up to at home."

"Right. Verci, get home, have a late supper with your wife with the shades open. Helene, you and Jules get home. Have your stick friend call on you."

"Asti, don't tell me what—"

"So you're seen at home," he said. "I'm going to have a few drinks at Kimber's. And Ken—"

"Wagon's already hidden in the back barn here," he said. "Jho and I will walk the horses to the Hodge and camp out there tonight."

"Good man," Asti said. Everyone got themselves together, starting for the door.

Verci put on a clean shirt. "Mila's got this?"

"She's got this," Asti said. "If she didn't, she would have told me to come."

"You better be right," Verci said. "Raych is going to be mad I got hurt. But if something happened to Mila, she'd skin us both."

Chapter 12

MILA RACED ACROSS FROM ROOF to roof until she reached the end of the block, and waited at the edge for the Thorn to catch up. She knew he'd be right behind, she had made sure of that.

"You move fast," he said as he came up to her. He pulled out a strip of dried meat from a belt pouch and started eating it. "You forget that I don't know where we're going."

"I wanted to make you run a bit, Vee," she said. She turned back to see him there, with the hood creating an unnatural shadow across the top of his face. But still that smile, that voice. Unmistakable. "You don't have to do that."

"Do what?" he asked.

"Hide your face. I already know, Veranix Calbert, or whatever your real name is."

"Fine, yes," he said. "Should have scouted in disguise before."

"Yeah, that's basic," she said. Then she realized what he really meant. "Saints, is your name actually Veranix Calbert?"

"Yes," he said. Then he stumbled, saying, "I mean, that's just a . . . I mean, you—look, it's . . ."

"You told me your actual name while you were pulling a job?"

"I don't pull jobs," he said. "I'm not some sort of swindler, like you all."

"I don't know what you think you are—"

"Exactly what I told you this morning," he said. "Are you really going to the University? Or was that some sort of scheme?"

"You talked to me," she said. "How is that my scheme?"

"I don't know what you people do."

"Oh, please," she said, rolling her eyes. "Like you are any less of an outlaw!"

"Outlaw? Is that what you think you are?"

"I think we do what we have to," she said. "But a college boy wouldn't understand that."

He pointed a finger at her, his hand shaking. "You have no idea what I understand."

She had touched a nerve. "So that whole bit on the street was real. Even the circus caravan?"

"Well, I didn't know you were part of this whole *efhân* in Seleth business. You said you were coming to the University, and I remembered what it was like my first year, so I thought—I just thought giving you a friendly face to look up would help . . . Never mind."

"No, no," she said. Now she felt bad. "It was sweet, it was. I appreciate it. I'm sorry to give you—"

"What is it you want to do?" he asked.

"Well, like I said, I was thinking law or policy—"

"I meant now. You want the Thorn to make some noise in this neighborhood, so what did you have in mind?"

Right. Business. "There's a gang that's attached to the bosses who were getting the drugs. The Scratch Cats. They've earned a bit of slaparound from me."

"So this is a personal score for you?" he asked. "But

you don't want the angry brothers or crossbow lady helping?"

"It's a bit personal," she said. "I have—I had—a group of boys under me. I didn't take care of them. So I need to make things right."

"Boys? As in, kids?"

"Yeah, kids. That's how it goes out here."

"And the Scratch Cats hurt these kids?" The shadow covering his face got darker. "Where are they?"

"Hold up," she said, putting the pack down. She took out the dress—a simple red work dress, the one she wore as the flower girl for the Pomoraine gig—and started taking off her boots. "Turn around."

He did so without question. "I'm not sure what the dress is for."

"It's character," she said as she stripped out of her blouse and skirt. "I can't be doing this with you as street girl Mila."

"With me?" he asked, turning his head just a bit back toward her.

"Eyes ahead," she said as she got the dress on. She took the hat out of the bag—a red page cap—and bundled her hair up under it as she put it on. Boots back on, then her belt. For this, she could wear her knives proudly on her hips. Then she coiled up her spare rope and put it over her shoulder. "So tonight, the Thorn has a partner. Maybe the Rose?"

He turned back to her. "You can't be the Rose, that's just silly—"

"Why not? You call yourself the Thorn!"

"I didn't actually call myself that, it's just a thing that stuck."

"Well, I like the Rose."

"Fine," he said. "But don't expect me to call you that. And if you're going to do this, you need to hide your face better."

"Right," she said. She drew one of the knives and sliced a strip of fabric off the dress, creating a slit up her leg. She glanced up at the Thorn, just to see if he was looking. Then she remembered she couldn't see his eyes. Damn it. She took the strip and wrapped it around her mouth and nose. "Better?"

"A bit," he said. He waved his hand, and Mila saw a flash of sparkles dance in front of her eyes.

"The blazes was that?"

"Just a little accent," he said. He spun his finger, and the air in front of her shimmered and turned into a mirror. She could see how she looked—and the whole look was quite excellent—and she now had a mask of red face paint around her eyes, with an intricate flower pattern woven into her eyebrows. It was truly spectacular.

"How—how—?"

"Mage," he said. "I thought you knew that."

"There's knowing and there's actually seeing it," she said. "That's amazing." She looked at it carefully in the magical reflection. "It will come off, right?"

"Probably," he said with an infuriating smile. "So, are we ready to hit these Scratch Cats?"

"Ready," she said. "You follow me—"

"Where are we going, exactly?" he asked.

"They're between Colt and Elk, about five blocks south of here. We'll have to . . ."

That was all she managed to say before he took a few steps back, and then dashed toward her, wrapping an arm around her waist as he leaped off the roof.

Mila screamed, and clutched him around his shoulders. Was he crazy? A jump from the roof would kill them!

But they weren't dropping to the street. They were soaring over Bridget Street, over Kimber's on Frost, over Holver Alley and Ullen Street.

"H—how?" she stammered out.

"I told you," he said. "Mage."

"You can fly?"

"No," he said, as she looked down at all of North Seleth below them—small and beautiful—and the rest of the city stretching beyond, a view like she'd never seen. "But I can jump really far when I need to."

They came down, landing like a feather on a roof of a shop on Colt Road.

"Saint Senea, that was a thing," she said as he put her back on her feet. Her heart might never stop thundering again.

"Try not to look so amazed," he said. "Or these guys will never believe you're the Thorn's sidekick."

"Partner," she said firmly.

"Well then, Rose," he said, bowing with a flourish. "Lead the way, and show me what you've got."

Verci split off from everyone else, and went home alone. Asti was going to Kimber's so he could be seen there, and had said it was best if no one attracted too much attention on their walk home. Verci kept his head down, avoiding corners where the streetlamps were still burning. He crossed into a few back alleys and took a long way around twice to avoid a group of boys who might be gangs under Lesk.

It was definitely later than he would have liked when he got back to the Gadgeterium.

He latched the back door and set the alarm trips. Even Asti wouldn't be able to get in without setting off the bells. Asti wasn't planning on coming back tonight, anyway.

Verci stripped off his gear and clothing and put them all in the cellar. Getting off his boot was the worst. His foot hurt like blazes, and he half wished he had gotten something from Almer for the pain. The shoulder wasn't much better.

He limped to the front of the shop, turning off the windups that made it sound like he had been working all night. He double-checked the latch on the door—secure—and blew out the lamps. Satisfied that everything was shut down in the shop, and the appearance of him having been working there all night had been maintained, he went up to the apartment.

"How bad are you?" Raych asked as he came in. She was at the stove, with her back to the door.

"Nothing broken this time," he said. "So that's something."

"Well, it's an improvement," she said, turning around. "So—oh, great holy!" She dropped the mug she was holding. Verci dove in and caught it before it shattered on the floor.

"Does it look that bad?" he asked, standing back up and handing her the mug.

"It looks like you were stabbed, so yes!"

"Well, I was. A little."

"A little stabbed?" she shouted.

"Let's not wake Corsi," he said, touching her gently on the arm. "Things went wrong."

She looked him up and down. "Did you get stabbed in the foot as well?"

"No, that . . . that was just careless. Stepped on a mussel shell."

"How did you—"

"Well, I didn't have shoes on, and I had just killed the Poasian—"

"What?" She blinked several times, and then put her mug down. "Cider isn't enough for this." She went to one of the pantry cabinets.

"It sounds worse than it was."

"I don't see how," she said, getting out a bottle of wine. She pulled out the cork and poured generously into a cup. "You killed a Poasian. Who I presume was trying to kill you."

"That's right."

"And why? I thought everything was supposed to be quiet and unnoticed. Was that all sewage you told me?"

"No, it was supposed to be. It definitely was! I wish to every saint it had been."

"So what went wrong?"

"On my part? I was scouting the boats coming in, and I skunked it. One of the Poasian bodyguards noticed me and swam after me. Chased me in an alley, we had a scuffle, I got away, back to the docks, put three darts in him. Not how I wanted it to go."

"Where was Asti during this? Or anyone else?"

"Helene showed up and took out the two sailors who came next."

"Helene," Raych said darkly, taking a deep drink of her wine. "Well, I'm glad she was there for you."

"We did succeed," Verci said. "We got the drugs, and Almer is destroying them, so they aren't going to hurt anyone."

"Until the next shipment," Raych said.

"Hopefully the failure of this one means they won't try again."

"Does that ever work?" Raych asked. She poured another cup of wine. "I mean, I don't know this Josie woman like you do, but is she the type to just throw her hands up and say, 'oh well,' and not try again?"

She had a point.

"No, definitely not," Verci said.

"So," Raych said, holding her cup of wine up. "What have you accomplished? Aggravated Josie, probably cost her money, and possibly made us targets."

"I don't think we're targets."

"Right, because you killed the Poasian."

"One of them."

"There were two? Did Asti kill the other one?"

"No, it was the Thorn."

Raych just stared at him for an eternity. "Who the rutting blazes is the Thorn?" she shouted.

Corsi started crying in the next room. Verci got up and picked him up from his crib. "He's a—well, he's a fellow from easttown who's got a grudge against Fenmere."

"And Fenmere is who again?"

"The drug boss who Josie must be dealing with," Verci said. He rocked Corsi in his good arm, trying to sooth him. The little boy just kept crying.

"I don't want to know any more," Raych said. "I just, I know this isn't done. It's never going to be done, is it?"

"I want it to be," Verci said.

"Then just be done," she said. She went into the

other room. "I'm going to sleep, because I have real work to do tomorrow."

"So do I!"

"Then you should get to sleep, too."

Corsi was calmer now, his cries eased down to heaving breaths. "Come on, buddy," Verci said to him. "Let's get some sleep, yes?"

He went to the other room, and Raych was already in bed, eyes closed. Verci laid Corsi next to her, blew out the last lamp, and got in bed himself.

Everything will be fine in the morning, he thought. *And things can get back how they should be.*

"Hey," he said quietly. "I'm going to go over those plans Carrigan brought us, take that consulting gig."

"That's good," she said back. "That's what we should be doing. That's what matters."

"And what we have right here," he said.

She turned over to face him, placing her hand on Corsi's chest, who was now cooing contentedly. "That's everything."

"I love you so much, Raych."

"I know," she said. "Go to sleep, Verci Rynax. Tomorrow's a big day."

Helene had left most of her equipment at the safehouse—no need to lug it all home, especially if the idea was to look inconspicuous tonight. The last thing she needed was some steve or gang boy spotting her walking home with a bunch of crossbow cases. She did leave one hiphanger—Orton—loaded and ready on her belt, but she would do that anytime she was out at night. Anyone who knew her would know that. Even respectable businesswoman Helene Kesser would protect herself.

"So we just go home?" Julien asked. "I wanted to check the smoke room before going to bed."

"That's the plan," she said.

"We were supposed to get pork cuts from Mister

Scall the day before yesterday. They haven't come yet. I didn't want to say anything while we had . . . other things happening. But now that's something that worries me."

"Scall hasn't been very timely, has he?" Helene asked.

"The past month, no," Julien said sadly. "His wife died."

"Why didn't you tell me that?" Helene asked, smacking Julie on the arm. "I'm not going to harass the man over being behind when that happened."

"Me either," Julien said. "He's been more and more behind, but if we don't get that meat, I can't start curing and drying, and then the sausages won't be ready by the time we're going to need them. It's a big problem."

Helene almost wanted to cry. She hadn't heard Julien talk so carefully, so thoughtfully, as he did about the work they did at the shop. He really loved curing meats, working with cheeses, telling their customers which went best together. "You know what we need. Do you want me to go talk to Scall?"

"I feel bad. I feel we need to find someone else who will deliver what we need. But that's so mean to Mister Scall." He lowered his voice. "She died because of the fire."

"What?"

"She never stopped coughing after that night, and it got worse and worse and . . ." He trailed off.

"That's terrible."

"I think we were pretty lucky that night. I was. You made me get out of the house."

"We did," she said. "I'm lucky I've got you, you know that?"

"I do," he said. "But you know I'm going to be all right, with the shop and all? Except for the books, I still need help with the numbers, but I can handle things."

"What are you saying, Jules?"

"That I know you're going to marry the lieutenant and want to move away."

Helene burst out laughing. "I'm not going to marry him."

"I think he wants to."

"Yeah, he can want to, but . . ." She shook her head as they reached the shop. "Can you imagine, me, wife of a constable? It's laughable, Julien."

"You like him, and he likes you."

"He does, and—" She should reach out to Covrane, like Asti said, so she could use him to establish being home tonight. Then she realized she wasn't entirely sure how to, at least at this hour. She hadn't been to his home, wasn't even sure where it was. Did he even live in North Seleth? Or was he a Keller Cove man? Saints, if he did ask her to marry him, would he want her to live in Keller Cove?

But her only point of contact had been him coming to her, or her leaving him messages at the Loyalty Waystation—not even the proper Keller Cove Stationhouse.

For all she knew, the man was married and she was the mistress.

"And what?" Julien asked as he unlatched the door.

"And that's enough for now," she said. "I ain't thinking of moving on from this or you, all right? We're a team."

"Yeah," he said with a shy smile. "Come on, I want you to try the spicy Prenkaw I made. It should be ready now, and I think it will be really good."

"I'm sure it will be," she said. No matter what, if she was with Julien, things would be good.

Kimber's taproom was relatively quiet when Asti came in, only a handful of folks nursing their beers, each one sitting alone. Asti sat down at the bar next to Jared Scall, who stared at his mug like he was expecting it to move on him.

"Evening, Jared," Asti said. "How's by you?"

"Horrid," Jared said quietly. "As usual."

Asti wasn't sure how to respond to that.

"You ever watch someone die, Rynax?"

"Yeah," Asti said. "More than a few times."

Jared turned to look at him. "Someone you loved?"

"Let's not do that," Kimber said as she came over. "I think that's your last tonight, Jared. Your children will be wanting you to come home."

"They don't," Jared said.

"Saints don't look kindly at the lies in your mouth, Jared Scall."

Asti had never heard Kimber be that blunt or harsh with anyone.

"Hey," Asti said. "It's all right. Jared and I, we were just talking. Nothing I didn't ask for."

"Sorry," Jared said. "I just. . . . I ain't been right." He got up and went to the other side of the taproom.

"It really was fine," Asti said as Kimber put a beer in front of him.

"He's in trouble," Kimber said. "And kindness wasn't doing anything. I tried talking, I tried bringing him to service, and . . . I only have so much."

"You do more than most would," Asti said.

"May the saints hear you," she said. "Where is Mila, have you seen her?"

"She's not around?" Asti asked, putting on a show of looking about the room. "How is her math?"

"Fair. But she's not in her room and I am worried."

"You know she's going to be on her own pretty soon, yes?"

"And that doesn't worry you?"

"All the time," Asti said. "But what did you need? She's been studying plenty. She deserves a day or two of break before leaving for school."

"Yeah, but I still have the boy upstairs."

"What boy?" Asti asked.

"One of those street boys, the ones who she would . . ." Kimber made an odd movement with her eyes. "I don't want to talk about whatever it is you all would do."

"You don't need to. But what about the boy? Was it Tarvis?"

"No, but . . . Tarvis was the one who brought him in. He was hurt real bad by some gang boys, and Tarvis found him, and Mila was watching over him for a bit, but . . ."

"Is the kid all right?"

"Gelson said he will be with rest."

"You need money? For the room, or for Gelson?"

"No, I couldn't," Kimber said. "You can't pay for every lost soul who passes under here. I don't know how you afford it."

Asti let that pass. She probably did know how he had money, but didn't want to think about it.

"But Tarvis is all right?"

"As all right as that boy could be, I suppose. He's not injured, which is something."

"It is," Asti said. He had felt an odd kinship with the violent little boy. He knew that if he had ever found Verci dead on a table, he would go on a rampage of blood and vengeance that would make every saint and sinner weep.

"Do you need anything?" Kimber asked. "There's a bit of bread and stew left, and if you need a bed for the night?"

Asti wasn't sure if she was offering him a room or her own bed.

"I actually think I might want to stay here," Asti said. "If that isn't trouble."

"For you, never," she said. She reached across the bar and put her hand on his cheek. Asti fought back the urge to flinch away from the tender contact. Such things were so rare in his life, and his every instinct—and the beast clawing on the chain—pushed away at such things. "I haven't given up on saving your soul. Not by a long shot."

Asti felt his throat dry up. "You've seen how broken it is."

"I know," she said quietly. "That's why it needs saving." She pulled away her hand, and looked at the ground sheepishly. "Stew and bread?"

"Please."

"Right away." She went off in the back.

Asti sipped at his beer and looked around the room again. Right now, things were quiet. But news of things going wrong tonight was surely reaching Josie, the mages, maybe even Fenmere. The morning would bring consequences.

But for right now, things were quiet, and Asti would take what small measure of peace and comfort he could get. No matter how small it might be.

Chapter 13

THE SCRATCH CATS HUNG AROUND a derelict workhouse on Colt Road. Run-down, broken windows, paint job over paint job with gang markers that probably went back to when Josie was Mila's age.

"Lovely place," the Thorn said as they hung back in an alley across the way. "So what sort of plan do you have?"

"What would you do?" Mila asked. "I mean, when you do this sort of thing?"

"This sort of thing?"

"You know, you—saints what do you do? Bust up drug sellers?"

"Mostly," he said. "Sometimes bigger dens and such. And as for plan—" He sighed. "I usually don't have much of one. And that doesn't always work out well."

Mila chuckled. "But what would you do?"

"Something like this?" He shrugged. "I mean, you got one or two dozen gang boys in there, right? So, we're outnumbered, we can't just thump them outright. We need showmanship."

"This is the circus boy talking, right?"

"Damn right," he said. "Like at the warehouse tonight, I hung back in the dark and quietly took out guys one at a time when no one was looking. When they realized guys were going missing, I hit them with a bit of voice echo, and everyone panicked. Your friend Asti just plain ran."

"Fear is the weapon," she said. It made sense: people in a panic were easier to fight. "That's why the whole disguise and the magic face and the bit where you disappear."

"Shroud," he said. "I like the word 'shroud.'"

"And can you shroud me?"

He shook his head. "It's . . . it's tied to the cloak."

"The cloak is magical, like the rope?"

"How did you—"

"That's not a normal rope. Texture is different, the metallic strands through the fibers . . ."

"You're really clever," he said appreciatively. "The cloak and the rope, they aren't magical exactly. In your hands, they'd just be normal things. But they can . . . how did Delmin put it?"

"Delmin?"

He muttered a curse. "Friend of mine. Real book smart. Anyway, they're receptive to and amplify magic. I could control your rope the same way I do mine, but it would be a lot harder, take more out of me. With this one, it's like an extension of my arm."

"It's the metallic part, right?" Mila asked. That was the aspect that stood out, it made sense. "Some metal that is magically attuned?"

"On the nose," he said. "I think you're going to do fine at Uni."

"And what are we going to do here?" she asked.

He scratched at his chin. "So the goal isn't to stop them so much as to be noticed. We want them to get away and spread the word that the Thorn is in Seleth—"

"North Seleth," she corrected.

"North Seleth," he accepted. "And so, we're back to showmanship. I'll go through those doors hot, and you follow up behind. Let me go big, and you keep them off my back."

"All right," Mila said. "There's one in particular I want a word with, so I'll make a point of pulling him down." Conor needed to answer for what he did to Nikey.

"That's a plan," he said. He took out his bow and nocked two arrows at once. "Nice and easy."

He walked across the road—just walked, calm and confident—while the air was filled with sound, a wind from the depths of the blazes, that grew into a horrifying howl. That howl then crashed down into the street, and the front door of the workhouse blew apart into a thousand splinters. The Thorn's cloak shimmered—not shrouding him this time, but surrounding him in storm and fire—and he dashed into the open doorway.

Mila was right behind, knives drawn. The Scratch Cats—however many of them there were—were in a scramble of confusion. Two of them were already on the ground, arrows sticking out of them. Others were grabbing weapons, diving under tables, or just shouting like madmen. The Thorn loosed three more arrows, putting down a few more Cats in the process.

"Which of you is selling?" he roared, his voice echoing like thunder. Mila was terrified herself, even though she knew it was just performance. Definitely some of the Cats were, because they went right for the door. "Who is putting that poison on the streets?"

"I'll poison you!" one Scratch Cat yelled, charging at the Thorn with a cudgel. The Thorn, hands like a rabbit, swapped his bow for his staff, and blocked the cudgel.

"See, that doesn't make any sense," the Thorn said, his tone lighter despite the magical thunder effect. He rolled out of the way of the next swing of the cudgel, and then cracked his staff against the Cat's knee, sending him down. "I mean, is that cudgel poisoned or something?"

"One of you get him!" a Cat yelled. Mila had seen him around before. Probably in charge. And Mila jumped at him, driving one knife low into his belly.

"You think you're going to get the Thorn?" she

asked. She pulled her knife out savagely and let him drop. She wanted him to hurt, to bleed, and die in a day or two. After he had told someone else about what happened today. Conor ran up, his face full of horror.

"Who the blazes are you?" Conor asked. The disguise was working.

"I'm the Thorn's bloody Rose," she said, holding up the knife as evidence. Pointing it at him, she said, "I hear you like to beat up little boys."

"Kids!" the Thorn shouted as he spun his staff about, cracking Cat after Cat across the head. "You go after kids!"

Conor drew out a knucklestuffer, but his hands were trembling. "This is our crash, you can't just—"

Mila swiped with both knives, slicing his arm. She didn't want to kill him, but she wanted him to pay. She wanted him to suffer, like he had made Nikey suffer. "Can't just what?" she snarled. "Smash in here and crack you boys up?" Another swipe forced him to drop the knucklestuffer. She moved in close and put a knife on his throat. "Isn't that what you do, boy?"

The Thorn's rope came whipping out, wrapping around Conor, and tore him away. The Thorn swung Conor about like a ragdoll, and used him to bowl over the Scratch Cats still standing. Most of them were on the ground now, moaning and crying. The Thorn threw Conor high in the air, sending him to the ceiling. As soon as Conor hit—with a very satisfying thump—the Thorn snapped his fingers with a magical flash. Conor was suddenly covered in goo, sticking him to the ceiling.

"Now," the Thorn said, pacing about the room. "Back to my point. Do you boys know who's selling the *effitte* in this neighborhood? Is it you?"

"No, we don't," one of the ones on the ground grunted. "We don't get a piece of that."

The Thorn went over to another one—one who was trying to get back up—and pressed the staff into his back. "So you know there is something to get a piece of. That's good."

"We don't deal with any of that," the one he was pressing said.

"But you report to people who do, don't you?"

"Sweet saints, get me down!" Conor shouted. "I just want to be on the ground!"

"He wants to be on the ground," Mila said.

"I should oblige," the Thorn said. He snapped his fingers, and the sticky gunk on Conor vanished. He fell—screaming the whole way—and stopped just before he hit the ground, hovering above the floor and surrounded in blue light. Mila went over to him—kicking another Cat in the head as she passed to discourage him from getting up—and crouched down.

"Now, repeat after me. I will never—"

"I will never!" Conor shouted.

"Beat up little boys."

"Beat up little boys!"

Mila grabbed him by the chin and whispered, "Especially ones who had been your brothers, traitor."

"I'm sorry, I'm sorry, I'm sorry," Conor cried.

Mila gave a nod to the Thorn, and the blue light vanished. Conor fell in a heap on the ground.

"Now, we'll let you get back to your evening," the Thorn said. "But tell your masters that the Thorn is here, and he does not want *effitte* in this neighborhood. Am I clear?"

"Yeah!" said the one whose back the Thorn was pressing. "We get it!"

"Good," the Thorn said, walking away to the door. Mila stayed close with him, knives still at the ready in case someone made a move.

They got out into the street, and the Thorn's shimmering aura faded, but the rope coiled around Mila, pulling her close to him. Wrapping one arm around her, he jumped high. Mila squealed, this time with excitement as they soared over the shops and landed on a roof a block over.

"Well, that was thrilling," the Thorn said as he let her back on her feet. While she was getting her footing, he looked in his belt pouches and frowned. "Already out." He muttered.

"Out?" she asked.

"I've got nothing left to eat, and I'm famished. You hungry? Where can you get a bite at this hour in this neighborhood?"

Mila had never been inside Jonet's Clay Bowl before—she hadn't ever really noticed it was there before—nor had she ever eaten Fuergan food, but it was open despite the late hour. She was also fairly certain she and Veranix were the only ones in there who weren't Fuergan. The two of them were looking normal now—he had removed the Rose mask from her eyes, and changed her red dress to blue, and had switched his appearance to his University uniform—but she felt that they were being stared at.

"There you go, children," Mister Jonet—or at least one of the Mister Jonets, as there seemed to be a few—said as he put two bowls in front of them. "Best *sradtikash* in the city."

"Thank you," Veranix said. It was funny, Mila couldn't think of him as 'the Thorn' right now, looking as normal as he did. Well, as normal as this disarmingly pretty boy could.

"You're forgetting the *afedhlan*," one of the other Misters Jonet said, coming out with a steaming teapot. "If you're going to eat this, it must be right."

"And the *hladac*," a Missus Jonet shouted from the kitchen. Mila didn't know much about Fuergans, but all nine of them in the place seemed to be in the Jonet family and in the fifteen minutes they had been in there, she had seen every single one of them kiss every other one of them in ways that made her blush. She was wondering if they had interrupted something by coming in here, but the Jonets all insisted that no, they must sit down, they must eat, of course they would.

"The *hladac,* I would not forget the *hladac*," the first

Mister Jonet said, going back to the kitchen while his co-husband poured two mugs of steaming, rich-smelling tea. The first came back with a plate of delicate, flaky flatbreads stacked high, and then poured spiced oil over the tower.

"Now, please, enjoy," he said. All the Fuergans retreated from Mila and Veranix's table to the one the whole Jonet family was at, where they laughed and ate and kissed in abandon.

"Quite the place," Veranix said, glancing back at them before turning back to his bowl. He smiled again as he stabbed his fork into the earthy-smelling dish, and Mila felt her heart hammer so fast she thought she might faint. Veranix blew on the steaming forkful, and then put it in his mouth. "Oh, by Saint Senea, that's good. And that's not just, you know, magical ravening talking." He took another bite.

"Really?" Mila asked, taking her own fork and gingerly probing the bowl. She wasn't sure what to make of it, but she had gone hungry so many times in the past years, she knew she could eat absolutely anything that was in front of her. She took a bite, which was an explosion of creamy, rich flavors that mingled with meat so tender it melted in her mouth, plus some other substance she had never experienced before but was utterly delicious.

"Sir," Veranix called back to the Fuergans, "You undersold this."

"Best in the city!" a Jonet shouted.

"Indeed," Veranix called back, taking a flatbread and biting into it.

"Magical ravening?" Mila asked.

"That's what we call it," he said. "Doing magic, it's like doing any other work. It wears you out, and it leaves you hungry. Most mages are very skinny."

"Most people I know are very skinny," she said. "But they aren't mages." But that was something she had noticed in the three at the Firewing house. "What do you know about the Firewings?"

He took another bite. "That's a Mage Circle, right?"

"They've started a house here in this neighborhood."

He shook his head. "There are few big circles—Lord Preston's, Red Wolf, Crescent Lights. And then there are, like, dozens and dozens of small ones. And they're, well, sort of like legal firms. Work together, jobs for hire. Some shadier than others."

"They're connected to this whole thing with the drugs and Fenmere and all."

He furrowed his brow in thought. "I wonder if that's what brought him out to this neighborhood." He took a few more bites, then went on. "So, a few months back, when I first really tangled with Fenmere, he was wrapped up with the Blue Hand Circle. Real nasty bunch, that Circle. They were who this rope was for, before I stole it."

"So you are a thief," she said.

"Guilty," he said. "Have some of the *hladac* before I eat it all."

"So what happened to the Blue Hand?" she asked.

"I busted them up," he said. "But Fenmere was in league with mages for a reason. Without the Blue Hand—"

"He goes to the Firewings."

Veranix frowned. "I'm of half a mind to go check on that place right now."

"But?" Mila asked.

He sighed and took another bite. "Between the scuffles at the warehouse, with your crew, and this, I'm pretty spent. And I've done some stupid things over the past few months, but 'take on an entire Circle chapterhouse while exhausted' would be a new level of stupid."

"Fair," she said.

"If you don't mind me asking," he said as he started to scrape the sauce on the edge of his bowl with his fork, "what got you to the University?"

"You're going to laugh."

"Maybe."

"We captured a mage who was part of this whole thing, and some folks from Intelligence wanted him, so . . ." She shrugged. "We got a deal to give us all clean, straight lives. A shop for Asti and Verci, another for Helene and Jules. Almer got his license back, and me . . . they got me into the University."

Veranix laughed. "What, they couldn't pull RCM?"

"Apparently that was not an option," she said. "Asti actually pushed for that."

"I'm serious about, you know, showing you around, whatever," Veranix said.

"I know you are," she said. "And we agree, we don't talk about our more colorful pasts."

"As far as I'm concerned, your past is whatever you say it is," he said. "But you should probably get your story locked down now."

"Do I look like an amateur?" she asked. She put on her Jendly Marskin voice. "I will have you know, several people in the various records offices in the city believe I'm a hard-working law clerk. I can maintain a pretense quite excellently."

He laughed full-throatedly. "Oh, that's excellent. Would you keep that up the whole time, though?"

"I'm not sure yet," she said, using her own voice. She had been trying to decide how much persona she would bring to her studies. "But no matter what voice I use, I'll be Mila Kendish. Though the details of who I am and how I got into school, I'll keep quiet."

One of the Jonets came over. "Everything was eaten, so it surely satisfied?"

"Quite," Veranix said. He dug a few coins out of his pocket. "Greatly appreciated."

"This is too much, sir," Jonet said, giving a coin back.

"It definitely is not," Veranix said. "We're grateful for your hospitality."

"It is what we give," Jonet said. "Please visit us again."

Mila got up from the table as Veranix thanked the family again, and they went outside.

"So now you—" she started to say.

"Should get back to campus," he said. "Like I said, exhausted. That meal should give me enough strength to get home. And if I'm not there soon, I have people who will come out here and start cracking skulls to find me."

"So you have a crew, too."

"I do," he said. "A small one, but good people."

"Is this it, then? Won't see you again?"

"Oh, no," he said. "I'm serious about looking into the Firewings, and there still is *efhân* out here, so I'll be back."

"Good," she said. "I . . ." Her mouth went dry, and her palms were suddenly sweating like crazy. "I liked teaming up with you."

He smiled again—that smile was fatal—and said, "I liked that, too. Never really had a partner before." He took a step closer to her, and her heart jumped into her throat. "Do you need me to walk you anywhere?"

"Oh, no," she said, then wondered why she said it so quickly. "I'm just over at Kimber's a block or so from here, and I mean, I can handle myself on these streets."

He stepped back. "All right," he said, his smile dropping just a little. "Then I really should get back. I'll probably see you tomorrow, Miss Kendish."

"Tomorrow," she said, even though everything in her head was screaming to say something witty, clever, or alluring. But no words came to mind.

He winked as his University uniform melted back into the Thorn outfit, the hood and shadow covering his eyes. Was that really there all this time? Was that perfect, beautiful face actually an illusion of some sort? With a last wave, he bounded up to the top of the restaurant, and then bounded off to the east, out of sight.

Mila turned and started her way to Kimber's. She was exhausted, but at the same time, she had no idea how she would get to sleep tonight.

Chapter 14

ASTI WOKE IN THE BACK room of Kimber's, in the bed that he was pretty sure was hers, even though he slept alone. At least, he went to sleep alone, and woke up alone. If Kimber had slept next to him, he didn't notice.

But he had slept peacefully through the night, which almost never happened. Maybe Kimber watched over him, and that was what he needed.

That and knowing they had kept a good chunk of *effitte* or *efhân* or whatever it was off the streets of North Seleth, and that meant lives were saved. That meant neighbors and friends were saved. And if more of the drug came, he would do something about it.

His thoughts drifted to the Thorn, with the hidden identity and noble cause. There was something romantic about that. Asti respected it. Maybe the Thorn had the right idea of how to handle things. Asti could deal with Lesk and his lieutenants, the Scratch Cats and the other gangs, Josie and her betrayal, the Firewings, the Andrendon Project—all of it—with the safety of anonymity. Verci and Raych and Corsi could be safe.

Of course, he knew that wouldn't work. He was a

man of singular short stature, with an unmistakable fighting style. Josie was no fool, she would know it was him.

Asti found his boots and jacket and got them on, checking them for the hidden knives. Still all in place. Belt on, with his two primary knives—the ones that had been Dad's—in plain sight. He knew Kimber wouldn't like that, but instinct told him that today he should be armed, and obviously so. Just in case someone got ideas. Too much went wrong yesterday, best be prepared for the worst.

He came out of the back to the taproom, where Kimber was serving breakfast to a few patrons. He didn't even get three steps in when she waved him to sit at the bar. She came over and presented him with tea, thick slices of bread, and a jar of apple preserves.

"Did I do something to deserve this?" he asked.

"Every day, your life is blessed by the saints," she said. "And they bless me as well."

"If you say," he said.

"I was going to service at ten bells, if you want to come." She smiled shyly. "I have a feeling you're looking for some guidance."

"You're not wrong," he said. "But I should check on Verci and the shop. Is it eight bells right now?"

"About," she said. "Mila got here late last night, by the way." She leaned in and lowered her voice. "I have it on good authority she spent some time in the company of a handsome young University boy last night."

"Who'd you hear that from?"

"Jonet ab Casmora," she said. The youngest wife in that Fuergan nontuple marriage. So Mila had made a public appearance, was seen doing normal things for a girl her age.

"Who's the boy?"

"I don't know, but Cass said he was quite fetching. So I guess Mila is already looking toward campus life."

"Good for her," Asti said, taking a few bites of his bread.

She had left with the Thorn. Was the Thorn the fetching University student? That might make sense—he was a mage, and from what Asti saw, a strong one, if a bit raw with his magic. Him still being a student made a certain amount of sense.

"I agree, though I do wonder a little about the character of a Uni boy who would come out here at such a late hour. Don't they have curfews on campus? I don't even know. She'll have to adjust to that, I suppose."

"Well, don't let her slack on her reading or her math," Asti said. "She's still got a bit to do before heading out."

"I know. I'll make sure she's awake before I go to service. And are you coming?"

Asti sighed a little. She really was set on saving his soul. "I will try. I can't promise there won't be a catastrophe I need to handle."

She scowled a little. "It seems there's always a catastrophe with you, doesn't it?"

"It does," he said. "I really wish that wasn't the case." He finished his breakfast quickly. "But all the more reason to go check on the shop, so I can get back here by ten bells, if possible."

"I'll always save a seat for you, even if you're late," she said.

"I appreciate that," he said, getting to his feet. "You know I—I appreciate everything you do, don't you?"

"I do," she said, reaching across the bar to take his hand. "And I feel the same way about what you do. Everything."

Her eyes were filled with such compassion, such honesty, Asti found it hard to believe that she had actually seen him in his red-faced murderous madness. It had been in the service of saving her and the pub from Lesk and his people, but still, it must have been terrifying for her. Despite that, here she was, looking at him with kindness, which he did not deserve.

"I . . . I should get going. I'll see you soon." He went out the door before she could say anything else.

Lesk, Sender, Poller, Ia, and five gang boys were all standing in the street.

"Rynax," Lesk said with an ugly grin. "The Old Lady wants a word. Can you come?"

"Easily," Poller said.

Asti looked at Sender, who was sporting a heavy bruise across his head. But he wasn't looking at Asti with any sense of specific malice or anger.

"Something wrong, Nange?" Asti said. "You could have sent a message. This all seems . . . excessive."

"We know there's no such thing as excessive when dealing with you. So, do you come, or do we have to make you?"

Asti would be quite entertained by Lesk trying to make him. But Asti didn't want to do that on Kimber's front stoop, and fighting all of them would definitely shatter any truce they still had with Josie. Probably the best play was to go talk to Josie and see how it all played out.

"Let's go have a nice chat," he said. "But I was planning on going to church in a little bit, so you all better respect that."

Helene swept the walkway in front of the shop, which was already as clean as it was going to be, but she had to put her energy somewhere. It had been an average day at the cheese shop. People came, bought cheese and cured meats, and Julien was thrilled to serve them. He chatted with each person about cheese, he let them try different things, and each customer walked away happy.

Helene had noticed four boys—Potato Boys, she was pretty sure—hanging around the corner across the way. Their eyes on the shop. Once she was certain they were casing her or the shop, she slipped upstairs, got the hiphangers and The Action, and put them all in place behind the money counter. She should keep a loaded hiphanger there all the time.

A fifth one came over. This one, she didn't know, but she had seen him about. Something about his bearing made Helene think he was being groomed for a street boss position in Lesk's organization. The Potato Boys, they were part of Lesk—part of Josie—she was sure of that. He talked with the other four for a bit, and then they all started to look like they were expecting something. Or expecting to do something.

Helene tightened her grip on the broom, and moved inside the shop. "Julie, be sharp."

"I got all the prices right," he said. "I did."

"No, sharp," she said, tilting her head in the direction of The Potato Boys. She glanced back, and they all were ambling across the street to the shop.

"Right," he said. He slowly came out from behind the counter as the boys came up to the door.

"Hey, hey, this the cheese?" The Potato Boss asked as they entered. "You the cheese lady?"

"This is a cheese shop," she said. "You boys looking to buy?"

"Don't know, don't know. Maybe. Definitely here for something."

"It's cheese and meats," she said. "That's all there is here."

"Not all there is," he said. "I mean, you're the cheese lady, right? So, there's you."

"Not for sale," she said. "You want some cheese, let me know. Else move on."

"Yeah, but," the guy said, looking back at his fellows, who were all chuckling like he had said something funny. "We're here for you, see. You should come with us."

"Not going to happen," she said. Saints, if that's what they were here for, that meant Lesk thought they had pulled something last night. Rutting blazes.

"Yeah, but there'll be trouble if you don't," he said. He walked over to the counter, and ran his fingers over the ledger where Julie wrote down his sales. "I mean, there might be accidents."

He pushed the ledger onto the floor.

"Is that the game?" she asked.

"It might be," he said.

Julien moved in, quickly now, getting right up to the boss and towering over him. "Pick that. Up. Off the floor." His voice was quiet, like he couldn't hold in his anger and speak normally at the same time.

"Hey, fella," the boss said. "That's no way to speak to a customer."

"You're not a customer," Julien said. "No cheese for you!"

"Listen," the guy said, putting a hand on Julien's arm.

Julien swept his arm out, hurling the guy against the wall. "Get out!"

The guy got on his feet, knife out. "That was a mistake."

"He asked you to leave the shop."

Lieutenant Covrane strolled through the open door, his uniform pressed and crisp, hand casually on his crossbow. Helene's heart skipped despite herself at the sight of him. "So perhaps you boys should move along."

The Potato Boss pointed his knife at Julien and Helene. "That was a mistake." He gave a whistle, and he and his boys scurried off.

"Trouble?" Covrane asked once they were gone.

"Nothing we couldn't handle," Helene said. She came close to him and kissed him. "But I'd rather not have to handle it. What are you doing here during the day?"

"There was some big action last night, near the river."

"Action?" she asked. "What kind?"

"I think a shady deal gone bad, but there's a lot of rumors flying. Some of our boys got hurt, and the folks involved mostly got away. Ugly business."

"Sorry to hear that," she said. "So you're just doing some extra patrol to make the peace?"

"There's something in the air. Like those boys right now. People are on edge."

"That's every day here, my friend." She started sweeping again, just to keep her hands busy. "Hey, I was thinking of calling on you for a change. How would I do that?"

"Leave word at the waystation," he said, pointing off to the south. "I keep a desk there."

"Do you sleep there?" she asked. "I mean, Jarret—" She let it hang for a while. "With everything we're doing, I would think I should know where you live."

"Oh," he said with a smile. "It's not much."

She glanced up to the apartments over the shop. "I am familiar with not much."

"I know," he said. He looked at the ground, a blush coming to his ears. "It's a little house in Keller. Off Colman. 182 Gladstone Way. But—"

There was a but. She knew it. She let her head drop and started to turn away.

"I take care of my mama there," he said, his hand gently touching her arm. "And my gran."

The smile came to her face despite herself. "Oh, saints, man, I know what that's about. Jules and I lived with our gran until she passed in the fire. And, I mean, we take care of each other."

"You'd want to meet the family, then?" he asked. "I wasn't sure if that was . . . you know, where we were at."

She swallowed hard. That wasn't where she was with him. She really didn't know where she was, or what she wanted it to be. She mostly just wanted to be sure there wasn't a Missus Covrane that she was doing wrong. But she had walked into it now. "Of course."

"I'd say tonight, but I want to do a double patrol around tonight. Like I said, there are some crazy rumors about. And—"

"You got a job to do," she said. "I understand that. And you want to give your mama more notice than that."

"Right," he said. "Next week?"

Next week, hopefully, all this action would blow over, and they'd be fully back to normal and boring.

Or, Lesk and his boys would kill her, and she wouldn't have to go to meet his mama and gran.

"Next week," she said, kissing him on the cheek.

"All right," he said. "I'm going to do a walk around by Elk, and then back to the waystation. I'll see you later."

"Later it is," she said. He strolled away.

"Are we in trouble?" Julien asked as she came back into the shop.

"We probably are," she said. "But what else is new?"

Raych had woken before the dawn, left some bread and preserves out for Verci, scooped up Corsi, and went to the bakery, leaving Verci to keep sleeping. He was clearly exhausted, as one would be after a night like he had. He had nearly been killed, and if she didn't love him as much as she did, she would have finished the job.

But she had a real job, and bread is a morning business. She had left dough rising, more dough proofing, the ovens needed to be lit and stoked. Plenty to do, and she set Corsi in his crib and got to work.

Having her hands in the dough, working and kneading it, helped her cool her head. The work was repetitive, soothing. She had been at it for some time when Lian came in.

"Good morning," Lian said as she came in the back door. "Where are we at so far?"

"I have the morning's loaves in the oven, they are just about ready to come out, and I've been kneading dough for tomorrow's. Pastry dough is cooling in the icebox, and that needs to be prepped."

"What pastries are we making?"

"I was thinking peach and apple crendolins?" Raych said. "We've got those preserves and we should use them now."

"What about something savory?" Lian asked. "I was thinking of—"

"Hal was thinking."

"Hal mentioned to me his thoughts of a cheese and summer sausage pastry roll."

That did sound good. "We'd need cheese and summer sausage for that."

"Can you get the Kessers to give you a discount on those?"

"Julien will trade some for bread," she said. "I don't know if he's making sandwiches for himself or selling them at the shop, but he does always want more bread."

"Do you want me to go?"

Raych wiped the flour off her hands. "No, I'll go." She could ask Julien about what actually happened last night, see what Verci hadn't told her. Julien would tell her, when pressed. He was always so uncomfortable with lying. She grabbed five loaves and bagged them. "Keep an eye on things, and I'll be back shortly."

"You better be," Lian said, going over to the oven. "We need to open the doors in an hour."

"I know that," Raych said, kissing Corsi on the forehead as he cooed in his playpen. "Get those pastries rolled out so we can add the filling right away."

"Yes, ma'am," Lian said, making a pretend salute. "I thought I was the bossy one."

"Then tell yourself to do it," Raych said. "Be right back."

She went out the back and came down the alley to Frost, where four rough-looking gentlemen were waiting.

"Look at that, she's got bread."

"I didn't even have breakfast."

"That's helpful," one said. "And the boss would like some bread."

"Gentlemen," she said tersely as she tried to get past them. "I'm on a delivery, if you please. If you want to make a purchase, the store opens in an hour."

"Oh, we're not here for bread," one of them said, grabbing a loaf out of her hands. "That's just a bonus."

The other three grabbed her arms and covered her mouth before she could scream.

"This isn't personal, Missus Rynax," the one holding the bread said. “We’re just looking for a word with the brothers, and we want them to behave themselves.”

She thrashed to get out of their grip, but they were holding her too tight, too close, as they dragged her over to a crate at the mouth of the alley. They threw her in and closed it up, and in moments, she was loaded into the back of a wagon. Now she screamed and screamed until her throat was raw, but the wagon rolled along without interruption.

Chapter 15

MILA HAD SLEPT WELL INTO the morning, which was probably because it had taken so long to fall asleep. She had been far too excited to even lie down. Accepting that, she had stayed awake deep into the small hours, burning lamp oil and reading *Beru the Crow* until she couldn't keep her eyes open any longer. She hadn't even remembered falling asleep, which explained why she woke with her neck in a terrible position and the book on her chest.

She got dressed and first went to Nikey's room, knocking before she went in. Nikey was awake but still in bed, his face now a mess of yellowed bruises.

"Didn't think I'd see you again," he said.

"Well, I'm around for a few more days," she said.

"Right, I heard you were easting out. And apparently you're going by 'Mila' now."

"I'm not—I always was Mila."

"So 'Miss Bessie' was the lie?" He shrugged. "I guess that's why you dropped it."

"It wasn't a lie," she said. "Just another name."

"I only had one name," he said. "Just Nikey, nothing else."

"Never had a family name?"

"Never had a family, except the boys. Now they're all gone."

"Tarvis isn't gone. He saved you, you know."

That seemed to give him pause. "I really thought it was Jede. That his spirit had come back for me."

She wanted to tell him about Conor, that she had put him in check, but she couldn't. Not without blowing her cover, putting everyone at risk. "Look, I know I didn't do you right, but I'm here now. Too late, I know, but still—"

"Too late," he said.

"Listen. This room is for you. And I'll make sure Kimber looks out for you."

"I don't need no mother," he said. "Been fine without one so far."

"Really, Nikey?"

"You're the one easting out. You don't need to worry about what happens here."

"I want to make—" She shook her head. "Never mind. You want a roof and a bed, Kimber will have you. She'll work you, but she'll have you. You want to end up like Conor, or worse, like Jede, that's your business. I've got enough to worry about."

She left, slamming the door as she went. She didn't want to hear any more from him. She went down to the taproom.

"You're alive," Kimber said dryly. "I was wondering if you'd sleep all day."

"Thought about it," Mila said.

"Where are your books?" Kimber asked. She waved to Mila to follow her to the kitchen.

"I left them in my room. I was up late reading, you know."

"Reading."

"Reading!" Mila felt her ears heat up. "What else would I be doing?"

"I don't know, what else *would* you be doing?" Kimber asked, her eyebrow raised. She put a teapot on the stove. "I mean, I hear things."

"What things do you hear?"

"Something about a University boy at Jonet's Clay Bowl."

Well, that gave her an alibi, at least. "He's—he could be a friend."

"Just a friend?" Kimber's grin was wicked. She got to work slicing bread and cheese.

"Just . . . I . . ." Mila's mouth was going dry. "I don't know, maybe? He's starting his fourth year at U of M and he's a magic student and . . . I don't know a lot more."

"But is he nice?" Kimber asked.

"I suppose," Mila said. "Do we have to talk about this?"

"No," Kimber said. She reached into her apron and pulled out an envelope. "But this came for you this morning."

The envelope was marked with a stamp of the University. Mila opened it up immediately. "You could have started with that."

"Is it from him?" Kimber asked. She seemed very excited at the prospect.

Mila scanned it quickly: hand-written, signed with a "V" at the end. "Yes."

"What did he say?" Kimber asked.

"Can it be private, Kimber?" Mila asked.

Kimber's smile waned. "Yes, sorry. I just . . . I'm just excited for you, everything that you're doing. I'm really proud. And I know Asti is as well."

Mila felt an ugly remark coming to her tongue, along the lines of "You aren't my parents." She held it in. There was no need to upset or insult Kimber, who had been nothing but kind to her. "Thank you," she said instead.

Kimber put bread and jam on the back kitchen table. "Now, after your breakfast, I think you should do a bit more numbers work. But just a bit. Your evening should be free, in case someone calls on you."

"Kimber!"

"It's possible!" Kimber said. "All right, I'm going to go to Saint Bridget's. If you see Asti, tell him I expect him."

"At church?"

"He needs some church," Kimber said as she went to the door. "Behave yourself."

"Sure," Mila said. The teapot came to a boil, and she poured herself a cup, sat down with her bread and jam, and got to reading Veranix's note.

I'll be back tonight. I've learned a couple things about Andrendon and your friends in the house. Maybe it'll help you, I don't know. Hope you're well. See you soon. Best, V.

Even though it wasn't a very long note, or very personal, the whole thing made her heart flutter. Perhaps because it was the first actual letter from a person she had ever received. She had received a couple formal missives from the University, telling her when to arrive, where she would live, what courses she would take—but this was written to her with personal intent.

It was a silly thing, but she decided to let herself feel silly about it.

She read it eleven times while eating her breakfast, and wondered if she should write a note back. Or maybe go out there. She did need to go out to campus eventually, maybe she should walk out there and look around. Maybe she could find Veranix, where he lived in the southern dorms—that was what he said, right—and then they could come back to North Seleth together.

She wondered if, when she was at University, taking her classes, she would still be doing anything shady on the side. She could still go be Jendly Marskin, finding out what she could about Andrendon, sending reports to Asti.

Or she could be the Rose, hitting the streets with

Veranix as the Thorn. Would that work? Would he want that? Would he really want to have anything to do with her once she got there? Was he just being polite to her out here?

Did he already have a paramour? Or a partner as the Thorn? He said he had people who would come looking for him. Who were they? What did they mean to Veranix? What did he mean to them? Would they like Mila?

Too many questions.

She went and got Kimber's cash books. Do the numbers. Let that be her focus. Deal with the rest later.

Verci woke well after the sun rose, Raych and Corsi already gone to the bakery. That was to be expected, but he was surprised how heavily he'd slept. Not that he didn't need it. He took a few minutes to check his injuries—both of them still hurt like blazes, his foot oozing blood despite the stitches. He changed out the bandages and tested his weight on it. He flinched as he put his foot down. That wouldn't do.

He went to a trunk and dug out the leg brace from when he broke his foot. The same foot. Why was he the one always getting injured?

That wasn't entirely true. But it seemed like his body took punishments to match the ones Asti's mind had.

That wasn't fair. If his body matched Asti's mind, he'd be confined to the rollerchair.

He put the brace on. It was designed to keep the weight off his foot, let him take it on his calf and knee. Less than ideal, but it worked well enough to get around and not put pressure on an open wound. Good enough to work in the shop today.

The shoulder was mostly stiff. He couldn't get it all the way up. That he'd just have to stretch and let heal.

He had the breakfast Raych had laid out for him, with a little scrawled note with a charcoal pencil saying. "Honest work! Love, Raych." He took the plans that

Carrigan had left behind and looked over them. Unfortunately, so much about the plans were meaningless to him. He understood the designs, in terms of the gear work and the moving parts, but all the numbers were just so much junk. Plus, he couldn't look at a set of plans and figure out what was wrong. He'd have to build.

He finished eating and went down to the shop. Today was supposed to be a building day—the front of the shop was ready except for merchandise to display, save a little sweeping and tidying. But he was not in a sweep and tidy mood. Asti could do that when he arrived. Asti was good at that.

So he settled into making a replica of the device on the plans. At worst, it would be a small waste of his time and he'd have an odd toy to sell.

Near as he could figure, the device was a central engine—gears and springs and steam pistons, it seemed—that pulled a series of wound cables, and then released them again. Each cable pulled a covered wagon of sorts, though it looked like it was designed to run on a track, like a mine cart. That made a certain amount of sense, but it was clear the main machine had an imbalance of power. Even at the small scale he was working, the cable kept snapping, or the wagon carts would crash into the machine hub. And he wondered if they expected manpower to operate every element, and where those controls ought to be. That seemed to be the major problem with the plans, he felt; no place for a person to work it. They designed the machine to a specific purpose, but forgot to include how to use it.

Maybe that's why these mechanical firm folks couldn't make it work—all education, no real application. So that's what Verci needed to bring to the project.

Ten bells rang in the distance. Had he been at it that long already? And Asti hadn't shown up yet?

Verci sighed. Asti was probably making more trouble for them somewhere. He wished that wasn't the case, but he knew his brother well enough to know better.

Asti was disappointed that Lesk didn't have a carriage. They all just walked down to Elk Road, surrounding him like a protection detail. It looked absurdly conspicuous. If they rode in a carriage, they would draw less attention.

Then again, maybe attention was the point. Maybe they wanted the neighborhood to see them marching Asti Rynax across town, so everyone would know what was going on. So Asti needed to play his part—helpful, cooperative, and utterly at a loss as to why they were taking him to Josie.

"Take his knives," Lesk said when they reached the Elk Road Shack, and Sender reached to take the knives from Asti's belt. Those had been Dad's knives.

"You touch those knives, you forfeit your fingers," Asti said. "I'm here politely, Nange. Don't test me."

Sender stopped, hand still outstretched. "Boss?"

Lesk looked at Asti, as if sizing him up for the first time. As if Asti hadn't already thrashed him soundly once. "Sure, Asti. If it makes you feel better, hold on to them." He put a hand on Asti's shoulder. "We're all just being friendly, right?"

"Right," Asti said, brushing the hand away. "Let's just do this."

They led him inside, and right away, Asti could tell that everyone there was a bruiser under Lesk. Most of them, he knew on sight from his research over the past months. He knew which gangs or crews they were in, who they worked under, what they did.

And near the back wall, next to a door to one of the storerooms, sat the Old Lady herself, Josefine Holt. She looked downright regal, clearly playing up the part of the Crime Queen of Seleth, with a stole around her neck and a wide-brimmed hat, and holding her walking cane—which was now embellished with silver trim and sapphires—in both hands with a tight grip.

"Asti," she said calmly. "It's good to see you."

"Josie," he said. "I have to admit, I'm shocked to see you in a room with a door that leads directly to the street."

"I've got nothing to fear in here," she said. "Do I, Nange?"

"No, ma'am. Especially not from Rynax here."

"Is he right about that, Asti?"

Asti sat across from her. "That depends on why you sent your lackeys to fetch me. I thought we had an understanding."

"I thought we did as well, Asti. I really thought you were going to be smart."

"I am very smart," Asti said. He needed to take control of the conversation right away, flip it on her to put her on the defensive. "Which is why I came here calmly. You have something to say to me, I'm willing to hear it."

"Willing?"

"I mean, I don't know if I can accept an apology, but I think it would be a good start."

She laughed, but the knuckles on her hands went white squeezing the head of her cane. "An apology?"

"I am definitely owed one," he said. He looked over to Lesk. "I mean, you and your folks all know what she did, don't you?"

"Asti—" she said sharply.

"I mean, I'm glad you're all so loyal that she feels comfortable sitting here with you all, but—"

"Asti!" she snapped.

"You betrayed me, Josie," he said. He made a point of keeping his expression controlled, his tone measured. "You betrayed me and all our crew, robbed us of what was ours. I don't think I can forgive that, but I am willing to hear your apology."

"You got paid," Lesk said.

"A token," Asti said. "And it's in the spirit of that token that you are still breathing right now." He said that to Lesk, and then looked back to Josie. "So in the spirit of our understanding, Josie, tell me why you've disrupted my day."

"Fine," she said. "We'll play this. Last night, my people had a delivery coming into the neighborhood. Things went wrong all around."

"I'd say I'm sorry to hear that, but I'm really not," Asti said.

"It's really quite incredible, though," she said. "Despite things going wrong—and I'm talking constables showing up, bodies on the ground, deeply skunked—we managed the exchange. We got our merchandise."

"Good," Asti said. "I still fail to see—"

"Because the merchandise was wrong. Someone switched it out for a fake. Somehow, in all the chaos and confusion, someone was able to get the real merchandise and skirt away with it."

"And this concerns me how?"

"How, indeed?" she asked. "Sender, you were there. What do you remember?"

"It's a bit of jumble, ma'am," he said. "I mean, we arrived with the money, and the captain was there with two of his crew. We start the trade, and then things turned left. Somebody attacked us all."

Asti turned to Sender. "Was it me?"

"Well, I—" He shook his head. "I don't think so."

"So why am I here?" Asti asked. "I mean, I'm really quite put out. . . ."

"You're put out?" Josie said, slamming her cane on the ground. "You have any idea what you messed up?"

"What I messed up?" Asti asked. "We've established I wasn't there. Let's be very clear, if I was the one who attacked Sender and your guys, Sender wouldn't be standing here right now."

"You're denying it?" she asked.

"He's denying it," Lesk said.

"I don't even know what I'm denying, but yes," Asti said. "I spent the night working in the new shop with Verci, and then I went to Kimber's to have a few drinks. Ask around, if you like."

"So, that's you and Verci. Where was Helene? Or Julien? Mila?"

"I don't know, I don't keep track of them," Asti said.

"So you say you didn't attack my warehouses. You say you didn't thrash the Scratch Cats."

"What the who?" Asti asked. "I don't even know what we're talking about now."

"You deny it all," Josie continued. "I want to be clear about that."

"Yes, sure," Asti said. "Is that all?"

"No, Asti," she said. "I just wanted to hear you say that first. Now, let's see if this changes your story." She snapped her fingers, and Lesk opened up the door she was sitting next to. Asti looked into the storeroom.

"How is an empty chair supposed to change my story?" he asked. That was all that was in there: a chair, knocked to the ground, some rope, and a broken window.

Josie turned and looked in the room. "Where is she?"

"She was there!" Lesk said, going in. He picked up the rope. "We had her tied up in here. You boys did it, right?"

"Yeah!" one of the thugs said. "The rope is right there!"

"Who?" Asti asked. The beast was growling in the back of his skull, and he was tempted to let it have its way.

Lesk came out with the rope. "Well, it didn't hold!"

Josie snatched it away from him. "This flimsy rope? You idiots! Do you know how strong she is?"

"What are you talking about?" the thug asked.

"Who is she?" Asti asked, now getting on his feet.

"The woman kneads bread every day, you idiots! She's stronger than most of you put together!"

Raych.

They had taken Raych.

He could just let the beast go, let it tear the room apart, but that wasn't what he wanted. He wanted to feel every ounce of this anger and let it fuel him. He wanted to leave every single person in the room dead on the floor and remember every single moment.

Asti picked up the table and smashed it into Lesk. Before anyone else could move, Asti had his knives out and on Josie's throat. She wasn't going to die just yet. He wanted her to feel it. He wanted her to fear it. He wanted her to know why it was happening. But feeling all that and still holding the beast on its leash, that took so much from him he could barely speak.

All he could do was whisper, "Our understanding is at an end."

Chapter 16

RAYCH RAN, NOT CARING ABOUT the scratches and blood, not caring about the bruises on her wrists. She ran as hard as she could, her lungs on fire, not even sure where she was or where she was going.

Where was she? Somewhere south of the bakery. Not far from Hal and Lian's house.

People were staring and pointing. Some were moving closer to her. No one she knew. Maybe more of the same people who grabbed her in the first place. She wanted to hide. She wanted to find a safe room and lock the door and never come out.

No, she shouldn't do that. Stay in the street. Stay seen. Make a commotion if someone grabbed her.

And run.

She ran to Lian's house. That was the closest place she could think of. She ran to the house as hard as she could, crashing through people, knocking over shop tables on the walkway, not caring about anything except moving.

She ran up the stoop to Lian's house, yanking on the door. Locked. Of course it was; Lian was at the bakery, probably worried out of her mind, and Hal was at work. She didn't have a key, that was back at the apartment.

Home. Get home.

No, they would look for her at home.

They would be looking for Verci. If they didn't already have him. Why did they take her? Did they take Lian? Did they take Corsi?

She looked around the street, looking for anything, anyone who could help her.

At the end of the lane: a constable.

She ran for him, even though she could barely breath, and her heart threatened to burst from her chest.

"Constable!" she shouted. "Please, Constable!"

He turned, and when he saw her, he moved quickly to her, catching her as she almost collapsed.

"Ma'am?" he asked. "What's wrong?"

"I was—I was—" She struggled for air. "They—"

"Are you hurt?"

"No, I—"

"Ma'am, you're bleeding," he said, helping her stand. "I think we need to have someone look at you."

"I was—I escaped—"

"Did someone abduct you?" he asked.

She nodded. No more words were coming right now.

"And you got away?" He looked her over. "For how long?"

"Just this morning," she said.

"Let's get you to the waystation," he said. "Have a Yellowshield look you over, get a statement, all right?"

She knew she should be worried about Verci, about Corsi, but in the moment, all she wanted was somewhere safe to sit down. The Loyalty Waystation was perfect.

"Yes," she said. "My . . . my husband—"

"Did he do this?" the officer asked. She was able to focus on his brass badge. A lieutenant. Covrane.

"No, no," she said. "But we need to tell him I'm all right. We need to let him know."

"We'll do that," he said. "Come on, let's get you safe."

Verci heard Saint Bridget's ring out one bell in the distance, and realized that Raych had not yet popped over to see what he was working on. Usually she would do that at around twelve, often with lunch. She had been a bit put out the night before, but that usually manifested in her being more present the next day. Especially when he was injured. She must be very angry to not even come see him.

So she wanted him to come to her. Fair enough, he could do that. He cleaned up his work—having built a small model of the Carrigan machine—and went out the back door. His foot was doing better, now that he wasn't putting direct weight on it anymore. He should change the dressing again, perhaps get an ointment from Almer. Maybe even have Doc Gelson look at it. Gelson had proved time and again that he could be trusted to not ask questions and just take care of things.

Mila was right, though—he should make a kit of bandages and medications to keep handy during runs. He wondered if that was something they could even sell at the shop. It certainly would be a good thing to keep in the carriage from now on.

He came around to the back entrance of the bakery, which was slightly ajar. He heard more than a few sounds of chaos inside: things falling, the occasional invective, and Corsi crying. He pushed the door open, ready for the worst.

The place was a mess—flour everywhere, including a dusting covering Corsi's crib and the boy. There was a distinct burnt smell in the air, and several trays of uncooked pastry askew on the counter. He heard Lian in the front of the shop, her voice on edge, as she was explaining to someone that things weren't quite ready and they would have to be patient.

Verci scooped Corsi out of his crib and dusted him off. Poor little guy, he was miserable.

"Hey, hey, you're all right," he said, even though the

boy was wet and needed changing. Rubbing the little boy's back, he went out in front.

Lian looked an absolute fright, hair a mess, covered in flour, ash on her face, and her hand wrapped in a bandage. Four customers were standing about, all of them looking angrily impatient.

"Hey, hey, what's the situation?" he asked. Where was Raych? "How can I help?"

"Verci!" Lian cried. "Thank Acser you're here!"

"What's going on?" he asked.

"Ain't no bread today!" one of the customers said.

"Yes, I see," Verci said, coming over to them. "And as you can see, things are a bit of a crisis, so I must beg your patience, please. I'll help sort this out as best I can."

Lian was clutching at his arm. "It's terrible. I don't even . . . it's just . . ."

"What is it?" he asked. "Where's Raych?"

"She . . . she . . ." Lian lost what little composure she still had, tears flooding her red eyes. Words poured out of her with the gasping sobs, "She went to run an errand and was supposed to come back and it was time to open the shop so I opened it but I forgot about the loaves in the oven and Corsi was crying—"

"Where is Raych?" he pressed.

"She never came back!" Lian wailed. "It's been hours!"

"She's missing?" Verci asked. That was all he needed to hear. He went to the counter and grabbed a few sheets of paper, signing his name on each. He gave one to each customer, "Thank you for your business, but I'm afraid we have an emergency and have to close for the day. Bring that in when we're open for a courtesy discount."

The customers all looked shocked and dismayed, but took the papers and shuffled out the door. Verci shut it and latched it behind them.

"But what will we—" Lian started.

"You will stay right here with Corsi," he said, handing the baby to her. "Snuff the ovens and take him upstairs."

"But—"

"And stay up there until Raych or I come back. Or my brother. If Hal comes to get you before any of that—"

"Stay here with him?"

"No, go home with him, take Corsi, and latch every door you have. If you don't hear anything from us, don't come back tomorrow." He went behind the counter and pulled out a crossbow. "You know how to use this?"

"No!"

There was no time to teach her. "Well, if anyone comes—anyone you don't know—point it at them and pretend you do."

"You're scaring me, Verci!"

"Good," he said. If what he was thinking was true, she needed to be scared. "I really hope it's nothing, but this could be very bad."

"What are you—"

"I'm going to find Raych."

He went out the back door, to the mouth of the alley. A discarded loaf of bread on the ground, kicked into a puddle. A few dirty boot prints. Possibly signs of a scuffle. Possibly Raych taken right here. Rutting blazes.

She was taken, he was sure. That meant Josie. That meant the truce was over. That mean retribution. He wouldn't let that happen, not today.

He needed Asti, he needed his gear, and then he would tear the neighborhood apart for his wife.

"Asti," Josie croaked. "Don't be stupid."

"Stupid is you've locked yourself in here with me!" he said. "You thought you'd drag me here and threaten my family and that would work out well?"

"There's more than twenty of us here, man," Ren Poller said.

"You think you can take us all?" Ia asked.

"Let's give it a try," Asti said. "Starting with you, Josie—"

He pressed the blade harder against her neck, about to slash it open.

"The mages," she said. That held him back for a second.

"What about them?"

"Insurance," she said. "If I'm killed, they'll kill Verci, Raych, Corsi. Lian. Hal. Kimber. The Kessers. Kennith and his girl and all her chomie family for good measure. Everyone in the West Birch Stage."

"What did I say about threatening my family?"

"Then get your knife off her neck!" Lesk shouted. "Saints, man. Everyone, everyone, weapons away." He waved to the thugs and heavies, and they slowly sheathed their blades and pocketed their knuckle-stuffers.

"You kidnapped Raych," Asti said. "How rutting dare you? I should kill everyone here for that."

"Yeah," Lesk said. "I get that. Bad play, I get it. But she's gone. She got away. So let Josie go, and no one needs to get killed."

"I get you're mad, Asti," Josie said.

"You have no idea where my head is at," Asti said. "Don't even try to guess."

"But we've got real trouble on us," Lesk said. "And we thought you made that trouble. But you're saying you didn't, so put the knife away. Just let her go."

Asti didn't want to. He wanted to make her bleed. He wanted her to suffer. But he knew her all too well. A deal with the mages to wreak havoc and retribution if she was killed was exactly like her. That was why she was willing to meet in the open.

"Fine," he said, letting her go and putting the knife back in its sheath. "Which one of these right bastards put his hands on Raych?"

"What?" Lesk asked.

Asti pointed at the thugs around the room. "Who

grabbed her? You tell me that now, or I find out if the insurance deal covers anyone but Josie."

Josie pointed to three blokes at a far table. "Those boys."

Asti took in their faces. "We'll have words later, chaps."

"Asti," Lesk said. "Like I said, we've got some trouble . . ."

"And you made some with me. If a hair on Raych's head—"

"Nothing, Asti," Josie said. "Now sit down."

"No, no, we're done," he said. "Things are not right with us, not by a bit." He went toward the door, but it opened before he got there. Ben Choney and Ka'jach came in.

"Asti Rynax," Ben said as they entered. "I thought you were out of this business."

"Trying to be," Asti said, glaring back at Josie.

"Ben," Josie said. "This the first time you've seen Asti in a spell?"

"Been years," Ben said.

"So you didn't see him last night, when things went bad?"

"No, no," Ben said.

"And you delivered the *efhân*?" she asked. "You're sure of that?"

"Yeah, we brought it to warehouse four, got the money, then the constables were there. Ka'jach and I barely got out of there. Our . . . escorts weren't so lucky, not that I'm all that broken up about it."

"That's part of the trouble we've got. Who killed them?"

"Didn't see," he said. "Blazes, I think one of them just plain fell in the river. May have drowned."

"And the other?" Lesk asked. "No clue?"

"Nope," Ben said.

"See, here's where we have something a little interesting," Lesk said. "See, our boys in warehouse four, they're kind of vague about what happened. Memory's a bit foggy. Right, Sender?"

"I mean, I was there, and Ben and his dark one there, and the other guy."

"The Poasian," Ben said.

"No, Druth fellow. Forgot his name, but, said he was your new chart man."

"I don't have a new chart man," Ben said.

"This isn't my problem," Asti said. "I'm leaving."

"Wait, Rynax," Lesk said. "Tell me about the chart man, Sender."

"He was a guy. I don't remember."

"Short, tall? Skinny, fat?"

"Short," Sender said.

Lesk glared at Asti. "Funny thing, that."

"I ain't the only short guy in this neighborhood," Asti said.

"But did Sender give you the money?" Lesk asked Ben.

"No, no," Ben said. "Sorry, I never saw Sender before right now. And we don't have a chart man."

"So who gave you the money?" Josie asked.

"Bloke who called himself Olivette."

Rutting blazes. Asti wanted to kill Pilsen. He had said the name just to give the old man a sense of what the ploy was about, how he should act. He wasn't expecting him to actually use the name.

Josie got to her feet. "Did you say Olivette?"

"Yeah, that was him."

"Rutting rutting blazes," Josie said. "What blasted sewage is happening?"

"Who's Olivette?" Lesk asked.

Olivette was no one. Literally no one. A trick Dad used to use back in the day when he had been running with Pilsen. A boss they pretended to answer to, a player no one met but whose name they could invoke. And then when Dad and Pilsen needed to get in good with Josie, when she was first taking over the neighborhood, they played a whole game to run "Olivette" out of Maradaine on her behalf. It was a brilliant scam, audacious, and Dad could never believe he had actually pulled it off.

"An old player," Josie said, her face pale. "The blazes is he doing back?"

Saints, Josie had never learned that Olivette was fake.

"So, what, you're saying he pulled a middleman?" Poller asked. "I ain't never heard of this Olivette before."

"I had," Kel Essin said. "My pops told me a few stories."

"If anyone could have pulled a middleman on us, it would have been Olivette," Josie said. "This is bad. Asti, you aren't going anywhere."

"Yes, I am," he said. "This is your problem."

"No, no," she said. "Your father was tight with Olivette. If anyone can help us deal with him, it's you."

"Why would I help you?" Asti asked. He was more than happy to let them chase a ghost right now.

"Insurance," she said. "You're coming with us."

"Where do you think we're going to go?" he asked.

"We need to see the mages," she said.

Asti paused. That changed things. He had an excuse to get in the mage house, see who they were, see what the deal was. If helping Josie—or pretending to help her reach out to Olivette—got him in the door, that was worth it.

"Fine," he said. "I will help you with this, but just me. Do not touch my family, or the old crew. And you are going to make right what you owe to us all."

"I will," she said. And for once, her face looked like she meant it. Then he saw it—she was terrified. Whether it was the mages, or the deal with Fenmere, or the specter of Olivette, Josie Holt was scared to death.

Good. He could use that.

Asti wasn't at Kimber's, and she hadn't seen him. He didn't know where to go next. Go for Kennith, or Helene and Julien?

Safehouse above Doc Gelson's. Verci's gear was there—the real gear for any and every kind of gig. If he had to, he'd take on Josie and Lesk and the mages and every other rutting bastard in Seleth to get his wife. Asti had warned him to be ready for war, and he had an armory waiting for him there.

Once he was ready, then he'd see if he could get any help. Maybe Almer was still there. Maybe everyone was there.

He didn't bother with sneaking or subtlety, just running as fast as his booted foot could handle to Doc's place, charging up the front stairs to the flop, kicking the door open as he went in. All the alarms rang like crazy, which startled the stranger in the middle of the room. Verci didn't even think, and fearing the worst, tackled the stranger. The two of them went right to the ground, Verci slamming punches into the stranger's side.

"Hey, hey, Rynax, stop!" the stranger yelled.

Almer came out of the water closet and grabbed Verci's arm, tried to pull him off.

"Verci, it's all right," he said. "Cool it down."

The stranger wasn't fighting back at all. Verci pushed off of him, getting to his feet, and realized it was the Thorn. Even though he didn't have his cloak or weapons on, his face was still shaded. Must be magic. Clever. "What's going on? Why are you here?"

"This was the only place I knew to find you all," the Thorn said, getting to his feet. "Found out a few things, thought you'd all want to know."

"He showed up about an hour ago," Almer said. "There's still plenty of *efhân* to destroy, so he was helping me."

"Where are we at with that?" Verci asked.

"Mostly done."

"Hold off on destroying the rest."

"What?" the Thorn asked, his voice rising. "Why do you want to do that?"

"Raych has been taken. Probably by Lesk's people.

Or who knows, even Fenmere's. They must know it was us."

"Oh, saints," Almer said.

"Who's Raych?" the Thorn asked. "The crossbow lady?"

"No, my wife," Verci said. He went to his trunk of gadgets and gear. "I'll tear them all apart to find her, but if I need to negotiate."

"Got it," Almer said. "How can I—"

"Wait, negotiate?" the Thorn asked. "You can't give a drop of that to them."

"What else do I have?" Verci snapped. He pulled out his coat and pants, the ones Asti had told him to make for just such an occasion, even if they were an absurdity. Heavy leather, the kind of thing that could keep a blade from finding its way between your ribs, useful if going into a real brawl. But the real thing that made them special was the pockets and pouches, for all his gadgets and weapons. He didn't think he'd ever actually use it. Then the dart bandolier. Two knives at the boots, two more at his hips.

"What do you need?" Almer asked.

Verci went into the trunk, taking out a box of small copper balls. Hollow ones. He handed it to Almer. "What can you fill those with? Smoke powder, boom powder, anything?"

"I got some things," Almer said. He sat down and started measuring out powders.

Verci took out a gauntlet, put it on his wrist. In theory, it was a launcher, using spring tension to hurl those copper balls over a hundred feet. In theory. He hadn't tested it.

A few other things went into pouches. Glass cutter. Spring line. Caltrops.

"Saint Senea," the Thorn whispered. "You're just charging in alone?"

"If I have to," Verci said. "Almer, once I'm gone, go find . . . everyone."

"This is it?" Almer said. "We're at war with Josie?"

"If they took Raych, then yes," Verci said. He was barely keeping his temper together enough to think clearly about what he needed to do. Was this how Asti felt all the time? Where was Asti?

What if they had grabbed Asti already? What if he had been killed, and Verci had been locked away in the Gadgeterium. If he lost both Raych and Asti, he couldn't—

He couldn't think about that right now.

"I won't let you go alone," the Thorn said.

"Don't try to stop me," Verci said, checking that everything was buckled and strapped. Couldn't have anything loose.

"That's not what I meant," the Thorn said. He had put his gear back on, and was fully the Thorn again, flowing crimson cloak and hood, shadow over his face, arrows and staff on his back, bow in his hand. "I mean you aren't going to be alone."

Verci stopped for a moment and really looked at him, letting what the kid was saying sink in. "Thanks, but I can't ask—"

"You didn't," the Thorn said. "What kind of hero would I be if I didn't help?"

The kid thought himself a hero. Verci didn't know what to make of that.

"Ready," Almer said, closing the last of the hollow balls. "Be really careful with these. Two of them are boom powder, which are the most sensitive. Don't blow your hand up."

"Got it, and the rest?"

Almer pointed them out. "Four smoke, four knock-out, one a phosphorous flash, one acid."

The Thorn let out a low whistle. "That's pretty sweet."

Verci loaded each one into the cuff of the gauntlet. Rotate the cuff to the right spot, lock in place, pull back the tension, aim and fire. Easy as anything. Assuming it worked.

Nothing like a field test to find out.

"Come on, Thorn," he said, pulling open the roof trapdoor. "We've got skulls to crack."

The Thorn grinned, perhaps a bit too much. "You're speaking my language."

Chapter 17

THIS TIME, THERE WAS A CARRIAGE. Not just any carriage, but the slow-rolling, heavily armored lockdown carriage that Kennith had designed. Asti wasn't sure if it was literally the same one, or if Josie had built one for herself. It was the perfect thing for Josie, though. Asti was amazed she agreed to sit in there with him, Ia, and Lesk. Asti knew he could slice all three of them to ribbons if he wanted to, and he wanted to. But Josie's threat of a deadman deal with the mages was enough to stay his hand for the moment.

"Tell me, Josie," Asti said, "Since we're riding in this monstrosity, what ever became of that statue we stole for that first gig? Who'd we take it from? Who got it?"

"Asti, you know it's bad form to reveal those things."

"I don't think you have any place dictating what's bad form," he said.

"What's this first gig?" Lesk asked. "Right after the fire, right? I knew you and your brother were up to something."

Verci. He must have discovered Raych was being missing by now, presuming Raych hadn't found her way home. But even if she was home safe, there was no way

Verci would just let it go. If he also couldn't find Asti, he'd come for blood. Smartly, calmly, and definitely deadly. Asti was counting on that.

Quite literally. He was being taken into the mage pit, and while he'd use that to get as much information as he could, he wasn't sure even he could fight his way out. His contingency plan right now was Verci. It was a plan built entirely on a foundation of faith, but he had complete trust in his brother to do that. It was only a question of how and when.

"That's impolite, Enanger," Josie said. "We don't talk about past jobs that may or may not have happened. That's how people get pinched."

"Sorry, ma'am," Lesk said.

"I'm just curious who would want that thing, where it came from. It was an Acserian statue, right?"

Josie shrugged, "I was told that, but I didn't really care, as long as they paid for it."

"But you know where it came from?"

"Are you in the business of art collection now, Asti?"

"Just trying to put some mysteries together. Something I thought you were interested in."

"I'm interested in holding things together," she said. "That requires resources to keep the wolves at the gate."

"The wolves were at the gate?" Ia asked.

"If they weren't, Rynax would still be living above Greenfield's shop," Lesk said.

"Shut it," Asti said. "I'm pretty sure you don't have a deadman deal with the mages."

Lesk went tight-lipped.

"Where is Mister Greenfield?" Josie asked.

"Win left this life and neighborhood, starting something new and real," Asti said. "He needed to be a whole new man."

"He did," Josie said. "I liked him. Really, Asti, I like all of you. I'll gladly have you on board with me."

"How could I trust you, Josie?"

"You don't. You never did."

"I got careless."

"Wait," Lesk said. "Have him on board how? Doing what?"

"Don't you bustle your hat, Lesk," Asti said. "What are we doing?"

"We're meeting with the mages and other interested parties, and you will tell them what happened to their goods."

"I don't know what happened," Asti lied. "Any more than you do."

"You know about Olivette. And you'll tell them how you'll help strike a deal to get the *efhân* back."

"Why would I do that?"

"Because you want to eat your meals without looking over your shoulder. Which you always will if you don't."

Asti didn't want to put up with any more of that. "Let's dispense with the theatrics," he said. "I'll tell these mages what I know, which isn't much, and they can do whatever they like."

"You aren't done until I have the merchandise back in my hands."

"I'm done when I say I am," Asti said.

"We're here," Ia said, unlatching the carriage door. "Try not to get us all killed, Rynax."

"Now that almost seems like a challenge," Asti said. He got out of the carriage, parked right on Holver Alley in front of the Firewing Circle House. It was hard to believe just a few months ago this was a pile of ash, and before that, Win Greenfield's locksmith shop. Win's wife and daughters died right here. Asti wasn't even sure if anyone found the bodies, had them properly buried. Win had never mentioned it. For all Asti knew, they were under the foundation of this house.

Josie stepped out of the carriage, Lesk offering her his hand until she was on the street and could use her cane. She looked up at the house and sighed deeply before working her way up the stoop. For a moment,

Asti considered just running, leaving this all as Josie's problem. It was clear she was in deep with the mages, with Fenmere, and losing the drugs was enough of a problem that it left her in a hole. That could be enough to collapse the whole foundation beneath her.

But what would it leave in her place? A hole for Fenmere to fill completely. Maybe strengthen the forces behind the Andrendon Project. For all he knew, Fenmere and the mages were the Andrendon project. His instinct told him they weren't—at least not the root of it—but he couldn't let pure instinct drive him. He needed information, and the best source was through those doors.

Plus, Josie had already shown she was willing to hurt Raych, and if she would cross that line, she was probably desperate enough to go further. Corsi. Kimber. Better to play nice for the moment. Especially since there were eight muscled goons just milling about outside the Firewing house. They weren't guarding the house, or even working the door. Just hanging about by the stoop.

"Asti Rynax!" an accented voice called from the street.

"Who is that?" Ia asked, coming closer to Asti. She moved like she was ready to subdue him if she needed to, which Asti found almost laughable. He was sure Ia was a capable fighter, but he also knew Helene had beaten her in more than one brawl. If she couldn't beat Helene, she certainly couldn't take him, either.

Khejhaz Nafath came over to them, large smile on his far too pale face. Asti had almost never seen him actually out on the streets here, and the Poasian man looked decidedly out of place.

"It's the spice guy on Fawcett," Asti said. "You don't know him?"

"He's a ghost?" Lesk asked. His hand went to the knife inside his coat.

"Chill yourself," Asti said, looking to Josie. She gave a nod to Lesk, who let go of the knife.

Nafath came closer. "Asti Rynax, I thought that was you."

"You were right, Nafath," Asti said. "Can I help you with something? I'm a little busy."

"I'm sure you are," Nafath said. "I know you don't have time to come to my shop, when I have so many things you need."

"You buy Poasian spices?" Ia asked.

"They're surprisingly robust," Asti said. Nafath was playing something here, and Asti wasn't sure what. Why was Nafath even here? Did he spot them just now? Had he been following after Asti? Possibly since Lesk and the others grabbed him at Kimber's? "Should I stop by later?"

"That would be beneficial," Nafath said. "But since I have you here, I can give you this *rijetzh*." He produced a cloth bag from under his coat. "I would normally deliver this to your charming sister-in-law, but I'm *certain* you will see her before I will."

Asti knew Nafath well enough to understand his message: Raych had gotten somewhere safe. And the *rijetzh*, Asti knew, disrupted mages' ability to tap into their magic. Nafath must be trying to help him for some reason. Nafath probably knew more about these mages, and their connection to Josie, Fenmere, and the *efhân*. He must want to give Asti some sort of weapon against the mages, which Asti took happily.

"I appreciate it," Asti said, taking the bag.

"I will put it on your bill," Nafath said. "Come when you can to settle up."

"Asti," Josie said sharply. "Enough."

"When you can," Nafath said, inclining his head slightly. He wandered around the corner and out of sight.

Ia muttered something in her native tongue, then, shaking her head, added, "Poasians."

Asti pocketed the bag, unsure of how he could deploy it if the need arose. But it was something that could be used against mages, so he was grateful to have it. Lesk knocked on the door.

The woman who wore the elaborate yellow and orange dresses answered the door. Larian Amalie, according to the file Mila stole. Thirty-two years old, graduated from RCM in 1201, after private schooling in Solindell. Granddaughter of a minor baron, but as the sixth child of a fifth child, utterly removed from contention to title. It was clear in her demeanor that she came from money and education.

"Why, Missus Holt, how delightful for you to grace us with your presence. And here I thought you were going to subject us to Mister Lesk." She glanced at Lesk. "Well, you still are."

"Ma'am," Lesk said with a nod.

"Such a coarse creature," Amalie said. She took a step out the door. "These two are new additions to your retinue?"

"Not exactly," Josie said. "Can we come in?"

"You are expected," Amalie said. She reached out to Ia, touching her on her cheek. "You should be the one she sends to us."

"Should I?" Ia asked.

"Oh, that accent," Amalie said. She took Ia by the arm and led her in. "It isn't Waish, is it?"

"It isn't," Ia said. Josie followed in behind them. Lesk shrugged at Asti and gestured for him to follow.

Asti had been watching the house from the outside, and had mapped out the rooms and furniture in his head, and now had to adjust that image to match reality. There was a wide staircase leading upstairs, and a door under the stairs that might lead to a closet, or to a basement. Asti was certain there was a basement, and a few steps on the wooden floor all but confirmed that.

The sitting room they were led to was richly appointed, a fact Asti had already been aware of from his scouting. The couches and chairs were Kieran, but upholstered with Turjin silk threading, and the wood inlaid with fire-gilded gold. Asti found it an ostentatious display of wealth, but then noticed that the table in the center of the room was listing, one of the legs bowed. The Imach carpet was frayed at the edges.

The picture became clearer. The Firewings had had wealth, but it was gone, and now they were scrambling to maintain the illusion. They'd held on to the few things they could that looked impressive, and put them all in the same room, where they entertained guests. The couch and the chairs did not match each other, each a different style.

Waiting in the sitting room were the other two mages: a man named Pria Mandicall, and a woman named Ecrain Jelsen. Neither of them showed the same pride of appearance that Amalie cultivated. Pria was mostly disheveled, dressed like a clerk who had given up trying to impress his bosses. Ecrain was downright slovenly, her blouse covered in crumbs and jam stains. She also had an eyepatch, and the name and the sight of her put the final pieces together for Asti.

She was the mage who had worked for Tyne when they burned it down. The eyepatch was from Helene shooting her.

One thing Asti didn't know from Mila's files was how powerful any of them were, or what sort of specialties they had. He wondered why they would be secretive about such things. As mages for hire, he would have thought they would proudly advertise their skillset.

Maybe that's why they had fallen on hard times.

Also in the room were the two professionals. Asti wondered if either of them would recognize him from the Drunken Steve bit he and Mila pulled the other night. Seeing them here made everything add up: they were Fenmere's people, the goons outside were his muscle, and they were all here to show North Seleth he was the boss here now. Neither of them paid mind to anyone except Josie.

"Oh, excellent," the man said. "This must be the infamous Josie Holt."

"Guilty," Josie said. "Remind me who either of you are."

"Of course," he said with a prim smile. "I'm Mister Corman. For all intents I am Mister Fenmere's right hand. And my companion is Miss Jads, who is our expert on the product."

"Charmed," Jads said flatly. "Shall we get on with it?"

"Certainly," Corman said, sitting down again. "It seems we've had a bit of a snag with the expeditious delivery of the product."

"In that we didn't get the product, you could say that," Josie said.

"You didn't receive it," he said, waving a finger at her. "I find that fascinating, since I know the delivery was brought to Captain Choney—your man, yes?"

"We've worked with him in the past," Lesk said. "But he's his own man."

"He did come well recommended. But he was given proper product and escort, and somehow the product is lost, and his escorts are killed."

"Tragic," Josie said.

"It's appalling," Amalie said. She was the only one of the mages engaged in the conversation. Pria flipped a coin absently, and Ecrain was far more invested in pastries. "We counted on you to handle your end of things."

"We handled our end of things," Josie said. "Just others intervened. We certainly weren't briefed about this Thorn character."

Asti raised an eyebrow. She knew about the Thorn, and still dragged him in like she thought it was his fault.

Of course, it was his fault, but it was clear that Josie didn't really know that. Maybe she just wanted the excuse.

Even still, she should not have touched Raych. No matter what else, there will be retribution for that.

"What about the Thorn?" Corman asked. "Is he . . ."

"Involved?" Josie asked. "Yes, deeply so. That's

something you should have briefed us on before a shipment came. We could have prepared for him."

"You don't prepare for the Thorn," Jads said with a shudder.

"You always prepare," Asti said. All eyes went to him. "I mean, that's how you make a plan. Learn everything you can, and prepare for each thing. But you can't do that without knowing everything you can."

"Who is this piece of scruff?" Ecrain asked.

"His name's not important," Lesk said.

Josie glared at Lesk. "His name is Asti Rynax, and he's one of the best in this neighborhood."

"Then why are we just hearing about him?" Amalie asked.

"Because he doesn't work for me," Josie said.

"She betrayed me," Asti added.

"Yes, well, we have our good days," Josie said. "He's here because we need him."

"Why?" Ecrain asked, taking another bite of her pastry.

"Because we have a lot of problems, and Rynax is a problem solver," she said. "First off, the Thorn. He's a problem for all of us now, yes?"

"Quite yes," Corman said. "I've gone through several people who thought they could stop him, and yet, here we are. I don't see how this Rynax fellow is any different."

"Nor do I," Asti said. Not that he had much interest, at least right now, in stopping the Thorn. Nor did he hold much loyalty to the kid, but between him and everyone else in the room, he'd go with the Thorn. "At least at the moment, because I don't have information. I'd make a point of figuring out the Thorn, studying him, learning everything about him before using that to cut him down."

"Well, that's brilliant," Corman said drily, his voice full of disdain. "I can't imagine how we never thought of that."

"Thinking of it is one thing," Asti said. "It's another to actually pull it off."

"And you would?"

"I never said that," Asti said. "I certainly didn't say I wanted the job."

Pria threw the coin high in the air, and then snapped his fingers, and it burst into flame. He then caught the flaming coin and threw it at Asti. Or, at least, in Asti's general direction. It missed Asti completely and hit the drapery, which caught fire. Amalie sighed and waved her hand, creating a gust of cold, magical wind.

"This is a waste of time," Pria said.

"I'm inclined to agree," Corman said.

"You'll get no argument from me," Asti said. He looked to Josie. "What are we doing? I'm definitely not interested in getting you out of trouble with them."

"You should be," she said. Pointing her cane at Corman and Jads, she added, "And you two should listen up, because this going to be your problem if you don't wise up."

"The Thorn is already our problem," Jads said. "We're handling it."

"I'm not talking about the Thorn, I'm talking about Olivette." She pointed a thumb at Asti. "He's going to help you get him."

"This looks like a real trash hole," the Thorn said as he and Verci looked down on the Elk Road Shack. "I mean, if any place here was going to be the center of a new *effitte* industry, it would be a place like that."

"Probably right," Verci said. "I don't suppose you've got a plan."

"Me?" the Thorn said. "I rarely do. It just works out."

"That doesn't match my experience," Verci said. Maybe being a mage balanced things out for him, but Verci hated the idea of not having a plan, and was used to making a move with Asti, who would have formed twelve plans and discarded ten of them by the time they had gotten here.

"Was what you all did in the warehouse a plan?"

"Of course it was."

"And that was how it turned out?"

"Imagine how it would have been without a plan," Verci said. "And if a vigilante hadn't have shown up."

"Your brother and Mila would have been carved up by that Poasian," the Thorn said.

Verci let that go. "Let's just focus on what we need to do here."

"Well, what's the goal? Bust them up, and get your wife out safe, about right?"

"Right," Verci said. There was no good way to see inside the shack, to get a sense of how many guys were in there, how they were laid out. "So what would you do? Kick the door in, crack skulls and hope for the best?"

"More or less," the Thorn said. "I mean, usually, you don't have to fight them all. Most scatter."

"I prefer to fight none if I can."

"I thought you were here to crack skulls today."

"I can fight, and I will, but I usually lean toward creep in, get what I need and creep out."

"So what you need is a distraction," the Thorn said. "Luckily for you, I'm very distracting."

Verci liked the idea here. "You make a lot of noise, I slip in and find Raych."

"You know your way around in there?"

Verci nodded. "Been in there a few times, back in the day. There are three different places where you would hold a prisoner, so that's where I'll check."

"That sounds like a plan," the Thorn said. "I suppose that's not too terrible."

"Give me five minutes to get into position, and then make some noise," Verci said.

The Thorn pulled out two arrows and nocked them. "It would be my genuine pleasure." He melted into shadow and leaped off.

Verci worked his way down to the street and slipped to the back alley behind the bar. There was a window to an old storeroom that made a good place to stash someone who was being uncooperative. That would work quite nicely for this occasion. Verci pulled out the glass cutter and went over to the window.

Broken already. Quite thoroughly, big enough to get through. That would save a bit of time. He put the glass cutter away. Now he had to wait for the Thorn.

Raych had to be here. And she would be fine, and then she'd be safe because he'd rescued her. And she won't be mad.

No, she'll be livid. And rightly so.

A splintering crack of thunder echoed through the streets. That must be the cue. Verci slipped through the window to the storeroom. There were signs that someone had been kept here: chair, rope on the ground. And a few splatters of blood.

Screams and smashes came from the main room. Verci wanted to check the kitchen and the basement, but there was no way to get there without going into the fray. If that was what he had to do, so be it. He loaded a smoke charge in the launcher, drew two darts, and opened the door, ready to fight his way through.

It was chaos. Several folks were bleeding and gasping on the floor, most with arrows in them. The Thorn was moving like a cat, dodging and leaping between the pitifully slow attempts to hit him. It took a moment for Verci to realize that it wasn't they were slow, but the Thorn was fast, like he was getting two clicks for every click of the clock. Verci took two steps out, hoping no one would notice him.

The Thorn saw him, and in a flash, his rope uncoiled and wrapped around a man behind the bar. Sender Bell. The Thorn yanked, and pulled Sender out onto the floor at Verci's feet.

"My friend has a question for you," the Thorn said, stomping on the man's chest.

"Where is my wife?" Verci asked. Sender knew damn well who he was.

"Answer him," the Thorn said.

"She got away!" Sender shouted.

"Got away?" Verci asked.

"Escaped! Out the window."

That explained the broken window. But it also confirmed they had her, and that needed to be answered.

"So, you all took her," Verci said, crouching down over the bartender. "You put your hands on my wife."

"Let's thrash these tossers!" someone shouted from the other side of the bar, where they were getting back on their feet. "There's only the two of them!"

"Knockout," the Thorn said. Verci understood, adjusted the gauntlet, and fired at the crowd. That side of the room filled with yellow smoke. The Thorn waved his hand, and the air shimmered, the yellow smoke stayed on that side like it hit an invisible wall. All those guys dropped back down to the ground.

"Handy," Verci said.

"So's that," the Thorn said, nodding toward the gauntlet. The rope tightened around Sender. "So why did you all dare to abduct his wife?"

"The Old Lady ordered it!"

The Old Lady. Josie Holt, despite everything in their past, dragged Raych into this. That would be answered.

"And where is she now?" Verci asked.

"She and your brother went to the mages!" the bartender said. "That's all I know."

"The mages," the Thorn said. "The Firewing house."

"My brother? Why did he go with her?"

"She made him! Said she'd take out all of you and your crew." Sender spat at Verci, but from his position on the ground, all he managed to do was spit on his own face. "And now we know you're in league with the Thorn, and that's who hit us last night."

The Thorn yanked Sender to his feet. "I'm not in league with anyone, I'm just against people who sell poison and abduct innocent women."

"You could say he's a concerned citizen," Verci said.

The Thorn moved in closer to Sender. "You look familiar. You have a brother or something in Dentonhill? Works for Fenmere?"

Sender looked confused. "I got a cousin who does."

"Bell, right?" the Thorn gave a chuckle that sounded almost evil. "He's my favorite. You should ask him what that means. And maybe you'll be my new favorite now."

Verci grabbed the Thorn's arm. "Let him down." The rope went slack, and Sender dropped to the floor.

"Are we done here?" the Thorn asked.

Verci nodded, and looked back to Sender. "Don't think this is over, Sender. You hurt my wife, threatened my brother, and there will be a reckoning."

"You weasels will—" was all Sender said before the Thorn's staff cracked against his face. He went down hard, his nose gushing with blood.

"There was no good ending to that sentence," the Thorn said. "Firewing house?"

Verci wasn't sure. He should find Raych, but if Asti was in there, he was in trouble. "You said you knew something about them."

"Not here," the Thorn said. "Let's put some distance from this place."

Verci nodded, and the Thorn swept the yellow knockout gas aside so they could get to the door. Once they were outside, the Thorn grabbed hold of Verci and launched himself in the air.

"Don't do that!" Verci shouted when they landed on a roof a few blocks away. "Saints almighty, that was terrifying!"

"Sorry," the Thorn said. "I thought some fast distance was in order."

"Just a bit of warning next time!"

"Right," the Thorn said. "So, here's the thing with the Firewings. A few years back, they were part of a thing called the Mage Rows."

"That doesn't sound good."

"Not good. A few small, mercenary Mage Circles fighting each other in the streets. Essentially over clients and territory."

"Like the Aventil Street wars," Verci said. Dad had told a few stories about that, even though he hadn't been a part of it. That was part of how Fenmere had gotten so powerful, when the Tyson brothers tried to make their own crime empire, and the in-fighting of their captains shattered the alliance they had formed against him.

"Not unlike it," the Thorn said, his voice chilling a bit. "But due to things with Circle Law, it got swept under the carpet, save some of those Circles got unbonded."

"Is that like being disbanded?"

"Not exactly," the Thorn said. "It's a whole lot of legal complications that go over my head, but bonding is how Circles police each other. If the other Circles say that one is shady or even illegitimate, they lose their bonding, and from there, lose business."

"Got it, sort of like getting blacked out of the guilds."

The Thorn shrugged. "And for mage-for-hire Circles like the Firewings, that's devastating."

"And the Firewings were unbonded?"

"They were supposed to be, but they basically cut a deal with a few other mercenary Circles, and kept a bottom-tier bonding. But that deal fell apart a few months ago. That's probably why they're working with Fenmere."

"Because they can only get work that's on the grayer side of the law."

"But here's the thing—at least this is what my friend told me."

"Your friend?"

"I have a friend at the University who's good with research," the Thorn said.

So he was probably at Uni as well. University of Maradaine, right next to Aventil and Dentonhill. That explained Mila's reaction to him yesterday. Had she figured out who he was somehow? Girl was whip-clever.

"Back when the Firewings made the deal, part of what they argued was that the city needed mages like them for things that went beyond the scope of what the bigger Mage Circles could do. They had a whole list of examples, including the Andrendon Project."

"So they are involved," Verci said. "What is it?"

"That, I don't know," the Thorn said. "It literally was just a name on a list. But 'Andrendon' comes from old Saranic mythology. You know about Saranus?"

"I never had much formal schooling," Verci said.

"Sure," the Thorn said. "It was an ancient city, somewhere in Druthal, before the Kieran Empire showed up. The dominant power in the area, and the Kierans defeated them. Most of what we know—even exactly where Saranus was—is more legend than record."

That really didn't mean much to Verci. "So is it just an old word to pull a pretentious-sounding name from?"

"Yes, probably," the Thorn said, laughing a bit. "It impresses scholars and city aldermen, I think. But here's the thing—Saranus was reportedly very magically powerful. And in the legend, the 'Andrendon' was this series of magical gates around the city, to instantly travel from one part to another."

Verci's eyebrows went up. "That's possible?"

"Not in any way that I know, and maybe it was just a legend. But maybe that's what this 'Andrendon Project' is trying to do."

Verci's head was reeling. "And they burned down our neighborhood for this? Why?"

"I can't answer that," the Thorn said. He looked off to the distance. "Mage house is over there, and your brother is in the heart of that. They're part of a thing that hurt you, they're part of a thing that hurt me. I want to take them down. What do you want to do?"

"Hit them," Verci said. "And we've got a chance at surprise right now, which'll be gone when Sender tells them what happened."

"So right now?" the Thorn asked. "Just you and me?"

Verci knew it was a risk, but there probably wasn't time to get anyone else. Nor was he comfortable dragging anyone else into it. Not even Helene, though she would definitely come if he asked. Plus, he knew Asti would be counting on Verci making a move to rescue him. "If Asti's in there, he's got nine plans to fight them. We make a move, he'll go at it as well."

"All right," the Thorn said, offering his arm. "Let's go."

Verci nodded, taking the Thorn's arm. It was the right choice. Raych had gotten away, and he had to trust she was safe. That this would keep her safe. He had to believe that.

Raych sat on a bench in the small waiting room in the Loyalty Waystation, hoping the fear and panic would cool down enough for her to no longer hear every beat of her heart pulse through her ears. She had never had occasion to go inside before, and it wasn't very impressive. There was a single desk, a small holding cell, and a small kitchen stove and table in the back. A set of stairs led up, presumably to bunks or another office. There was no proper station in North Seleth, for the Constabulary or Fire Brigade, and the closest hospital was Mandell Ward in Keller Cove. This was just a place where constables, Fire Brigadiers, and Yellowshields—sticks, sparks, and shields, as Verci would call them—would wait around if they needed to be in the neighborhood for one reason or another. Right now, there were two constables, one Yellowshield, and one brigadier, all of them in shirtsleeves around the table, playing cards. One kid—looked like a page, but hard to say for which organization—sat at the desk, absently throwing an apple in the air and catching it.

Lieutenant Covrane brought her a cup of tea and told her to wait.

"What am I waiting for?" she asked. "Can you take me home?"

"You were taken near your home, yes?" he asked. "I'd like to have some men check out your place first, and also get a formal statement to the City Protector."

"Formal statement?"

"I think it's best," he said. "Hey, Renns?"

"Yeah?" the kid asked, throwing the apple in the air again.

"Go run to the Protector's Office, have him come with a clerk."

"Do I have to?" Renns asked, catching the apple.

"Yes, Renns. Tell him I've got a witness who can help us crack the Elk Street gangs."

Renns sighed and got to his feet. "Waste of time." On a look from Covrane, he shrugged and went out the door at a leisurely pace.

"I need to get some things from the office upstairs," he said, squeezing Raych's shoulder. "I'll be right back. Just try to relax." He went up.

Relax. That was impossible. But the rush of fear had faded, leaving Raych with a shivering chill despite the hot autumn air.

"You hear that?" one of the constables asked, putting down a card. "I think it was a Burn Call."

"I didn't hear anything," the Yellowshield said.

"No, I heard it," the other constable said. "Pretty sure."

"Rutting blazes," the brigadier said, putting down his cards. "I'm not hearing anything."

"You know how most of the whistleboxes here are," the first constable said.

"Yeah," the brigadier said. He knocked the Yellowshield on the shoulder. "Come on, someone might be hurt."

"Even if there wasn't a call, that's probably true," he said. They both got up from the table, and with a leisurely, even languid, air, grabbed their coats and went out.

"Shouldn't you go as well?" Raych asked the other two.

"Nah," one of the constables said, getting to his feet. "There might be something else we need to do."

"Can't all run out," the other said, also standing.

"Right," Raych said. "So do you live here?"

"Yeah, this is our neighborhood," the first said. He strolled over to Raych. "Why we keep getting posted out here."

"It's not too bad," the other said, walking across the floor. "Usually just do a few strolls around the block, play a few cards."

"But," the first said, moving even closer. "We can't have anyone giving testimony against the Elk Street fellows."

He grabbed Raych by the arm, and covered her mouth before she could scream. She did the first thing she could think of—bit down hard on his hand. He cried out, and in a moment, he had out his handstick and cracked it across her head. Everything went hazy and gray, and she dropped to the ground.

She felt herself being picked up, and pulled along the floor. Her eyes wouldn't focus, and then there was another sound—a shout, a scuffle, she couldn't make any of it out—and she fell to the ground again. Hands grabbed her and hauled her up, dragging her out the back. She tried to push and hit whoever it was, but she couldn't get her arms to work. She spun about dizzy, only seeing colors until a pair of hands grabbed both sides of her head.

"Missus Rynax," a voice said.

Her eyes focused on the face of Lieutenant Covrane. He looked panicked, a gash over his eye, blood on his lip.

"Lieutenant," she slurred out.

"Can you hear me?"

"Yes," she said. Sounds and sights were coming back. They were in the alley.

"I'm so sorry," he said. "I had no idea they were—I should have known."

She looked behind her as he helped her to her feet. The other two constables were on the ground in their own blood. Neither moving. "Did you—"

"I did what I had to," he said, his voice cracking. She tried to walk, but her legs wouldn't obey, and her senses were going gray again. He scooped her up into his arms. "Let's get you somewhere I know I can trust."

Chapter 18

TODAY HAD BEEN A QUIET day at the cheese shop, at least in terms of customers. Helene had kept an eye out for other gang boys watching the shop, but if there were any more, they weren't being obvious about it. The day lazed into the afternoon, and Helene had swept the stoop as many times as she usefully could. Julien was in the back, salting and spicing meat for curing. She was about to just sit behind the counter with her feet up when Covrane came bursting in the doorway, carrying Raych Rynax on one shoulder. Both of them were bleeding.

"The blazes?" she said, coming out to them. "What happened?"

"My men," he said. "My own rutting bastard men, they must have been in the pocket of Enanger Lesk!"

"Helene," Raych slurred. She looked in terrible shape. She reached out to Helene, but she didn't seem to have the strength to manage even that.

"Julie, I need you!" Helene shouted.

"You know her?"

"It's Raych Rynax, she runs the bakery," Helene

said. Best to make a guarded description. "I know the whole family."

"I know this is a lot to ask," Covrane said. "But I don't know who else to go to right now."

Julie came out front, and immediately ran to Raych, scooping her up in his giant arms. "What happened?"

"What do you need?" Helene asked.

"I know you—" he hesitated. "I know you're . . . capable. You can keep her safe."

"Absolutely," Helene said. What had happened? Had Lesk hurt Raych? Did Verci know. "Where's her husband? Or his brother?"

Covrane shrugged. "I hadn't gotten to finding them yet. I don't even know them."

"What do you need from me?"

"Lock yourselves away somewhere safe, keep those crossbows loaded." His hands started shaking. Only now did she see the caked blood on his knuckles. "I . . . I had to stop them, Hel. They were going to kill her and . . ."

"Hey," she said, grabbing his head with both hands, letting her fingers run into his hair. "You did your job, all right? You protected her."

"They were fellow constables," he said. "But they had rutting—forsaken their duty to do the petty—" He was fuming, sputtering, almost unable to speak clearly. "How . . . how could they . . . how could I?"

"Julien and I have her. No one is going to touch her, you hear?"

"Yeah," Covrane said, eyes to the floor. "I'm going to make this right. For her. But I'm going to have to—no, need . . . I need to go to the City Protector, my captain, report what I did." He took a deep breath and composed himself. "I'll have the whispermen investigate me. Those men were corrupt, but I—I can't be above the law here."

"You're too good for this neighborhood," she said.

He looked up at her and kissed her. He kissed her like he wasn't going to see her again.

"I'll . . . I'll be back," he said halfheartedly. "I just need to—"

"Take care of what you need to," she said.

He nodded, head back down, and went off.

"What are we going to do?" Julien asked as Helene started pulling down the metal grates.

"I'm going to get my crossbows," she said. She went back over to him, checking Raych. "How are you?"

"Hel—" Raych said. "Where am I?"

"You're at my shop," Helene said.

She chuckled and spoke dreamily. "That's where I was going. To trade bread for meat and cheese."

"We'd do that," Julien said.

"We'll worry about that later," Helene said. Raych was still dazed.

"I need to get back," Raych said. "Corsi, Verci, they're—"

"We'll get to that," Helene said. "I'm getting my crossbows and then we're taking you to Doc Gelson."

"You mean—" Julien started.

"I mean the doc. Then I'll figure out what's next."

She ran upstairs and put on her purple coat, her belt for the hiphangers and extra quarrels, and loaded The Action. Then she put on her cap—the green one she took from Ia after they brawled. For luck.

Back downstairs, Julien was holding a wet cloth to Raych's head. "She's hot and dizzy," he said. "Her head got hit bad."

"Why we're taking her to Gelson," Helene said. "Let's stop wasting time."

"Who is Olivette?" Corman asked. He looked at least a little concerned now.

Josie smirked. "He's the player who took the *efhân* out from under your noses . . ."

"*Your* noses," Jads said. "We hadn't gotten hold of it yet. You are responsible."

"We're going to get it back!" Lesk snapped.

"Oh, merciful saints, Lesk is talking," Amalie said. "We certainly don't need that."

"Hey—" Lesk started, but Amalie waved her hand and a series of red ribbons appeared out of thin air, wrapping around his face. Lesk fell to the floor clawing at the cloth around his mouth and nose.

"Next time I'll let Pria do it," Amalie said. "He prefers fire."

Asti hadn't tangled with mages often, and that was a sharp reminder of how dangerous they could be. He let his hand drift its way to his pocket, wrapping his fingers around the *rijetzh* that Nafath had given him.

"Olivette," Josie said sharply, "is an old player. Hadn't been heard from in twenty years, but now he's back."

"Where was he?"

"I don't know," Josie said. "Hardly anyone does, which is why we need Rynax."

"You know him?" Corman asked, his attention on Asti now.

"No," Asti said. "Let's make something clear, I have never met Olivette. I just know a bit about him, because my pop would run gigs for him back in the day."

"Asti's father helped run Olivette out of town when he worked for me," Josie said. "I don't know how or why he's back, but he is, and we need to deal with that now. Especially since he took your drugs."

"We know that for certain?" Jads said, giving a pointed look over to Amalie and the other mages.

"Fairly," Josie said. "And maybe he's in league with the Thorn, we can't really say."

Corman drummed his fingers. "That actually makes some sense."

Asti wasn't sure how to take that, but he nodded and masked his confusion. Right now, he had the opportunity to seize control over the situation. "I'm not going to guarantee anything, but I'll see if I can reach out, arrange a meeting, maybe you all can make a deal."

"A deal?" Corman said. "No, we're not interested in

a deal. A meeting, yes, so we can then put an end to what he's doing. But there will be no deal."

"Well, he's got your merchandise—"

"Which we will find," Corman said. "We were discussing that very thing when you arrived."

"Oh, you were?" Josie asked. Now she looked quite nervous. Of course, if she wasn't part of the solution to finding the *efhân*, she wasn't of use to Fenmere. Asti almost felt bad for her.

"Indeed," Jads says. "Apparently, the drug has unique magiochemical properties, so they can find it."

"I doubt that," Asti said. "If that was the case, they would have found it already."

"Have to prepare," Ecrain said, finishing another pastry. She got up from her chair, brushing the crumbs off herself. "It's not just a snap of the fingers."

"Are you ready now, Miss Jelsen?" Corman asked.

"Yeah," she said. Then she looked up at the ceiling. "You feel that, Larian?"

"Feel what?" Asti asked.

Amalie looked up, and went over to one of the support beams of the house, placing her hand on it for a moment. A wicked grin crossed her lips.

"Uninvited guests," she said. "And one's a mage."

Corman jumped to his feet. "The Thorn!"

Asti moved back so no one was behind him. The Thorn was here, and he wasn't alone.

Things were about to get dangerous. He reached into his pocket, wrapping his fingers around the bag of *rijetzh*. He had no idea how effective it would be if he walloped one of these mages in the face with it, but he didn't have any other choice. There was about to be a brawl with these mages, and if he didn't even the odds a little, he would have no chance of walking out of here.

Mila didn't end up leaving Kimber's back room until late in the afternoon. Kimber had come back from church annoyed, muttering about men never keeping a promise, and piled more bookkeeping on top of Mila.

Mila decided to do it with grace—Kimber had basically put her up for the whole summer, asking nothing but that she focus on her studies. Grousing about doing math—which Mila agreed she needed work on—seemed petty. No need to act that way, and there was no rush. Asti knew where she was, as did the Thorn, so if something was urgent, they would seek her out.

She finished with the bookkeeping and sums, and in doing so realized that Kimber was in some trouble with her city taxes and license fees and dues to the Bed Guild. She made a point to talk to Asti about getting some coins in Kimber's pocket in a way she would accept. She knew Kimber was too proud to just take it.

Mila wrote down some account numbers and addresses. Maybe they could pay off the taxes and other debts directly on Kimber's behalf. Kimber couldn't politely refuse that.

Mila went up to her room to get her pack. Ropes and knives tucked away in there, as well as the Rose dress and cap, which were still blue. For some reason she expected the magic to fade, and they would change back to red.

Not that it mattered, she wasn't going to be the Rose again. Probably not.

Even still, she changed into the blue dress. It had the advantage of looking inconspicuous on the street, but was also comfortable to fight or sneak in, had places to hide her knives and rope, and was dark enough to be hard to see in the shadows.

Plus, she thought she looked pretty damn good in the dress, especially with the cap on.

Satisfied with that, she slipped downstairs and out the front door before Kimber spotted her and asked her where she was going.

People were walking in the streets tonight like they were expecting trouble, a tension Mila could sense. Everyone had their guard up, everyone had suspicion in their eyes. A good pickpocket stayed aware of that sort of thing. Mila wasn't snatching purses anymore, but she wouldn't even try right now.

Mila kept her own eyes down as she walked to the safehouse, but noticed two men talking on the corner while one of them smoked a pipe. She knew who they were: Kel Essin and Ren Poller, both lieutenants who worked with Enanger Lesk. Would they know her? She had met them once in her Miss Bessie guise, but that didn't mean they'd recognize her.

Still she walked by and stopped at the walkway curb to adjust her boot.

"We're going to be shoeless in winter over this," Essin said. "I want a drink."

"So go get one," Poller said.

"I didn't say I was going to get one. I said I wanted one. Always do. Especially with this sewage."

Poller sucked on his pipe. "I hear you. Hide out at the Birdie Basement? At least the view's not bad."

"Good enough place to rest our feet until this Olivette business is settled," Essin said. "Let's go."

Mila snapped the boot buckle shut and moved away before they noticed her. Not that that was very useful scouting, but she knew those two were nervous over something, and that could be good.

She made her way to the safehouse, taking the wrought iron back stairs up to the window and letting herself in that way. She was surprised how many people were there.

Helene paced about nervously, her two crossbows on her hips and two more laid out on the table, loaded and ready. Almer was drumming his fingers on the table as he jotted something in his notebook. Julien and Kennith were in the kitchen, working away at something, and Jhoqull sat at the table, polishing and sharpening a wicked-looking Ch'omik blade.

And, oddest of all, Raych Rynax was sleeping on the couch.

"What's going on?" Mila asked.

"You tell us," Helene said in a snap. "What's the word out there?"

"Out there?" Mila asked. "Did I miss something? Are you hiding?"

Helene huffed.

"You haven't heard from Asti?" Almer asked.

"Haven't all day, though he was supposed to go to church with Kimber and didn't."

"Blazes," Helene said. "When did Verci say he was coming back?"

"He didn't. It wasn't exactly a well-planned thing." Almer closed his journal and wiped off his glasses. "Let's start at the beginning."

"Please," Mila said.

"At some point this morning, one of the gangs under Lesk grabbed Raych—"

"What?" Mila shouted.

"Quiet," Helene said. "Saints, you don't need to scream."

"Sorry," Mila said. She looked over to Raych, who looked to be sleeping peacefully, but had a large bruise on her head.

"They grabbed her, but she got away, I think," Helene said. "She managed to get to Lieutenant Covrane, who took her to the waystation, but the sticks there were in league with Lesk and tried to grab her again."

"Oh, sweet Saint Senea," Mila said.

"Covrane brought her to me, I had the doc check her out and then brought her up here to keep her safe."

"Good," Mila said.

"And I gave her something to rest, because she was in a state," Almer said. He looked at Raych and shook his head. "Maybe a bit too much."

"All right, where are Asti and Verci?"

"No one's seen Asti today," Helene said. "But we think Lesk grabbed him too."

"You believe Raych got away but Asti didn't?"

"That doesn't track," Kennith said from the kitchen.

"I just know we haven't seen him," Helene said. "We

were all hoping he was with you, since he supposedly crashed at Kimber's last night."

Mila shook her head. "And Verci?"

"He came here when he realized Raych was missing, ready to tear the town apart," Almer said. "He went off with the Thorn, armed for a fight."

The Thorn was here? Mila blinked a few times trying to get her head around that. "He was already here?"

"Came here about midday, to look over destroying the drugs," Almer said. "That boy, he's passionate about getting those gone."

"Yeah," Mila said. She wondered why Veranix had written he was coming tonight, but came earlier. "So he and Verci left together? To where?"

"Tear up Lesk and his folk," Almer said. "Elk Road Shack, I presume."

"Shouldn't we do that too?"

"That's what I said," Jhoqull said. "And if you need more, I'll call on my cousins."

"We don't need that," Kennith said. "Saints, last night went poorly enough, you bring a dozen armed Ch'omiks across town, every constable in the city will descend on us."

"They will come if I call," Jhoqull said sternly, to Mila and Helene.

"We should do something," Mila said.

"I am," Helene said. "I'm keeping Raych safe, and I'm thinking we should stay here until we hear from one of the Rynax boys about what's going on. Julien is staying here with me. Anyone who wants to do something else, you're welcome to it."

Mila didn't know how to answer that. Helene was right, but Mila didn't like it, or the useless feeling that burned in her belly. She knew she *should* do something, she had no idea what. Asti, Verci, and Veranix were all out there, but she didn't know where, or what they needed. She should have come over sooner. She might have been here when Veranix was, gone with him and Verci.

Almer cleared his throat. "For the record, I've destroyed most of the *efhân*. I've got about fifty vials left here." He patted the leather case on the floor. "Verci told me to keep it intact in case we need collateral."

"For?" Kennith asked.

"At that point, he assumed Raych was still in danger. I don't want to destroy the rest until I know what he wants, though."

"Anything else we should know?" Mila asked.

Almer pointed to the barrel in the back room. "That's got the product from destroying the drugs. A lot of it."

"What is it?" Kennith asked.

"Would probably make a pretty good rat poison," Almer said. "Or, you know, person poison."

"I thought the point was to make it not dangerous," Helene said.

"No, the point was to make it *not drugs*. You won't get your brain blitzed off of that. You'll just die."

"But we should get rid of it," Helene said.

"Take it back to my shop, I can actually sell it as rat poison. That ain't too bad."

"You need me to carry it?" Julien asked.

"Not all the way to the shop, not right now," Almer said.

"The carriage is in the port of the back alley," Jhoqull said. "Horses are back in the Hodge, but I can go around and get them. And maybe bring some muscle back?"

"No," Kennith said firmly.

Jhoqull looked to Helene. Helene gave her the barest of nods.

"Fine," Jhoqull said, giving Helene the nod back. "Just the horses. I'll be back in a bit." She got up and tossed the Ch'omik blade to Kennith. "In case you get into trouble."

"I don't—" Kennith started, but Jhoqull was already out the door.

"Are you in trouble, Kennith?" Helene asked.

"I don't even know," he said. "She got in a scuffle with one of her cousins last night because I can't recite the heritage of my House, and . . . it's Ch'omik sewage. But it matters to her."

"I don't know what half of that means, man," Helene said. "But if it matters to her, and she matters to you, get it sorted."

"Said the girl being courted by a stick," Kennith said. "I don't know how you square that."

"I really don't either," Helene said quietly. "Hey, Mila. You want to do something useful?"

"Yes," Mila said in a snap.

"Take a stroll around the blocks, from here to my shop and back. If you spot Covrane, let him know we're safe here, and—"

"Tell a constable about here?"

Helene frowned. "No, I mean . . . blazes, we can move her down to Doc Gelson's office. Tell him that."

"All right," Mila said, going to the door. "If I see him."

Maybe down on the street, she'd find Asti or Verci. Or Veranix. And then she could do something useful.

The gable roof of the Firewing house was precariously steep, which Verci did not like one bit. It was not a style of roof that was common in this part of the city, and he wondered if the mages had built the house this way specifically to keep people like him off their roof, attempting to crack inside.

He admitted it made sense from their point of view, but he didn't have to like it.

"What's the plan this time?" the Thorn asked. He was more at ease on this roof, crouching with one leg extended, like he had been born on a high ledge. He was so at ease, he was casually eating strips of dried lamb he had in one of his belt pouches.

Verci glanced about. "I'd like to get some sense of who and what we're dealing with." He spotted the chimney flue. "Maybe that'll help." He pulled the flue scope out of one of his pouches and lowered it down, putting one end to his ear.

"Where was he?" a man asked.

"I don't know. Hardly anyone does, which is why we need Rynax." That was the Old Lady. She was here. Saints, this must have been a bad situation if she actually came out of whatever hole she'd been hiding in. And she was talking about Asti. Or was she talking about him? Were they discussing something they needed Verci for?

"You know him?" the man asked.

"No." Asti talking now. So he was here, and he wasn't in immediate danger. "Let's make something clear, I have never met Olivette. I just know a bit about him, because my pop would run gigs for him back in the day."

"Olivette?" Verci muttered. Olivette wasn't a real person. The blazes was happening?

"What's going on?" the Thorn asked.

"They're talking about something that doesn't make a lot of sense," Verci said. "But Asti is in there, sounds like he's trying to run a play on them or something."

"How so?"

Verci shrugged. "I don't know, other than I know my brother. If he hasn't just killed everyone in the room, it means he's got an angle to work, and a reason to work it."

"And if we came just charging in there, we'd bust that up," the Thorn said. "I've screwed up enough out here already."

"Right," Verci said. He listened again. "Does 'magiochemical properties' mean anything to you?"

The Thorn's shadow mask flickered briefly, and his shocked face was visible for a moment. "How could I be so stupid?"

"What is it?"

"The drugs, they—I'm not going to explain it well, but . . ." He looked like he wasn't sure what to say, then just blurted, "The explanation doesn't matter, but they might be able to magically track the *efhân*."

"You can do that?"

"I can't, but it could be done."

"You feel that, Larian?" A new woman's voice came through the flue.

"Feel what?" Asti asked.

"Uninvited guests," another woman said. "And one's a mage."

"Oh, damn," Verci said, pulling up the flue. "We've just been made."

"What do you mean?"

"I mean the mages sensed you, me, us, and they know we're here."

"Oh, damn," the Thorn said. "Your brother is in there?"

"Yeah."

"Same plan as last time. I make some noise, you get your brother."

"But—" There were, what, three mages who lived here? At least. Plus Josie would have muscle. It was too much for the Thorn to handle on his own.

But one word was all Verci got out before the Thorn was jumping off the roof, bow drawn and arrows flying.

Verci looked down to the street below. A handful of goons were already pulling crossbows and handsticks, trying to tangle with the Thorn. He was a jackrabbit, never in the same spot for half a tick, cracking wise and cracking skulls all once.

Breathtakingly stupid, but Verci had to admire how the kid went at it full bore.

Verci pulled a line out of a pouch, spiked a piton into the chimney, and belayed himself down off the roof to a third-floor window. At this point, he should just break it open, but he did still have some pride of being a window-man. As the Thorn kept up his scuffle with the thugs, Verci took out his jimmy tool from his belt. A slide, twist, and pop later, the window was open.

Still had it.

Verci jumped inside the house to an upper hallway landing. A few doors to bedrooms, he assumed, and sweeping stairs down the two flights to the main floor. He glanced out the window just in time to see the front doors burst open, and a streak of flames fly outside and slam into the Thorn.

No time to be subtle anymore. Loading a smoke pellet in the gauntlet, he fired it down the main floor. Smoke plumed up from where it hit, green and purple. Verci attached a line clamp to the overlook railing, and jumped down, belaying himself to slow his descent until he hit the center of the smoke. Feet on the floor, he drew out two darts.

His shoulder picked this moment to flare angrily at him, reminding him it was injured. Push through the pain.

"The blazes is this?" someone shouted.

"The Thorn's outside!"

"Pria will get him! Clear this out!"

A gust of wind almost knocked Verci off his feet, and the smoke cleared away. In front of him was a woman in a bright yellow gown, lightning and ice crackling off her fingers.

"You're not the Thorn," she said. "But we'll take care of you just the same."

Verci let the darts fly at her, but with a wave of her hand, they went into the wall to her side.

"Asti!" Verci shouted.

"Verci!" Asti came into view from the sitting room, and a moment later he was tackled by Ia Estäan and Enanger Lesk. Verci saw Asti tussle with the both of them while the yellow woman threw a blast of white light at him. He jumped out of the way, just before the floor under him was turned to ice.

"Mages," he muttered.

"Thieves," she sneered back.

Asti had a knife out, and got a solid slash on Lesk, and then another. Blood gushed from Lesk's belly, but Ia then got a solid punch at Asti's head, sending him to the floor.

Another blast of icy magic came at Verci. He slipped

to one side, throwing another brace of darts as he moved. This blast clipped him in the shoulder. The cold was intense, so strong it was like burning. Verci cried out, but so did the mage. His darts hit her in the chest and stomach.

"Ia! Get me out of here!" Josie's voice.

Ia was off Asti and ran out of sight. Verci gave his best punch to the woman mage, knocking her square on the chin. At least his right arm was still good. His left arm hung useless at his side as he closed the distance to Asti. Asti was getting back to his feet, rage in his eyes.

"You all right?" Verci asked.

"I'm still me," Asti said back.

"Someone get them!" A man in a well-tailored suit shouted. Verci saw the rest of the room. Josie was limping toward another door, Ia dragging her along. A woman in a similar suit to the man hid behind him, and another woman with an eyepatch sputtered and swore while wiping some powder off her face.

Before Verci could act, there was a deafening crash as the front window burst in, and a whirling dervish of fire and shadow flew onto the floor in the middle of the room. When the fire and haze cleared, the Thorn stood over a man, his magic rope constricting around him. The Thorn was breathing heavily, his clothes scorched and smoldering, as he looked around the room.

His attention locked on the well-dressed couple.

"I know who you are," he said darkly.

"Run!" the man said, and he and the woman dashed past Asti and Verci and toward the door. The Thorn leaped at them, his rope coiling up and striking as they all raced outside.

The Thorn and his quarry were gone.

Josie and Ia were gone. The woman with the eyepatch stopped rubbing her face and looked spitting mad, sparks and pops coming from her. The man the Thorn was fighting got up, and a nimbus of flaming wings burst out of his back. The woman in yellow was on her feet again, despite the blood covering the front of her dress.

"These two," she said in a throaty whisper. "They're going to hurt."

"We won't be alone." Asti had both knives out, looking ready to spring, but also swaying uneasily. Ia's punch was still clouding his head.

"Cover your ears," Verci said. He lifted up his left arm with his right hand—it was still hanging numb—and turned the cuff to load a new ball.

"Stop him!" the yellow dress shouted.

Verci pointed the gauntlet at the wall and let it fly.

"Boom," he whispered, and ducked his head down to cover his ears as best he could with one arm.

The ball exploded in a terrific burst of fire, smoke, and noise, louder and brighter than Verci was ready for. Still, he managed to keep his feet, as the fiery man and the eyepatch woman fell over. Verci grabbed his brother and pulled him through the hole in the wall he'd just made.

Asti was coughing up a storm as they stumbled out into the street, fire and carnage all around them.

"This looks familiar," Asti muttered. "Good old Holver Alley."

"Can you run?" Verci asked him.

"Yeah," Asti said. "I think—Raych!"

"We'll find her," Verci said, pulling Asti down the back way behind a building. "First let's get safe, brother."

Asti stopped and took Verci's hand, squeezing it. "Get safe, get our heads together, and then . . ."

"Then we'll deal with what comes next," Verci said. But he knew what it would be.

War had come.

Chapter 19

DOC GELSON WASN'T AROUND. Of course he wasn't here, he'd far rather be at Kimber's, drowning in beer and cider. Helene lit a lamp while Julien laid Raych on Doc's cot.

"She good?" Helene asked.

"Think so," Julien said. "I'm going to get that barrel out to the carriage port now."

"Good idea," she said. "Don't dally out there too long."

"Nope," he said.

She looked about—everything in here looked respectable enough. The doc might be a lush, and not much of a sew-up, but he ran a legit office that he kept clean and ordered. This was a decent enough place to bring Covrane, if he needed to come. She wondered how he was holding up, what he was doing right now. He had killed his own men, constables, and she wasn't sure how a decent soul like him would be able to reckon with that.

"You all right?" Julien asked.

"I'm fine," she said. "Just . . . just worried for Jarret."

He nodded. "I hope . . . I hope you can be happy with him. If that's what you want."

Helene took her cousin's hand and squeezed. "I'm happy if you are."

"I'm not happy that things have gone badly. I want Asti and Verci to show up, let us know everything is all right. It isn't right what happened to Missus Raych. I know you . . . I know you don't like me fighting."

"You're not fighting."

"But if Asti and Verci need help. If people are getting hurt, like Missus Raych, we gotta do something. Even if it's the things we don't like."

"You're right," she said. "Hopefully it won't come to that."

He went back upstairs. Helene sat down at Doc Gelson's desk and put The Action on it.

"Won't come to what?"

Raych looked over at Helene with sleepy eyes.

"This whole neighborhood at war," Helene said. "How's your head?"

"Better," Raych said. "I . . . where are we?"

"Doc Gelson's office."

"Oh, is . . . did Doctor Gelson see me?"

"He actually did, but then he went off to his nightly haunt. Mostly said you needed to rest."

"I do," Raych said, pulling herself up to sit on the bunk. "But I need . . . I need to get home. My baby needs me. Verci needs me."

Helene shook her head. "Verci's not there."

Raych raised an eyebrow. "Where is he?"

"He went off to rescue you."

"And my baby?" She shook her head. "No, I have to—" She stood up, and immediately stumbled. Helene jumped up and grabbed her hand.

"You need to rest and wait. You're in no shape to go home. We don't know what's going on out there, but someone has their sights aimed on you."

"You mean Josie Holt and her gangs," Raych said. "Why me?"

"I'm guessing they wanted to get the boys' attention," Helene said.

Raych looked around. "There were constables who—when did we?"

"Your head took a wallop, and your memory must be a mess," Helene said. "Just stay calm, and when Verci gets back here . . ."

"How do you know he's coming back?"

"Well, I know he won't stop until he finds you. And you're here."

"How would he know that?"

"I sent Mila to find him. She'll come through."

Raych chuckled. "That girl always does." She patted Helene's hand and sat back down. "Why are you the one watching over me?"

"Jarret asked me to," Helene said. On Raych's confused look, she clarified, "Lieutenant Covrane."

"He's 'Jarret' to you?"

"Well, we've been, I don't know, 'courting' for some months. If that's what you call it."

"That's good, Helene," Raych said. "That's a good, stable man."

"Who'll do the right thing, no matter how much it hurts," Helene said. "Which means I have to keep him at a length."

Raych sighed and nodded. "When Verci and I were going to get married—he had told me early on that he was involved with 'dangerous things,' and that was exciting—but before we got married he sat me down and told me everything. I mean *everything*. From his dad teaching them things to the scraps he and Asti would get into . . ." She shuddered. "But no secrets, he said, even if that chased me away."

"And you didn't run away," Helene said.

"Of course not, I love that idiot," Raych said. "Even when that love puts me in positions like this."

"Sorry," Helene said. "But there's a difference between telling a clean lady like you, and telling a *stick*."

"That stick, when he saw his fellow officers were

corrupt, came to you," Raych said. She smiled warmly. "He knows who you are."

Helene was tempted to say something bitter. She wondered if Raych was being so encouraging of her relationship with Covrane because it kept her from flirting with Verci.

She kept that in. "You should lie down," Helene said. "It won't be—"

The bells upstairs started ringing. Someone had set off the roof alarms.

"What?" Raych asked.

"I don't know," Helene said, grabbing The Action. "I'm going to go see. Lock the door behind me, don't open it for anyone you don't know."

Helene went to the stairs, and the door shut with a rushed slam. Raych had the sense to not argue. Helene's stomach soured, a warning of what might be coming upstairs.

Mila circled the blocks around the safehouse, not wanting to go too far. There was trouble a few blocks away, she could hear that. Was that trouble Verci was in the middle of? Or Asti? Or Veranix? She had no idea, and as much as she wanted to find out, she shouldn't dive into what was sounding like an actual battle.

Booms and thunder came from the distance. Mages. It must be. If it came to an actual fight with the mages, what would she do? She had no idea how to fight that.

She doubled back to Kimber's, if only to make sure Asti wasn't there. Maybe he had been there all this time, and this fight in the distance had nothing to do with him.

No, there was no way they were that lucky.

Rounding the corner to Kimber's, she saw a man in a suit far too nice for this neighborhood coming out of an alley, clutching his hand to his chest as he gasped for breath. He took a few moments, and while his attention was on gathering himself, she got a good look at him.

Same fellow from the other night, the suit working with the mages, the one they took the *efhân* from. This fellow was trouble, and he was running from it. She moved closer. If she was able to subdue him, tie him up, maybe that would help.

Or she could just stay close, find out more about him.

That would be what Asti would do. Get information, learn everything she could, then decide an action.

The man went into Kimber's. Mila followed behind, keeping her head down. She reached into the pouch of her purse and took out the dry history text Asti had given her. She sat down near the table where the suit went and listened.

"Things have gone poorly," he said to the other folks at the table.

"That shouldn't be my problem," one of the men there said. Harsh accent. Poasian. She recognized that. She dared to glance up, and the other folks at the table—eight of them—looked like garden-variety thugs, except for the one Poasian man in an embroidered cloak. "I shouldn't even have to be involved at all."

"I agree," the suit said. "Your people insisted on sending you."

"I go as I'm ordered. Your incompetence made such orders necessary."

"By all means, let us continue with the insults," the suit said. "It's an effective use of time."

"So there is urgency," the Poasian said.

"The Thorn is here, and he's already gotten Jads. I barely got away."

"You left your female?"

"I couldn't stand up to the Thorn. That's why you're here."

"Very well," the Poasian said. "These ruffians of yours will get in my way."

"Or his," the suit said.

Another person burst into the bar, blood dripping from a gash in his head. His presence made other folks startle, and Kimber gasped from behind the bar. "Sir, the mages say they've got it. They're ready to move."

"What's this?" the Poasian asked.

"It means it's time," the suit said, waving for them all to stand. "The mages were about to track the *efhân* when things went bad. Let's find them, and then get to work routing out these people."

"Yes," the Poasian said, getting to his feet. He moved with a fluid poise that was somehow both animalistic and divine. Everything about him screamed *danger* in the back of her skull. He snapped his fingers at Kimber, and she, uncharacteristically quiet, came from behind the bar carrying a beautiful sword with a carved ebony handle. The Poasian took it from her and dropped a coin in her hand. "Let's be about it."

The suit, the Poasian, and the rest went for the door. Kimber locked eyes with Mila for a moment, shaking her head desperately.

Despite that, Mila followed them out.

When they were outside, the sounds of fighting in the distance had subsided, but now the sky was filled with flashes of light and fire.

"Oh, I think they've found it," the suit said. "Let's investigate. And hopefully end our time in this pockmark of a neighborhood."

He and the Poasian went toward the source of the fire and light. And Mila knew exactly where they were headed.

The safehouse.

"They're coming," Liora whispered, as the specter of her leaned against the brick wall. Asti tried not to even look at her, focus on Verci, who was shaking out his left arm.

"You all right?" Asti asked.

"It's not so bad," Verci said. "I mean, in a way, it's numb and doesn't hurt."

"You have any fight left in you?"

"I don't think there's much choice in that matter," Verci said. "The fight's here."

"I doubt he'll make it to dawn," Liora said. "I'm actually impressed how well you both held up against three mages."

"And the Thorn's here? He's with us?"

"He is. But it looks like he went after Fenmere's men. Hopefully he's still about."

"Less people for us to fight," Asti said. He hadn't gotten a full read on the Thorn, but Verci seemed to like him. Good enough. "Ready to move?"

"Are you?" Verci asked. "You got a good hammering from Ia in there, and I don't know what else."

"I'll get by," Asti said. "I've held it together so far today, and I'm ready to extract some retribution on these people." Ia had hit him pretty blazing hard, and then she got away. So did Josie. If Asti could count on one thing, it was that she would now go underground and not come up for air for some time. He had blown a shot at her, so the only thing he could do now was dismantle every bit of power she had, so she had nothing to touch them with. "They're going to pay for the line they crossed."

"You mean Raych," Verci said. He started walking down the alley toward the safehouse. "That's not on you to exact."

"Yes, it is," Asti said. "I promised that your family would be safe, and it's on me to do the ugly things required."

"So very ugly," Liora said.

"Not alone," Verci said.

"It's fine," Asti said. "I'll burn them all down if it means you get a—"

"Stop it, Asti!" Verci shouted, turning on him. "Please, for the love of Saint Senea, stop pledging to dive into your madness and die for my sake, or Raych's, or Corsi's." Verci grabbed Asti's head and pressed their foreheads together. "When are you going to get it, brother? That safe, happy life for my family includes you."

Asti felt hot tears threaten to burst forth. "You don't

get it, Verci. I don't get that life. I definitely don't deserve it."

"We're going to have it," Verci said. "Together. Even if we have to run to the north side for it." He let go of Asti and started back up the alley.

"North side?" Asti asked.

"Turns out there are things called 'mechanical firms' of college boys doing big business," Verci said. "If you like, we can pretend we're conning all those swells out of their coin."

Asti wasn't sure what that even meant. "You're going to have to—"

He cut himself off. They could see the safehouse over Gelson's, and it was no longer remotely safe. Lights and flashes were on the roof, and at least a dozen men were approaching the front door. Mister Corman was with those men. And Larian Amalie strolled up the road, casually adjusting the stray hairs out of her face as she approached Corman.

"This isn't good," Verci said.

"Not at all," Asti said. He had to believe the other two mages were on the roof, having tracked the drugs and their magiochemical properties. Stupid of him to not think mages were capable of such things.

"Plan?" Verci asked.

A dozen ideas went through Asti's head, and not one of them was good. "We don't know who's in there, but the priority has to be getting our friends out. Everything else can hang at this point."

Larian was talking to Corman, they all looked so confident, so assured they had won.

"Infuriating, isn't it?" Liora asked.

"So how do we—"

"I'll draw these bastards," Asti said. "You get to the back stairs, get everyone out."

"All right," Verci said. "But let's not be completely stupid about you taking them all on alone."

He drew up the gauntlet launcher, adjusted the cuff, and fired. Then again, and again. Bright flashes of burning light and massive plumes of colored smoke filled the street. He pulled out three darts and tensed his body like he was about to run.

"Hey," Asti said. "I love you."

Verci relaxed for just a moment, letting a slight smile creep in. "Love you, too. Let's get on it."

He dashed out, vanishing into the smoke. Asti ran behind him, drawing out his knives. He acted on instinct, on memory, to lead him to Corman's goons in the cover of the smoke. He grabbed one, and took him out with a few slices and swipes. Someone yelled out, and Asti stabbed at him. A scream let him know he hit true. Someone was near him in the smoke, and Asti thrust both knives at him.

Both knives were deflected with a metallic clang. A blade swiped dangerously close to Asti's nose.

A great gust of wind rushed through the street, and all the smoke flew off out of sight. Amalie, now looking drawn and haggard, held her hands out at them. She at least had the decency to look out of breath after that.

Asti was face to face with a tall Poasian man, armed with a glorious sword. He launched into a perfect series of attacks, which Asti barely had the opportunity to dodge and parry with his knives. This fellow was far from a typical goon.

"Get in there!" Corman shouted to the others. He led the goons as they smashed down the front door and charged into the building, leaving Asti on the street with the Poasian blademaster and the angry mage.

"Poor Asti," Liora said from behind the Poasian. "This looks like it's actually a fair fight for once."

Verci was through the smoke and down the alley, hoping he had hit one or two of the goons with his darts as he dashed through. Hoping Asti could handle himself. Hoping this wasn't it for them.

Hoping Asti wasn't ready to let himself be killed out

of some stupid sense that he needed to give his life for Verci.

Verci was up the back stairs, jumping three at a time, not caring about the noise he was making with each step. Stealth was long since abandoned.

He reached the window, where he could see total chaos inside the flop. The front door was knocked down, and the only thing keeping the goons from pouring in was Helene. She had thrown the table on its side and was crouching behind it, popping up every few seconds to fire crossbows at the goons trying to come in. Kennith was next to her, reloading her crossbows as fast as he could, while Almer stood on a chair, trying to hold the roof trapdoor shut.

Verci opened the window. "Let's move!"

Helene popped up, firing another shot before she dropped back down to look at Verci. "You need to get your wife!"

Raych. He didn't see her anywhere. "Where is she?"

"Down in the office," Helene shouted.

"I can't hold it!" Almer yelled. There was a horrific sound from the roof above. Verci didn't dare climb higher to see what was making it, but Almer was straining to keep the trapdoor from flying open.

"You all got to run!" Verci said.

"Get Raych!" Helene said, switching her crossbow with a fresh loaded one from Kennith. "We're right behind!"

For a moment, she turned to him, locking eyes. He saw her fear, but also understood what she meant. She wasn't going to be able to hold off the goons much longer, and she didn't dare stop until she knew Verci had gotten Raych out.

She popped back up and fired, hitting the goon charging in square in the chest.

Verci hated himself for doing it, but he went back down the stairs. There was a back door to Gelson's office. Verci knew he couldn't kick it open, and didn't have time to pick the lock. He had the spring-line clamp, though. He cranked it tight, shoved it into the crack of the door and popped it. It snapped open, crunching through the door frame. He pushed it open and ran in.

"Raych!" he shouted into the darkness.

"Verci!"

That was all he needed to hear.

Verci was gone. Hopefully that meant he was getting Raych out of here. The only reason Helene was keeping up the fight in the flop was to keep the attention away from Raych in the office below.

Kennith handed her The Action. "We're running out of bolts," he said.

"I'm aware," she said. She popped up from behind the table—the goons had crossbows as well, but they were bad shots and slow loaders, so she had been able to keep them bottlenecked in the doorway.

For now.

She fired when one of them came out to take a shot, nailing him in the arm. He groaned and fell back, and Helene swapped The Action for Orton. Another shot in the chest, since that guy had the decency to stand in place when he had been hit. Now there were two dead bodies in the doorway, and that should be enough to block the entrance long enough to escape.

"You two get out the window," she said to Kennith and Almer as she dropped back into a crouch. "I'll cover you."

A loud bang came from the trapdoor, pulling it up a couple inches, almost taking Almer with it. Kennith lurched and grabbed his ankle, holding him down.

"I can't let go of this!" he said. He pointed to his case on the ground. "Kennith, there's a green crystalline powder in a glass container, and then a copper flask. Get them!"

Helene reloaded all three crossbows. Only three bolts left after that. She had to make them count.

"We don't have much time," she said. "Just run!"

Kennith rummaged through Almer's case. "I'm not finding the green powder!"

"Saints," Almer said. "Get up here, keep this shut!"

Helene popped up with both hiphangers and snapped her shots off, scaring away the mooks who were about to go through the doorway. Kennith scrambled up on the chair and grabbed hold of the trapdoor handle. Almer jumped down to his kit and grabbed a couple vials.

"Whatever you're going to do, Almer," Helene shouted. "Right now!"

"On it," he said. He poured a powder into the copper flask, slammed the lid shut, and shook it. He then tossed it at the doorway, and it burst open, filling the hallway with billows of sickly pink smoke. All the mooks out there started coughing and retching.

"Now run," he said. "And shoot whatever comes through there!"

Kennith let go of the trapdoor and dove for the window, Almer dashing toward it as well. Helene reloaded The Action and moved right behind them.

With a wrenching groan, the trapdoor tore open. Helene took aim and fired blindly. As soon as she shot, a plume of flame cracked through the trapdoor, scorching the floor. It was followed by a blazing figure, who swooped into the room and out the window, taking Almer with it.

"Rutting—" Kennith started, but before he got another word out, a woman dropped down into the room, and with a wave of her hand, he flew up in the air and slammed into the wall.

Helene reloaded The Action as fast as she ever had, bringing it up and firing at the woman.

The woman's hand came up, and the bolt stopped dead in the air, inches from her throat. She turned to look at Helene with her one eye—the other covered with an eyepatch—and smiled. "None of that, girl."

Helene dropped The Action and wound back her arm to clock this mage in the face. She swung hard, the sort of punch that she could take down Ia or Sender with. But just as her knuckles were about to graze the woman's cheek, she moved impossibly fast out of the way. Helene's punch swung wild, and she almost fell to the floor.

She got a kick to the ribs, and then a blow to her head that felt like a whole wagon had hit her.

"Keep it up," the mage snarled. Helene couldn't move, but received another kick that flipped her over on her back. A booted foot pressed into her chest, so heavy it pinned her to the floor.

"Are we secure?" a man called out.

"Got them all," the mage said. "At least all that were in here."

A man in a suit strolled in, with a few mooks at his side. "Find the *efhân*. And then kill these two."

"Do we have to?" the mage asked. She looked down at Helene. "I remember you, girl."

"Did I used to smack you around in preparatory?" Helene asked.

"Oh, no," the mage said, tapping her eyepatch. "I remember the last thing I saw with this eye."

Saints. Ecrain, from Tyne's Emporium.

"I owe you dearly, girl," Ecrain snarled. "And I will pay you back."

Chapter 20

RAYCH HID UNDER GELSON'S COT while a cacophony of shouts and echoing booms assaulted her ears. She had no idea who was there or what was happening, and she prayed to the Sixth Prophet to deliver her from whatever terror had befallen her.

"Raych!" she heard from outside the door. A voice she knew better than any other.

"Verci!" she called back, scrambling out from under the cot.

The door rattled, and she could hear him muttering on the other side. "Hold on," he called.

"I got it," she said, releasing the bolt and opening the door.

There he was, looking like he had been through nine kinds of horror, his beautiful face scratched and smudged with soot. His shoulder was bleeding, seeping through his torn shirt.

She grabbed him and kissed him like she had been walking through the desert and he was water.

"Raych, Raych," he tried to say before she let him extract himself from her lips. "We have to go."

"What's happening?" she asked.

"Everything bad," he said. "Come on."

He twisted something on the gauntlet he had on one arm, and took her hand and led her through the darkened corridor to the back door. Upstairs, she could hear fighting and chaos.

"All right," he said. "There's the back courtyard here, and on the other side is an alley that comes out on Heel. When we get outside, we're going to run like every sinner is behind us. Just keep running until you get to Heel, and then we keep on running until we get to your sister's."

"My sister's?"

"I told Lian to stay upstairs with the baby until Hal came for her, and then go home and lock themselves in. At this hour they've already gotten there."

So Verci had taken care of Corsi. Good. "But why are you telling me?"

"In case we get separated."

She grabbed his hand and squeezed it tight. "We are not getting separated, Verci. No chance."

"All right," he said. "Ready?"

"No," she said. A horrific crunching sound came from above. "But that doesn't matter."

"Run!" he shouted, and they both tore out the door, across the courtyard, and down the alley. As soon as they were out in the street, Raych stopped short, startled by the appearance of two great horses in front of her, and the Ch'omik woman she nearly crashed into.

"Heya, what?" the woman shouted.

Raych reacted, throwing the first true punch she had ever thrown in her life. She hit the woman right in the chest, sending her reeling back.

And possibly smashed her own hand in the process.

The Ch'omik woman recovered, and moved back at Raych while pulling out a terrifying blade.

"Whoa, whoa!" Verci shouted, getting between them. "It's all right, it's all right!"

"What the blazes?" the Ch'omik woman snarled.

"She's my wife," Verci said.

"I know who she is, why did she hit me?"

"How do you know me?" Raych asked.

"I was up there while you were sleeping," the woman said. "What is going on?"

"We're compromised," Verci said. "Jhoqull, I need you to get Raych out of here."

The woman looked up toward Doctor Gelson's office. "But who is there?"

"Fenmere's heavies and mages," Verci said. Raych gasped at the sound of that. "Just get her out of here. Her sister lives on Colt Road, right by the creek—"

"And where will you—" Jhoqull started.

Raych already knew the answer. "No, Verci, you are not going back in there."

"But Asti—" he said.

"Will also run if he has any sense. So will everyone else. I'm not letting you leave me."

"Over there!" someone shouted from down the alley.

"Your wife is very correct," Jhoqull said. "We will need to ride."

"Ride?" Raych asked. She could hear several footsteps running toward her.

Jhoqull grabbed her by the waist and hoisted her up onto one of the horses. "You can ride, Verci?"

"Yes—"

"Then do so," she said. She jumped up onto the other horse and kicked it. Verci scrambled up in front of Raych on her horse just as three men were coming up the alley. Verci pointed his gauntlet at them and let it shoot. The alley was filled with yellow smoke, and those men coughed and dropped to their knees. Verci grabbed the reins and kicked the horse to a gallop, catching up with the Ch'omik woman.

"Who is she?" Raych asked over the thunder of hoof beats.

"Kennith's paramour," he said.

"And where's Kennith?" she asked.

She saw his face as he looked back. "Let's just get you safe."

She wrapped her arms tighter around his waist, never wanting to let go again. The cost of that, she'd worry about later.

Let me.

The beast kept growling at him as Asti's attention was split between Amalie's magic and the Poasian's blade. All he could do was parry and dodge, and in the process pull them farther away from the safehouse. Their fight was halfway down the street now.

"Talented," the Poasian said as Asti blocked a slash with both of his knives. The Poasian kept moving in close, not giving Asti the distance he needed to switch to the offensive. And Amalie was all offensive, keeping far enough away as she hurled blasts of magic at him. He could probably take her down with a well-thrown knife, but the Poasian assured that he never had the opportunity.

"Isn't he?" Liora's specter strolled around the fight like a drill inspector from Intelligence. "I mean, darling, that's a Poasian Thurgir. Like a King's Marshal and an Intelligence Assassin all in one man."

Asti had to agree. The man's skill was on par with a Spathian master. Asti was barely holding his ground, and dodging Amalie's blasts didn't help.

Let me.

The beast wanted to take him, wanted the chain to be dropped. Asti was more than tempted. But he didn't dare. He had to stay in this fight, in his head, so he would be ready for whatever came next. From the corner of his eye, he saw Corman and his goons coming out of the safehouse.

And not alone. One of his goons was dragging Kennith, and Ecrain held Helene by the back of the neck.

He didn't have time to waste.

He dodged and parried the next series of blows, taking two steps closer to Amalie in the process. It left him open, and the Thurgir took full advantage. Instead of dodging this next thrust, Asti reached out and grabbed Amalie, pulling her toward him. She screamed as the Poasian sword went through her side—all the way through, slicing Asti as well. But that didn't matter.

He pushed her onto the Poasian as he pulled away. If he moved quickly, he could dash back to the safehouse, tear his way through those goons, and get Helene and Kennith free. Then he could—

"Run, Julie, run!" Helene shouted.

Asti's gaze went to where she was looking. Julien was in the mouth of an alley across the street, and for a moment he looked unsure of what to do. Then he bolted down the street.

"Get him!" Corman shouted.

Let me.

A group of goons—three of them—gave chase to Julien. Asti dashed after them all as Julien ran down the street and around the corner. Asti had no idea where he was running, but the goons were running faster. It took all Asti had to close the distance, but he rounded the corner just as those goons were on top of Julien. The three of them had managed to pull him to the ground.

Asti didn't waste a moment, leaping in with both knives. Going straight for hearts and throats, tearing them up.

Let me.

Julien looked terrified, collapsed on the road. "You all right?" Asti asked.

"I don't—Hel—"

"We'll—" was all Asti could say before a scuff of boot warned him of an attack from behind. He slid to the side and turned around, earning a shallow slice across his belly. At least that was better than being run through.

The Thurgir was there, and all his attention was on Asti.

"Enough of this," he said.

"I agree," Asti returned. Now he didn't have to also

dodge a mage, he gave the Thurgir everything he had. Slices and swipes like lightning, too fast for the eye. But each of those swipes was met with an expert riposte, every attack parried.

"Even now, you hold back," Liora said. "When everything is on the line. Fascinating."

The Thurgir danced around Asti, his sword going for Julien's throat.

LET ME!

Asti didn't hesitate any longer. Even as he moved in to block the attack, he let the chain holding the beast at bay free.

And everything went red.

Mila watched everything unfold from the safety of an alley half a block away, unsure of what she could do, how she could help. Now it seemed too late—Asti was gone from sight, Helene and Kennith were captured, and there were far too many of them for her to fight. She had no idea what she was going to do, how she could do anything.

But she had to do something. She slowly started to move closer. Do what Asti would do: gauge the enemy. Figure a plan.

The suit who worked for Fenmere was there—Corman. Seven other goons. Two of the mages—the fancy woman and the one with the eyepatch. Larian and Ecrain, she remembered from the records. Pria was the man—where was he?

He dropped down out of the sky, flaming wings on his back, carrying Almer.

"I'm assuming they're alive for a reason," Pria said as he landed.

"Only a little bit of the product in there," Corman said. "We have to determine where the rest of it is."

"Gone," Almer said.

"You couldn't have sold it that quickly," Corman said.

"Not sold. Destroyed."

"Really?" Ecrain asked, grabbing Helene by the hair. "You destroyed it?"

"I don't believe that for a moment," Corman said. "They only had a little, right? Olivette has the rest."

"Who?" Helene asked.

"Don't be stupid, we know all about him," Corman said. He walked past Helene in a deliberate pace. A little away from the mages or his men. Vulnerable.

"I don't know what you mean," Helene said.

"You two gentlemen want to echo that sentiment?" Corman asked.

"I just drive," Kennith said. "She's just a sniper, and he's a chemist. We don't know the plan."

"Ah, the chemist," Corman said. "Now it makes sense. You had a little to analyze it. And Olivette has the rest."

"No, I don't know who Olivette is," Almer said.

"You're making a big mistake," Helene said.

"You're right about that. We should get off the street. Let's go back to the house to work through this."

He started walking, as if he expected the rest to follow him. That put him just a couple of paces from Mila. She pulled out her rope and dashed out onto him, wrapping it around his neck.

"All right!" she shouted, tightening the cord around his throat. "Here's how it's going to go. You're letting those three go, or he dies!"

"You're not serious, little girl," Larian said, holding on to her bleeding side.

"She's got brass, I'll give her that," Ecrain said.

Corman gasped and clawed at the rope as she pulled it tighter, and he dropped to his knees.

"He doesn't have long," Mila said.

"No," Larian said. "Pria?"

"Aye?"

"Kill her hard."

Before Mila could do anything else, Pria's fiery

wings burst from his back again, and he launched at her with terrifying speed. He grabbed her and flew up, up above the rooftops, above all of North Seleth, above the whole city. Higher than she ever imagined possible.

It was breathtaking.

She couldn't breathe at all.

"It's amazing, isn't it?" Pria said. "Enjoy the view, last you'll ever get."

He let go.

Mila tried to scream as she plummeted, but her voice failed her. Or she did scream, but the wind rushing past her ears made it impossible to hear anything. Impossible to see anything except the city, the buildings, the ground, all coming at her.

Faster.

And faster.

The ground kept rushing up to meet her. She should have just studied and gone to the University now she never will go to school or kiss anyone or anything else she'll just be—

She was struck.

But not by the ground. Not crashing into the unforgiving cobblestone street, but struck, body to body, arms wrapped around her. She was suddenly cocooned in red cloth, as she careened sideways, not down.

Then she crashed, crashed into the body holding her as it crashed into something else.

She was alive.

Impossible but alive. Breathing, heart pounding, barely able to contain herself but feeling every muscle and bone *alive*.

She looked up, and saw how.

Veranix, still holding her, his strong arms clutching tight as a warm glow surrounded them both.

And then the glow sputtered and faded. He let her go, his embrace just falling open.

Mila got to her feet. They were in an alley, five blocks from the safehouse.

"Ver—" she said, then held her tongue. He was the Thorn, couldn't use his name, not here. "Are you—"

He looked like he could barely breathe, lying on the ground.

"Are you"—he wheezed out— "You all right?"

She nodded. "But you?"

He was a mess. Cuts and singes all over his clothes, bruises and burns and scorches on his hands and face. He looked like he couldn't even stand.

"Took—took—took more out of me—" he stammered out.

She grabbed his arm and hauled him to his feet. "We need to move." No telling who was about. She wasn't even sure where they were. She should get back, try to save Helene and the others still, but—

But he was in no state, and she couldn't leave him.

"Where—" he asked.

"I don't—" She stopped. There were three figures at the end of the alley. It was too dark to make them out. But if she had to fight all three right now to get away, so be it. "Clear off, you blighters!"

"Miss Bess?" one of the figures asked.

"That really you?"

"Who's that?"

The figures moved closer . . . now she could see they weren't gang boys, but kids. Her boys. Enick, Telly, and Nikey. Nikey was up and about.

"Boys," she said. "Good to see you."

"You've been in a scrap," Nikey said. "Who's he?"

"A friend," Mila said.

"He's the one who right slapped Conor and the Scratches," Telly said.

Nikey nodded. "So he is a friend."

"And he needs help," Mila said. "Something to eat, somewhere to rest."

Enick and Telly came over and helped support Veranix, who looked like he couldn't even stand on his own anymore. "We know just the place."

Mila was dead. Stupid girl. Helene should have scared her off completely before. Helene wanted to cry, but she couldn't, not in front of this crowd.

The winged mage landed again. "That was fun. Do we do another?"

The boss had gotten back up, untangling Mila's rope from his neck with the help of one of his stooges. "No, let's get back before there's any more surprises."

"A little insurance against that," Ecrain said. Suddenly they were engulfed in darkness. Helene couldn't see anything, could only feel Ecrain's hot breath on her neck, her grubby hand squeezing her arm.

"Follow me," she heard the dressy mage say, and she was dragged along through the darkness. After several stumbling steps, the dark melted away, and they were all in a well-appointed sitting room. Or at least, it had been well-appointed, but there had been a knock-down brawl here.

And that brawl had put Nange Lesk down, as he was lying on the carpet, moaning and bleeding.

"Help," he said weakly.

"Blazes happened to him?" Almer asked. Almer seemed to not care one rutting bit about what was happening. Captured and abducted by mages, about to be killed or tortured? He looked like that was an average day to him.

"That Rynax fellow did," the lady mage in the yellow dress said. She was in the process of peeling the dress off, as it was caked with blood. Someone had gotten a good piece of her, at least. "He is an associate of yours?"

"We've met," Helene said cautiously.

"You've met," the suit said, shaking his head. "I think it's more than that. You work for Olivette—"

"Who is Olivette?" Helene asked, but then the memory kicked in. Pilsen was a bit out of sorts, not sure what he was supposed to do. And Asti told him, "You're playing Olivette." Somehow Pilsen's performance had spiraled out of control to the thugs out here thinking he was a real guy, a player.

"I've never heard of him," Kennith said.

"Me either," Almer said. "Someone going to get him a doctor or something?"

"Aren't you a doctor?" the guy with the flaming wings said.

"No, I'm a chemist. Don't handle the same things at all."

"Please, help," Nange said.

"Saints," Helene said, crouching in front of Nange. She didn't like him, but there was no need to be cruel. "You want to be treated or just choke you out of misery?"

"Doctor, please."

Ecrain grabbed Helene by the shoulder and pulled her up, and in the same moment there was a singe and spark of heat and energy that tore through her shoulder, down to the pit of her stomach.

"Don't touch him," she said.

"The woman has a point," the suit said. "We should either kill him or treat him. Send for a doctor, if for no other reason than to use as a bargaining chip."

"Shame you tore up the doctor's office," Almer said.

The suit's fist flew out, cracking Almer in the jaw, sending him down to the ground in a heap.

"Hey!" Kennith shouted.

"Be glad you are all useful enough to keep alive!" the suit shouted. "I want my merchandise, and one way or another you will help me get it. And if you're very lucky, you'll still have your black skin at the end of it all."

Kennith jumped at him, but the goons grabbed him and tore him back down to the ground with punches and kicks.

"Enough, enough," the suit said. "No need to belabor this. You, miss? Are you smarter than your friends?"

"Not particularly," Helene said. "No one ever accused me of being smart."

"Smartest thing anyone's said here tonight," the suit said.

Two more goons came into the house. "Nothing, boss."

The suit's face fell. "Then get back out there. Find her! All of you!"

"And these folks?" one of the other goons asked. The suit looked to the mage in the yellow dress, who was now half out of the dress, far more interested in the wound on her side.

"In the basement," she said dismissively. "Solid doors and stone walls."

"And no screams will be heard," Ecrain said. She grabbed Helene by the hair. "Which is good, because I want to play with this one."

Chapter 21

VERCI RODE TO HAL AND Lian's house, telling himself over and over that he was taking care of the most important thing, getting Raych safe. That was what Asti wanted him to do. What Helene wanted him to do. He wasn't abandoning anyone, he was doing his job.

This was his job.

They reached the house with no small amount of spectacle. They were quite a few blocks away from the brannigans at either Gelson's office or the mage house, the folks around here surely weren't expecting anyone to gallop up the street at this hour.

"This is it?" Jhoqull asked as Verci dismounted.

"Yes," Verci said. "I'll make sure she's settled here, and then you and I—"

"You are not going anywhere, Verci!" Raych said.

"I need to—"

"I will tell you—" Raych started. She looked about at the passersby. Several people were staring at them, which made sense. Verci was armed for bear, with darts and gadgetry unlike anything most people around here had seen. Raych looked like she had been through the blazes, with a bandage on her head, her clothes covered in dirt and blood. Jhoqull stood out just being a Ch'omik woman, let alone one with tattooed and scarred arms and several wicked blades. "You need to get in that house and we talk about it there."

"We're going in."

"Go in faster!" she said, pushing him up the stoop to the door.

He opened the door carefully. "Hal, Lian, are you there?"

Raych gave no such caution, pushing past him into their sitting room. "Lian!" Verci found himself pulled along inside, and then Raych ran into the kitchen in a state. "Lian! Hal!"

Verci realized Jhoqull was standing next to him. "I didn't think you would—"

"Those horses need water and care," she said. "They aren't used to being ridden, they're not happy."

"Lian!"

Hal and Lian came down the narrow stairs, Lian carrying Corsi, Hal holding a knife. He held it like it was the first time he'd ever picked one up.

"Raychelle!" Lian exclaimed, pushing past her husband and almost leaping upon her sister. "I thought you were—"

"I almost was—"

"But you're—"

"What is going on?" Hal shouted. He was staring at Verci. "I mean, I mean, saints almighty, what is this?"

Verci wasn't sure where to start. "A lot has happened today."

"But—what are you wearing? What is *that* on your arm? What the blazes—"

"Language," Lian said.

"I think this is a moment where I am entitled!" Hal said. "And, I mean, who is this woman you've brought into my home?"

"Begging your pardon," Jhoqull said, the harsh tones of her accent now almost melodic. "But the horses out there need water, and rubbing with wool if you have a blanket you could spare."

Hal stammered in confusion. "Well, I—that is . . . horses, you say?"

"I know it's an inconvenience," Jhoqull said. "If they could be secured in the back garden, that would be ideal. I fear their safety on the street."

"I—yes, of course—that is—I think I can—" He shook a finger at Verci. "I'm not done with you, mister." He led Jhoqull back outside.

"I understand," Verci said. He looked back to Raych, who was now sitting on the couch, Corsi in her arms, looking like she would never let him go.

"I should—" Verci said.

"You will do nothing that involves leaving my sight," Raych said. "May Acser help me, you aren't even going to the water closet without me, Verci Rynax."

"I can't—"

"What happened?" Lian asked. She looked at Verci, her eyes wide. "You said you were going to find her, but . . . by all the prophets, I didn't think you would . . ."

"It's madness," Raych said. "And it's the trouble your brother brought on us."

That was it. "Asti is still out there."

"And Asti can handle his own business."

"What about Helene, Julien, Mila . . ."

"I didn't marry them!" Raych said. "I'm sorry if . . . all of this means everyone is in trouble now, but we have to think about our own."

"All of our own," Verci said.

"Right here, this is all that you need to take care of," Raych said. "I was almost killed at least twice tonight, thanks to Asti's little war."

"Little what?" Lian asked. "What is going on?"

"Tell her, Verci," Raych said. "Tell my sister, tell Hal, what exactly you and your brother have been up to. And why that put our lives in danger."

Lian looked up to him, her eyes piercing. "You knew

what was going on this morning. As soon as you heard she was missing, you knew."

Verci couldn't hold back anymore. "That's because I am exactly what you always feared of me. I am exactly the thief and conman and killer that you've always presumed I really was."

"My—" Lian said.

"Verci," Raych started.

"No, if we're going to do it, we're going to do all of it. I am the guy people call upon when they want something stolen. Or smuggled. Or forged. Or if you need something built to help you do those things."

Lian was fanning herself. "Raych, you . . . you knew this?"

"Always," Raych said. "But he had given that up. All of it, to start the shop."

"And then there was the fire, and we lost everything. So Asti and I went back into the old life."

"Asti," Hal said from the doorway. "So he's just the same. That story about him working for the government, is that sewage?"

"Hal, language!"

"Is it?" Hal insisted.

"No, it isn't," Verci said. "But . . . that work took its toll on him. A harder toll than you can even imagine. That's why we took him in."

"That's why he's dangerous," Hal said. "And you are as well."

"Yeah, we are," Verci said. He went over to the cabinet where Hal kept his stash of brandy, brought out the bottle. "But you know who else is? The folks who started that fire. The folks who burned out a hundredsome people on Holver Alley, and killed dozens more, just to buy some land."

"Wait, what?"

Verci poured two brandies, and gave one to Hal. Hal looked perplexed by the gesture, but took it.

"The fire, part of a scheme. Those riots on election

night, part of a scheme. And the drugs coming into this neighborhood now, part of a scheme."

"Drugs? Scheme?" Lian asked.

Verci took a swig of the brandy. Hal had good taste in the stuff, he'd credit him that.

"There are people looking to bleed out this neighborhood," he told Lian. "I can't tell you who they all are, but the people who grabbed Raych this morning work for them. The people I went after today work for them."

"But drugs?" Hal asked.

"They were coming in last night. Asti and I got in there and got hold of them, destroyed them. So those people came for us. Came for Raych. And it's now a war in the streets."

"A war you started?" Hal asked.

"A war that was coming." Jhoqull came in from the back through the kitchen. "The Rynax brothers were the ones who were willing to fight in it. The rest of this neighborhood clearly cowered, hoping it would slip away."

"Who is she?" Lian asked, looking to Raych.

"I . . . just met her," Raych said. "You're Kennith's friend?"

"Kh'enta is my lover," Jhoqull said. "And I am Jhoqull-Ra of House Gheqham, daughter of Hejha-Cha, daughter of Kecelle-Amra, daughter of—"

"I think I get it," Raych said. "You were part of this drug robbery. You brought her in?"

"Needed a driver," Verci said.

"So, let me get this clear," Hal said. "You stole from the drug sellers, so they couldn't sell the drugs in this neighborhood. And now those sellers, they abducted Raych this morning. But you rescued her."

"No, she rescued herself," Verci said. "But then she went to the constables, and stumbled on crooked constables who tried to drag her back—"

Hal drank his brandy and then poured himself another glass. "This is too much. This has been happening all this time?"

"All this time," Verci said.

"And you stood for that?" Lian asked.

"I know it was necessary," Raych said. "But there needs to be a line, Verci. We need to stop all this."

"I would love for it to stop, Raych, you know I would." He took the gauntlet off his arm. "I would love to not have one more gig, and just build toys and raise our son." He put the gauntlet on the table, then took off the bandolier of darts, and laid it there as well. "I would love all of that. But that's not what we have right now."

"Just walk away," Raych said.

"Can he?" Hal asked. "Can you?"

"If we get this mess settled, maybe," Verci said. "But I need to go—"

"I don't want you to go!" Raych said. "I couldn't bear it."

"Rynax," Jhoqull said. "The horses need to rest, or they'll be no good. The same is true for you."

"I need—"

"No," Raych said, standing up and coming to him. "Let's just . . . get some sleep. Figure out the next thing in the morning."

Verci wanted to argue. He wanted to tell her he wasn't about to abandon anyone to the night. But she was right. His head was pounding, his eyes heavy. "But Asti . . ."

"Can take care of himself," Raych said. "For tonight, he can."

Verci didn't agree. Didn't want to agree. But he didn't want to fight with her right now.

Because one thing was true—she was here, she was safe, and so was Corsi. His family was safe, and he wanted to stay with them.

He took his wife into an embrace. "You're right. I'll stay here."

He hoped Asti would forgive him. He hoped they all would forgive him.

By the time Mila had finished dragging Veranix up to the flop, his magical disguise had faded. No shadow covering his face, the scratches and scorches on his costume all plainly visible. Fortunately, none of the boys seemed to care too much about who he was.

"I think he needs food," she told Nikey. "You boys have any?"

"Not a lot, I don't think."

Mila handed him a few coins. "You know Jonet's Clay Bowl? The Fuergan place. They should still be open."

"I know where it is, never been in."

"Well, go in, and tell the Jonets that Mila and . . . and her friend from last night need what they had last night. Twice as much. Or whatever they can give you." She looked at Nikey, Enick, and Telly. All three of them looked like bones. She dug a few more coins out of her pocket. "As much as they can give all of you."

"Thanks, Miss," Telly said. "Best save a few coins. Mister Cobie ain't here right now, but when he comes back, he'll be a bit salted about you being here. A few ticks will ease his rile."

That was good to know. These boys were living under someone's grace, probably grifting and picking to earn their keep. "Mister Cobie, how is he?"

"He's decent," Enick said. "For a gruff bastard. He don't leave here too often but he will thrash folks who cause us trouble. He's off with Peeky right now to lay into a Potato Boy who robbed Peeky."

"Potato—that'd be good," Veranix mumbled. He pawed at the pouch at his belt, which Mila opened up. A couple scraps of dried meat, just slivers. She put them in Veranix's mouth for all the good it would do.

"Any food you have now," Mila said. "And run for Jonet's."

Telly came over with a half loaf of stale bread. "All we got right now."

"We'll run for more, though," Enick said. "Glad you're back, Miss Bessie."

The boys all ran off.

Mila tried to feed the bread to Veranix, who ate it

from her hand, like he was too exhausted to move. While he ate, she looked around. She realized this place had been burned out in the Holver Alley fire, but not so badly that one couldn't squat here. It wasn't too different from the one she and Jina had been staying in the night of the fire.

"Better," Veranix said weakly. "Are you all right?"

"Me?" she asked. "You're the one as weak as a kitten."

"I'll recover," he said. "But get the cloak off me."

She helped get it off, him wincing as he moved his arms. "Why do you want it off?"

"It draws magic to me, but in an unnatural way. Hard to gauge when I'm too far in. Better to have it off to recover."

"If you say so," Mila said. "How bad are you hurt?"

"I'm not sure. Nothing stretches and *oxaym* won't cure."

"Oxaym?"

"Racquin healing brew. Disgusting stuff, but it works."

"If you say so," she said. He took the rest of the bread from her and ate it. Again, he winced when he moved his arm. "You're bad off, should I look at that?"

He sighed. "Help me get the vest off."

She did so, and in getting that off, his shirt came open. His chest—lean and muscular—was a mess of bruises and scars.

"Saints, how—" She hesitated to touch it.

"Nothing that won't heal," he said. "I asked if you were all right."

"I'm fine," Mila said.

"You nearly died."

"You caught me," she said. "Which was . . . where even were you?"

"Verci and I were at the mage house, and I went after Fenmere's people, and I got drawn away from the rest of the fight. By the time I realized they had all gotten to your safehouse, it was too late. I saw that guy with the wings—and what's with him taking the Firewing name so literally?"

"I know!" Mila said, laughing despite herself. She found her hand on his chest now, his warm skin just under her fingertips. She imagined she could feel the flow of magic through him, but maybe that was just . . .

"He launched up with you, and I couldn't—I don't know how to fly. But when he threw you down . . ."

"There you were," she said.

"And thank every saint I didn't miss." He smiled as he said this, too perfect, too pretty. She moved closer on instinct, and before she even knew why, she was kissing him.

Kissing and her hand on his chest and then her hands moved on his skin and his hands were on her hips and she had never kissed anyone or touched anyone like this and all she wanted was to touch his skin and him to touch hers and she moved on top of him pulling up her skirt—

"What in saints and sinners is this?"

Mila launched off of Veranix's hot and beautiful body like magic and everything holy compelled her. A paunchy man was in the doorway, Peeky by his side.

"Miss Bessie, your shirt's open," Peeky said.

Mila grabbed her blouse and turned around to fix the laces.

"You know this spread of butter, Peeky?" the man said.

"She's Miss Bessie. Don't know the steve."

"I'm no steve," Veranix protested.

"Cover yourself, boy, I don't need to see that," the old man said. "And I don't know why I shouldn't beat you both into tar and blood."

"Nikey and the others brought us here, Mister Cobie," Mila said, turning back around once she was satisfied she looked presentable. "We've been in something of a tussle and needed a place to lay low."

"This is my place," he said, raising an eyebrow. "I don't run an inn or nothing."

"I understand," Mila said, coming over to him. "But I think you should be properly compensated nonetheless." She handed him a few coins. Not all she had, but nearly a whole crown's worth.

"Hmmm," he said, looking at the coins. "Well, that's easier than the beating."

"Appreciated," she said.

He raised an eyebrow. "This tussle wasn't that whole fracas that ran from Holver and up Fawcett to Heel? I heard a whole lot of ruckus that ways."

"That was us, sir," Veranix said, now shakily on his feet.

"Do you mind if we lay low here a bit, Mister Cobie?" Mila asked. "Rest for a few hours?"

"You paid me, and you're decent polite," he said, scratching at his beard. "And the boy likes you."

"Today I like her," Peeky said. "And he's got a bow, that's neat."

Cobie nodded, and grabbed a jug from the cabinet, taking a swig from it. "So you two can stay a bit. But there's just the one bed."

Mila looked over at Veranix, her heart suddenly pounding. "If that's all there is . . ." she started.

"There is, and it's mine. You two get that patch of floor, and stop making a spectacle of yourself." He shook his head as he went to the back room. "There's young boys in this place, by the saints."

Chapter 22

ASTI WAS AWARE OF SUNLIGHT and pain before anything else. His head hammered, and he didn't want to open his eyes. The light was already too bright.

"Close the shade," he muttered, not sure of who he was talking to. Not sure where he was, what had happened. The last memories were a blur. He was on the street, fighting the Poasian Thurgir, with Julien. And he lost control. No.

He had surrendered control. He let the beast fight for him. He didn't control the situation. He had no idea what he had done, where he was, where anyone else was, or what else had happened.

He had no idea if Verci or anyone else was still alive, or even safe. It was morning, so it had been hours. Anything could have happened. Anyone might be dead.

"I got it." Julien's voice. So whatever else had happened, he had stayed with Julien. Or more correctly, Julien had stayed with him. As Asti heard the shade closing, he wondered what Julien had gone through over the course of the night.

"Where are we?" Asti asked. "Where is everyone?"

"Everyone?" Julien asked. "I don't know. Are you still you?"

Asti opened his eyes, and even in the dim candlelight, it was still like a knife stabbing into his head. "I guess that means I wasn't for a while."

"Not really," Julien said.

"Sorry," Asti said. "I must have terrified you."

"No, I—" Julien sat down next to Asti. Asti realized he was on a cot in a small, unremarkable room. The only thing of note was the scent, which Asti couldn't quite place. "I know I'm . . . I know a few years ago I got my skull kicked in, and before that happened, I was a different guy. I know that I will never be that guy again. But I do remember being him. Sometimes, little bits of the memory of him come up. Is that what happens with you?"

"Sometimes I think I'm just the memory, Jules," Asti said. "I didn't hurt you, did I?"

"No," Julien said. "You went wild fighting that Poasian, like an animal. And it was a great fight, I—I ain't seen nothing like that."

"Not sure what that means."

"But then the other Poasian showed up, and he said something in Poasian, and the first one ran off. Then he said something to you and you stopped fighting. You fell down, like you fell straight asleep. He told me to carry you here to recover, and here we are."

"A Poasian told you—where—" The smell made sense now. "Nafath!"

The door of the small room opened. "Ah, gentlemen, you're awake." Khejhaz Nafath came in, a disturbing smile on his face. "I trust you have recovered what wits you have, Asti."

"I'm here and talking," Asti said. "Though I wonder why I am here, of all places. This is your shop?"

"This is my home, Asti, which I have welcomed you and your large friend into. But it is adjacent to my shop, so the confusion is reasonable."

"Why—"

"Last night was quite the fracas, and I presumed you were in a state which demanded you rest and be kept safe from potential assault. Since we are old friends, I provided that."

"So you know him?" Julien asked.

"I do," Asti said. "Jules, this is Khejhaz Nafath, spice merchant and spy."

"I am only a spice merchant, my friend. You of all people should know that 'spy' is a tenuous job you don't get to keep when mistakes are made."

"Is he a spy?" Julien asked.

"Yes," Asti said. "So, you just showed up when I was fighting that other Poasian."

"That other Poasian was a Thurgir, and not just any Thurgir, but part of a *nazhnet adjh.* Do you know what that is?"

Asti's Poasian was limited to a few phrases. "That's 'kill crew,' yes?"

"A crude but functional translation," Nafath said. "I have no idea why such a man would be in Druthal, and certainly do not know why he was trying to kill you, but any reason is terrifying."

"But you told him to go," Julien said.

"Is that what I did?" Nafath said. "Asti, you didn't tell me your large friend is fluent in Poasian. He would be the first of your people to achieve that."

"That's not what you did?" Julien asked.

"Not exactly," Nafath said. "I know a few phrases of authority—a remnant from my previous career—to establish that you were a part of my mission for the *Pankchamnta*, so if he killed you it would be . . . troublesome. So he left you breathing."

"You saved me," Asti said. "Saved both of us, and protected us. And you've gotten *rijetzh* to me twice to help deal with mages."

"I didn't do anything of the sort. I simply thought your sister-in-law's baking would benefit from its inclusion."

"I don't—"

"And so you know, your brother and his wife are both alive and safe, at her sister's home. As is that *mnegh* woman."

Asti wasn't sure what that insult meant. "Helene?"

"No, the Ch'omik one." Nafath made a horrifying noise from the back of his throat.

"You wouldn't happen to know anything about the rest of my crew, would you?"

"Not at this time. I only know about the Acserian sisters because I have an ear tied to this community, and people were, of course, concerned about all the goings-on last night."

"You know what the mages and Fenmere are up to, and how that ties to having a Poasian secret policeman keeping guard."

"Who can say what I know," Nafath said. "I do know that if a Thurgir is involved, then the Poasian parties interested in this affair are looking for a final solution, if you will."

"Meaning?"

Nafath sighed, like he was annoyed by having to spell out explicitly what he was talking about. "Second chances are not the way of my people. So if smuggling the *efhân* through here is a failure, they will not be interested in backing it any further."

"So the Thurgir represents the 'either this works or it doesn't' phase of things?" Asti asked.

"If he decides it's not worth it," Julien said. "They don't sell the drugs here?"

"Without the Poasian backing, that's almost enough to draw a line in the street against Fenmere," Asti said.

"He needs their partnership," Nafath said. "Or at least, that's what I would guess, given how my people behave. I'm just a spice merchant."

"Who saved me," Asti said.

"I told that Thurgir the truth, Asti Rynax. I find you useful to my ends."

"Which are?" Asti asked.

"Mine," Nafath said. "For now, I'll just say that neither the Firewings nor Fenmere in this part of town are things that suit me, and as my own capacity to deal with them is limited, I'll happily enable yours."

Asti didn't trust that at all. Especially since Julien said Nafath's words put Asti to sleep when he was in beast mode.

The beast was silent right now. Asti hadn't realized that.

Right now, neither the beast or Liora were speaking to him. That was a relief, even if it left him feeling oddly disconcerted. Almost empty. But he liked the quiet, for once.

There was far more to reckon with Nafath, but this was not the moment.

Asti got up from the cot, seeing that his boots, waistcoat, belt, and knives were in a neat pile on the floor. "You didn't need to do that, Julien."

"I just wanted you to rest," Julien said. "Are we going?"

"We're going," Asti said, gathering his things and getting his boots on. "Nafath, I appreciate your hospitality."

Nafath opened the door that led out the back stairs to the alley behind his shop. "I will be available for all your spice needs, my friend. Above all else, I would never want to lose such a good customer."

Asti walked out into the harsh morning sun—how was it so hot so early this late in the year?—squinting as he oriented himself. Julien came up behind him.

"So where are we going?"

"To end this."

Verci had slept far heavier than he thought he would. The sun was well up when he woke, and he heard voices downstairs. Raych and Lian. And Jhoqull.

He took a few moments to check himself over. His left arm was doing better, though he didn't quite have the full range of motion he wanted there. The wound was no longer seeping, though it could probably use a salve from Almer to avoid infection. The cut on his foot was much the same way. It looked a bit frightful, but it no longer hurt to bear weight. It should heal cleanly enough.

He found his clothing and equipment had been spirited away while he was asleep, and in its place, a set of clothes that had to be Hal's. Charcoal gray slacks and waistcoat, with a linen round-collar and white cravat. Verci put it on, surprised that it fit relatively decently. It must have been a few years old, from when Hal was skinnier. Shined work shoes were waiting for him as well.

Verci had to admit, looking down at himself, that he looked exactly like a respectable shopkeeper should.

He went downstairs to find the ladies in the kitchen, listening enraptured as Jhoqull told a story of some grim battle. He came in just as she said, "and cut his heart out, to present it to her lover."

"Well, that's something," Verci said. "Good morning."

"Morning," Raych said, getting up from the table to kiss him. "Jhoqull was telling us about her great-great-great-*great*-grandmother's victories against the Shekum Tar."

"That's a lot of greats," Verci said. He had no idea who the Shekum Tar were, but that was the other side of the world.

"And she earned them," Jhoqull said. "What are your intentions, Verci?"

"That's a very good question. I noticed my weapons and gear are . . . missing."

"I put them in a trunk," Raych said. "I would hope you don't need them today."

"I would hope that as well, but I don't know," Verci said. He poured himself a cup of tea from the pot on the table. He noticed Lian, who was holding Corsi, made a point of not looking at him. "I don't know anything. I should find, well, everyone, and see what's happening out there. For all we know, Josie's people are combing the streets for us."

"Or the constables ironed them up and the streets are clear," Lian said.

"Doubtful," Raych said with an ugly scoff.

"I would love to be that fortunate," Verci said. "But the main thing is, I cannot hide in here all day."

"Should we?" Lian asked, still looking at the ground.

"We weren't sure if we should get to the bakery today or not," Raych said. "Saints and prophets, the place is likely a mess."

"I want to tell you everything is going to be normal again," Verci said. "But I need to find out what's going on, and then see how to get things right again."

"What'll that take?" Raych asked.

"I don't even know," Verci said. He scowled. "I mean, the easier thing to do is go to Josie, beg forgiveness, and hope she decides to go back to how things were."

"Beg forgiveness for what?" Raych said.

"Doesn't matter. Josie likes a good display of humility. I don't like it—Asti would *hate* it—but if that keeps you safe."

Raych scowled. "I'm guessing that *safe* would only last so long. Until Asti punches the bear again, or Josie or someone else decides to cross the line."

"That's about right," Verci said.

"What's another way?" Raych asked.

"I would like to know as well," Jhoqull said. "I'm anxious to find Kennith and make sure he is well."

"Maybe you take the horses to the carriage house at the North Seleth?" Verci suggested. "I could go with you if you needed."

Jhoqull chuckled. "I think you are needed elsewhere. Do I leave word for you here if I find anything of note?"

Verci looked to Lian. "Is that all right?"

Lian got up from the table, now not looking at anyone. "If that's what has to happen I suppose that's what it's going to be."

Jhoqull nodded. "I will be in touch. And if this

comes to a war, I will call on House Gheqham, such as we are in this city—"

"Let's hope it doesn't come to that," Verci said.

"Thank you for your hospitality," Jhoqull said to Lian. "That kindness will be paid back to you, by me or my house."

She went out the back.

"So, what is the plan, then?" Raych asked. "Where are we going?"

"We?"

"I'm not leaving your side, I've been very clear on this," Raych said.

"But what if—"

"Not. Leaving. Your side." She smiled demurely. "Lian is quite happy to lock herself in here and take care of Corsi."

"Yes," Lian said quickly.

"So, are we going to the bakery, to the Gadgeterium, to Missus Holt? Because if it's the latter I will have words for her."

Verci bit his lip to hide his smile. "I think we need to find Asti first. So start at the Gadgeterium, and then—"

Someone pounded on the door.

"They're here!" Lian shouted. "We'll be killed!"

Verci instinctively shushed her. "Where is that trunk?"

"In the sitting room," Raych said.

Verci slipped into the next room, popped open the trunk, and took out the bandolier of darts, palming three of them. Signaling to Raych to stay back, he went to the window, as another series of pounds came.

Verci slid the shade a bit to look, and when he saw who it was, let out a sigh of relief.

"Asti and Julien," he said to Raych as he opened the door.

"Well, that's one thing solved," Raych said.

Asti grabbed Verci in a tight embrace as soon as he came in. "I'm sorry, I'm sorry," he said. "I should have looked for you sooner, I should have been—there's no excuse."

Verci found himself hugging his brother just as tightly. "No, I did the same thing. Just, we got separated, we got skunked, we didn't have a plan . . ."

"We need to always have a plan."

"Get out of the doorway and let Julien come in," Raych said, pulling Verci and Asti inside. "You hungry, Julie?"

"Sure," he said, coming in and taking off his cap. "Who's here? Just you?"

"Jhoqull was here," Verci said. "She just left to see if she could find Kennith."

"And Helene?" Julien asked. "You haven't—"

"Julie, we'll find her," Asti said. "Last we saw, Kennith, Helene, and Almer were grabbed by the mages and Fenmere's men. We're going to need to do something to rescue them. If it's not too late."

"Don't say that!" Julien shouted.

"Sorry," Asti said.

Verci brought Asti into the sitting room, noticing Lian still in the kitchen, watching all of them with concern. "So what do we do?"

"That doesn't involve a war in the streets," Raych said.

"Raych," Asti said, going over to her. He made like he was going to take her hands, but then pulled away, like he wasn't sure if he should make any sort of tactile gesture to her. "What happened to you was unforgivable. We're going to make sure Josie and Lesk's crew all know that, no matter what."

"I think I want to draw a line somewhere before 'no matter what,'" Raych said. "But I appreciate the thought."

"You know what she did to escape, don't you?" Asti said, turning to Verci. "Your wife was tied up, but she just broke through the rope. She's that strong."

Raych didn't say anything there, but she gave Asti a small nod of acknowledgment.

"She's pretty incredible," Verci said. "So how do we get out of this mess?"

"I've been thinking," Asti said. "The Fenmere cartel and the mages are in our territory, and we've got to make them want to pull out. Give up on North Seleth."

"How, when Josie is welcoming them?"

"Because they think another player is on the scene, the one who stole the drugs."

"That's us, though," Verci said.

"But they—and Josie—think it's Olivette."

Verci burst out laughing. "Was that what that was?"

"Who is Olivette?" Raych asked.

"He—" Verci could barely control his laughter. "He doesn't exist. He was a ruse Dad had cooked up to fleece people with. A boss no one saw."

"But Mister Corman thinks Olivette has his drugs," Asti said. "So I'm thinking we arrange a meeting between Olivette and Corman, use that meeting to muscle them out of the neighborhood, rescue Helene and the others, and draw some new lines that maybe we can force Josie to respect."

"That's a scheme, all right," Verci said. "And it would need Pilsen, wouldn't it?"

"Pilsen and Vellun, going against Josie," Asti said. "I think we can trust them, but . . ."

"Keep it to just them," Verci said. "Don't drag the whole theater troupe into it."

"You say that like you're not coming," Asti said.

"Because I shouldn't," Verci said, a plan coming together in his head. "We've don't have a lot of time, and there's only the four of us."

"Four?" Asti asked, looking to Raych. "You're in?"

"I'm not leaving Verci's side," she said.

Asti nodded. "So what's your idea?"

"You and Julien get to Pilsen and Vellun. Get them ready to meet later today. Meanwhile, Raych and I go to Josie to arrange the meeting."

"You're up for that?" Asti asked.

"We can do it," Raych said. "It'll be better coming from us. They won't have their guard up as much."

"All right. Make it two bells at Kimber's," Asti said.

"Why Kimber's?" Julien asked.

"It'll give the sense of a neutral space, but we'll have the advantage," Asti said. "Though what other assets do we have?"

"Jhoqull and House Gheqham will answer our call to war," Raych said. "For what that's worth."

Asti scratched at his chin. "A dozen Ch'omik warriors wouldn't be the worst thing. And is the Thorn still a player in all this?"

Verci shrugged. "He's a good kid, and we shouldn't count him out, but we certainly shouldn't count on him, either. We don't know what happened to him last night, or how to reach him."

"Right," Asti said. His face went pale. "Do we have any idea where Mila is?"

"Hey, hey, you kids going to sleep all day or something?"

Mila woke, arms wrapped around Veranix, his around her. She wasn't sure when in the night that had happened, but she liked to wake up that way.

"What?" Veranix said groggily. "What time is it?"

"I don't know," Mila said.

"About eight bells," Cobie said. Mila looked to see he had the boys—Nikey, Enick, Peeky, and Telly—sitting around the table eating the remains of the Fuergan feast. For a moment, it made her think of her father at the breakfast table. Way back, before Mama was sick, before they lost it all, before he—things she tried not to think about, but the memory hit her so clearly. She realized she had been staring and shook herself out of it.

"Didn't mean to sleep that long," Mila said, looking for her boots.

"Definitely not," Veranix said, looking about for his gear.

"Going back out there?" Peeky asked. "It's pretty wild after last night."

"Define wild," Mila said.

Nikey answered. "There's a whole mess of Scratch Cats camped around the Elk Street, Crease Knockers at the Honey Hut, Potato Boys and Three-Fingers at Holver Alley. Just out there in the street."

"Constables?" Veranix asked as he put on his clothes.

"Staying clear," Nikey said.

"You boys should do the same," Mila said. "Don't get involved."

"You sure?" Enick asked.

"Look, boys," she said. "I screwed up with you. And I let the Old Lady get her fingers in you all."

"Got us sent to Gorminhut, you did," Peeky said. "But we got out."

"Tarvis got us out," Nikey said. "That kid, he—" He shook his head. "Deep down, he still believes, I think."

"I thought that was just you," Mila said.

"Still do," he said.

"Even in Conor?"

"Even," he said with a grin. "Though I'm glad you two sponked him."

"Mila," Veranix said, now fully suited up as the Thorn again. "I need to get back to campus *now.*"

"We need to sort what's going on here," Mila said.

"I agree," he said. "But I need to check in or else my people will raise some hell. Possibly with constables."

"Right," she said. "Then let's go."

"Together?"

"Quick jaunt east, and then back. Let's do it." She turned to Cobie. "You—be good to these boys or you will answer to me."

"Yeah," he said. "I got them, ma'am."

Mila wasn't sure, but her gut told her he was being legit. He cared for these boys. Good.

"Mila," Veranix said at the window to the iron back stairs. "Let's go." He offered his hand, which she took gladly.

In moments, they were soaring over rooftops, crossing North Seleth and Keller Cove and Dentonhill before reaching the University of Maradaine. They landed behind a grove of trees near the northeastern wall, and Veranix's appearance magically altered to a school uniform.

"What about me?" she asked, looking at her own outfit. It was shabby, but fortunately not torn up or too dirty.

He scowled. "I can't do too much about that. Besides, we aren't exactly here to be seen by the general populace."

They came out from behind the trees onto a walkway, and for a moment, Mila thought her heart would explode. The whole place was a miracle of green. Trees and grass and perfectly manicured walkways and grand brick buildings with ivy growing up the side.

"You all right?" Veranix asked. She had stopped dead in the middle of the walkway.

"Sorry, I just . . . I didn't know what to expect but—" Her eyes were tearing up.

"You're here in what? Two days?"

"Yeah," she said.

"You're going to do great. But let's move."

He led her to a storage shack behind one of the buildings, and with a wave of his hand, the door unlatched, and he let her in. Once inside, he moved a tarp-covered box, revealing a trapdoor. He opened it up and went down, calling for her to follow.

"Kai?" he called out as he went down the ladder. "Are you here? Delmin?"

"Is this your safehouse?" Mila asked as she got to the bottom. It wasn't quite decked out like the Old Lady had the warehouse, but it did have a table covered in files and papers and a basket of apples, a wall of faces and names and maps that looked like the kind Asti would make, and a weapons rack, mostly with arrows.

A young dark-skinned woman was at the weapons rack, selecting a fighting stick from there. "I was about to bring in the brigade," she said. She turned and noticed Mila. "Who's she?"

"This is Mila—I didn't catch your family name."

"Kendish," Mila offered, extending a hand to the young woman. "Mila Kendish."

"Kaiana Nell," the woman said, accepting it, though her eyes looked skeptical. "You bring just anyone down here now?"

"She's, you know, the Rose," Veranix said.

"Oh, the *Rose*," Kaiana said. "Well, that's different. You decided to come out here."

"Well, I am coming here," Mila said.

"What, as a student or something?" Kaiana asked incredulously.

"Yes, exactly. I start the day after tomorrow. Presuming we survive."

Kaiana made an odd noise. "So what's going on?" she asked Veranix as she grabbed an apple off the table and tossed it to him.

"Mostly, just letting you know I'm all right," Veranix said, catching the apple without even looking. "And to double-check a few of the notes."

"On?"

"Fenmere's man Corman, and the rest of the main bosses," Veranix said, going over to the table as he greedily ate the apple. "Corman is running things on this, it looks like."

Mila glanced at the papers he was looking through. "Are these Constabulary files?"

"They are," Veranix said. He grabbed two more apples and tossed one to Mila. "I've got a contact with them who—"

"Who wants to see Fenmere taken down as much as we do," Kaiana said. "Is that what you're interested in?"

Mila nodded. "I'll be honest, I hadn't even heard his name until a few nights ago. But his people and his drugs are pushing into my neighborhood, which has enough problems already." She looked about the room, which seemed to be some sort of old bunker or wine cellar. "How did you get this safehouse?" She took a bite of the apple, which was ridiculously sweet. Sweetest one she had ever tasted.

"It's a safehouse?" Kaiana asked. "I mean, I guess that works."

"Kai found it," Veranix said, thumbing through the file. "She's in charge of grounds on campus—"

"Second in charge," Kaiana said.

"And she lived in the old carriage house when she was one of the gardeners—"

That perked Mila's ears up. "Oh, you take care of the trees and lawns? They are gorgeous."

Kaiana's stern expression softened a little. "I supervise the people doing that now. But, yes."

"So the carriage house was where I would hide my gear, work out of . . ."

"Safehouse," Mila said. "That's the term."

"If you say," Veranix said. "But when Kai got promoted, she had to move out. But she also got access to charts and keys and archives, so . . ."

"So I found this chamber which dates back to when this part of campus was a monastery, and here we are."

"All right," Mila said. She wondered how much of this was an invitation. She was going to be on campus soon, and while she should be focused on studies, she had already proven to herself she could excel at learning without giving up the other activities in her life. Would the Thorn need a Rose? She couldn't tell if Kaiana filled that role at all. There certainly seemed to be friendship between her and Veranix, but nothing really more. After kissing and other things last night, how much was that just last night, how much was an intention for things to continue?

Right now, Veranix was all business, which she respected—they were in a crisis that needed to be resolved—but she couldn't help but have a burning need to know what he felt.

"I was right," he said. "Corman is Fenmere's closest lieutenant. He's basically the one who ran things while

Fenmere was out of town last month. We eliminate him—"

"You mean kill," Kaiana said.

"It's not like I can deliver him to the constables," Veranix said.

"Maybe I can, though," Mila said. "Lieutenant Covrane is one of the good ones, supposedly."

"Even the good ones can't move the whole system," Veranix said, tapping the files. "That's why I have this."

"Veranix," Kaiana said. "Where is your rope?"

"What?" Veranix asked.

"Your rope," Kaiana said, her voice rising. "Your unique, irreplaceable, napranium-weave rope? You don't have it. Where is it?"

Veranix's face went white. "I completely forgot."

"You forgot where it is?"

"No, I know where it is, and I'm sure it's safe, but—"

"But?" Kaiana asked.

"But Mila and I need to get back to North Seleth right away." He grabbed another file and handed it to Mila. "We'll need that."

"What's this?" Mila asked, looking at it. The charcoal sketch of a woman's face at the top of the file looked vaguely familiar.

"That is Miss Jads Farrell," he said. "Another top lieutenant in Fenmere's organization."

The woman in the suit at the mage house. "All right, and—"

"And I sort of left her tied up in a rooftop water tank all night, so let's get back."

Chapter 23

ASTI WASN'T SURE HOW THIS was going to play out. He was driving forward—like Dad always said, if it isn't skunked, drive forward. But driving forward meant sorting out his goals. First was rescuing Helene, Kennith, and Almer, assuming they were captured and still alive. Problem was, he had nothing to actually trade for them. No drugs, hardly any money. Which meant he had to use guile and bluster to negotiate.

What else did he want? What did winning look like right now? Mages out, Fenmere out, some sense of who or what was behind Andrendon, what they wanted. Josie paying them all back, paying for her sins. Lesk and his gangs out of North Seleth.

That wasn't going to happen today.

Julien didn't say much as they made their way to the West Birch Stage, slipping their way around the Scratch Cats and other gangs to avoid being spotted. Julien wasn't great at that part, but he followed instructions well. Even still, Asti would have preferred Verci at his side, with a lifetime of instincts keeping them on the same page.

Verci was right about the plan. Someone had to arrange the meeting, and someone had to get an Olivette.

Asti walked into the West Birch Stage—the doors were open now—to hear Vellun give a speech to the rest of the troupe.

"I need every one of you hungry in this. That's the crux of it. You need to perform with salivation."

"You want us to drool?" an actor asked.

"No, I want you to perform as if you are hungry for every word of the text, that you haven't eaten in weeks, and that stage is the table where you'll lay out your lust supper."

Pilsen waved him off. "You make this too complicated, dear. Just say the words clearly, with clear intention. The rest follows. Oh, look, there's Asti. Everyone, go about your business."

"Final rehearsal?" Asti asked as Pilsen and Vellun approached.

"Just about," Pilsen said. "So you finally came to check on us after the other night."

"We almost died, Asti," Vellun said sharply. "And it took you this long to make sure we were all right. Let alone pay us for the job."

Pilsen chuckled. "And he's not here for that. He's here because he needs us again."

"I do need you again," Asti said. "And I'm sorry I didn't—"

"Not one performance!" Pilsen said. "You haven't come out for one!"

"I'm coming to the opening of this on the eighteenth," Asti said. "But I can't if I'm dead, or Verci is, or North Seleth is all on fire. And I didn't check on you yesterday because Josie grabbed me, and then I was dragged about until sunrise this morning."

"Why are you here, Julien?" Vellun asked. "You don't usually—oh, saints, it's that bad, isn't it?"

"It's pretty bad," Julien said. "Asti and I escaped, and Verci and his wife are safe, but everyone else?" He shrugged. "We don't even know."

"So it's been a bit of business," Asti said. "Down here on West Birch, you're away from the war of North Seleth, so you don't know."

"We had a good taste the other night," Vellun said.

"Well, I need you. The crew needs you. You need money to help me, I'll get you money. You need me to apologize for how the other night went, I'm sorry. I didn't want anything to go that way. You want me to beg, I'll beg. I will get on the knee and cry to your saints, but help me."

Vellun and Pilsen looked at each other, and then gave polite applause. "A very good performance, Asti," Pilsen said. "Modified from one of the Whit romances, no?"

"*A Magician's Dalliance*," Vellun said. "And well done at that. Why is he not onstage?"

"Better things to do," Pilsen said.

"A busy man, so many tricks and ploys."

Asti looked about. "Do I need to join the troupe? Will that help?"

"It will always help," Vellun said.

"Did he come to audition?" Pilsen asked. "The show is cast."

"No, damn it," Asti said. Was Pilsen messing with him, or was he so addled that he had lost track of the conversation? "I came because everything is terrible, and I need you to play Olivette."

The name hit Pilsen like a snap. "What did you say?"

"Olivette," Asti said. "I told you to play him the other night."

"I remember," Pilsen said, though Asti wasn't sure he actually did. "But why do you—"

"Because Josie still thinks he's real," Asti said. "And you said the name the other night, they think he's got Fenmere's drugs."

"Rutting blazes!" Pilsen shouted. He looked about, seeing if anyone was marking them, and then lowered his voice. "That business the other night was fleecing Willem rutting Fenmere? Are you mad?"

"Yes, that's been established," Asti said.

"And Josie is in league with him now?"

"There's a tenuous partnership that's teetering off the bridge right now, thanks to the drugs being stolen. I'm hoping to push it all the way and keep Fenmere out of North Seleth completely."

"That's ambitious, Asti, I'll give you that." He looked to Vellun. "I think we should help."

"You sure?" Vellun asked.

"Yes. For a sizable donation to the West Birch Stage."

Asti wasn't sure whether to laugh or scream. "I . . . I can work that out. I don't have many crowns on me right now, but—"

"Oh, I'll trust you to be good for it. I imagine this all rests on Josie never finding out who Olivette actually was, or that you are pulling it on her again."

There was the canny conman. Asti still wasn't sure how much of Pilsen's doddering brain-addled persona was performance, but it was good to see the man he used to be—the man he needed—was still in there.

"Now," Pilsen said. "I assume you need to be there as yourself. But Julien here should be disguised as Olivette's muscle."

"Same as always," Julien said.

"It's how it goes," Pilsen said. Looking to Vellun, he added, "As for you, beauty, I think we need to do something you're going to hate."

"I don't want to be your son."

"You're going to be my son," Pilsen said. "Because I can see how we need to work this. Olivette left Maradaine for twenty years, and he came back to reclaim what was his, with his heir apparent."

"I like this a lot," Asti said.

"Good, because you'll be paying well for it. And *Corringshire* opens in two days; I expect you in the audience."

Asti let himself smile. "If my throat isn't slit before then, I'll be there."

Verci had kept the respectable outfit—he did look quite stylish in it, even if it was a few years out of date—but he still wore the gauntlet and his bandolier of darts. Somehow, the look still worked.

Raych had changed into one of her sister's dresses, the kind she would wear to church when she and Hal went. Raych augmented that look with an apron and a matching ribbon in her hair.

Raych had come up with a plan, and it was a good one, which meant stopping by the bakery. "I have pie in the icebox that will be just the thing to bring."

"A pie?"

"My father had a saying—an Acserian one—some people deserve a slap with a velvet glove."

"I'm not sure what that means."

"It means we bring a pie."

The next stop involved breaking into Almer's shop through the back door. He made a point of breaking in cleanly, so the locks wouldn't be damaged. It was crucial to lock it back up as well as possible, for Almer's sake. He would pay Almer back for what they took. This part of Raych's plan was delightfully devious, and fortunately everything in the shop was well organized and labeled. They found what they needed in a matter of minutes.

"Are we set?" Raych asked when they came out, ready to face Josie.

"I think so." He was quite on edge, but the streets were oddly subdued. Except in a few places, like on Holver Alley and near the Honey Hut, where gang boys were congregating far more brazenly than they usually did at midday. This was doubly true at the Elk Road Shack, where three dozen Scratch Cats were milling about around the door.

"I don't like this," Raych whispered as they approached.

"Just follow my lead," Verci said. He just kept walking until they were a few steps from the door of the Shack, and one of those Cats put a hand on his chest.

"What are you doing, pops?"

"I'm going to see the old lady, boy," Verci said. If they were going to be disrespectful, he'd throw it right back. "And no one who likes their face should get in my way."

The Cat turned to his fellows. "He thinks he's a tough—"

Verci aimed the gauntlet at the wall of the Shack and fired the acid. It hit the wall and sizzled hard and fast, quickly eating an ugly hole.

"So, who doesn't like their face?"

That was the only acid shot, but Verci hoped they weren't going to risk testing it. Scratch Cats weren't the type to call a bluff like that.

"Go on," the Cat said, waving him to the door.

"Thank you so much, gentlemen," Raych said as they approached the door and went inside.

The place was dim, and still something of a mess from yesterday's brawl. Even still, there were a few heavy drinkers already on the premises. One stood out.

"Kel Essin," Verci said. "Are you in charge here today?"

"I wouldn't put it that way," Kel said. For what it was worth, Kel had been a decent enough window-man, when he stayed sober. Verci wasn't sure why he had fallen in with Lesk's crew. Kel turned to one of the other boys. "Get us a table, some tea, and the Old Lady."

"Really?" the boy asked.

"Yeah," Kel said. The boy snapped his fingers, and a table was cleared off quickly. Kel sat down, and offered seats to Verci and Raych.

"So we're going to get to talk to her," Verci said.

"Ain't my job to be in between her and the rest of the world," Kel said. "Let me tell you, Rynax, none of this is how I wanted things. Nange said come do some jobs, Nange said we could be the bosses, that sounded good. I wasn't looking for any of this mess."

"With the Old Lady and mages and Fenmere?"

"The whole thing was Nange wanted to move on from the Old Lady. Now we work for her. Not my plan, Rynax."

"Stop your yammering, Essin," Ia said, coming out of the back with Josie. "What are you doing here?"

Raych spoke up. "Well, I thought we could talk civilized. So I brought pie."

"Pie?" Josie said. "Well, I appreciate that Missus Rynax." She limped over to the table and sat down as plates and tea were brought over.

"I'm afraid it's not the best pie, as it's a few days old," Raych said. She cut slices of the pie and served it to everyone at the table. Her voice darkened just a little as she said, "I wasn't able to bake anything yesterday." She served herself last and then took a bite.

"Josie," Verci said sternly, taking a bite of the pie. "You broke the truce. And you did it in the most deplorable way possible."

"I did?" Josie asked. "You and your brother were the ones who—"

"You abducted my wife, Josie. There is a code to these things, and you—"

"A code?" Ia asked with a mouthful of pie. "What is this code? We all do business, and do what we have to do, *sjat*?"

"*We* had an understanding, Verci," Josie said. She took a bite of the pie. "You and your brother were out of my business. Retired back to normal life."

"What is *your* business, Josie? Is it now smuggling drugs into the neighborhood? Working for Fenmere?"

"I do what I have to," Josie said. "I wanted that to involve you boys, I wanted that to take down the people who burned the alley, but I have to be practical. You of all people should understand that."

"No matter who gets hurt? You don't even come talk to us first. You thought Asti and I had done something, and your first move is to touch my family. You never would have done that before."

"You were supposed to be done!" Josie shouted. "And then you and Asti team up with Olivette of all people? Work with the Thorn? You and he came in here and tore the place up!"

"I came here because *you took my wife*. The Thorn had shown up to smack your people around, so he made a convenient ally."

"Then you hit the mages."

"Which all started because, once again, *you took my wife*."

"Try to take some responsibility, Josie," Raych said primly. "You have a whole organization at your command, and you keep trying to blame Asti and Verci for all your trouble. You brought it on yourself."

"You have no idea, Missus Rynax, what I've done or what I'm capable of. And I'm tired of your hypocrisy, Verci." She snapped her fingers, and Ia grabbed Verci, twisting both his arms behind his back. Two other goons stepped behind Raych, knives out.

Raych didn't flinch, bless her. Instead she took another bite of pie. "This came out quite good, don't you think? I was worried about it. It wasn't fresh, and I'll be honest, I didn't know how the flavor would be affected by the—Verci, what was it called?"

"Calnidonna," Verci said.

"That was it."

Josie's eyes went wide. "But you both—you couldn't—" She stood up and knocked her plate of mostly eaten pie to the ground.

"You poison all of us?" Ia asked, twisting Verci's arm further. "I should break you for that, *sjat*?"

"Problem is, you'll never get the antidote," Verci said. "If I recall, it takes about an hour before you're quite ill, and then you die in about six hours, horribly."

"You said it was very painful, yes?" Raych said coolly.

"I think Almer said it's one of the worst ways to die," Verci said.

"Give us the antidote," Josie said.

"I'm afraid we took the last doses," Verci said.

"There wasn't much left in Almer's shop, so we took what there was. Tasted terrible."

"Quite awful," Raych said. "But the poison itself has an almost flowery note to it, really brings out the richness of the pie."

"You will—" Josie sputtered.

"Here's the thing," Verci said. "Almer could probably make more antidote, but I'm given to understand he was grabbed by Fenmere's goons last night. With Helene and Kennith. So, here's what's going to happen. Asti has been kind enough to reach out to Olivette, and he'll meet with you all at Kimber's at two bells. You will make sure Fenmere's man is there, you will make sure he releases those three, and you will make sure your *business* never comes close to touching anything with those mages or the Andrendon Project again."

Josie's expression cooled, and she sat back down. "You don't even know what that is."

"I don't care what it is, Josie. I only care that my family, my friends, and my neighborhood are left in peace. If they aren't, you will discover exactly what I'm truly capable of. I will make my brother's violence look like swift mercy."

The gauntlet on his arm starting ticking.

"For example, there's my failsafe kicking in. If you want to find out what happens when the ticking stops, please prevent Raych and me from walking out unmolested."

Josie's eyes narrowed. "Let them go. And we'll see Asti at two bells."

"Have a lovely day," Raych said as she got to her feet. Ia let Verci go, and he stood next to his wife. Gently holding her hand, he walked backward to the door, all the goons stepping away as they went.

Kel Essin gave Verci a little approving nod as they went outside.

They walked calmly past the Scratch Cats and around the corner, going half a block before Raych pulled him into an alley and grabbed him in a mad embrace, kissing him intensely.

"It worked," she said when she broke away. "I don't know how but it actually worked."

"You were amazing," he said.

"I was terrified. How are you not terrified?"

"You didn't look terrified," he said. "You were incredible."

The ticking on the gauntlet stopped without any additional consequence, but Raych squealed in surprise anyway. She laughed, nervously at first, then explosively.

"How sick are we going to be?" she asked through her laughs. Now they faced the worst part of Raych's plan. The pie was not laced with calnidonna, but a mix of Almer's laxatives and emetics. Josie and Ia wouldn't die, but for the next few hours, they would feel like they were going to. Long enough for Josie to believe it.

"The curative we took should stave off the worst of it, but I think we'll want to get to a place with a water closet sooner rather than later."

"Home?" she asked.

"Home."

"You put her in there?"

Mila was amused that the rooftop water tank in question was the one on top of Kimber's. She knew Kimber wasn't one to check the tank unless there was a problem, and she wouldn't even know of a problem as long the well taps were running. Kimber wouldn't switch over to the tank unless the wells were dry, and given how little rain the hot summer had given them, it was far more likely for the tank to be empty than the wells.

"I had to put her somewhere quickly since, well, you were half a mile in the air."

"Fair," Mila said. "But how do you know she didn't get out?"

"I coiled her in the rope, and magicked it to be as hard as steel. It should stay that way unless another mage took control of it. Now, mind you, I wasn't planning on her being there more than a few minutes, but . . . well, the night got away from us."

"She must be spitting mad."

"I feel really terrible," he said flatly.

Veranix had fully engaged in the Thorn persona, and given Mila the look of her Rose disguise. There was no need for Miss Jads to see who she really was.

"Shall we?" she asked.

Veranix hopped her up to the top of the water tank. At the bottom, laying in a few inches of water and wrapped nearly head to toe in the Thorn's rope was that same woman from the other night. She was lying there in a pathetic lump amid the musty odor of stagnant water.

"Morning, Miss Jads," Veranix called down to her. "Did you have a good night?"

She looked up and started thrashing and yelling, but her cries were muffled by the rope around her mouth.

"Sorry, couldn't quite get that," Veranix said.

"Thorn, this is just cruel," Mila said. "You were not thinking of the people who rely on this tank for water. Now infected with her filth."

"It was a hasty decision on my part. I should get her out."

More thrashes and muffled cries.

"It's the decent thing to do. For the people who use this tank."

The Thorn hopped down and grabbed the rope, uncoiling just a bit of it from her as he leaped back up, bringing the poor woman up with him. He had her dangling over the water tank as he landed back at the top.

"Now, I'm going to loosen the rope on your mouth, Miss Jads, because I'd like to ask you a thing or two. You scream, and Rose gets to practice her carving. Are we clear?"

Jads made an attempt at a nod. The rope uncoiled off of her mouth.

"Fenmere is going to skin you for this."

"Oh, please," Veranix said. "The man already wants to enact vicious and public murder on my body. I doubt there's any further for him to go, and I seriously doubt you'd be the catalyst to push it."

"Do you have any idea who I am?"

Mila took the cue, remembering the information in the Constabulary file. "Jads Farrell. Born 1187 in Hechard. Studied elemental science at the University of Hechard, no Letters of Mastery. Apparently expelled after an arrest and scandal in 1206. Came to Maradaine and denied entry into both the Apothecary Guild and the Physicker's Guild. Arrested again in 1209 for—what was it?"

"Accounts fraud," Veranix said. "It was quite a fascinating scheme. She worked as a secretary and clerk at the University of Maradaine and created a fake courier service, which she would hire to send letters that didn't exist, using the University's courier payment accounts to line her own pocket."

Mila whistled. "I hate you because you're drug-peddling sewage, ma'am, but I will give you full respect for that play."

"You imagine how much your respect means to me, little girl," Miss Jads said. "Are you going to kill me, Thorn?"

"It seems unsporting," Veranix said. "I mean, in the midst of a fight is one thing, but like this? Just uncivilized. But I'm not interested in keeping you prisoner, either."

"You'd need a cell," Mila said.

"And someone to guard the cell."

"And feed her."

"Probably twice a day," Veranix said. "Can you imagine how much work that would be?"

"So much work," Mila said. "I wouldn't want to do it."

"What do you want?" Jads shouted at them.

"For one, I want to know all about the plans for this

neighborhood. You and Corman, Fenmere, the drugs, the mages, all of it."

"And Andrendon," Mila added.

"And what?" Jads asked, genuine confusion on her face.

Mila swore to herself. Jads didn't know what that was. So it didn't connect to Fenmere's involvement.

"Just talk," Veranix said.

"There's no plan," Jads said. "With the Blue Hand gone, Fenmere needs mages for hire. So he formed an alliance with the Firewings. They need more capital, and have to be out here now, so Corman and I are setting up a new district for them to supervise with the chowderheads who think they're crime bosses out here. It's drug trade, Thorn, not anything more."

"It kills people, Jads," he said raising her up higher. "But it's good to know there's not anything deeper than that."

So they weren't invested. That was good. The mages might be invested in this part of town, invested in Andrendon, but the Fenmere part of the equation could be eliminated, and then without it, the rest would fall apart.

Mila tapped Veranix's arm. "Put her back down there. I need a word."

"Certainly," he said, and the rope coiled around Jads's mouth before she could protest. Her muffled yells became more muted as he put her back in the bottom of the tank, and then he lowered himself and Mila to the rooftop.

"What's up?"

"All right, I'm thinking, Corman and the mages, they grabbed my friends last night. We have her. So let's negotiate a trade."

"A trade?"

"Her for Helene, Almer and Kennith," Mila said.

He scowled. "I don't like the idea of negotiating anything with these heels."

"I get it. But for—"

"For the sake of saving your friends, of course," he said. "So how do we do it?"

"Well, we have to send word that we have what they want, and we want to trade. So we need a page."

"And you know where to find that?"

She certainly did. And there was no time to waste. No telling how long Helene and the others had.

Helene didn't know how long it had been. She didn't know what time was anymore. Had it been hours or days or what, she didn't know. Maybe that rutting one-eyed mage actually had made a few minutes seem like days. But for however long she had been strapped to the table in the basement of the Firewing house, every minute had been agony.

Every minute she was pummeled with lightning, singed with flames, scalded with ice. Every minute, the source of pain, the method changed, so she could never acclimate herself to any of it.

She had tried not to scream, but that resolve had crumbled long ago. Now her throat was raw from screaming.

Then it all abated. For a moment, there was only the memory of pain, writing stories on every nerve in her body.

"That . . ." she wheezed out. "That . . . all you . . . got?"

The eye-patched face came into view. "Not at all. But it's time to get a little something to eat. I'm just famished."

A splash of water hit Helene in the face from nowhere.

"Drink up," Ecrain said, shuffling out of view. "I don't want you to pass out yet. I have days and days of fun planned."

"Ecrain." Another voice. The man with the wings. The man who killed Mila. He was going to pay for that. "What's your status?"

"Taking a break. Let her remember what not being in pain feels like to give it some contrast."

"Well, Corman says we're going to talk with Olivette about a trade, so we need some proof we have her and the others."

"I'm not giving her up yet. I have so much pain planned, and I haven't even gotten to crippling her body."

"No, no," the winged guy said. "I would never ask you to give something like that up. I can get my proof without giving anything up. For her and the other two."

"Oh," Ecrain said knowingly. "Be my guest. I'll be back down in a bit."

Helene heard her shuffle off, as another face came into view.

"Hello, Miss Kesser," he said. "I'm afraid that this is going to hurt quite a bit."

Chapter 24

"JUST SO YOU'RE CLEAR," Cobie said. "These are my boys doing a favor for you. They ain't your boys, and you're not swiping them from me. And you are not putting them in danger."

"I'm not going to do that," Mila said. They had brought Miss Jads to his flop—bound, gagged, and blindfolded now—which he wasn't happy about, but Mila had paid him enough to balance that out. Veranix had offered to cover it, but she didn't feel right about taking his money.

That was after trying to find either Asti or Verci, with no luck. For all she knew, they were both dead. Or also captured. It might all be on her shoulders.

"You better believe you won't do that."

"I wasn't a good boss for them, and I'm not going to be around much longer."

"I'm thinking no one should be around much longer," Cobie said. "Benson Court is starting to look real appealing."

Veranix whistled low at that one. "How much waiting are we going to do?"

"The boys have run off to deliver the message, we wait for them to get back," Mila told him.

Veranix scowled and paced away. "It's not my money, you know."

"Hmm?"

"The money I would have used. It's not like it's from my school stipend."

"I don't know what you mean."

"I mean . . ." He shrugged. "When I'm in Dentonhill, taking out dealers or the big game, I usually take their money, and then use it against them. Or donate it to the church."

Mila chuckled. "You give it to the church?"

"It's the least I can do to balance out what I put on my soul."

That was unexpected. "You're serious?"

"Very," he said. "Plus there's a reverend who's helped me more than once. I . . . I wouldn't be alive if it wasn't for him."

Mila didn't know how to respond to that. Her own experience with the church—that old reverend repeatedly wanting to put her and Jina back with her uncle despite . . . everything—left her far from endeared to the institution. But she couldn't argue that his good experiences with his reverend didn't help him.

"I'm fine," she said. She lowered her voice a little. "It's not like my money doesn't have similar ill-gotten origins."

"Oh?" he asked. "More like that hustle in the warehouses?"

"All in the name of getting those behind the fire," she said.

"And making those bastards pay." That came from the boy who had crawled in the window—Tarvis. It amazed Mila how small and innocent he looked, until one saw the hate in his eyes.

"Tarvis, what are you doing here?" she asked.

"I told you, I keep watch on Nikey and the others,"

he said. "That Cobie seems pretty good to them. But if he gets out of line, I stab him."

"Damn," Veranix said. "How old are you?"

"Six, I think," Tarvis said. "But I've been stabbing folks who deserve it half my life."

"Prices on souls, indeed," Veranix said under his breath.

"I got something to tell you," Tarvis said to Mila. "You're trying to cut some sort of deal with the mages and the bastards they work with?"

"Yeah," Mila said. "They've got my friends, hoping to get them back."

"I heard some talk, they're already meeting some new cat called Olivette. Prisoners being traded to him."

"Who's Olivette?" Mila asked. "I heard that name on the street last night."

Tarvis just shrugged.

"I heard Verci say that name at the mage house," Veranix said. "Something he overheard while listening in."

"Olivette?" Cobie said. "He's not a new cat. He was a street boss around these parts, about twenty years back or so. Josie Holt ran him out of town."

Mila swore. The last thing this business needed was another player. And why the blazes did he want to take Helene from the mages?

"Do you know when?" Veranix asked.

"In just a bit, over at the death place."

"Death place?"

Mila realized. "He mean's Kimber's Pub."

Veranix paced a bit again. "I don't think we can wait."

"But—" Mila said.

"If they're already meeting Olivette, this is the chance to hit them and save your friends."

"But without a plan—"

"Saints," Veranix said, his magical shadow enveloping half his body. "You all keep talking about plans, and look where it ended up. I've got a plan, it's called

I'm the goddamned Thorn. Time to show these bastards what that means."

"Vee!" Mila said, but Veranix was already out the window.

"That kid has style," Cobie said.

"Rutting saints," Mila said, scrambling out after him. "I can't do this alone."

"Why ain't the brothers helping you?" Tarvis asked.

"Brothers?" Mila said, not sure if she should climb down the back stairs or wait here with Jads. "You mean Asti and Verci. I don't know where they are. Maybe they were killed."

"Not the one with the bad foot."

"Verci," Mila said. She reached out, almost grabbing Tarvis before she stopped herself. Tarvis wouldn't want to be touched. He might even cut her. "You know where he is?"

"He and his wife went into their shop a bit ago."

Verci and Raych were all right. They were home.

Verci would know what to do.

Verci and Raych had taken turns in the water closet, until Raych had reached the point where she couldn't give up her place in there. Verci didn't argue with her. It was clear she had been hit far worse than he had.

He took some small comfort at the thought that this was how they felt after taking the pills to diminish their symptoms. Josie and Ia must be feeling so much worse now.

"I'm making some flower tea, that should settle us a bit," he called out to Raych. He dug the jar of dried flowers out from the back of the cabinet.

"I will never be settled again," Raych said back. "My body will always hate me after this. Why are you still standing upright?"

"I should tell you the story of when Asti and I did get poisoned."

"Please." She made some horrible sounds. "I want to hear all these stories."

"Flower tea first," he said, putting the kettle on the stove.

The apartment door suddenly opened. Verci, despite his stomach doing somersaults, dove for his darts and took aim at the intruder.

"Just me!" Mila shouted.

"Mila," he said weakly. "You're all right." Though she was wearing all red, including some odd masking face paint around her eyes.

"I'm uninjured," she said. "All right is far away."

"I'd embrace you, but the scent of me would probably kill you." He went back to the cabinets to get two cups and add the dried flowers to them.

Mila's nose crinkled. "Scent is right. Is Corsi sick or something?"

"We're sick," Raych called from the water closet. "Let us be."

"It's bad," Verci said.

"Everything is bad," she said back. "Why are you both sick?"

"The consequences of tricking Josie into thinking we poisoned her."

"You poisoned yourselves in the process?"

"Yes," Verci said, sitting down at the table. His stomach threatened to expel everything still in his body, which logically shouldn't be anything at this point, but yet there seemed to be an endless supply of vile material. "But Josie will feel much worse."

"How does that help?" Mila said. "You know Helene and the others are captured, yes?"

"Yes, of—"

"And I don't know where Asti is and the mages are going to sell Helene to some crime lord and the Thorn has already gone off completely uncocked and—"

"Slow down," Verci said. "Asti is working the problem. What's this about selling Helene to a crime lord?"

"Some new cat—or old cat, I don't even know—named Olivette."

"Oli—" Verci got half the word out before his stomach rebelled. He barely got hold of the bucket before it all came out.

"Saint Maria," Mila said.

"Olivette is us," Verci said quietly. "Old, old scam, from our pop. Asti and I arranged a meeting between Fenmere's people and 'Olivette,' but it's just going to be Pilsen."

"Why didn't you tell me about this?"

"We weren't sure what happened to you," Verci said.

"Well, the Thorn is probably going to bust in there and screw a lot up," Mila said. "Let's move."

"I'm not moving," Verci said. "I have done enough already."

"Verci!" Mila shouted. "Would Asti say that if it was you? Would Helene?"

"They don't—" he said reflexively. But that wasn't fair. He knew they wouldn't. He knew he shouldn't.

"Go," Raych called out.

That was a shock.

"I thought—" he started to say.

"We had a plan," she said. "But that plan was founded on Asti being able to control the situation. He's not ready for the Thorn to foul it up."

"What about not leaving my side?"

The teapot started to whistle.

"I don't want you to go," Raych said. "But . . . Asti is going to need you."

"Fine," he said to Mila, taking the teapot off the stove. He poured the hot water over the flowers, letting the scent hit his nose. "But give me a click to get myself together."

"Well, the meeting's at two bells, and the Thorn will probably smash in a minute after that," Mila said. "But, please, take your time."

"I will," Verci said, picking up his teacup. "I like this look of yours, by the way."

"What's she wearing?" Raych called out.

"It's a whole red and pink ensemble, including face paint."

Raych opened the door of the water closet and stuck her head out. "Oh, Mila, that is something. How did you do that face-painting?"

"The Thorn did it. With magic."

"Good eye, he has."

"Good lips, too."

"What?" Raych said. She came out, wrapped in a drycloth. "Are you saying he kissed you?"

"I kissed him," Mila said.

"Good for you," Raych said, taking a seat at the table. She took Verci's hand and squeezed it, telling him a thousand things at once. She understood. She hated it, but she understood.

Verci drank down the tea, not caring how hot it was. He strapped on the bandolier and gauntlet. "Enough of this, let's go."

"Don't die," Raych said as he kissed her cheek quickly.

"Love you, too," he said.

"I know you do, idiot," she said with a tiny laugh. Then she grabbed at her stomach. "Go save your brother." She ducked back into the water closet.

"It's what I do," he said. Following after Mila, he hoped it would be that easy.

Asti wished a carriage had been an option. Without Kennith, without Jhoqull, there was no way to take a carriage to the meeting. Walking through the streets was far too vulnerable.

He wished Verci was with him. Or Mila. Or saints damn him, even Liora. As fond as he was of Julien, Pilsen and Vellun, none of them were planners.

"We shouldn't walk?" Julien asked.

"If I were in their place, I would put Helene in a nest outside Kimber's and pick off Olivette before the meeting even started. I would want to do that now, but—"

"Yeah," Julien said. "So how do we get there without walking in the street? Not like we can go under."

"Actually, we can," Asti said.

With the supplies needed for their disguises packed up Asti led them through back alleys through Benson Court—it was amazing how the streets turned into a slum of shambles in just a few blocks—and then slipped over into the back of the bakery on Frost. Fortunately, no one was in there today. Asti unlocked the entrances into the basement bunker and let them all in.

"Doesn't Josie have a way to get in here?" Vellun asked.

"Maybe," Asti said.

Pilsen added, "Josie and her old crew used these tunnels extensively, and they never knew how far it all went. One of her cousins just plain got lost for weeks down there."

"We don't have weeks," Julien said very seriously.

"I mapped out what we need for this," Asti said. "Path from here to the root cellar of the shop next to Kimber's. We'll be able to come up in the alley, through the back door."

"Then let's get to work," Pilsen said, unpacking his face paints, wigs, and costumes. In short order, he and Vellun were dressed in matching outfits, heavy wool suits, in checkered plaid. "I think Olivette has been in Hechard all this time. He'd go to the north coast." Blond wig for Vellun, gray for Pilsen, tight curled hair. Shading and coloring contoured their faces, and before long, Asti wouldn't have recognized either. The same care was taken with Julien, slicking back his hair and dressing him in a thick-necked pullover of a similar plaid.

"Do I need an accent or something?" Julien asked. "I'm not that good at that."

"Just be quiet, be ready if things go poorly." Asti told him.

"Ready how?" Julien asked in a low whisper. "You need me to fight?"

Asti knew the last thing Helene would want was to have Julien fight, even to rescue her. He needed to respect that, for her sake "No. Things go bad, you get them out of there. Fast as you can."

"If Helene is danger . . . if you need me—"

"Jules," Asti said. "The last thing we need here is a fight. If it comes to that, we've already lost."

Ready in their disguises, Asti opened the secret door to a cool, brick-walled passage, and led them through to the root cellar. Asti closed up the passage behind them, and they went up into the alley and into Kimber's.

"Asti!" Kimber said as they came in the taproom. "Where have you—are you . . ." She let it hang.

"I'm not at all," he said, taking her hand. "In fact, things are quite bad."

Fear and concern flashed over her face, but then her expression hardened. "What do you need?"

"Thank you," he said quietly. "Get everyone out of here, and then go yourself."

"You want me to abandon my business?"

Asti squeezed her hand. "I wouldn't ask, but I . . . I can't have you in danger. You could be used as leverage against me."

"How bad is this?"

"I'm going to ask you to pray, that's how bad."

She nodded, and clapped her hands loudly. "All right, people, we're clearing out. I don't care where you go, but it can't be here."

The few patrons grumbled and went to the door. Jared Scall collected his mace from behind the bar and hung back for a moment.

"Rynax, if you need me."

"Jared, I couldn't ask that," Asti said.

"Whatever this is, I know it—I know you're holding a line down for folks like us. I can help if you need."

Asti wanted to tell him that the best help would be to go home, to be with his daughters. But instead he just said, "We've got this. Just be safe."

Jared sighed and went out.

Kimber took one last look about, gave Asti a solemn nod, and left.

Asti set up a table near the back exit. If things went bad, they could run out that way. Of course, they would surely put a few men on the back door. Asti would carve his way through them. He had Pilsen and Vellun sit at the table, with Julien standing guard over them, and Asti took position standing in front of the table.

After a few minutes, several people came in the front door. Corman, looking haggard and unrested, in the same suit from the night before, led the group, which included Pria, the Poasian, and half a dozen other goons.

"Well," Corman said as he approached. "This must be the legendary Olivette."

"It must be," Pilsen said. "And you must be the bastard who wants what's mine."

"What's yours?" Corman asked. "What do you think that must be?"

"I'd say it's North Seleth. Every square foot of it is mine. I ceded it to Josie Holt some years ago and dealt with some other business, but I see she's run it all to the ground. Letting it get burned out, letting in mages, making deals with easttown bastards." He sneered at the Poasian. "Ghosts, even. No more of that."

"We're the easttown bastards, I presume?" Corman asked.

"You are," Pilsen said.

"We've tolerated this incompetence for too long," Vellun said. "So we are back."

"And you accept this, Rynax?" Corman asked.

"I just arranged a meeting for you," Asti said. "But between you and your drugs, or Olivette taking control of this neighborhood, I'd take this sinner over you."

"And thus you plan to run us out?" Corman asked. "I don't think so."

Asti noticed a shimmer out of the corner of his eye, moving through the room slowly. He remembered having seen that shimmer once before. The Thorn. What was he playing at?

"Well, let's make sure no one does anything foolish," he said a bit louder than he had been speaking. "And we can work out a deal that's good for everyone."

"The deal that's good for me is my merchandise back," Corman said. "And I'm willing to let you all live in exchange for that."

"And my people?" Asti asked.

"Yours?" Corman shot back. "Not Olivette's, but yours."

"My people now," Pilsen said. "Like the neighborhood, the people you have are under my protection."

"They aren't. They're under my grace." Corman looked around. "Where is the proprietor? My throat is parched."

"Rynax had this place emptied before we came," the Poasian said.

"Asti." The voice was right in his ear. "Scratch your nose if you hear me."

The Thorn.

Asti scratched his nose as he said, "I thought it best to keep this conversation private."

"Foolish," the Poasian said. He stood up, moving like a dancer. "Which of these swills do you want?"

"What's good here, Rynax?" Corman asked.

"I've got an arrow trained at Corman's throat," the Thorn's voice said at the same time. The shimmer was over by the bar. "Say the word."

"I've found the cider is the best for saving my throat," Asti said.

"Cider," Corman said. "Now, Mister Olivette, let's say I'm amenable to a deal. I'm not, but I am curious what you're bringing to the table."

"What I'm bringing?" Pilsen asked. He glanced around a bit nervously. "What am I bringing? Why don't you tell me?"

Asti bit back a curse. Pilsen was losing focus.

"We aren't here for a deal," Vellun said, picking up on Pilsen's falter. "We're here to tell you what's going to happen. You get to decide how you're going to take it, easy or hard."

Corman laughed and clapped his hands. "I'm impressed. Are you impressed, Pria?"

"No," Pria said. "Not impressed at all."

"I am," Corman said. "They come in here with nothing. Nothing. And they act like they set the terms. I do admire that courage."

"We don't have nothing," Pilsen roared. "I ruled these blocks, and I will again!"

"We could thump all of you right now and not even sweat over it," Corman said. "And then roll over these blocks. Which we will."

"Tell him you have Miss Jads," the Thorn's voice said.

"Pardon?" Asti asked.

"We will take all of this," Corman said.

"Jads. The woman he was with. I've got her tied up."

Asti nodded. "We hardly have nothing. Olivette has the merchandise you need. I know how badly you need it. And he also has Miss Jads in his possession."

"What?" Corman asked.

"You heard him," Pilsen said.

"So, we will trade, Jads for my three," Asti said.

"If you've hurt her—" Corman said sharply as he stepped forward.

"She's fine for now," Asti said, holding up his hands. "That can change, though. Or we can bring her here safely."

"Well, I didn't bring your friends," Corman said, reaching into his pocket. "All I brought was proof I have them."

He pulled a kerchief out of his pocket and put it on the table, unwrapping it carefully.

Inside were three bloody fingers. Easily recognizable: Helene, Kennith, and Almer.

"Now, we can definitely continue delivering them in

pieces," Corman said, with a disdainful chuckle. "If that's what you—"

That was all he was able to say before the hand was around his throat.

"You hurt her!" Julien shouted.

Two thugs jumped on Julien, but he swatted them away and continue to squeeze Corman's throat.

"Where is she?" Julien asked.

Pria released a plume of magical flame on Julien's arm. Julien screamed and dropped Corman, his arm on fire.

Pria raised a flaming fist, but then he screamed. An arrow through his arm. He cried out and fell to the floor.

The shimmer materialized into the Thorn, bow raised.

"Hello, Corman. I'm here to give your boss my best."

Corman saw him, and shouted with almost inhuman rage.

"Get him!" Corman shouted. "Five thousand crowns for his head!"

"Is that all?" the Thorn asked. "I'm insulted, Corman."

Vellun whipped off his coat and used it to tamp out the flames on Julien's arm. Pilsen stumbled up from the table, looking terrified.

"Run!" Asti shouted, drawing out his knives.

All at once, a handful of the goons came at Asti and Julien. In the same moment, the Poasian vaulted over the bar and charged at the Thorn. The Thorn drew and fired three arrows like a blur, each one a true shot for the Poasian's heart.

The Poasian reacted with similar speed and grace, catching one arrow, drawing his sword and knocking the second away, and stepping out of the path of the third without losing pace. While the Thorn drew a fourth arrow, the Poasian grabbed his bow and with it twisted his wrist, tearing the bow out of the Thorn's hand.

"A child," he snarled. He smashed the bow on the floor.

"Stop all of them!" Corman shouted, running for the door.

Asti fought off two of the thugs, and Julien was slamming the others around like they were dolls. Red-faced with rage, Julien was screaming and crying as his massive arms flailed about.

"Run!" Asti shouted, too busy fighting two of the goons to do anything else.

Vellun didn't need further prodding, grabbing Pilsen by the arm and tearing out the back.

The Thorn dodged several of the Poasian's swipes with his blade, drawing out his fighting staff and starting to parry the blows. He was out of his league.

Pria snapped his fingers, and the arrow in his arm turned to ash. "Let me kill him!" he snarled. His hands burst into flame, and his wings of fire unfolded from his back.

Julien had smashed in the heads of three goons, and shoved a fourth against a wall. "Where is she?"

"The mage house, the mage house!" the goon shouted.

Julien threw him to the floor and ran out the door.

Blazes, Julien was going after Helene. Asti couldn't let him go alone.

The Thorn was dodging sword and flame, but he couldn't keep it up for long. And Pria and the Poasian were between Asti and Julien.

"Thorn!" Asti shouted. "Let's take this outside!"

"Capital idea," the Thorn said. He flipped backward to the door, and Pria and the Poasian pressed after him. Asti dove in at them, tackling the Poasian to the ground as they went out the door.

The Poasian slammed his fist into Asti's chin, and then another blow to his ribs. Asti flipped over, trying to drive a knife into the man, but he hit steel instead of flesh. The Poasian pulled a knife, but before he got that into Asti's chest, Asti was yanked away by a rope that had coiled around his body.

He landed on his feet next to the Thorn.

The Poasian and Pria were on their feet again as well, ready to square off against them.

"Well," the Thorn said. "Looks like someone wants a fight."

Asti let a smile creep to his face. "Then let's give it to them."

Then the beast, which had been silent all day, woke up screaming.

"So," Liora said, suddenly standing next to the Poasian with a light sword in hand. "You thought you could hide us away."

Chapter 25

THEY REACHED FROST LANE TOO LATE. Mila cursed herself for taking too long, not forcing Verci to move faster.

Mila had no idea what was happening inside Kimber's but in the street, Asti and Veranix were fighting the fire mage and the Poasian swordsman.

No—Veranix was fighting both of them. Asti was fighting no one. Literally, parrying and stabbing into open air.

"What is wrong with him?" she asked Verci.

"I don't know," Verci said, rotating the cuff of his gauntlet. "But we can sort that out later. Deep breath."

He launched a ball out of the gauntlet, that struck the Poasian square in the chest. Purple smoke erupted out of it, engulfing the Poasian, Veranix, and the mage.

Mila had her rope out, and lassoed it around Asti, pulling him out of the smoke, the sickly-sweet smell of it hitting her nose, making her head reel.

He grabbed her, terror in his eyes. "Mila, run. She'll kill you."

"Who?"

Before he could answer, the mage with the fiery

wings launched out of the purple smoke, entangled in the Thorn's rope, with Veranix grappling him madly. As they flew in wild circles, the two of them exchanged punches, punctuated with fire and thunder.

The Poasian lurched out of the smoke, stumbling with each step, but still with his sword up. He moved towards Asti with intent.

Asti, though, despite being bound with Mila's rope, fought against his invisible attacker. Fought like he was keeping himself between them and Mila.

"You're too much trouble, Mister Rynax," the Poasian said, his words slurring. "I don't care who it inconveniences."

He thrust his blade at Asti, but Mila pulled him out of the way before he was stabbed.

"You've got to run!" Asti said. "I can't hold her off much longer."

"Worry about him!" Mila said. "There's no her!"

Another strike from the Poasian, and Mila couldn't drag Asti out of the way fast enough. But this attack was parried.

Verci, armed with the Thorn's fighting staff.

"That's my brother you're trying to kill," Verci said. "I take that personally."

Verci shoved at the Poasian, putting distance between him and Asti.

Mila took the chance to further bind Asti's arms.

"No, no!" he cried out, thrashing at the binding. He tried desperately to protect himself from blows that weren't there.

"Asti!" Mila shouted. His eyes were still focused on the empty air in front of him. Then he looked at her, but it was like he didn't see her. Bound as he was, he still managed to lash out and get his hands around her throat.

"Asti—" she whispered.

"I won't let you hurt them!"

Unsure of what else to do, she slapped his face as hard as she could.

That got him to blink.

"Where'd she go?" he asked.

"Who?"

"Liora, she—" He looked around wildly. "She was here, with—"

"Asti, what happened?" Mila asked.

"Julie!" he said. "He went wild, running—we need to get to the mage house."

Suddenly a ball of light and fire crashed into the ground, kicking up dust and dirt around them. When the air cleared, the Thorn stood over the battered body of the fire mage, surrounded in a glowing halo of magic.

"Untie me," Asti said quickly. "We need to move."

Mila looked in his eyes. Whatever had happened, the moment had passed. He was in his right head, or as much of it as was normal.

Still struggling to catch her breath, she uncoiled him from the rope.

"Thanks," he said. His voice a bit lower, he added. "I don't know why that happened but . . ."

"A little help!" Verci called out.

Asti and Veranix both sprang into action, Veranix hurling a magic blast at the Poasian that knocked him back from Verci. Verci tossed Veranix his staff and reset the spring trigger for his gauntlet.

The three of them stood shoulder-to-shoulder in the street: Asti with his knives, Verci with his gauntlet, and Veranix with his staff and magic flowing shadows all around him.

"Another time," the Poasian said, and ran off.

Veranix moved like he was about to chase after him, but Asti grabbed his arm. "He doesn't matter. The mage house. Julien."

Veranix glanced back to Mila, taking a cue from her as she still struggled to find her feet. "You're right. Let's go."

They ran. Mila wanted to go with them, but she knew they were going to need more help than she could provide alone.

And she knew where to find it.

❂

"It's a delicate art, you know," Ecrain whispered while Helene screamed. "Figuring out exactly how much pain you can handle, pushing you to the limits, changing its methods so you don't acclimate."

Helene didn't respond. She couldn't put anything to her voice except screams. Magic wove through her body, burning and shredding her, pinning her to the table.

"I will make you beg for death, girl," Ecrain said. "But not for a long time, I think. First—"

Ecrain was interrupted by a resounding crash, somewhere in the distance. She stopped her magical assault for a moment, turning toward the door. Putting Helene in her blind spot.

Helene took the opportunity, swinging her legs up and hooking them around Ecrain's neck. With all the strength she had in her legs, she pulled Ecrain to her and pummeled her head with multiple blows from her right fist.

"Never turn your back on the person you're torturing!" Helene whispered, her throat already shredded, punctuating each word with a punch.

She dropped Ecrain to the ground and kicked her one last time before pushing herself to move away, go through the door.

Her body was a memory of pain, except her left hand, which was beyond pain. That was numb with loss. She couldn't think about that right now. She had to just find the others and get out. The rest she would sort later.

"Helene!"

Her name echoed from above. Julien. She didn't care that he was in the thick of things, that he was fighting. It was the last thing she wanted for him, but he was here for her.

"Julie!" she tried to call, but her voice wouldn't obey. She had nothing left in it, having screamed it raw. "Down here!"

The hallway was dark, several doors along it. No

sense of the way out, where the stairs were. Helene stumbled blindly, trying a door at the end of the hall.

There were stairs here, going down even farther into darkness.

Last thing she wanted to do.

"Helene!"

"Julien!"

That was Almer's voice, from behind one of the other doors. Thank the saints. She heard a scuffle and smashing above her. She couldn't get to Julien, but she could get Almer out, and be together when Julien came. She opened the door of that room—a storage closet—to find Almer and Kennith tied back to back. Kennith looked in a bad way: pale, sweaty, and out cold. Almer didn't look much better, and his spectacles were smashed on the floor.

Also, dried blood on the floor. Their hands bandaged. Just like Helene's.

"Hold tight," she said, her voice little more than breath. "Julien's coming."

Her body exploded in pain.

"He's not," Ecrain said behind her. "And if he does, he'll suffer as much as you."

"I take it everything is bad," Verci said as he ran with Asti and the Thorn to Holver Alley.

"Everything is bad," Asti said.

"This is when Dad would say the gig is skunked and bail."

"Bail?" the Thorn asked.

"Not an option," Asti said. "Not with our crew at stake."

"Do you have a plan?" the Thorn asked as they rounded the corner onto Ullen Street. "I'm given to understand you're a planning man."

Asti stopped just in sight of Holver Alley and the house. The front door was wide open and several goons were on the stoop, rubbing at their chins, looking about like they expected trouble. Fenmere's. "We've got who knows how many goons—Fenmere's, Three-Fingers, Potato Boys—as well as at least two mages between us and our friends. So my plan is to kill them a lot."

"I'm not against that plan, but—"

"Where's your bow?" Verci asked.

"That Poasian broke it in half," the Thorn said. He tapped Verci's gauntlet. "What's left?"

"One smoke, one knockout, one boom, and the phosphorous flash."

"We need to get in there," Asti said.

"Yeah, yeah," Thorn said. "The Scratch Cats are working with them, right?"

"No Scratch Cats here, though," Asti said.

"Not yet," the Thorn said, and with a wave of his hand his appearance changed to look like a Scratch Cat, complete with the scars on his face, as did Asti's.

"How does that help?" Verci asked.

"Because we're running from the Thorn," he said. He put his hand on Verci's shoulder, and Verci's clothing melted into looking just like the Thorn's outfit, complete with cloak and hood.

"Useful," Asti said.

"I can't hold this long," the Thorn said, almost as if he was holding his breath. "Smoke, flash and knockout, and they won't know you're not a mage."

"And the boom?"

"Last resort," Thorn said. Tapping Asti on the shoulder, he said. "Let's run, Cat."

Asti dashed off toward the house, the Thorn right with him.

"Oh, saints, the Thorn is coming!" Asti shouted. "Run, run, he's crazy!"

Verci cocked the gauntlet, ready to take these bastards down.

The Thorn's plan got them up the stoop and in the door. Asti was amazed that it had worked at all. Shouts and yells outside made it clear everyone outside was far too concerned about Verci's assault as the ersatz Thorn to worry about them. But they were hit with a blast of light as soon as they were in the parlor, and their disguises vanished with it.

"You thought I wouldn't see through that?" Larian Amalie stood in the archway to the sitting room, nimbuses of magic around her hands. Corman was beside her with a half-dozen of his goons.

"You get the one on the left," Asti said to the Thorn. "I'll get the seven on the right."

The Thorn's hand moved faster than Asti's eye could follow, drawing and throwing arrows like they were darts. Amalie batted them away maniacally, and the Thorn leaped on her. Asti would have loved to have watched the whole fight between the two of them, but he had his own situation to deal with.

Carving through Corman's muscle was not that situation. That was the dance, and Asti knew the steps all too well.

Let me, the beast cried out. *I can kill them all. Let me.*

"Who do you think you're saving right now?" Liora asked from the couch. "Helene and the rest are surely dead. The neighborhood belongs to Fenmere now."

"Not while I live," Asti said.

"We're happy to change that," Corman said, though he was backing away from the fight.

"No one elected Asti Rynax as the savior of the neighborhood," Liora said.

"No one needed to," Asti said.

One thug's blade got a bit too close, slicing Asti's side. The beast howled, pulled at its chain.

"Just surrender, Asti. You're not a hero. You're not even a man. You're an animal on two legs."

"Never!" Asti shouted. He drove his knives into the belly of the last goon. Only Corman left, who had pulled up a crossbow.

"You stay back, Rynax," Corman said. "Don't think your madman act scares me."

"Then shoot," Asti said.

"You ready to die for this neighborhood?" Liora asked.

LET ME! the beast screamed.

"Shoot me," Asti said. "Because then I'll die for this neighborhood, and be the one thing you can never stop. A legend."

"I'll stop him," Amalie said. Suddenly the Thorn was hurled into Asti, the two of them tumbling into the parlor and half out the door.

"I am disappointed by this Thorn," Amalie said. "He almost seems distracted."

"I was," the Thorn said. "You wouldn't believe how hard it was keeping track of all these arrows."

He brought his hands together with a flourish, and from every direction, arrows converged on Amalie. Eight of them penetrated her on all sides. She screamed an unearthly howl, a wave of magic bursting from her, and she fell down, lifeless.

"I had wanted nine," the Thorn said. "Do a whole 'Acser against the legionnaires' thing. Didn't have time."

"No one appreciates the classics," Asti said, getting to his feet.

Corman came out to the parlor, crossbow trained on Asti. "Do you think you've won? Do you think you've stopped us? I'll bring more mages, more muscle. Fenmere will own all of this, and crush you beneath his boot. You would need—"

One of Verci's darts struck his hand, and Corman yelped, dropping the crossbow.

"Were you about to say we'd need an army to stop you?" Verci asked, popping in between Asti and the Thorn. "Because I've got one outside."

Asti glanced out the door, where the brawl was now a full battle. Mila—still dressed in a crazy disguise that mirrored the Thorn's—was taking down goons with her rope and knives. Jared Scall, armed with a mace, was braining them left and right. Kel Essin was even in the mix, taking down Fenmere muscle. Cobie Pent—when did he get out of prison?—was knuckle-dusting a pair of them. A dozen other neighborhood folks that Asti had known all his life.

And Jhoqull-Ra, leading a squadron of Ch'omik warriors. The mere sight of them made half the Potato Boys and Three-Fingers run in terror.

The Thorn grabbed Corman by the front of his suit. "You tell them where their friends are."

"Or you'll kill me?" Corman sputtered.

"No, you get to live, to run home to Fenmere and tell him that North Seleth is off limits to him. Everywhere but Dentonhill is off limits. And soon, that will be as well."

"So why would I—"

The Thorn ignited his hand in a nimbus of red magic. "Because you want to have your teeth and tenders when you tell him."

"Basement," Corman said quickly. "Door's over there."

Asti didn't waste any time running to the door, Verci by his side.

"Have to admit, the Thorn has style," Asti said.

Helene was being torn apart, bit by bit. First by Ecrain's magic, and then when Julien came into the basement. Ecrain wrapped him in yellow light and dragged him down the hall with it.

"Let him go!" Helene said through the pain. She would endure it, but Julien should never have to.

"Look at this one," Ecrain said. "I remember him as well. I'm so glad I get to play with you both."

"You—will—not—" Helene forced herself to say.

"You care about him?" Ecrain asked. "Maybe I should make you watch while I tear him apart. Or make him watch you. Or keep you both alive long enough to watch each other almost die, over and over."

Julien started smashing his mighty arms against the yellow light, harder and harder. "You! Will! Not!"

His pounding was hard enough that the light around him shattered like a porcelain plate. Ecrain focused her attention on him, doubling her effort to hold him.

Helene jumped at her. No quips, no smart mouth, just punch after punch. Break her concentration. Break her magic. Break her.

Helene kept going until a hand touched her shoulder. Julien.

"She's down," he said.

Helene looked at the bloody mess in front of her. Her hand was covered with it, and her knuckles were scraped raw. She might have broken some bones in her hand.

Ecrain wasn't getting up, though. Not this time.

"I'm good," she told Julien. "Get them up."

"Your voice," he said.

"It's fine," she rasped.

Julien untied Almer and Kennith. Almer got to his feet, brushing off his clothes. Kennith stayed on the ground.

"Ken," Julien said. "We need to move."

Kennith didn't speak, but shook his head.

"What did they do to him?" Helene asked.

"He hasn't said anything in hours," Almer said. "They took a finger, like they did to me."

Helene held up her bandaged hand. "Same."

Julien scooped up Kennith in his massive arms.

"Help me!"

That was behind another door.

"Who is that?" Julien asked.

"Lesk," Helene said, opening the door. Lesk lay curled up on the floor, dried blood and vomit surrounding him.

"Helene," he said. "You've got to get me out of here."

"I don't have to do anything," she said. "Let's go."

Asti and Verci came running down the stairs, both looking like they had fought every sinner to get here.

"Hel," Asti said, grabbing her in an embrace. For once, she didn't mind. "I'm sorry it took us so long."

"You're here now," she said. "Never doubted it."

"Rynax!" Lesk cried out. "Save me."

Asti let Helene go and looked to Lesk. "Give me one good reason why."

"I know about the fire," Lesk said. "I know about Andrendon."

Asti swore. "Who can carry Nange?"

Julien sighed and passed Kennith over to Verci and Almer. "I got it."

"You better not be lying to me," Asti told him as Julien scooped him up. "Or you'll wish I left you here."

"I'm not," Lesk said. "This whole house is part of it."

Chapter 26

"THIS WHOLE HOUSE IS PART of it."

Asti took that in. How much did Nange know? How much did Josie? How deep did it all go?

"The house itself, or the Circle?" the Thorn asked at the base of the stairs.

"Yes," Nange said, looking as pale as a Poasian. "All of it. But we need to get out."

"Let's discuss it later," Verci said, holding Kennith up with Almer's help. "We should be running, yes?"

"Go," the Thorn said. Then looking at Verci, "You use that boom powder?"

"Wasn't last resort," Verci said.

"Is now," the Thorn said. He pointed to the door at the far end of the wall. "Shoot it at that and run like blazes."

"But—" Almer said.

"I got it," Asti said, taking the gauntlet off Verci's hand. "Get them all out. Get them all home."

Verci nodded. "Let's move."

Helene and the others needed no further prodding. They ran up the stairs, Verci going last.

"Asti," he said quietly.

"Right behind you, brother," Asti said. Looking to the Thorn, he asked, "Is this safe?"

"Not remotely," the Thorn said. His face was screwed up in concentration, with magic building around him so strongly it made the hairs on Asti's arm stand up. Even his shaded face had faded, showing a young kid, the same age as Mila. "Best if you not look back once you start running."

"And what'll you do?"

"I'm not planning on dying today," he said through gritted teeth. Sweat was breaking on his brow, and he was breathing harder and faster. "Now, Asti!"

Asti brought up the gauntlet and fired. The shot flew down the hallway and exploded into a ball of fire. But then the ball stopped in place, churning in an aura of magic. The fire surged and swelled, going from orange to yellow to blue to white.

"Run!" the Thorn shouted.

Asti didn't wait any longer. He dashed up the stairs, through the ground floor, and out the foyer. Mila was standing in the doorway, looking confused.

"What's going on?" she asked. "Where's—"

"No time," Asti said, tackling her as he went out the door, spinning to land on his back so she wouldn't hit the cobblestone.

Seconds later the whole building erupted in blue-white flame. The fire launched up into the sky and then pulled back down, taking the house with it. Asti covered his eyes, and, when the glare subsided, all that remained were glowing embers of the bare structure, ash and brick.

"Vee!" Mila shouted, clawing at Asti.

"Don't, don't," Asti said, holding her back. "Nothing you can do."

"You left him there?" she asked.

"He said to run," Asti said in the gentlest tone he could manage. "He said he'd be all right."

Asti looked around. Most of the gang boys and thugs were laid out on the ground, moaning. Verci was sitting on the ground, looking exhausted, one hand on the back of Nange's neck. Julien had Helene wrapped in his big arms. Almer was looking about and squinting, his spectacles missing. Kennith just stood there in the road, looking at nothing.

"Kh'enta!" Jhoqull came over with her squadron, the rest of them carrying one of their own. She went to Kennith, still standing with a haunted, vacant stare, and grabbed him in an embrace. "Ken, I'm here. You're all right."

Kennith turned to Jhoqull, and, in a blink, folded into her and started weeping. He looked at the fallen Ch'omik man.

"Who was he?" he whispered.

"Och'me-ra, son of Neqram-cha, son of Genoch-am'ra."

"Rest with your fathers, Och'me-ra," Kennith said. "Watch over your sons."

The other Ch'omiks, including Jhoqull and Kennith, started to sing.

"Mi yang go, dja guraga, djayaye, ch'omiye, dja guraga."

"What now?" Mila cried, still clutching Asti's arm.

"I don't know," Asti said quietly.

The whole alley was filled with the song when the Constabulary whistles started blowing.

"What in the name of every saint is happening here?"

Constables had swarmed the alley, grabbing anyone and everyone, slapping irons on whoever was still breathing. One exception was Helene and Julien, but only because Lieutenant Covrane had put himself between them and his fellow officers. Mila wasn't being ironed, because she had ditched her weapons and disguise, and looked like a passerby who had been caught up in the action.

Verci had been too tired to even struggle with the constables as they put irons on him. Asti had taken the cue from him, accepting his without a fight. More constables and lockwagons and Fire Brigade and Yellowshields all arrived. Verci had never seen anything like it in North Seleth.

And then the Constabulary Captain had arrived, demanding answers.

"Captain!" Covrane said, moving himself in front of some of the other officers. "We've got a lot to sort out here."

"We certainly do," the captain said, glancing around. "How many people do you have in irons?"

"About thirty," Covrane said. "Though I think some of them might be innocent bystanders."

"And the house?"

"It was a mage chapterhouse. Who knows what they were doing. You know how they are."

This earned a sidelong glance from the captain. "I don't appreciate talk like that, Lieutenant."

"Apologies, Captain," Covrane said. "I'm familiar with some of the people here, and I can tell you who are most likely the malefactors, and who were victims and the innocent bystanders."

"I'm sure you can," the captain said, pacing about. "But given your situation, Lieutenant, I shouldn't even let you be here."

"I appreciate you believing—"

"I'm mostly just short of decent officers to handle this much mess, Jarret. Don't push me, or I'll iron you to a desk myself. What's going on over there in the rubble?"

Verci craned his neck to take a look, and something was moving in the ruins of the fallen house.

"Help, anyone!" a nasally voice called out. "Anyone!"

A couple constables ran over and helped move charred panels of wood out of the way, revealing a scrawny young man in a University of Maradaine uniform.

"Oh, thank every good saint," he said as he was helped to his feet. "I was certain this was the end for me."

"Who are you?" the captain asked as the kid was brought over.

"Oh, me?" the kid asked, pushing cracked spectacles up his nose. "Kendall Parsons, natural sciences at U of M."

"And what was your involvement in all this?"

"I can't speak to involvement. The mages of this house abducted me and abused my person something horrible. And they did the same to that gentleman, and the Ch'omik fellow, and the woman over there. Quite terrible folks, these mages were, I can tell you."

"Hmm," the captain said. "And where are these mages?"

"One's over on Frost, unless he woke up," Verci said. "The other two were probably killed when the house fell."

The captain came over and squatted in front of Verci. Now he got a look at the man's face, and there was something familiar about it. "All right, you. Tell me who should get dragged off to Quarry, and who's innocent in all this."

"Well," Verci said, clearing his throat.

"Captain, surely that's not the best—" one of the regulars started.

"I'm very interested in this man's opinion," the captain said. Verci remembered where he had seen him before. In the man's own home, and the name on the brass badge confirmed it.

"Like the kid said, the mages had abducted several neighborhood folks, the ones he pointed out. My large friend over there was distraught over it and sought to rescue his cousin. My brother and I, seeing he was having difficulty with the variety of malcontents around the house, aided him in his fight. As did several of these other fine people, pillars of the neighborhood."

"Show me," the captain said, signaling to one of the officers to take off his irons. Once Verci's hands were free, he pointed out those who were friends—or innocent enough—including all the Ch'omiks, Nange and

Kel, and Jared Scall. Each person he named, the captain signaled to take the irons off of them, and slowly they were each allowed to go. Nange tried to slip off, but Mila and Helene were both on hand to grab hold of him. Helene mouthed "Kimber's" to Verci as they left. Soon gang boys and thugs were loaded into lockwagons, and Verci was the only one left besides the constables. Covrane looked very out of sorts about the whole thing, but was biting his tongue.

The captain strolled over to Verci and shook his hand. "My instincts are usually right, so don't let me down, hmm?"

"No, sir," Verci said.

"Good," the captain said. "But you can consider that a debt paid, for my niece's sake."

Verci nodded, gave a small salute to Covrane, and went off toward Kimber's.

Halfway down Ullen, Asti grabbed Verci and pulled him into an alley, where he was waiting with the Thorn, still looking like the nebbishy student.

"What the blazes just happened?" Asti asked. "Why did that stick captain listen to you?"

"Remember that constable's daughter I saved?" Verci asked. "Captain Welling is her uncle."

"Welling?" the Thorn asked. He blinked in confusion and muttered, "What are the odds?"

"Come on," Asti said. "After all this, I definitely need a drink."

"Three beers," Asti told Kimber as he came in with Verci and the Thorn.

"And, like, three strikers or whatever you've got that's like that," the Thorn said.

"That's really all you're going to say?" Kimber asked. "After what happened in here?"

"I am sorry about that," Asti said. "But hopefully the worst has passed."

"You believe that?"

Asti sighed ruefully. "I have to believe we did something good today. Time will tell. But right now, I'm calling it a victory."

"We could use that," Kimber said. "Where are you staying tonight?"

"I hadn't thought that far ahead," Asti admitted.

"Start thinking ahead, Asti Rynax," she said with a sad smile. "Two beers and cider. He's a child."

"What happens if they look up the name you gave them?" Verci asked the Thorn as Asti sat down with them.

"They find a student at U of M who's been in an effitte trance for months," the Thorn said. "I wasn't about to give the constables my real name or face. Especially if Corman still lurked about."

"This isn't your real face?" Asti asked.

"Not even remotely," the Thorn said. "I was careless enough that Mila knows who I am, I think—"

"We understand," Asti said. "This is a good level of trust between us for my comfort."

Kimber came with the drinks and a plate of sandwiches. The Thorn wasted no time cramming one into his mouth. "By the way, every room upstairs is occupied. Helene, Mila, Lesk. No one looks in good shape."

"It has been a day," Verci said.

"That it has," the Thorn said.

"And hopefully, things will calm down in this neighborhood," Asti said. In his head, the beast growled quietly on its chain. Across the bar, Liora held up a beer in a toast.

Neither are real, he reminded himself. *And neither of them are you.*

"What's next for the Thorn?" Verci asked.

"Well, the semester starts soon, so, classes," he said.

"Saints, you're young," Asti said.

"And I'll be wanting to keep hitting Fenmere now. Hopefully topple his whole empire."

"Ambitious," Verci said. "We just plan on opening a shop."

"The Rynax Gadgeterium," the Thorn said, working on his second sandwich. "I saw it. That's what's in store? The simple life?"

"Can't do revenge forever," Asti said.

"I don't intend to," the Thorn said. "I've got other things going on. There any reports of missing kids in this part of town?"

"Kids around here are all missing," Asti said. "It's a neighborhood of orphans and truants. Even the ones with parents are orphans."

Verci frowned. "That something Fenmere has his fingers in?"

"Maybe," the Thorn said. "It's all stories. Kids vanishing, grabbed by a giant. Sticks busted up something northside, but it's still happening in Denton."

"We'll let you know if we hear anything," Asti said. "Mila knows how to find you on campus?"

"She does," the Thorn said, picking at the crumbs left by the last sandwich. "I should probably say something to her before I go."

"Yes, you should," Verci said. "We like you, but she's a sister to us and we will cut you if you hurt her."

The Thorn drank his cider down. "Rynaxes. It's been a pleasure. Let's not do this again soon." He went up the stairs.

"He's a good one," Verci said.

"Smart kid," Asti said. "He should stay in school, get his letters, and do something real with himself."

"Absolutely," Verci said. He smirked a little. "I do feel bad about his bow, though."

"Oh, totally," Asti said. "He lost it fighting with us."

"Never made a bow before."

"It'd be a challenge."

"Hey, boys." Helene stood at the landing of the stairs. "If you're done congratulating yourselves, Nange is ready to talk."

Chapter 27

DOC GELSON PASSED VERCI AND Asti on their way up. He gave a heavy sigh as he saw them.

"Boys, I said I didn't want to know anything. Still don't. But some real mess happened—"

"We will make you whole," Verci said quickly. He had done a fair amount of damage in the heat of the moment, he felt more than responsible. "Might take a few weeks."

"I appreciate that." Gelson looked down the hall. "Real mess tonight as well. Lesk, he should stay in bed for weeks. Might get an infection. Might not make it."

"Do what you can," Asti said.

"I've done all I can for now, but I'll keep an eye."

They went into the room, where Lesk was on the bed, pale and drawn. Helene, Julien, and Almer were all there. Verci embraced all three of them.

"I'm so sorry," he said to Helene. "I should have done more, sooner. I should have been there for you."

"You'd have been nabbed and lost a finger as well," Helene said.

"It's just the little one," Almer said with an odd resignation. "To be honest, I'm shocked I hadn't blown one off yet. Most guys in my profession have less than nine."

"That's ridiculous, Almer," Helene said.

"We'll do what we can for you," Asti said.

"Don't mind me, just dying here," Lesk said from the bed.

"Doc Gelson says you're not dying," Asti said, going over to the bed. "At least not tonight."

"Slow death. Fun," Lesk said. He chuckled hollowly. "You got me good, Rynax. Fair fight and you got me good. And I saw what I was worth to them all."

"Ia and Josie left you behind," Asti said. "That must have stung."

"Well, that earned this betrayal, I suppose. I said I'd tell what I know, so I will."

"Josie has her hands in Andrendon, whatever that is?" Verci asked.

Asti followed with, "Do you know what it is?"

"Only in a vague sense. Some sort of project to 'renovate the city.' Improve the value of life here in Seleth and westtown."

"That means raise rents," Helene said. "Chase us out to Benson Court or even the Old Quarry."

"You said it had to do with the mage house," Almer added.

"So, I never fully trusted the Old Lady. Specially since she burned you all, and started using me and mine to rebuild her place."

"You thought you would be on top," Asti said.

"Yeah. But when that ponce Treggin took over my gangs, he was linked into all the Andrendon stuff. When Josie took the top spot back, they looked to her. That hooked her to the mages and all."

"And Fenmere and the drugs?" Verci asked.

"Far as I knew, that had nothing to do with Andrendon," Lesk said, taking a moment to cough fiercely. "That was just for some fast money, since Andrendon wasn't flowing any our way yet."

"Yet?" Asti asked.

"I found some letters, promises made, that sort of thing. In one of Josie's desks. Things were delayed with the magic and the technology, and they were behind schedule."

"Magic and technology?" Verci asked. "Like, together?"

Lesk shrugged. "I don't understand what that's about, but that's why things weren't moving as fast yet. The mages were cash poor after building the house, and reached out to Fenmere."

"This isn't much, Nange," Asti said.

"Here's the big thing. Whoever is behind it, they're working through a law firm. Colevar and Associates."

"We know that one," Asti said. Verci knew that was a dead end. In the past months Asti had done more scouting on Colevar and Associates, and on Heston Chell, the lawyer handling it. But the law offices had pulled up the defenses. Whatever connection they had to Andrendon was being well hidden, and Chell was too protected to get direct answers from.

"And the bankrolling is being done through three goldsmith houses. That's the big key, the funding is coming through them. It's tied up in paperwork and secrecy in such a way that, without those houses working the money, it all falls apart. Josie has a plan to ruin those three houses if things don't go right."

"She told you that?"

"She told Ia that, Ia told me."

"What are the three houses?"

"Rynax," Lesk said, his voice lowering. "I tell you, you can't just cut me out. If I die from this belly slice, so be it, but if I live, I got nothing. Bring me into your crew here."

Asti looked up to Verci, and Verci couldn't quite read what he was saying. No use of signals or codes.

"I got to be honest, Nange. I don't know how much this will be a crew after today. But you'll have my word that you will be under my watch."

Lesk nodded. That seemed to be good enough. "The Neville House. Caton & Smedley. Lester & Sons."

Verci let out a low whistle. Those were pretty big houses. Exchange offices all over the city. Hundreds of thousands of crowns worth of currency.

"All right," Asti said. "We'll let you rest."

They started to leave, but as they went out, he said, "Hel, hang back a second."

She gave a nod to Julien that it was all right, and everyone else left. They waited outside in the hallway for her, and in a minute, she came out too.

"Everything all right?" Verci asked her.

"He just needed something. I'll have Kimber take care of it. Come on, we all need a few beers." She went down the stairs, Almer and Julien behind her.

"What do you think it was?" Verci asked his brother.

"A priest," Asti said. "He might have confessed to us, but there's still his soul. And right now, I think he's clearing all his accounts."

"You think so?"

"He didn't call either of us a 'pirie' the whole time," Asti said. "That's a first."

Mila's heart jumped when there was a knock on her door. She threw it open to Veranix standing there, looking a bit too sheepish with his grin.

"Thought I'd check in on you," he said.

She grabbed him by his beautiful face and kissed him.

"Ow, wait," he said, pulling away. "Not that I don't like that—I really do—but I'm a mess of bruises."

"You don't—"

His face shimmered to reveal so much purple and yellow on his face. "Pria and Amalie could throw some punches, let me tell you."

"You worried they'll come for you?"

"Amalie definitely will not," he said as his face changed back. "And hopefully Pria got picked up by the

Constabulary, and there's surely enough to charge him even with Circle Law."

Mila wasn't sure what that meant. Maybe a mage thing. Something to learn at University.

"So, about the kissing thing," Mila said.

"I am very for the kissing thing," Veranix said. "Just, gently."

"Right," she said, giving him a gentler one. "I just . . . I'll be on campus, well, tomorrow."

"Tomorrow," he said, with a bit of a foreboding tone.

"And I don't . . . that is . . . is this just an excitement of the gig thing? Is it just a North Seleth thing?"

"What do you want it to be?" he asked cautiously.

Mila wasn't sure how to answer that. "I will need to focus on my studies. I may have had a door opened for me to go, but I don't think it will be held open if I screw up."

His face fell a little. "Sure. That makes sense."

"But . . ." she said. "I think it's clear that the Thorn could stand to have a Rose at his back. Once in a while."

A shy smile crossed his lips. "I'd like that."

"Now," she said, putting her palms on his chest to establish a bit of boundary. "You've got all your gear this time. Cloak, rope, staff, bow?"

"Bow was wrecked by that Poasian," he said. "Though that's a thing that keeps happening."

"Well, I don't want Kaiana mad at you when you get back," she said. "Or at me."

"No, she likes you."

"I did not get that impression."

"She likes anyone who keeps me from getting killed." He sighed. "I should be getting back, I think."

She nodded. "Asti and Verci downstairs?"

"Yeah."

"I should—I mean, today was a mess, and . . . I'm leaving tomorrow."

"They're family," he said. "I get it."

"You do?"

"I know a bit about the families you find when your first one was taken from you."

She gave him one more kiss. "See you around campus, Thorn."

"Yes, you will," he said, and his appearance shimmered to his full Thorn look—staff and arrows on his back, shaded face. With a wave of his hand, the window opened. "See you soon." And out he went into the night.

Mila went down to a near empty taproom.

"Asti and Verci here?" she asked Kimber.

"They went upstairs," Kimber said. She leaned in closer. "Was that the boy?"

"That was the boy," Mila said.

Kimber's face cooled a bit. "He went to your room—"

"Very respectfully," Mila said. "But I will be seeing him at school."

"That's tomorrow," Kimber said wistfully.

"That's tomorrow."

"You feel ready for it?"

"I'm ready for a change," Mila said. "Thank you."

"Always," Kimber said. "There will always be a room for you here. And the saints will watch over you."

"I'm still breathing," Mila said. "Given what I've gone through, they must be doing something."

Helene came down with Almer and Julien, who sat down at a table. Helene came over to Mila and Kimber at the bar.

"You holding up?" Helene asked.

"I really feel like I should ask you that."

Helene gave a half shrug. "I'll adjust. Kimber, can I get a word?"

Mila took that as a cue to step away. "I'll go to the table."

"Can I bring you something?" Kimber asked. "Glass of wine?"

That was the first time for that. "I'd like that a lot."

Kimber gave a small wink. "Glass of wine it is."

Mila went over to the table. Time for one last drink with the family.

❂

"Can you do that?" Helene asked Kimber. "He seemed to really mean it."

"It's only out of faithful spirit he's under my roof," Kimber said. "That man . . ."

"I know," Helene said.

"I'll go up to Saint Bridget's and ask the reverend. He might not come himself. Send a brother or a cloistress."

"Fair enough," Helene said. She was trying desperately not to let the weight of the past two days crush her. "What's a beer cost for a nine-finger girl tonight?"

"Tonight, she gets it on me," Kimber said. "But Julie smashed one of my tables so he's going to have to pay."

"Also fair," Helene said.

She sat down with Mila, Almer, and Julie. Almer had forsaken beer and ordered a pair of Fuergan rums. Just the smell made Helene's head dance.

"You're all right?" Julien asked.

"Saints, yes," she said. "Everyone needs to stop asking me that."

Asti and Verci joined them at the table, and Kimber brought another round of beers, and wine for Mila.

"So," Helene said. "Did we do it?"

Asti clucked his tongue. "I think we did enough damage to Fenmere's enterprise here to dissuade his interest. And sabotaged Josie's empire enough to keep her off our backs for a bit."

"A bit?" Julien asked.

"And I'm going to have words with her," Asti said. "Establish a new understanding between us."

"She holds a blazing heavy grudge," Helene said.

"That she does," Verci said. "But so do we, and she knows that."

"Do we?" Almer asked. "Are we still—Ken!"

Kennith and Jhoqull came into the taproom, his

head hanging down, her hand on his shoulder. Asti got up.

"Kennith, hey," he said. "I'm glad you're here."

"We figured this would be the place to meet," Kennith said. "Made odd sense."

Jhoqull spoke up. "We had to go back to the Hodge first. Take care of Och'me-ra."

"I'm so sorry," Asti said to her. "I—I can't thank you and your family enough. Is there—"

"There is no debt, Rynax," she said. "We came because we were needed. Och'me-ra chose the risk. Chose it for Kh'enta."

"Well, sit, have a drink," Asti said.

"No, no thanks," Kennith said. "I wanted to tell you that I don't think I can do this anymore. I need to just . . . just do honest carriage driving. Build and design things. Work with Jhonnie in her forge."

"Jhonnie?" Helene asked.

"I allow him to call me that," Jhoqull said. "Do not press your luck."

"No, ma'am," Helene said.

"That makes a lot of sense, Kennith," Verci said.

"It does," Asti added. "I know Lesk told us something about Andrendon, but . . . saints almighty. I can't do this to you anymore. Any of you. The three of you could have been killed. Raych could have been killed."

"You're going to drop it all?" Helene asked. "Or is this another masquerade of an honest life?"

"No masquerade. You all . . . you all have something better than you did at the fire. I won't be responsible for any of you losing that."

"We agreed every time," Helene said. But she looked at the other faces, and saw—save Mila—they were all a bit too broken, too ready to accept. "All right. If you don't have anything, no plan, no gig, I guess that's fine."

"I really don't," Asti said.

"But if you need a crossbow aimed at someone . . ."

He laughed a little, and Verci did as well, then everyone did.

"I wouldn't ask anyone else." He picked up his beer and handed it Ken.

"No, I—"

"One toast," he said, signaling to Kimber to bring two more. She was over there with more drinks in a snap. "To the Holver Alley Crew—"

"You're really going with that?" Helene asked.

"Absolutely," he said. "To the Holver Alley Crew, the best group of—"

"Miscreants?" Helene offered.

"Orphans?" from Mila.

"Lunatics?" from Verci.

"Friends," Julien said solemnly. "The best friends to have your back."

"The best family I've had," Asti said. He drank, as did everyone else, and then he grabbed Verci and kissed him on the forehead. "Let's get you home to your wife."

"Agreed," Verci said.

They shook hands and embraced everyone, and they were out the door. Kennith and Jhoqull went right behind them. Mila finished her wine, gave Helene a half embrace on her side and went upstairs. Almer mumbled something and went off into the night.

"Home?" Julien asked.

"Home," she said. Cheese shop. Simple apartment. Honest life. Honest woman.

Perhaps for real this time.

Jarrett was at their stoop when they arrived.

"You're all right," he said, grabbing her in a passionate embrace when she approached. "I'm so sorry, I dragged you into this."

"No, you didn't," Helene said. "Don't hold that on yourself."

"If I hadn't brought Missus Rynax to you . . ."

"I would have still been in it," Helene said. "You know, you *know*, Jarrett, that's who I am."

Julien awkwardly moved around them and went inside.

Jarrett took a step back, nodding. "I suppose I do."

"I understand if that's something you can't live with."

He nodded his head, a bit solemnly. "I've had to think a lot the past couple days about what I can live with. I killed two men. I imagine you know what that's like."

"You know I do," Helene said. "Those three in the bakery that night."

"Right," he said. "You did what had to be done. And I know I did as well, but . . . it's a lot to reckon with. And I'll have some time to reckon with it."

"Your captain said something about putting you on a desk," she said.

"A full inquiry with the Protector, investigators from the GIU, maybe even from the archduchy office. And it's best if I'm not on street duty for that."

"And who will patrol North Seleth?" she asked.

He looked at her very seriously. "I imagine you know all too well who will look after this neighborhood."

She looked away, not sure what to say to that.

He got back to his feet. "Like I said, I've been thinking about what I can live with. And what I can't." He reached into his coat pocket and took out a pair of bracelets. "Is there a chance a lawless, dishonest woman can become a constable's wife?"

All Helene wanted to do in that moment was cry, and she didn't even know why. She certainly didn't know the answer.

She held those tears back and kissed him. "I don't know. Ask me tomorrow."

"Of course," he said. "You—it was stupid of me to—"

"No," she said. "It was honest. And I . . ." the right word failed her. It wasn't love. She knew that. "I respect that so much. It means everything to me."

One more kiss.

"I'll see you tomorrow."

She went inside and upstairs. Julien was at the table.

"Did he just—"

"I do not want to talk about it," she said. "I am going to bed. If you open the shop tomorrow—your call—but if you do, do not wake me."

"Of course not," Julien said.

Helene went into her room, latching the door behind her. Only now, alone, would she let herself fall apart.

Tomorrow she would put herself back together.

Raych waited up for her husband.

Her stomach had settled itself shortly after he left, and she decided to put her energy into tidying the apartments above the Gadgeterium to make them as homey and livable as she could. Vinegar and oil and sweeping and absolutely scrubbing the water closet. With Corsi at her sister's—and Lian could darn well watch him another night—she was able to do the work quickly and efficiently. It helped her focus her thoughts, decide exactly what she would say when Verci got home.

Asti and Verci came in the apartment, both in subdued good spirits. Having been drinking, but not drunk.

"Hello, my love," Verci said with a kiss. "How are you feeling?"

"Better," she said. "I've been thinking."

"Good," he said.

"Asti," she said, making a point of keeping her voice calm. "I'll be getting the second apartment into a livable state, so you can move in there soon. I think—I think it's important for us to have some distance, between us and you."

"I agree," Asti said. "And I need to be spending my nights in a proper bed in a proper place from now on. Like respectable shopkeepers do."

"This isn't a joke, Asti."

"It isn't for me, either," he said. "What happened to you, what happened today in this neighborhood, that—that's on me."

"No, brother," Verci said. "That's on them, who brought in the drugs and—"

"No, as much as I talk about a plan, as much as I scout and watch, when it came down to it, I didn't have anything but a wild run that should have gone much worse. And it went so bad."

"How bad?" Raych asked.

"Well, Hel, Almer, and Kennith each lost a finger, for one," Verci said.

"Sweet prophets," Raych said, kissing her knuckle. "How?"

"The mages tortured them or—I'm not clear."

"Corman did it as proof of having them," Asti said. "And my fault for them getting captured in the first place. I've got no right to ask any of you to do any of this if I don't have my head on, and it is not right now."

"So you're committed to just . . . honest business?" Raych asked Asti.

"I'm committed to keeping us safe," Asti said. "I think that means not doing anything but honest business."

"Good," she said. She went over to Asti and gingerly touched his hand. He flinched away for just a moment. "Asti, I know . . . I know you are a good man trying to do good things for us. And I know . . . I know I don't know the depths of what you've gone through, what's wrong with you. But you need to share that with someone, and that can be me if you need it to be."

"No," he said quickly. "You don't want it."

"Then find someone you can talk to. Please. Promise me that."

Asti's lips got very tight, but he nodded. "All right, Raych," he said in a quiet whisper. "I promise."

Verci poked at an envelope on the table. "What is that?"

"That," Raych said. "That is part of honest business. The folks at Carrigan, Fisher and Elvert delivered that."

"Who now?" Asti asked while Verci opened it up.

"They called themselves a mechanical firm. Wanted to hire Verci to consult on the build of something."

"And pay for it?" Asti asked.

"Pay handsomely," Raych said.

"Rather," Verci said, looking at the letter. "It's an agreement of terms if I work with them. Good money, too. We certainly need good money to pay back Doc Gelson."

"Good," Asti said, getting to his feet. "I guess we should be settling down. We've got work in the morning."

"We all do," Raych said, with a smile. "Honest work."

"Honest work," Asti said back.

"Nope," Verci said over the letter.

"What?" Asti and Raych said together.

"I said nope."

"Explain," Raych said, hoping the tone of her voice made it clear to Verci he needed to tread carefully.

"We're starting a new gig. The last gig . . ."

"Verci, no . . ." Asti said.

"This one is just us, Asti. Long game. Slow con. No break-in, no fighting."

"What are you talking about?" Asti asked.

Verci slid the letter to him. Asti picked it up and read, his eyes going wide. Then he laughed a little and put the letter down.

"Explain to me what's going on," Raych said, picking up the letter.

"We're going to work with Carrigan and the rest," Verci said. "We're going to use them to get to the heart of the Andrendon business."

"How is working for them going to do that?" Raych asked.

"The terms of payment make it clear," Verci said, a downright wicked grin crossing his face. "Because now it all makes perfect sense. The work they've been commissioned to do, the work they need my help on . . . that *is* Andrendon."

Chapter 28

THE BELLS OF THE SHOP door indicated a customer, but Khejhaz Nafath didn't look up from his notebook. He knew exactly who had just entered by the absence of the repulsive odor of Druth sweat invading his nose.

"Hello, Frojiur," he said, so pleased to be able to speak the dancing, lyrical tones of his mother tongue for once. "I assumed you would have come to see me by now."

Frojiur—like all members of the Thurgir he had forsaken his lineal name, under the pretense that he served Poasia as a whole, rather than any one of the Pankchamtir families he might have blood ties to—came up to the counter. However Nafath had known the man long enough to know Frojiur's family name was Cthellian, and held no power. Frojiur had been more than ready to shed it.

"I'm still wondering how you had fallen so low, Nafath. Did you displease the Espionage Bureau so profoundly? Is that why your phrases were out of date?"

"All I had available," Nafath said. "Though I wonder why you've been so chastised to come to this ghastly city just to aid petty drug peddlers."

"It serves the interest of the state, and thus I serve it," Frojiur said. "Do you still serve the state? Or are you feeding Druth Intelligence to stay alive?"

"I do what I have to in this cesspool," Nafath said. "If that means being a humble merchant, so be it. Can I interest you in some *ghetziil*?"

Frojiur's expression softened. "Actually, yes. Nothing in this place is palatable."

"A gift, then," Nafath said, measuring out a vial of the delightful powder. "For your surely less than eager acquiescence to my proposal the other night."

"And why does Asti Rynax need to keep breathing? Or you, for that matter?"

"The *Khol Taia Śaricca*."

"That project is dead," Frojiur said. "It was decided that even if those Druth men had intervened, and even if they had all survived the reclamation of Khol Taia, they'd now be long dead, and—"

"I believe the list of ten exists," Nafath said. "And there is a faction in this city who are planning on utilizing it."

Frojiur blanched at that, which for any Poasian was almost impossible. "Presuming you're right, that is a horror. Let alone in Druth hands."

"So, tell your masters that I am here, that I am forsaking everything, including my right to return home, pursuing it."

"If there's even a chance you're right—"

"I hope to the winds I'm not, believe me," Nafath said. "But if I am, I need Asti Rynax for the time being. I need this part of the city to be a sanctuary."

Frojiur took the vial of *ghetziil*. "I will do as you ask, even though surely it will mean I will be ordered to remain here."

"I thank you," Nafath said. "And my inventory is at your disposal."

Frojiur opened the vial and inhaled. "How pathetic it is, that the small comfort of home I will find here comes from a traitor like you."

"Your future company leaves me as displeased, Frojiur," Nafath said. "But we do what we must for the glory of Poasia."

"May the world realize the glory," Frojiur said, and he left the shop.

Nafath went back to his writing. He hoped he was wrong. Being wrong would be jubilation.

But when he had seen the effect five simple words had had on Asti Rynax, he knew that everything he feared was true.

"And winter falls on Corringshire, with no promise of spring, no stirring from his dreamless sleep."

Pilsen Gin hated the final part of the show. Dying on stage was a triumph. He had been magnificent. Being dead on the floor while five more pages went on was a bore. He thought about cutting lines but Vellun wouldn't hear of it. Beautiful boy knew he had Pilsen's heart so fully ensnared. And that devious bastard made the most of it.

"Bear him to his tomb, and we must bear the sins of gracelessness. We fools. We madmen. We who forget that we play in summer, but autumn always comes."

The curtain went down, and Pilsen got to his feet, ready for it to rise, for his well-earned applause.

And it was thunderous.

He bowed, noting that the Rynax boys were in the front of the audience, just like they promised. Kelsi's sons were good boys, indeed. Asti and—

Saints be damned.

Holsi?

No that couldn't be right.

The short one was Asti, and the pretty one . . .

No, wasn't there.

He shook that away and took another bow, and the rest of the actors went down off the stage to get their adulations. Which usually meant kisses and more from whichever willing pretty flesh suited their fancy.

Vellun—always the willing pretty flesh that he was—waited backstage.

"Perfect, love," Vellun said. "Though—"

"Act Two dragged with the sea speech," Pilsen said. "I'm aware. Give me a few minutes, and then we'll go get a drink with the Rynax boys. Asti and, you know, the other one. Verci." There it was.

"All right," Vellun said, giving Pilsen a quick kiss. "I'll make sure none of the cast gets their costumes torn out there."

Pilsen went into his dressing room. Tiny little closet, but his.

But not unoccupied.

"Hello, Josie. Glad you made it to the show."

"You, doing Corringshire?" Josie said, leaning against the wall. "Wouldn't miss it. Had to be almost as good as your Olivette."

That got his eyebrow up. He sat down in his chair and started taking his greasepaint off. "You knew?"

"I've always known, but I did enjoy the game of it with Kelsi. And I was curious to see exactly what the boys were playing."

"You aren't mad at them," he said.

"Oh, quite mad. Enraged. Everything would have been easier if they had just been loyal from the beginning."

"So why let them play the charade?"

"Because I was up to my neck in mages and Fenmere. I figured at worst, they'd get killed, and that would be sad. Instead, their gambit got me out of this mess without costing me anything with Gemmen and the Neighborhood Kings."

"So you aren't going to come at them?"

"I never wanted to," she said. "They're the best arrows I have in my quiver. But I had to put on the show. I need everyone—including them—to think they're on their own. You know how that goes."

"I do," he said. A flash of a memory came up. "For the goldsmith houses?"

"Surely Lesk has pointed them toward the houses by now. They'll be my wild cards in this game." She touched his face gently, "Don't let the boys know."

"Of course not," he told her. Though he had already forgotten what it was to not tell them. So many things were just so much smoke in his mind. He couldn't recall what not to tell the boys, or even how this conversation began. He was in his dressing room. He had just done the play. Had he? He was nearly certain. "Did you enjoy the show?"

"The best, old friend," the old woman said, patting him on the shoulder. Something familiar about her. She reminded him of a box girl from back in the day, one of the best window crackers. What was her name? Jessie? Jolie? It would come to him. "A rare pleasure for me. Watching someone else bear the weight of responsibility."

"And . . . the boys?" He had a sense someone—Kelsi's sons, yes—they might be in danger, but he couldn't remember why.

"They'll have their own weights to bear," she said. "Sooner than they realize."

Classes began shortly. Mila was amazed to think that. She was here, on the grounds of the University of Maradaine, and it was glorious.

Her room in Intaria Hall was a good, solid room. Heavy brick construction. No leaks in the ceiling or cracks in the wall. No drafts or rat holes. The best bed Mila had ever slept in.

The meals at Redfern Hall—at least the three she had had since arriving—were abundant, filling, and delicious. Mila hadn't eaten like that ever in her life.

She even loved the uniform, even if the wool skirt was a bit scratchy for her taste.

Her two roommates—Jadonne and Livvie—both complained. The room was small, the bed hard, the food disgusting, and most of all, that they had to share with two other girls. Both these northside girls had lived the pampered lives of private schools and estate homes. Both whined that they shouldn't have to live in the dormitory for a year before applying to social houses.

Both were lucky that Mila wasn't going to slit their throats in their sleep. She knew that wouldn't look good, and she'd have to deal with actually cleaning all that up. Not worth the trouble.

Mila decided to use her Jendly Marskin voice after all. She knew her westtown accent would not fly with these girls, or anyone else in Intaria. Too many questions would be asked. Ones Mila didn't want to answer.

But she had her knives, her rope, and every aspect of her Rose outfit in a case under the bed. Plus the one knife she always kept hidden on her person. No telling when she might need to use it. Especially with these girls about.

Mila had made a quick assessment of Intaria and Redfern. Doors, locks, windows. Hard and soft points of entry. Hiding spots, blind spots. Still just preliminary work. If the building had deep secrets, she had not discovered them yet. But she had time.

"Where's Almers Hall?" she asked Livvie.

"Isn't that on the south end of campus. The boys' dorms?"

"It a boy's dorm, yes. So, south?"

"South lawn," Livvie said. "Why, are you meeting a boy there?"

"She has a boy to meet?" Jadonne almost screeched from her bed. "How did she do that so fast?"

"I already knew him," Mila said. She went under the bed and took out the box Verci had given her. "I'm just delivering a gift."

"Delivering?" Livvie asked. "Like some sort of page?"

"No, like a friend," Mila said.

"What else do you have under there?" Jadonne said, glancing under Mila's bed.

"Don't touch my stuff," Mila said as she left the room. She stuck her head back in. "I will know, don't doubt that." It was probably best to instill a little bit of fear in these girls right away. Just enough to keep them out of her hair.

She wandered to the south side of campus, asking directions from the campus cadets when she got disoriented. She needed to learn the campus.

Her campus.

Her new home.

She found Almers just as boys were crossing to go to dinner. So many boys in their school uniforms walked in packs, and Mila had to keep her eye on the whole crowd for a while before she spotted who she was here for.

"Veranix!" she called out. He was walking near the back of the crowd, talking with a boy who was almost impossibly skinny. He noticed her when she called, and left the crowd with his friend to join her.

"Mila," he said awkwardly. He did look adorable in his uniform. "I didn't know if I'd see you here."

"Of course you would," she said. "I only have one friend on campus so far."

"Let's make it two," the skinny boy said, extending his hand. "Delmin."

"Mila." She looked cautiously to Veranix.

"Oh, he knows," Veranix said. "Hiding things from your roommate is a challenge."

"I have two," Mila said.

"Condolences," Delmin said. "We're about to go to dinner, so . . ."

"Right," Mila said, turning to Veranix. "It's just, I have something for you."

"Do you?"

"It's a gift from Verci," Mila said. "He was . . . he felt bad about your bow."

"It happens," Veranix said, guiding her farther way from the crowd. "I've gone through too many this year."

She presented him the box. "Hopefully this one will last you."

"Who's Verci?" Delmin asked. "Wait, is she from—is she the one who—"

"That's enough, Del," Veranix said, a hot blush coming to his tan cheeks. He opened the box, looking at the bow inside. "That's beautiful. And arrows as well?"

"The arrows have special heads," Mila said. "Verci said to tell you he made them with Almer."

"He's the—oh!" A smile broke across his face. "Oh, that's very interesting."

"What is?" Delmin asked.

"I told you about the guy with the gauntlet, remember?" Veranix said. "I think he sent me arrows that are similar." He looked through the box. "Good, he labeled them."

"Maybe this isn't a standing in front of the dorm conversation," Delmin said. "I'm going to get dinner."

"Go ahead," Veranix said. "I'll catch up."

"Sorry," Mila said as Delmin left. "This wasn't the best place to bring that to you. I know you're—"

"Keeping my identity a secret?" he finished. "We should probably get this to the safehouse."

"See?" Mila said, flashing her best smile. "Now you know it's a safehouse."

"It's a good term," he said. "You want to come with me?"

"If you don't mind," she said.

"Never." His smile lit up. "And then I'll take you to dinner."

"I thought I'd take you," she said.

He laughed, crooking his arm into hers. "That's fine too."

It was definitely fine. Mila didn't know what the next months would bring, but she was excited for all the possibilities.

Tarvis kept his distance from the others. Nikey, Peeky, Telly, Enick, they were a good bunch, he knew. Almost like brothers. But not his brother. He would never have a brother again. But they were who he had left.

Right now, in the cover of moonslight, they were back at the abandoned factory, where they had started. Before they were with Bessie, before they were anything other than a bunch of hungry kids who needed a pack. They had clung together out of mostly boredom then. Tarvis had only stayed because Jede wanted to. He had done whatever Jede had wanted back then. He'd play any trick, stab any fool, if Jede needed it.

Now he had these four, and Mister Cobie. Mister Cobie was all right, Tarvis had figured him out. He had been a father once, like Tarvis had been a brother. He needed the boys, and the rest of the boys needed him.

Tarvis wasn't going to let himself need him. He wasn't going to let himself count on anyone else.

But he would let his boys, his pack, count on him. He knew he would never be like the rest of them, but he would be there for them. No matter what.

"This ain't too bad," Cobie said, looking about. "I mean, it ain't cozy or nothing, but we won't be on top of each other, and it's not a building that's gonna fall down."

"Told you," Enick said.

"It's good, boys. Good place to start."

"What are we gonna start?" Nikey asked.

"Nothing that ambitious," Cobie said, pacing about the yard. "That's where most of the trouble in this town happens. People get hungry for too much. Nah, boys, we just want to live well, with full bellies and a warm place to sleep. Ain't too much to—"

Tarvis hadn't been paying attention. He would have seen the giant before it walked up to Cobie and smacked him with an arm the size of a horse.

"Great saints!" Enick yelled.

"Children," the giant said. It moved so fast, Tarvis couldn't believe it. It grabbed Telly, picking him high up off the ground.

"Run!" Tarvis shouted. The other boys scattered.

Good. Now he only had to worry about Telly. He had his knives out as he charged the monster.

And it was a monster. Tarvis thought those were just stories old boys told, but there it was. Almost twice as tall as a grown man. Skin gray and sickly wet, eyes jet black, and every tooth too big for its mouth.

Didn't matter, Tarvis was going to cut it. He jumped on the beast—on its leg—and drove both knives into the pockmarked flesh. Except they didn't break the skin. No blood, no cut, not even a scratch.

"Two children," the beast said, grabbing Tarvis by the back of the neck and lifting him to his eye level. "Gurond finds two children."

Tarvis wasn't having any of that, stabbing both knives into the creature's wrist, over and over. Like stabbing into stone.

"Let us go!" Telly shouted. "Just leave us alone!"

"Gurond finds children for the Brotherhood." His lips curled into a grotesque smile. "The Dragon will be pleased."

He walked away from the warehouse to the creek bed, carrying Tarvis and Telly like they were just a pair of sticks. Tarvis stabbed and kicked like mad, but nothing he did even drew the creature's notice.

The giant bastard stopped at a creekside entrance into the sewers. "Children be calm," he said.

"Like rutting blazes I'll be calm, bastard!" Tarvis shouted.

"Be calm," the bastard said as they went underground. "Children will serve the Brotherhood."

Chapter 29

VERCI HAD WORN THE SUIT he had appropriated from Hal. "Stolen" was an ugly word, and besides, not only did it not fit Hal anymore, but Verci looked fantastic in it.

Asti looked fine—his suit was one Kimber had in storage, from a trunk left behind by a guest a few years back. It fit well enough, it was all the same color and pattern, so it was a better look than usual for him.

The two of them looked exactly how Verci wanted them to look for this: like poor businessmen trying to look their best by wearing out-of-date suits that didn't belong to them. Fit the plan perfect.

They took a series of tickwagons from Seleth across to Inemar, then up the bridge to the north shore, and another tickwagon to North High River, and the offices of Carrigan, Fisher and Elvert. The whole way, Verci carried a crate in his lap, while Asti had a valise full of documents and paperwork.

Neither of them were armed, not for this.

Verci had to admit, the offices were quite intriguing. It was as if a lawyer's office and a warehouse had had a baby, with a forge and tool shop in the middle of it.

"Quite impressive, isn't it, Mister Rynax?" Mister Elvert had asked. He was a Waishen-haired fellow, working in the tool shop when Verci and Asti came in through the barn doors. Not a stuffy swell in a full suit, but stripped to shirtsleeves and wearing goggles. "A lot more resources than your tinker shop, huh?"

"That is quite true," Verci said.

"Let's go see the others," he said. "Glad you came out."

"You made too intriguing an offer to ignore," Asti said.

"Hmm," Elvert said, barely giving Asti a glance. He led them to a lounge, away from the heat and noise of the tool floor, where Carrigan was waiting with the man Verci presumed was Fisher—tall, skinny, and spectacles. "Look who came by."

"Verci Rynax," Carrigan said, shaking his hand. "I guess you got our formal offer letter."

"I did," Verci said.

"Who's your friend?" Fisher asked.

"My brother and business partner, Asti," Verci said.

"He's the talent," Asti said. "I handle the details to help him work. Paperwork, finances, that sort of thing." He was doing just a little bit with his voice. Hint more educated, a breath more nasal and subdued. For once, Asti wasn't trying to intimidate.

"Glad to meet you," Carrigan said. "I missed you when I came out before."

"Always running about, that's me," Asti said.

"So," Verci said, putting the crate on the table. "I've made a scale mockup, based on what I understood of your plans. Frankly, I based it more on what it seemed you are trying to accomplish, rather than what the plans said."

"Sure," Fisher said. "Results are what matters most, isn't it?"

Verci opened up the crate, taking out the mechanism. "Could I get a taper to light the burner here?"

"You made it with a burner that lights? At that size?" Elvert asked.

"Well, this is the scale I'm used to working," Verci said. He lit the tinder in the burnbox, which quickly caught and started smoking. Soon, like a tiny teapot, the water in the tank started simmering. "It struck me you were going to have a power distribution problem. You want the engine here to pull these carriages at speed, but also slow down to stop when you need them. One cord was too much, too hard. Kept snapping, right?"

"Right," Carrigan said.

"So instead of one cord being pulled, it's a series of cords in parallel, that can be put on or taken off the gear shaft as needed." He flicked the tiny levers, and the threads started pulling the toy carriage toward the engine. "Obviously there's a lot more going on here, but that's the gist of it all."

"This is great," Carrigan said. "Now, we've recently been informed there's been some setbacks with other aspects of the project. Some sort of challenge with the build site."

"Oh, that's too bad," Asti said, putting so much sympathy in his voice even Verci believed it.

"They assure us that things are moving forward on a new timetable. We would love your help in developing the full-size prototype."

"Here?"

"Not here," Elvert said. "Even this place isn't big enough. The backers have purchased a factory in Shaleton—near your part of town—and we're going to convert that into the workhouse we'll need to build the real engine and carriages."

"Now, this isn't my field," Asti said. "But I do have some questions. The actual engine will be pretty sizable. And these carriages will require tracks, something like a minecart uses. Where's that going to be built?"

"The site for the engine has been selected, land acquisition being handled by the clients."

"The clients, yes," Asti said. "And the tracks? Building through the streets? Raised platforms?"

"Oh, no," Fisher said. "That's the genius. Do you know anything about the old quarry and catacomb tunnels under the city?"

"Heard some stories," Asti said.

"That's already the network in place to build the tracks. Some work to be done, but the infrastructure exists. I've not seen it, but we've been assured it's impressive. In a few years, we'll have a whole system of carriages going at high speeds, bringing people all over the city in a snap." He snapped his fingers for emphasis.

"Like the Andrendon," Verci said, looking to Asti.

"The what?" Fisher asked.

"It's an old Saranic legend," Verci said. "Read about it once. A magical transport around the city, according to the myth."

"Oh, yeah, I heard one of the money guys call it that once," Elvert said. "I didn't know what it meant, either."

The money guys.

From the goldsmith houses.

"Don't worry," Asti said. "We won't hold it against you all."

"Well," Carrigan said, going over to a desk and getting out some papers. "This is a great start, and we're looking forward to working with you. Though I presume you will also keep working your own shop."

"Right," Verci said. "Your proposal mentioned silent consulting. We're not supposed to talk about this or acknowledge our work on it."

"It's for proprietary reasons," Carrigan said. "Foolish, but the client and the money people don't want what we're doing going beyond involved parties before it's to be unveiled and—"

"We're very good at secrets," Asti said. "Worry not." He took the envelope from Carrigan.

"Well, thank you," Carrigan said. "We'll be in touch. And you're opening the shop this week?"

"Just in time for Terrentin," Verci said. "Toys for the children."

"We'll have to stop by to get some," Fisher said.

"Wonderful," Verci said.

Hands were shaken, empty pleasantries exchanged, and soon they were ushered out into the street.

"Was I right?" Verci asked Asti once they were a block away.

"Notes from the Neville House, Caton & Smedley, and Lester & Sons," Asti said. "And Elvert seemed to confirm it. This underground carriage thing, this is Andrendon."

"And the mage house, and the stairs leading farther down that Helene saw, were a part of it as well," Verci said.

"I would bet that's exactly where the engine is supposed to go when it's built," Asti said. "Right below Holver Alley. Now we have an in. Now we take our time."

"Until we're in position to sabotage." Sabotage all of it: the engine, the goldsmith houses, and the client behind it all. Verci glanced around at the North High River shops and houses. "Lovely place, this all is."

"Very nice neighborhood."

Verci felt the bile rise in his throat, but he held it down. This was not the time for anger. This was the time for patience. Long, slow burning patience. "They'd never burn it down to build their engine here."

"No, they wouldn't," Asti said. "Let's get home. We've got a shop to open."

Appendix

The History of the Fifty Year War

The Fifty Year War—also called the Island War—occurred primarily on the various Napolic Islands that lie approximately midway between Druthal and Poasia, where both nations had been establishing outposts and colonies. The exact beginnings of the war in **1150** are unclear, since both sides claim the other was the offending party that had broken the uneasy peace between the two nations. Druth scholars hold that the inciting incident was when Poasians invaded the freshly established colony of New Fencal—actually more of an isolated private club for Druth nobility than a proper colony—slaughtering all the residents and the token military presence of twenty archers and pikemen. Poasians contend that no such slaughter occurred, that they found a dead colony when they arrived and were then attacked by a Druth armada with no provocation.

For the first few years, the two militaries were engaged in island-hopping campaigns, gaining ground on one island, then losing on another, Poasia having advantage on land, Druthal on sea. A degree of balance in the war was achieved, as neither power gave full commitment to the war.

The war first shifted in **1156**, when Poasian forces brutally assaulted the civilian colony of New Marikar. All the citizens were killed and the buildings burned to the ground. The Druth considered this an utter violation of the Rules of War and Engagement, which they had held to be universal truths. The Poasians believed in no such constraints. This atrocity enraged the Druth populace, and the Parliament voted to fully mobilize its forces against the Poasians. Additionally, they attempted to engage the rest of the Trade Nations against their enemy.

The response of the Trade Nations was less than the Druth had hoped for. The Kieran Empire officially declared itself neutral in the affair, going only so far as to write stern letters of protest to the Poasians. King Keshynn VII of Waisholm pledged his support to the war, but this support took the form of but a token force of a few hundred men. Acseria lent no support at all, for it was more concerned with the possibility of war with its Imach neighbors to the east. No request for aid was sent to Kellirac, as many Druth leaders, including King Maradaine XV, held prejudices against them from the minor war with Kellirac in the 1140s.

The mobilization of the army was underway, and a full third of the Druth forces were sent to Poasia itself, to bring the war to its soil. The mighty Druth armada raced west, delivering thousands of soldiers to the Poasian shore. The Poasians were ill prepared for such a full-scale invasion, so the Druth landing forces quickly captured the coastal city of Khol Taia.

The Druth victory was short lived, as the Poasians, gravely offended by the invasion, would brook no further defilement of their land. Khol Taia was isolated and surrounded by the Poasian Army, as well as their allies the Cthellians and Xaminics, so all attempts by the Druth to push deeper into Poasia failed. Khol Taia was held until **1161**, when Poasian assaults forced a retreat from the mainland. The Poasians then destroyed Khol Taia, burning it to the ground and salting the earth.

The Druth Navy, however, did have a degree of success with the other aspect of their mission: blockading the Poasian ports. With superior Druth ships just outside their few harbors, the Poasians were effectively stopped from sending support or forces to their outposts in Napoli.

The following year, a Poasian assassin infiltrated the royal palace in Maradaine and killed the king and two of his sons. With the only other option being Pomoraine, the eldest prince's infant son, the crown went to the king's youngest son, Escarel, who was serving as an officer in the war. Escarel refused to abandon his place at the front, despite the pleas of the Druth lords and Parliament. He was crowned at the Napolic outpost colony of Fendrick, taking on the name Maradaine XVI (1162–1184).

The new king had already married: a young woman from the local Napolic village, and they already had had a son. As mortified as many Druth nobility were at the idea of a foreign queen and a crown prince of mixed heritage, they were spirited off to Maradaine to protect them from the frontlines of the war.

The war continued unabated throughout Maradaine XVI's reign. He coordinated the war effort from Fendrick, and it is noted that throughout his reign he never once was in the palace in Maradaine. Druthal continued to have the upper hand until **1177**, when Bürgin vessels began making their presence in the Napolic waters known, sinking many Druth ships. While it was never confirmed, many believed an alliance had formed between Bürgin and Poasia.

No longer the dominant naval force in the area, Druthal began to lose ground, abandoning many of its colonies and strongholds. The worst came in **1184**, when the Poasians assaulted Fendrick, and the king was killed.

News reached Maradaine, and Crown Prince Maradaine was primed to take the throne—he had been an active part of the government for some time. Several nobles and members of Parliament objected, citing his

Napolic heritage as reason to question the legitimacy of his rule. Many wished to put Pomoraine on the throne. Pomoraine, however, loved his cousin dearly, and felt that he would make a better king. Thus the prince was crowned Maradaine XVII (1184–1213).

Shortly after he came into power, the Poasians had their strongest victory, when their forces landed on Corvia and laid waste to the city. As the Druth forces responded and strove to get the Poasians off the island, Maradaine XVII began to feel that the war was pointless. His desire to concede, though, was blocked by the Parliament—they would agree to a peace treaty with the Poasians if one could be reached, but they would not agree to a surrender or concessions of defeat.

The fighting continued, as Druth forces tried to reclaim the territories they'd had at the beginning of the war, while emissaries were sent to Poasia with peace proposals. Every emissary was killed until **1195**, when Maradaine XVII contacted the Tsouljans for assistance. After years of negotiations, in **1199** Maradaine XVII met with Adjatkal, the head of the Poasian Council, at Tek Betor, a Tsouljan outpost in Napoli. While they were in deliberations, small battalions from both sides engaged with one another on the beach outside, the final battle of the war. This battle was brutal, and ended with no decisive victory on either side: Maradaine and Adjatkal announced that a treaty for peace had been reached.

In the years since, Druthal continued to maintain colonies on three of the Napolic Islands, as did Poasia, with the agreement that neither country would form colonies or outposts on any other islands. There has been little in the way of formal diplomatic relations between the two nations since. In an attempt to foster peace and openness, Druthal has allowed Poasian spice traders and other business interests access to the country, but almost no Druth interests have touched the Poasian mainland. Poasia and its culture remains almost a complete mystery.

Edward Willett

The Cityborn

"Willett wraps his capable new adult science fiction adventure around the fate of a mysterious many-tiered city and its inhabitants.... [*The Cityborn*'s] spunky protagonists and colorful world will entertain SF adventure fans."

—*Publishers Weekly*

"Set in a metal city at the center of the mountain ringed Heartland, *The Cityborn* is sprawling space opera centering on Alania, born to the City's privileged caste, and Danyl, a lowborn scavenger.... This is one suspenseful sci-fi thriller not to be missed." —Unbound Worlds

"Willett brings J.G. Ballard's *High-Rise* into the distant space age in this dystopian tale of class, power and freedom that will entertain devotees and non-genre fans alike. The worldbuilding in this book is impressive, creating an atmosphere that is both fascinating and oppressive, and characters who are magnificently complex." —*RT Reviews*

ISBN: 978-0-7564-1178-7

DAW 174

Jim C. Hines

Magic Ex Libris

"[A] love letter to science fiction and fantasy, with real emotional weight at the center…. A rollicking adventure story full of ridiculous little touches. It's a seriously fun ride for anyone who's loved geeky books their whole life." —io9.com

"A rich backstory and mythology that weaves history and magic and science fiction across centuries, between cultures, and around the globe." —*Wired*

"Sharp wit, rapid-fire action, and strong characterization have become Hines's trademarks."
—*Publishers Weekly*

Libriomancer	978-0-7564-0817-6
Codex Born	978-0-7564-0839-8
Unbound	978-0-7564-0969-2
Revisionary	978-0-7564-0971-5

To Order Call: 1-800-788-6262
www.dawbooks.com

DAW 195